C ... **up to** ... ... **Richard Winert Reported Missing Only One Week after Being Released from Jail."**

Joey's hands left her shoulders, taking the newspaper. Claire rubbed her neck while she watched her partner pace the room, absorbing the information. Her eyes flicked across the ceiling and walls, as she tried not to feel the queasiness rising inside. The skin on her arms rose into goose flesh as an involuntary shudder occurred deep within her, causing her to rise. She crossed to a dying plant in the corner and absent-mindedly fondled its leaves until two dropped to the floor.

Joey shifted focus from the newspaper to catch the downward flight of those leaves, then focused on the sight of Claire's shoeless feet. One stocking bore a tiny run up one side, probably caused by Claire impatiently banging her shoe against the desk. That nervous tapping was a noise Joey had learned to live with over the past few years.

"I still don't get it. What's this got to do with Mad Maxx? The guy probably just took off."

"I don't think so."

That comment commanded Joey's full attention. Claire never turned that phrase lightly and there was too much history between them to deny this warning. The sheer weight of its impact hung out over them in the form of a pregnant pause. Joey's eyes searched Claire's. It was clear that something ... something was tugging at Claire's brain.

"It's coming, Joe. There's something ... *out there.*"

PUBLIC ENEMY

V. I. LAWRENCE

POCKET STAR BOOKS
New York London Toronto Sydney Tokyo Singapore

An *Original* Publication of POCKET BOOKS

A Pocket Star Book published by
POCKET BOOKS, a division of Simon & Schuster Inc.
1230 Avenue of the Americas, New York, NY 10020

ISBN: 0-671-89561-3

First Pocket Books printing February 1996

10 9 8 7 6 5 4 3 2 1

POCKET and colophon are registered trademarks of
Simon & Schuster Inc.

Front cover illustration by Don Brautigam

Printed in the U.S.A.

For the Men in my life . . .

my father
an old lover
a good friend
and my beloved husband

Each of you have taught me
that the difficult questions in life
are the ones *worth* asking

Some of you are dead
and already know the answers

Prologue

The Welcoming Committee
June 19th—The Central Arizona Desert
01:13

A man's got to do what he thinks is right.

The desert, particularly at night, holds in store only one kind of quiet ... the kind that works its way into your bones, into the very soul of a man.

It was here, in the deep dark quiet of the Arizona desert, that Champ finally stopped the truck and untied the man. He was slow and methodical as he removed the ropes, carefully monitoring the man's expression at all times. He wanted to be sure that he could see the little spikes of terror appear on his face.

Of course, there wasn't much of a face to see past the large patch of duct tape strapped across the mouth and nose. Champ had covered the nose of his victim on purpose, deliberately leaving a feeling of suffocation, which made him struggle less during the long ride.

The man was all right.

Champ wouldn't let him die of suffocation! He kept a watch on those eyes—eyes that now had taken on a panicky kind of glare as they darted in search of some sort of expla-

1

nation, some sort of reasoning behind the madness that had taken place in the past few hours.

But, in fact, this man had all the answers. He knew damn well why he was out here in the desert with a stranger, and he expected the rest of the lynch mob to show up at any moment.

Richard had come home from work.

That's all he did.

Thursday, wasn't it? One last day until payday. That money was sure gonna feel good in his pocket. His first real money since he got out. The only stinking job he could find, buffing up bumpers at the Octopus Wash for minimum wage, which, for this state, was lower than fly shit.

"Need a hand job, mister?"

Jerks with Beemers and Jags telling him what to do, what not to do ... then leaving him without a word when he waved his towel to signal he was through. Nobody wanted to tip these days.

"... And don't get so close when you do the windshield—someone put a scratch in her with a belt buckle last time I was in here!"

Jesus Christ! Richard didn't even own a belt yet. He was lucky to find a job that would supply him with clothes, period! But not everyone was that way. There had been a couple of folks who were working people, who knew that a bumper guy like him had to be down on his luck to be working a line like that and would handshake him a buck or two. That made him feel good. It was one of the few things that did.

So Richard worked from seven till four-thirty, and then went back to that rattrap of a hotel room to stare down the grainy images on a small black-and-white TV until he could fall mercifully asleep.

The hotel room had no heat and no air-conditioning. The bathroom reeked of vomit and urine, and looked like it hadn't been swabbed out since last Christmas. So, with summer coming on, this place was a stinking inferno. Flies buzzed and alighted briefly—making it hard for him to keep his mind on the two channels he could get decent reception on, so far out here in the sticks.

Two channels.

No fucking antenna, either.

Sometime on Tuesday night he had begun to imagine what it would be like to hold that first cold beer against his chest, allowing it to make his skin uncomfortable. He would have to shift it, or drink it down, to relieve the chill.

Yup, he couldn't wait till payday.

Of course, that would violate his parole—purchasing alcohol. But he would have to do it, just have one good tall one while the heat was around him.

He hadn't quite worked out yet how he would get the beer. That might be a problem. Nearly everyone knew about him. They knew what he had done and why he was stuck here, instead of a real town. It wasn't easy, getting out. The newspapers and the TV had made it a real tough go, but Richard had always been a lucky man. And lucky men get even luckier when their face goes national. So it seemed that for Richard, he'd won it big in the little community.

"Yes, we'll take him," they cried to the reporters and the review board. *"We don't care what his crime was. We believe in rehabilitation! We believe in the American Way! We've even baked him an apple pie . . ."*

Yeah, and I bet they still clap for Tinker Bell, don't they . . .

So Richard was released for good behavior into the little community of Cortez Bend, Arizona.

The Bend, as they called it, only clung to life because of its proximity to I–10 and the fortunate fact that for the next fifty or so miles in either direction there was nothing but cactus and asphalt . . . unless you want to include the sand.

You could always wait until you hit Phoenix to buy a Coke or get gas, but that could be an eternity. Cruel and unusual punishment to be trapped in the summer heat, out in the middle of nowhere, without even so much as a rock to pee behind. Weary travelers *need* pull-down sani-shield dispensers and five different kinds of soda on tap at the self-

3

serve fountain. In fact, *they demand it!* And Cortez Bend was there to cash in on it.

The new, giant, walking-word sign didn't hurt, either:

"CORTEZ BEND WELCOMES YOU! ONE STOP FOR COLD DRINKS, FOOD, GAS, AND TRAVELER'S AID. EASY ON, EASY OFF—NEXT EXIT."

"CORTEZ BEND WELCOMES YOU! ONE STOP FOR . . ."

Well, someone had stopped at the Bend today, and it wasn't for tourist information. It didn't take long for him to overhear the locals talking about the insect they had adopted, and how he was working for peanuts at the local bubble barn and slept nights at a hotel they affectionately referred to as the "BendOver."

And there, Champ waited for Richard. Champ blended in quite well with the clientele of this joint. Right about now he resembled a lone biker-type in search of his next blow job.

His dark hair had grown too long, and he had begun to wear it strung up in back with a rubber band. He usually favored a hat, but it changed from time to time. Today his head was covered by a bandanna, worn kerchief-style over his forehead, the triangular point of it just topping his crown. Sunglasses conveniently withheld secrets he might otherwise have had to work to keep hidden. The rest of his attire had been discovered right alongside the highway—that's how he found most everything he wore.

Except, of course . . . the boots.

His boots were the thing. They were tailored to fit and had lasted ten hard years. The scuffs and tears in the leather didn't do much to soften the image. They were his shit kickers all right. Even had a bloodstained left toe, if anyone cared to examine it.

Though it was damn hot today, no one questioned why a man sat cooped up inside a dirty Ford 4×4 in front of that shitty little hotel for nearly five hours. No one even saw him there.

Richard had arrived home around four-fifty and showered down, using a hand-spray contraption someone had rigged to the bathtub faucet. It wasn't adequate, but Richard was tired from being on his feet all day and just wanted to stretch out on his back. On his way back to the hotel, he had picked up a small package of Chee•tos at the gas station. That would be dinner. He only had enough change to buy that and maybe a cup of Joe in the morning. Tips were nonexistent today, and they had been working like dogs. Tomorrow started the Memorial Day weekend. Everyone was going to be going places, and some had already started. That meant double time on the bumpers.

Richard didn't bother with the uniform. He left it on the floor of the bathroom, soaking up a puddle he had created with the spray. He figured Friday would come and he could slip by with the same dirty set. He'd do laundry on Saturday.

Yeah, fuck the clothes.

He wasn't going out anymore tonight. He just wanted to stretch out, watch some tube, munch some Chee•tos and imagine once again that cold brew against his chest, even if it was just a lonely mind game he was playing.

His naked body flopped against the sheets, and a week's worth of sweat and smell rose to greet him. He punched back the pillow so that he could get into a better position. The news was on, and Richard wanted to see what other poor slob besides himself might be in it tonight.

With a hefty tear, the Chee•tos bag burst and a few flew overboard, leaving fluorescent orange dust on the sheets where they landed. Richard gathered them up, even bending to fetch the ones that went on the floor, before the roaches got to them. Without hesitation, he popped them one by one into his mouth with delight, allowing the salty cheese puffs to consume his senses while he masticated away, turning the mouthfuls into a gummy orange paste that would embed itself into every available nook and cranny his teeth could provide.

5

Meanwhile, the tubes warmed on the old black and white, and the Phoenix channel was starting to unblur nicely. The sound always came on first, and the blond lady newscaster was describing some wonderful new appointment the governor had made to the State Board of Education. When the picture emerged, her face barely blurred at all! Perhaps he wouldn't have to mess too much with the set tonight.

"And turning our focus to Cincinnati, a late-breaking story is just now unfolding as police there have stumbled upon a real-life house of horrors. This gruesome discovery took place during the arrest of thirty-one-year-old Kenneth P. Marlovich, for suspicion of kidnapping a fifteen-year-old neighborhood boy, Mikey Rodriguez. After searching the premises, the police discovered that Marlovich, a neighbor of the missing boy, had dismembered the fifteen-year-old, along with several others, and was storing numerous body parts in his kitchen refrigerator."

What luck, an interesting news story! Richard finished up his bag of Chee•tos and listened intently as the pretty little newscaster droned on.

Champ waited on the sun.

He slumped in the truck's cab patiently, until the dark of the hills had swallowed the valleys whole. The illumination from Richard's shitty black and white played across the windshield and made funny, lightning-type images in the cracks where a stone had kicked up and laid to waste a perfectly nice piece of glass. It fascinated him for a few moments until he shook it off and looked outside. The streetlights were sparse, as was any outside illumination in the Bend. So that was not going to be a problem. With no moon, Arizona nights can be dark—pitch-black.

Rabbits think twice on nights like this. As well they should. Predators didn't need a moon by which to hunt— just a warm, quivering little body, making its way through the darkness.

Champ welcomed such darkness.

Not because he was afraid of being seen—that wasn't a concern. Champ was invisible now. He could move through this world without hesitation because his hands were being guided. His life had become a mission.

And he could use all the terrible blackness the sky could afford.

For the performance.

For the full effect.

He had waited for this night. He had two nights, actually, but he was anxious to get this over with, so he chose the first night without the moon to do the job in Cortez Bend.

And now it was time to go to work.

Champ started the truck, put on the parking brake, and removed his sunglasses, tucking them neatly up under the visor. He climbed from the truck and allowed the door to remain open while he stepped to the rear, unhitching the tailgate. The back was covered over with a taut canvas cover, pulled across the top to make a box out of the bed. From inside, he fetched out a length of rope and a utility belt similar to one a carpenter or construction worker might possess. He slipped the rope over one shoulder as he casually adjusted the utility belt about his hips. Like a professional, he patted the right-side hammer head and the left-side flashlight before deciding it was right. He then reached for the large roll of duct tape and peeled back a swatch, slapping it onto his own shirt.

It was time.

He left the tailgate down as he stepped away. The large round roll of tape swung clumsily to and fro, knocking Champ in the hip and buttocks as he approached the step to the hotel room door. The shitty green, peeling paint job of this dump showed badly, even in the dim light.

Champ didn't pause. He tried the door, found it locked, and stepped back. There was going to be no contest. This same door had been kicked in a dozen or so times before and gave up without resistance.

Richard had fallen asleep on the bed, but the noise from the door rebounding off the wall was enough to roust him.

"Huh?" was all that came out.

Champ fell upon him.

The duct tape stuck quickly, making semicircles across his

cheeks and up into his hair. No chance to scream, no chance to fight. The weight of the attacker was tremendous. And he was solid, like brick. The first thing that Richard thought was:

"Okay, they chose the biggest guy in town to sit on my nuts, so where are the others?"

Richard had been waiting for this. He expected to be beat up by someone in this town, it was just a question of when. One day, he imagined someone would say to him at the car wash, "Say, weren't you the guy they let out of prison on good behavior? Aren't you that sick *fuck* we've been hearing about on TV?"

Then a fight would start, and perhaps there would be two or even more men kicking the snot out of him. He had accepted this possibility and lived with it. But quite frankly, he hadn't expected it to go down like this.

Champ had him rolled over and hog-tied in expert time, sheet and all. Then, with one shove, he rolled Richard back and looked into his frightened eyes.

His victim's lungs were already screaming for more air. His nostrils worked in furious little strokes, *in—out—in—out.* That's when the second piece of tape came out. Champ slapped the strip rudely across Richard's nose, clipping dangerously close to his left eye as he did so. The reaction was immediate. Richard began bucking and screaming behind the tape.

Champ smiled as he lifted Richard over one shoulder in a fireman's carry. It was a short haul back out to the truck. He had parked strategically so that the few steps from the doorway to the passenger side of the vehicle were shielded from any inquiring eyes that might be watching.

But none were.

Champ dumped the body onto the tailgate, whose metal hinging groaned loudly with the weight. He then shoved the cargo up under the canvas. Richard's bare feet were exposed between swatches of the sheet, tangled with the roping. It was the last glimpse Champ had of his quarry before . . .

Up came the tailgate. Champ bounded back up the steps to the hotel. As he did, he removed the utility belt, shut the door as best he could, then crossed back to the truck and tossed the belt on the passenger's seat as he climbed behind the wheel. He paused a moment, listening for any signs of trouble, but it was already clear this insect wasn't going to be any trouble. He was going to be a piece of cake.

A piece of flaming, fucking birthday cake.

A man's gotta do what he thinks is right.

The desert, particularly at night, holds in store only one kind of quiet ... the kind that works its way into your bones, into the very soul of man.

It was here, in the deep dark quiet of the Arizona desert, that Champ finally stopped the truck and untied the man ...

Richard was shivering as his captor began loosening the rope. He turned his head, looking this way and that, trying to figure out where they were and what was going to happen next. All he could see was the few cactus and scrub trees that the headlights illuminated before them. The man he was with had a flashlight that was balanced on the canvas top of the truck bed, so he could snatch a glimpse of his attacker as he moved in and out of the light.

They had driven a long way. Richard guessed hours. And for quite some time, they had been on a dirt road full of bumps. Riding as cargo, he had been tossed about by the truck's bouncing movements on the washboard lane, his face, hands, and feet colliding with the various angles of the truck bed. It stunk of gasoline back there, and now he stunk of it, too.

He searched the horizon for the signs of surface light—damn, it was dark! No light out there at all; no moon tonight.

No way of knowing where the hell they are going to find me—if they find me, Richard thought.

Once he was unloaded from the truck and the ropes were removed, Richard clutched at the sheet, positioning it like a toga about him. His bare feet were dangerously close to a length of cactus spine that had long since dropped from the plant, but he didn't have time to notice.

His captor approached, pulling a set of shears from his

utility belt and raising them toward Richard's face, forcing him to back up. His foot grazed the cactus, but no painful contact ensued. It was just enough of a distraction to make him stop short and reassess his situation.

Smiling in an understanding sort of way, his captor motioned for Richard to stand quietly and allow the cutting and peeling of tape from his mouth and nose.

Suddenly hope ran through Richard's mind:

No lynch mob! No one else is here. This guy is just the Welcoming Committee. He's trying to tell me to find another town to live in. That's all. He's just gonna dump me out here with a "get lost and don't come back" speech, and that'll be it. I can handle that. I can definitely handle that.

Richard moved forward reluctantly. His captor went to work on cutting the tape as he spoke quietly. His voice was friendly like.

"She was five, wasn't she?" After a moment, the man clarified his statement. "Your daughter."

At first, Richard didn't react. He held still until the tape was free. The sting and smack of the removal was still smarting. But he could breathe freely now, and he gulped in a few clean breaths. The gasoline was stronger smelling now. He noticed it was all over the sheet.

"Answer me," Champ demanded after a moment. The friendliness was fading from his tone.

"Yeah . . . yeah, she was five."

Champ replaced the shears in the utility belt and crossed his arms, resting lazily against the tailgate, like a good ol' boy. He was now wearing a straw hat with a small chunk missing out of the back, another roadside attraction that he'd stopped to pick up a month or so back.

"They're cute at five. Aren't they?" The friendly tone returned.

Richard didn't comment. He was growing impatient with this and just wanted whatever he was going to get from the Welcoming Committee, even if it was a committee of one.

He spoke hastily. "What do you want from me? You want me to leave town? Fine. You wanna kick the shit out of me, then get on with the program. Quit fucking around. Everyone knows what I did! I spent the past eight years in the joint. I was—a different kind of person back then. Everything was different."

Instead of replying, Champ reached for the utility box and slid it forward, producing a can of beer. He offered it to Richard.

Richard paused before reaching for it. It wasn't completely cold, but it was cool to touch. He popped the top and then looked to the man in the hat for what was expected of him.

Champ's beer was already open, and he gulped down a swig in a hurry. He raised the can in salute to Richard and then drank again.

Richard took his first sip.

It tasted good. Real good. He took another quick gulp.

Then a welcome thought crossed his mind:

Perhaps this asshole isn't the Welcoming Committee. Maybe he was in the joint, too. He probably saw all the brouhaha on the tube about Cortez Bend taking me in as a charity case, and just wanted to sit down and talk about it. Talk about the joint or something. But why all the . . . treatment? Why the mind fuck? No telling what this one has done. So play along. This could be a good thing.

"You wanna see her? Your daughter?"

Richard stopped in mid-gulp.

"Can't. Never. I see stuff on the tube. They did interviews. When I was going to be released, they were doing a lot of them. I watched the TV in the community room a couple of times."

"How did she look?"

"She looked . . . she looked okay. I mean there's a lot they can still do for her. But, you know, it's been awhile now, and just from seeing her on the tube . . . there's been a lot of changes in eight years."

"Yes. A lot of changes."

The two men drank deeply this time. The beer was hitting Richard fast. The Chee-tos he'd had for supper weren't holding much back. He was beginning to feel secure, convincing himself that this guy meant him no harm.

11

He wouldn't be doing this—it would already be done if it was a bad thing.

Champ crumpled his first beer can and tossed it back into the utility box. He reached for a second.

"You got kids?" Richard inquired, hoping to open a door or two.

"Nope."

"Married?"

"Nope."

"So you bring me out here to play twenty questions?"

"Nope."

"Then . . . what?"

Champ smiled as he popped the second can and began spraying Richard with it. In defense, Richard swung a armful of sheet up at the spray and stepped away.

"Arrrrrh!" Richard cried out as those cactus spines pierced the soles of his bare feet.

He hopped onto his left foot, dropping his beer in the dust. He was vaguely aware of laughter as he struggled to regain his balance. His dancing side step brought him closer to the truck. He reached out for support on the tailgate.

The spray continued.

And beyond the pain shooting into his foot, Richard was becoming aware of something else. There was a smell here, too. That beer must have really hit him hard, because with the adrenaline and all that was happening to him, it wasn't until he was hit in the face with a stream of liquid that he finally became aware that he was being squirted with . . .

Gasoline!

"Fuck! Fuck!" he cried, hobbling away from the tailgate.

"No man—*fuck you!*" Champ stated flatly as he raised up the canister and pumped out another stream of gasoline.

It sprayed against Richard's bare chest.

It was at this point that Champ always recited his litany: when the insect knew he was trapped and there wasn't gonna be any going home . . . not this time, *not ever*.

"Did you know that when they found her, she was still *screaming* for you? Did you know that for months afterward, while she was lying in the hospital, she was begging the nurses to take her to you? She was convinced that the same thing had happened to *poor daddy!* They had to tell her that you were the one who did that to her and then, like the chicken-shit piece of scum-fuck that you are, you left her there to die. They had to explain it to her as she grew older and could understand such things, that her own precious *daddy* was capable of kidnapping his own five-year-old daughter, and then, while she slept peacefully in some anonymous motel room in Nevada, he was also capable of pouring gasoline on top of her and setting her on *fire.*"

Richard had fallen in his flight.

Blinded by the gasoline and crippled from the spines in his foot, he had let go of the sheet. It was only a few steps from where he lay, crumpled in the dirt next to a small pile of brush.

Champ crossed to him and kicked the sheet closer. It grazed his feet, and he fanned it away, sobbing.

"God ... no! Please!"

He was past words. Way past words now.

"That kid has had over ten operations in the last eight years. The last one took twelve hours to perform. And afterward, the recovery was so bad that she cried for days on end—but not because of the pain. You'd be happy to know your kid is no quitter. She was crying because she was afraid that the skin grafts wouldn't be healed in time for her to start junior high *with her friends.* That is to say, those few kids who don't run in fear from her or point at her in the store or talk about her incessantly, like she's the *town freak.*

"But let's talk about the inside, now—shall we? The nightmares? Nobody could stop her from screaming then ... not even her mother. When you're five years old, man, there ain't nothing but good or bad. No in between. You fucked her up good. You fucked her up real good. And there ain't nothing anybody can do about it. But there is something we can do about you. Something we can do *to* you."

Champ kicked Richard in the legs with his custom-made boots. *Hard.* The naked man cried out in pain, clutching his kneecap and shin.

"Isn't there? To allow you to understand, even if it is only

13

for a brief moment, just how that five-year-old girl felt." Champ pulled a blue-tip match from an inside pocket and held it up.

"I . . . I . . ." Richard struggled to say through tremendous gulps of breath. "Please! Please, don't! I'm sorry!"

"I know," Champ replied as he flicked his nail against the match head in poetic motion. He dropped it on the sheet, which caught fire quickly.

"I know you will be."

Champ dug down with his boot tip and kicked the wad of flaming sheet at Richard, who was already trying to crawl away, pawing at the line of scrub brush in front of him, raking his hands raw on the razor-like tubers as he tried crawling under . . . and away.

Like a dog, Champ thought. What a naked, sobbing excuse for a human being.

Champ remembered having a dog once. When the poor animal got too old, Champ and his little brother had to take it out and shoot it so it wouldn't feel any more pain. It was merciful that way, he told his little brother.

But this was not going to be merciful.

The gasoline trail jumped from the sheet and started up the man's leg. That realization made Richard leap up suddenly and start running. He batted at the fire that quickly covered the hairy areas of his back and chest, working its way quickly toward his face.

Champ had noted Richard was not a particularly hairy fellow.

So he squirted a few more jolts at the guy for good measure.

Richard fell to the ground and rolled, trying to suffocate the fire with dirt. Seeing what his prey was up to, Champ kept careful watch. A little squirt here, a tiny squirt there . . . until finally, Champ emptied the canister in one big blaze.

Motionless, the body continued to burn.

Champ returned to the truck and leaned against the tailgate, resting the empty gas canister next to him. Head raised, he turned his attention upward to the faraway canopy of twinkling fires in the sky, each running its own course in the way of things.

A sigh.

And so it continues.

"Do you know that she will never grow hair on the right side of her head? And that her left eye has only twenty percent sight left?"

His mind raced on. This one had really gotten inside of him. He reached into the pocket of his pants and pulled out a key chain that bore a lucky rabbit's foot. It was a faded blue—one that had seen a lot of use in the past.

He stroked it, almost subconsciously while he cursed himself for not having remembered to include each and every devastating fact of this tragic case into his litany.

Oh well . . . nobody's perfect.

1

Life in 'The Dicks'
June 20th—Cincinnati, Ohio
16:49

"Cooperation is everything in an investigation. From the beginning, through the middle, and then straight on into the bowels, my friend ... that's when the case *finally* finds itself down the toilet—as if anyone around here ever flushes."

Bennie Sarkissian huffed, puffed, and pontificated as he led a new babe in the woods up the fire stairs to the fourth floor of the suspect's apartment building. A babe consisted of anyone not having more than five years in homicide detail, and this "young gun" didn't even have one week's worth of investigative toe jam inside his Reeboks.

But the babe was in shape, which Bennie was not. So this young officer found himself waiting on Bennie at every landing while the seasoned detective caught his breath between speeches.

"If you got cooperation, then you got an easy case, but that's where that theory floats—belly-up. From the lips of criminal investigation instructors right down the old commode, baby—because this ain't gonna be no easy case."

And with that, Bennie made his way through the door to

the fourth floor and followed the hallway down to the nearest open doorway. Policemen stood about idly, watching the activity inside apartment 414. The smell alone nearly melted the buttons right off the babe's snappy Le Tigre shirt. Bennie graciously tossed a plain white kerchief at the kid's chest, but it bounced off and fell to the floor. The poor kid just stood there, gaping.

"Better pick that up. My wife will wonder where I left it."

Bennie quickly searched the crowd for signs of his partner, but didn't connect. He started into the room, motioning to the kid to follow as he spoke.

"Now, as I was saying ... with this case, we got plenty of cooperation. But who needs it?"

Bennie watched as a fellow officer left the apartment in an obvious hurry to find fresh air.

"What we need in here is some goddamn fresh air! A shitload of fucking barf bags wouldn't hurt, neither. Aw, such is life in 'The Dicks,' kid, welcome to it."

The Cannibal's apartment was crammed with every kind of public servant the taxpayers could provide. And most of them were wearing coverage on their nose and mouth because of the unspeakable stench that permeated the place. There were the coroner's people and the people from the Department of Public Health. There were regular cops, and then there was Homicide.

And in Cincinnati these days, when you spoke of Homicide, you were speaking about the newly famous Lt. Daniel G. Traask.

"Traask!" Bennie called.

"Yeah, Bennie, over here" came the reply.

A tousled dark head of hair popped out from behind the kitchen half wall ... but only for a moment. Even Traask was wearing gear to cut the stench. Bennie threaded his way over to him, careful not to disturb two guys bent down on all fours over some spot in the carpet, gathering samples. He left the babe lost in the new woods, fumbling to fold Bennie's hanky into some kind of triangle to cover his nose and mouth.

"Hey, hon, my dinner ready yet?" Bennie asked casually,

taking note that Traask was supervising the inventory of the refrigerator contents personally.

One of the bag men turned in response.

"We was gonna save you some, but Traask told us to bag it up quick when we heard you was coming."

"Yeah, no in-between-meal snacks, now!" the other bag man chimed in. They chuckled between them, but one look from Traask cut it short.

Traask had been losing his sense of humor lately, and there were lots of reasons for it. Over the past year, the thirty-five year old cop had worn a dozen furrows in his previously flawless brow. Still, he was one of those men that women loved ... well built, darkly handsome, with playful blue eyes that spoke to you of things he couldn't say. Sometimes they were things you didn't need to know.

"Put some speed on it. I want to get this shit out of here before the press arrives."

"Yeah, well ... somebody's been earning their tips today. There's already a half a dozen of them out there," Bennie reported uneasily. Then he leaned into Traask and added, "And they know you're here."

"Great ..." Traask moaned, eyes rolling to the ceiling. His left hand moved by reflex to the back of his neck to rub a dull ache that still lay deep inside, but it was building.

"I thought you'd be pleased."

"Is *she* down there?"

"No. So far, no sign of the Twat Leader."

Traask turned to Bennie with an expression of disdain. "Come on, Bennie ..."

"I'm sorry, I'm sorry! I forgot you don't have an appreciation for pet names." Bennie sounded sincere, but Traask knew otherwise. "But if the name fits ..."

"Okay, Lt. Traask, we're finished here."

The bag men had begun to move the two large containers that held the evidence from the refrigerator out of the kitchen.

"Look out, you guys, coming through!"

The coroner's department wasn't ready to be moved. One

guy blocked the path of the bag men. "Hey, back it up, back it up; can't you see we're workin' here!?"

"How're we supposed to move this shit outta here, then?" the first bag man replied. "'Levitate it?'"

"Levitate this . . ." the coroner tech replied testily, grabbing his crotch and grinning to his partner.

"Yeah, nobody else will . . ." his cohort chimed in. This prompted both of them to burst out in hiccuping laughter at the inside joke. It drew attention.

The bag men exchanged a pained look. Their levity was not shared by the rest of the group. They were losing patience.

"Arnie, you're a real asshole, *you know that?*" the first bag man snapped.

The coroner boys stopped laughing. Suddenly, it was a standoff.

Traask's red flag went up, and he stepped between the two. "Okay, all right—hold on. Jerry, how much more you got left to do here?"

"Well," the seasoned toxicologist replied from his position on the floor, "it's hard to say."

"A rough estimate, please?" Traask held his tongue for the sake of diplomacy.

"Maybe another fifteen minutes."

"Thank you." Traask turned to the bag men. "Set them down. We'll wait."

"What?" the bag men complained.

"You heard the man," Bennie said as he pulled Traask away. He finally barked, "Sit on it!"

Bennie led Traask to the only clear area in the whole apartment at the moment, which was the now empty kitchen. The newsworthy refrigerator had its door left wide open. With its light on and motor still humming, it appeared as a violated, gaping mouth, hungering to be filled again.

Bennie thought of his own fridge at home and shook his head. That kind of thing will follow you home, nights. It's shit like that got to the forty-six-year-old, overweight detective—not the blood and guts at the murder scene or the grisly evidence when discovered. Not even the rancid smell was a problem for Bennie. He couldn't breathe too great out of one nostril, and the other one wasn't on speaking terms most days, so he wasn't offended in the least. But this ... this nightmare figure of an ordinary home appliance was beginning to bite him in the ass.

Traask followed his gaze. He knew this partner. They had worked around each other for over five years, but had been assigned together as a team for only five months. The past year had seen some of the worst cases Cincinnati had lived through in decades—newsworthy cases that demanded a lot from the people assigned to them.

That's how Traask had gotten to know Bennie and his wife Lottie. He had also got to know a lot of the men and their families on the force because of the Cop Killer. Suddenly he had become the Man of the Hour—the man who had brought the news to the people of Cincinnati as they sat before their television sets every night—glued to the outcome of who and where and when.

Cincinnati's notorious Cop Killer had gunned down seventeen cops, one by one in cold blood, and reigned as the top news story for over a year. Six months ago, they finally got that son of a bitch. But not without a price. To capture him alive nearly tore the police force of Cincinnati apart. Things were definitely out of control there near the end. Vigilante task forces comprised of off-duty police officers were secretly meeting to search for the killer on their own. These were men who had families and wives who knew what they were doing.

Traask was the one who stepped into the limelight after one such task force—since nicknamed "The Enforcers"—had been exposed and subsequently all suspended without pay, pending an internal investigation. It was Traask who had pulled the force back into a team and then tracked that cop-killing bastard until, finally, they got him.

It was good police work that resulted in that kind of outcome. Of course by then, the media was busy whipping up a frenzy within the public to support gunning down this criminal whenever or wherever they found him. It was Traask's job to keep the cool head. It was Traask's job to turn his fellow cops around and keep them focused. And it was Traask who had brought Eddie Jefferson, a.k.a. the Cop Killer, through the station house doors that night in one piece and booked him. Everybody knew it was Daniel Traask who had made it so.

So stumbling across the Cannibal's lair in the middle of a routine investigation was fuel enough to nominate Traask for sainthood in the eyes of the press. The citizens of Cincinnati were sure to eat this one up.

Hell, they'd lick his plate clean.

And Bennie knew that Traask wasn't ready for the added pressure. Traask had been reaching his limit in his unsolicited role as media hero. If they wanted to do their jobs and do them right, Traask could not be seen as a figurehead here.

Bennie knew the best thing was to get him out of there, fast.

"Look, why don't you just take off?" Bennie casually suggested.

"What?"

"Get lost, before the circus starts. Go back to the station. We'll manage. I'll make some sort of nominal statement to the bozos downstairs, and they can get the rest from a press statement in the morning. It'll give us a chance to get this thing together . . ."

"Are you trying to get rid of me?"

But Traask's eyes met Bennie's for a moment, acknowledging what they were talking about.

"You know what's gonna happen if they see your face. It's gonna start all over again," Bennie explained. "And we need you with us right now. Not in TV land."

Publicity over the Cop Killer trial had Traask's name being mentioned every night on the news. His presence here would spark off more media fireworks than a Fourth of July carnival, and that was the last thing Traask wanted right now.

"Maybe you're right. We're almost through here, anyway. Where'd they take him?"

Bennie knew Traask was talking about the Cannibal. They

had moved him out fast to avoid the usual photo opportunities.

"He's back at the ranch. They've already turned him and burned him. They're just waiting for you to get down there so they can begin taping. That fucker talks a mile a minute, you know."

"I noticed. Okay. I'm gone. Is there a back way out of here?"

Bennie turned and nodded to the doorway. "I think your best bet is the fire stairs. I took them on the way up. They empty out onto the street—west side. Most of the press is in the lobby."

Bennie held out his keys. "Take my car. It's parked at the bottom. They know yours already, and I think they've got it surrounded."

"Gee, maybe they can take a statement from my mechanic," Traask smirked as he dug out his own keys and traded with his partner.

"At this point they'd settle for a statement from your mechanic's mother."

And the sad thing was, Bennie was right.

Deborah Morrison was running late. By the time she got to the school to pick up her youngest, the teacher in charge of "After School Activities" already had her car keys in hand and a nasty expression on her face.

"I'm sorry," Deborah apologized as sincerely as she could.

After all, it was the first time in a long while that she had been late to pick up her daughter. The teacher escorted them out of the school without a word. She didn't even say good-bye.

Well, Deborah was used to getting "the treatment," as she had taken to calling it. Her mother and grandmother used to tell stories about their own battles with discrimination, but it had all seemed a million miles away from the here and now. But as a black, single mother of two, Deborah had begun to realize a lot of people gave the treatment to you without even knowing they were doing it.

In the last six months, Deborah had learned that people were capable of doing all kinds of things.

Meanwhile, her son had reset the radio station while waiting for them in the car. It was now blasting rap music, and he was pounding the monotonous beat on the dash with his palms. He didn't blink as they entered the vehicle. Even when Deborah demanded he turn the music down. He was revved for the holiday weekend and hadn't bothered to say three words to Deborah since she picked him up from basketball practice.

She really needed someone to ask her how her day had gone ... someone to take at least half this load off her shoulders. She was tired, dead tired, of carrying it. And it had only been five-and-a-half months since she had started doing it alone. But she didn't want the kids to see her fatigue, so she drove home on autopilot, doing her best to pick up her spirits.

"So, what's the haps?"

"Mom, don't forget, I invited Joe and Bobby over. We're having a *Nightmare on Elm Street* marathon, so I get the VCR in my room on Saturday, okay?"

Deborah bit her lip. Her thirteen-year-old son and his friends had taken on an abnormal affection for those slasher films. God, she hoped this was a phase.

"John ... how long is this marathon gonna be? You're not the only person who might want to use the VCR, you know."

"Yeah," Kathy chimed in.

John's ten-year-old sister used to be kind of fun. Lately, she was a pain.

"Oh, like you're gonna have anyone over? Your friends don't need to use the VCR. You just chase each other out of the bathroom every fifteen minutes. I can hear them calling for backup on the phone." With a mock telephone to his ear, he turned his voice falsetto. "Be sure the curling irons are loaded! Send in the SWAT team, we need more hair spray at this ten twenty. You copy?"

"Mom!"

"Look!" Deborah stopped the fight in midstream. "I don't

know what's gonna be happening this weekend yet. I gotta make a few phone calls when I get home."

"But, Mom, he *always* hogs the VCR!"

"And *her* friends always leave the bathroom armed and dangerous. It's disgusting!"

"Stop it!" Deborah shouted as they pulled into the driveway. She turned to reach for the garage door opener, but John had bent forward with lightning speed and activated it. As the Suburban rolled to a halt inside the garage, Deborah turned to face both of them.

"I promise you, I'll make some phone calls and find out what's going to be going on. But for now, can we just have some cooperation between the two of you and help me hustle up some dinner? Okay?"

John and Kathy reluctantly nodded and anxiously piled out of the car, heading for the door to the inside. It was always a race between them to see who could get to the TV remote first, for it is written somewhere that he whosoevereth hath the remote control, hath the power. Then it would be MTV for the next hour or until Deborah was sick of it and made them turn it off.

Deborah didn't pile out of the car so fast. She gathered her things together in tired, undisciplined motions and then heaped them all into her arms, closing the car door with her hip.

By the time she reached the kitchen counter and dropped her load, she was in no mood for the dirty morning dishes and collection of overnight glassware that greeted her. She was tempted to call out for pizza, but that just wasn't in the budget these days. Besides, she was saving a pizza coupon for use over the weekend when the kids would want it most.

"Mom! Mom, come here! Come quick!" John called, the tone in his voice sounding serious.

The first thing that crossed Deborah's mind was that she would round the corner into the living room and find all of their worthwhile possessions gone—victims of some daytime burglar who needed some quick money for drugs, or worse.

But when Deborah got there, everything was as it should be ... except for the fact that John and Kathy were standing together, side by side, glued to the images before them on the television set. The news was on. And although she couldn't see the reporter's image through the bodies of her two children, she could clearly hear who it was.

"Excuse me, excuse me, Lt. Traask—Holly North, WKLX Channel Thirteen News. Can we get a comment from you on the findings inside the apartment building? Is it true that there were multiple bodies found decomposing in the suspect's apartment?"

"It's Dan on the news again, Mom. Let's see how he handles the Twat Leader this time!"

Deborah's mouth opened to comment on her son's vulgarity, then shut just as fast for two reasons. First, she knew where he'd learned that nickname. It was from his father, and she wasn't going to provoke John into defending the memory of his father again. She knew damn well that Frank would have said almost exactly the same thing, using those same words, had he been standing in this room tonight. This was something that John needed to imitate, and it was something that helped them all heal just a little, even if it was a vulgar term—which brought her to reason number two.

The bitch deserved the title.

"Quiet, John!" was all she managed to say as she studied the image of Daniel Traask trapped on some strip of sidewalk, standing next to—was that Bennie's car? Yeah, she recognized Bennie's car all right. It had been parked in their own driveway more than its fair share over the years.

Traask appeared to be running off of reserves, too, thought Deborah. His face was a bit pale and, as he shifted uneasily before the camera, he was thinner than when she saw him last. Everyone in Cincinnati had seen Daniel Traask on TV at one time or another during the past fourteen months, but that was the *only* place she had seen him. And this was a man who used to reach into her own refrigerator on a daily basis and ask why there were never any jalapeños in the house.

Suddenly Deborah felt ashamed.

It didn't have to be this way.

"I have to decline comment. We all should know it's still

25

too early to tell what we've got happening here. We'll have a statement for the press later in the day or maybe tomorrow morning."

"... But surely you've been inside, supervising this gruesome discovery. Can't you at least confirm for us that the bodies were indeed dismembered? I mean, rumor has it that the suspect is a member of some sort of cannibalistic cult and that the killings were just part of a ..." The reporter was cut off in mid-sentence.

"I really don't have anything to say at this time. It wouldn't be right for us to speculate before all the evidence has been brought in and examined. So let's give the men a chance to do their jobs here, and then we'll be getting back to you on just what we've learned, okay?"

Traask moved away from the reporter and unlocked the car, climbing inside, but this didn't stop the Twat Leader from giving pursuit. If she was anything, Deborah thought to herself, she was consistent.

"Can you just confirm for us that the man has given you a full confession to the killings? Can you confirm that he is, indeed, a cannibal—engaging in ritualistic activities inside the apartment? Is he part of a cult?"

Traask tried waving her off, but she wouldn't budge, even motioning to the camera crew to block the car's exit. So Traask was forced to back the car out—away from them, driving in reverse for nearly half a block until he could turn around safely and burn some rubber in the opposite direction.

Deborah didn't need to pay attention to the rest of this broadcast.

"Too cool! Did you hear that, Mom? Dan's got another big case! I guess this means we'll be seeing him every night on the news again." John strutted about the living room as if he were a proud son, then he pointed the remote control at the screen and pressed MUTE—shutting out the incessant chatter that issued forth from the mouth of Holly North.

"Take that, Twat Leader!" John smiled, thoroughly satisfied with himself. Raising the remote, he blew away the imaginary smoke from the imaginary barrel.

If it were only that easy, Deborah sighed. She turned to leave the room just as Kathy spoke. "I don't get it. A man was cutting up *people* in his apartment?"

"He was *eating* them, stupid! Don't you even know what a cannibal is? God, are you stupid!"

"I am not!"

"John! Knock it off," Deborah ordered. She really didn't need Kathy thinking about that one. "Let's just get going on the dishes, please? Kathy, will you get a salad started?"

Deborah headed for the kitchen, and the kids followed suit without delay. They were getting hungry, and it was pretty late. But Deborah could hear Kathy ask John as they entered the kitchen, "Gosh, now does Dan have to question that guy? I mean, gross!"

"That guy is nothing next to Freddie Krueger, man. Freddie would take on that cannibal and make him hurl his lunch back in one heave."

"Gross!"

"Yum yum, eat 'em up. Hey, man, that's the way it is on *Elm Street!* Only the sickest survive!"

I'm gonna call Dan, Deborah thought to herself. I'm gonna call him right now and leave a message on his machine.

Something about the way he looked. Or maybe it was just time . . . she wasn't going to fight the feeling. Calling just felt right. She crossed into the bedroom and sat on the bed, dialing the familiar number by heart and without hesitation.

"Hi. Leave a message after the beep or you can have me paged at the department. If you know me, then you know that number too. Thanks." Then the long tone sounded.

And just like that . . . it was Deborah's turn.

"Uh, hi, Dan. It's Deborah. Morrison. I was just wondering how you were, uh—doing. Can you give me a call? I'll be home tonight—I know you have the number. Or you can just give me a call before the weekend, if you're busy."

If you're busy?

Of course the man was busy. "Well, talk to you later then. Bye."

Deborah hung up and held the phone in her lap for a

moment trying to picture him after he got that message. Would he be surprised? Would he smile and pick up the phone right away, or would he re-cradle the receiver just as fast, thinking it was still a bad idea?

God, she hoped it would be a smile.

She needed to talk.

2

Message in a Bottle
June 22nd—Phoenix, Arizona
Approximate Time 14:30

The temperature inside a closed vehicle sitting in the direct sun of a Phoenix parking lot at midday can cook an egg inside the carton.

Residents have reported milk product spoilage as fast as five minutes after grocery shopping.

Televised public service announcements warn that leaving a car's windows cracked for a pet is not enough to keep the animal from serious dehydration and even death within fifteen minutes when left inside a vehicle in Arizona's summer heat.

And you'd better believe that many a surprised owner returned to his car to discover Fido had fried into a crispy critter while he was inside a cool and comfortable air-conditioned mall "... for only a matter of minutes ..."

The kids in the back of the van had no way of judging how long it was since they had been left inside to die. Both the boy and girl lay on their stomachs, facedown—barely able to suck in the scorching air to refill their laboring lungs. They had stopped squirming at least five minutes ago when the girl felt a wave of blackness overtake her, causing her to drop her full weight to the van floor.

The rocking motion should have brought someone running, the boy thought.

He dove for cover as well. He waited for the doors to open and the horror to begin. His eyes darted quickly to the makeshift panel that separated the driver's seat from the cargo area. Only tiny cracks of light made it through the seams.

After several moments, those small indicators of light remained undisturbed. It seemed that the rocking motion had not been detected. No one was coming for them.

Jimmy raised his head for one last survey around before struggling to drag his weight toward Carly's lifeless body, avoiding—if he could—any motions that would cause the van itself any more movement.

The T-shirt of the sixteen-year-old girl was streaked with perspiration, old and new. Clumps of cloth, soaked through with sweat, clung to her skin in wet Rorschach-like patterns. Her hands, bound behind her with yards of duct tape in the same fashion as Jimmy's, were closed and motionless against their bonds. She was no longer struggling against them, no longer hoping the sweat from her arms and hands might work down to loosen the sticky bonds, freeing a hand with which to claw toward freedom.

Jimmy tried whispering, but heard the ineffectual noise and knew it would not arouse her. He cleared his dry throat and tried making a slightly louder sound. The duct tape across his mouth would not allow passage of any comforting words—merely garbled, M-sounding warnings.

"Mmmm, Muh Muh," Jimmy tried.

He butted Carly's shoulder with his head, leaning over her awkwardly, hands restrained and legs bound at the ankles. His dirty Nikes were in the exact same shape as the day he had first noticed the beat-up van outside the convenience store where he was playing video games with his best friends, Bobbie and Ron. Little had he known what that van meant. How could anyone guess the horrors that awaited inside those doors? How could Jimmy have known that this good-bye would become his last reported position when he parted from them and started home late for dinner?

That had been over a year ago. When they had got tired of "playing" with Jimmy, they had run into Carly. And suddenly Jimmy had someone to share his fate with. This gave him tremendous hope that was dashed all too quickly. The combinations were now infinite. As an eleven-year-old, Jimmy had not yet known that sex could be used as an instrument of punishment, pain, and when they felt so inclined, pure torture.

But Carly was a fighter. This is what had saved her—not her ability to block out the painful, savage attacks upon her body. It was Carly's true spirit that had made her a struggling survivor of this nightmare. And as she turned now, she fought the swirling blackness of the heat and fatigue to reach Jimmy.

"We have to get out of here!"

"I know," Jimmy nodded in return. He jerked his head toward the panel that hid the driver's seat. He shook his head violently, nodding toward her to indicate his intentions. Then he fell to the floor, purposefully sending the vehicle into a rocking motion. He shook his head violently once more, nodding toward the driver's side.

Carly's eyes grew wide. Their captors had not seen the van move! They had always maintained that they could see or be within earshot of the van whenever they left Jimmy and Carly inside alone. This occurred very rarely. There was usually one of them around to keep watch anytime they stopped. But on the odd occasion that they both left, any movement inside the van was grounds for swift and severe punishment.

Carly had been delivered a concussion from one incident within recent memory. And yet she still wanted to try. She knew that someone had to see them eventually. Someone had to see something, for Christ's sake!

Carly's nightmare had begun as she ran along a lonely stretch of road between her school and home, as she did every day. She was a member of the cross-country team and had taken some medals to reward her hard work. No one had ever thought that this small and remote town was in danger from kidnappers or creeps until that day. The day before Carly's sixteenth birthday.

Her parents retraced the steps with the police and found one running shoe and a clump of hair. So it was deduced that she had been kidnapped and the long sad wait began. Carly's aunt had taken the reins at that point, calling kids and explaining that the big birthday party had been canceled. There were no explanations necessary. Everyone in the little town of Antelope Hill, Nevada, had watched the news or heard that Carly was missing. But no one had actually seen anything that day. And Carly was determined that someone, somewhere, was going to find them by having seen something!

At this moment, she struggled to sit upright, falling backward, then forward, until she could balance her weight properly. The heat was sucking the life from them. She worked her nostrils in large breaths, weighing their position. The back of the van stank of urine, feces, vomit, and rancid leftovers, as this had been their sixty-cubic-foot "hell cell" for many excruciating months. They ate only when the tape was removed and scraps were finally tossed to them. Most of the time the half-eaten food lay just inches from their taped-up mouths while the two men laughed. Once this food "game" went on for two days and when the tape was finally removed and the scraps consumed, both Carly and Jimmy vomited it up for hours, later receiving a massive beating for being sick inside the van.

Frequently they were forced to urinate (or worse) in their clothes, for lack of attendance to their bodily needs. This also brought on the beatings, but they had learned how to hold on until their usual nighttime relief out in some deserted area, in full view of each other, of course. Jimmy didn't even want to think about how they had handled Carly's periods. It was too humiliating.

In her attempt to sit, Carly's shoulder made contact with the metal wall of the tire well. Using that as an indicator, she could deduce that they would not be able to last much longer in this oven on wheels constructed by Ford.

It wasn't likely that anyone was standing around watching them in this heat—but it was hard to tell. The van was devoid of windows in the cargo area. Their only indicator of night or day had become the rays of light that bled through the seams of the paneling at the cargo head. That indicator was a friend, because it allowed them to know when someone was near, trying to peek in on them. So they slept whenever they could—or pretended to be asleep so that the torture factor diminished.

But they knew they were in a city now. The sounds of many cars and trucks—the vibration of activity and frequent stops, indicated they were in civilization once again. So there was hope. Carly was from Nevada, Jimmy from New Mexico—and both had experienced hot summers. There was no telling where they really were until last night when the back end of the van was opened to reveal a desert terrain and Carly recognized the familiar outline of a saguaro cactus—something that grew only in Arizona, around the Phoenix and Tucson areas.

So now she knew something! But she had no idea if Jimmy was aware of this or not. Perhaps he had gathered it from movies he'd seen ... she had little information about her partner except his name, age, and that he was from New Mexico. She knew he had been here before her, but exactly how long? Could her captors somehow be related to this boy through an unfortunately twisted root in a family tree?

That was too gross to think about. Relatives that could do this kind of thing might mean that Jimmy would have nowhere to run to—nowhere safe to belong when this was all over. She wanted to believe that he was once a regular kid with friends and a family. Carly wanted to believe there must be someone out there searching for him. But many times the look in his eyes became lost—almost dead. As if this were his fate without end. She guessed his spirit had been broken long before her arrival, but the deadness she saw staring back from within him frightened her. She was afraid his hopelessness might be catching.

But they possessed a chance here. A remarkable chance, in fact. And damn the Fates if they didn't agree.

Carly and Jimmy had searched the van many times for something sharp or pointed to help cut the tape that held them. Many times they had tried using saliva to loosen the sticky hold across their mouths, which only resulted in severe punishment upon discovery by the powers that be, for their bonds were regularly checked and often replaced—usually when the "games" began, which had been every single night.

But nothing had turned up to be a useful tool for their escape. For escape was foremost, discovery a close second. It would be nice to be discovered, but they knew the men who had taken them possessed guns and they were afraid that anyone discovering their presence in the van would be taken a prisoner as well or perhaps just be shot dead right there. For those guns had been positioned outside, as well as inside, their own bodies at various times—and several times discharged in their presence, just for effect. Once Jimmy had spontaneously urinated when they aimed at his head and played "Russian Roulette." That was the night they made Jimmy lap at their urine with his tongue as they pissed, laughing and calling him "the Piss-Sucker."

But something was catching Carly's attention now. As she inched forward, she could see that there was an object, a corner of white, peeking at them from under the paneling. She moved by swinging her legs sideways, using her knees to inch forward. Jimmy voiced a warning, and she knew he was concerned about movement—they could come back at any time. But Carly didn't care. She needed a break, and she felt this might be it.

Reaching the paneling, Carly saw that it was loose. She bent down to the small item to get a better view. It appeared to be a paper something—perhaps a corner of a map or . . . a matchbook cover! That could really do them some good. A car on fire could lead to discovery, all right. Carly was determined to get at it and pull it through, under the paneling.

She began to brush her cheek against the board, picking up slivers in her skin, but she knew this technique worked well at the corners of her taped mouth and soon she had peeled away a small piece. She bent down once again and turned her head in, wedging it against the paneling and the floor of the van, attempting to connect the peeled-away tape with the white object. She prayed for some semblance of sticky matter to be left so she could use it to pull—but she wasn't able to connect with the object due to the angle of her head in relation to the object.

After several attempts, the black swirl of unconsciousness was again knocking on her senses. She continued working, however, until the blackness came and swallowed her whole.

When Carly went down the second time, Jimmy realized he had to get her away from the object of discovery or their captors would certainly figure out what she had been up to. He moved to her with difficulty and butted at her with his head, shoving against her while bracing his sneakered feet against the van's side door. With all his effort, he only managed to push her a little ways toward the opposite wall.

But this revealed that she had made progress with the object, for now there was clearly more of it appearing under the partition wall.

Jimmy knew he would never be able to bend as she had and labor for the object; he was nearly spent himself and would black out if he bent over. But he could try for it with the sticky strip he had managed to produce around his bound hands.

As he positioned himself, he gained hope. His bound legs were in front of him, his hands just grazing the floor in the right position, taped side toward the object. He used every one of his senses to determine where to place the sticky edge, and then fished for it.

It was a prize almost too easily won! Jimmy pulled forth the object with an exhale of shuddering triumph and turned quickly, dropping it to his left side so he could see what sort of item he had recovered.

It was a Polaroid photo. The square white edges were matched perfectly with an interior block of black backing. But it lay facedown, so there was no telling what image was on the film. Jimmy scooted over, positioning himself to pick it up again, and flipped it over.

The image there startled him. His own face peered back at him, alongside Carly's. It was taken during one of their "game" sessions not long ago, when the captors were particularly high on some drug or drink, and a Polaroid One-Step camera had appeared.

Flashes of light had illuminated their faces for a few moments while the one of them cut the clothes from their bodies with a long buck knife. More flashes and a few touching sessions—*"Here, lemme touch that, there! Ohhhh, that's good! That's right. You're gonna like this!"*

Jimmy had not seen his own face in over a year. The frightened eyes of the boy in this photo were his, all right, but they tore right through him. His tears welled up as he turned to Carly's image. Her expression was much stronger, more angry than his ever would be. Their taped mouths indicated their fate, although their bound hands were behind them and their feet were not pictured at all in the photo. It was obvious that they were being held captive in the back of some vehicle—perhaps someone could guess it was a van.

And then it came to him, just as he heard the first sounds of the men returning. Instinct made him reach for the photo, shoving it behind him and inching for a good position. The voices grew closer, but Jimmy did not panic. He knew he held the answer to their salvation.

The captors were just outside now, fumbling with keys and swearing about the excessive heat. While they worked the door lock, Jimmy settled in a natural position beside the side door, photo well hidden behind his back. From where he sat, when they opened the side door, he would be able to drop the photo down the side of the van between the door and the step there, perhaps without them noticing his covert actions—if he was very, very lucky. He decided at that moment that perhaps a little diversion was necessary.

The door opened, and the rustle of grocery sacks brought the captors closer as they loaded a few bags just inside the door. Jimmy pretended to be startled from a nap. His rolling eyes and struggling shoulders drew their attention. In a well-orchestrated performance, he pretended to struggle away from them. But in reality, he was merely drawing their attention up and away while he let go his valuable prize below.

It dropped downward, skimming the van door and flipping over—coming to rest facedown on the parking lot's sweltering asphalt surface.

"You cooked up enough yet?" the younger one quipped, adding a jaunty laugh to the comment. He enjoyed the terror on Jimmy's face. "Knew we'd have no problem leaving you here in this kind of heat. Surprised you're still alive! Whew!"

Then he turned a bit suspiciously to Carly, who appeared dead in the position she was in. He poked at her leg.

"They ain't even medium well yet, jackass," the older one responded. "Come on—let's get going. I wan' outta this town. It's too *fuckin'* hot!"

"Yup! Too hot for *fucking!*" the younger one agreed.

They moved away from the interior, and the younger one manned the door. "Now don't be messing with them groceries iffn' you want something to eat—you know how it goes. We'll feed ya'll when we make camp."

And with that, the side door came crashing back into a closed position. The two men entered the cab of the vehicle and the engine started, after some more comment on the vehicle's interior heat. The van pulled away slowly, bouncing Jimmy back from his precarious post at the doorway.

Jimmy was jubilant. They had won! A testimony to their presence had been left behind. A cry for help from those who could not cry out loud. He had no idea the photo had landed facedown, nor had he any clue as to where the van had been parked. Would foot traffic indeed pass that way? Would the clue be discovered and ultimately delivered to the proper authorities? He knew there was no guarantee that anything they had accomplished that afternoon would pay off for them, but still he felt hopeful.

And even as the van proceeded toward the I-17 on-ramp, their luck was changing.

A three-year-old girl and her young mother stepped carefully in the heat of the afternoon. They made their way along toward the grocery store. As they progressed down the sidewalk, they noticed the van pull away, leaving the far end of the parking lot. The mother took the child's hand and held on tightly as they crossed over a small embankment, entering the far end of the parking area in an attempt to cut down their walking time.

The mother was thinking hard about working the two books of food stamps in her purse into the long list of items that they couldn't afford but needed anyway. The three-year-old wasn't as distracted. She was staring down at the hot pavement, noticing the way the white lines struck at the rich blackness of the perspiring asphalt. It was a game to jump occasionally over the lines on one side or the other as they walked along.

When she spotted the curiosity lying a few steps ahead, she let loose her mother's grip and headed for it, snatching it up in no time. She knew what it was, for she had seen her mom with this kind of thing. Pictures were her very favorite! The Polaroids of her grandmother and aunties taped to the refrigerator at home were an object of constant comment in her daily ritual.

But the faces that stared back from this photo were not happy. There was something wrong here. Something not right. She held it out to her mother, with a questioning frown.

"Put that down, Carmelita." Her mother spoke in rapid Spanish. "That is dirty trash! How many times must I tell you not to pick up such things!"

"But Mama, it's a picture!" she protested.

The mother took a conditional glance only out of courtesy to her daughter, but what she found there spoke to her. It was difficult not to listen. Suddenly her mind swam in a series of connective activities.

She remembered the van and her mild curiosity that it had parked so far from the store on such a terribly hot day. It had to be two football fields to the front door from here. And then it had left—but for where? Had she noticed which way it had turned?

Quickly, she scanned the choking traffic in the street and wondered—was there a connection? Or was this merely a joke kind of photo. But those eyes . . . these were someone's children! Children in trouble. Awful people had to be doing this to them. They needed help.

The young mother stepped up to the service counter inside the nicely air-conditioned supermarket and waited her turn. The service lady did not seem overly helpful to the man in front of her, but this was important. She would wait. Carmelita pointed to the candy machines by the entrance. The mother shook her head negatively in response.

"¿Habla Español?" the mother asked the service lady when it came her turn.

In response, the lady merely rolled her eyes in protest and called to a manager behind the next register. The mother could tell immediately he was a manager, because of his brightly colored vest. He diverted his attention from his work. "Yeah, whaddya need?"

"Can you help this lady? I don't speak *Mexican.*"

He nodded with a sigh, asking for a moment to finish processing an order.

The young mother was not going to wait. She stepped up to the vested man, thrusting the photo out at him.

"Mira—los niños! Mira!"

The manager stopped his work as the hair on the back of his arms rose in response to a feeling—danger had walked in with this woman. Hesitantly, he took the Polaroid from her and saw for the first time the desperate look on Carly's and Jimmy's faces.

"¿Donde?" he inquired.

She pointed to the parking area and spoke rapidly in Spanish.

"What does she want?" the service lady nagged from behind the desk.

"Call the police," said the manager, quietly.

A woman purchasing groceries in the next aisle peeked over the railing to get a glimpse of the photo.

"Oh my God!" she choked.

"What is it? What's going on?" the service lady demanded.

"Call the police, *now!*" the manager ordered, turning to

39

the young mother and her child. Carmelita shyly smiled, then hid behind her mother's skirt, playing peekaboo.

The manager nodded to the mother in recognition. He had children too. He then called to another checker to finish processing the order for the tall man who'd been patiently waiting in line during the commotion.

But the tall man didn't respond. He understood her Spanish all too well, and now knew that a white van had just left moments ago, taking the freeway on-ramp south.

The children might be inside.

It may have been coincidence, but the tall man was Champ. And like always, he did not question what needed to be done. At that moment, he realized that being there, in that particular store was exactly where he had been called to be. The forces at work in Champ's life were turning into forces that could tell him where to go and what needed to be done. Something was guiding him along—tugging at that part of him that allowed tugging.

And now, there was a new mission. He felt chosen, ordained ... given *permission*.

The manager made sure the lady at the service desk was dialing the phone before leading the mother and child up a half flight of stairs toward the business office to await the arrival of the police.

Champ stepped toward the exit and did not turn back. He appeared to be a disgruntled customer, unwilling to wait until some other checker could ring his order. But Champ didn't care about the groceries anymore.

He pulled out his blue rabbit's foot key chain, ready for the challenge.

There were more fish to fry. This lake was full of them.

3

BBQ's and the Early Bird
June 20th—Cincinnati's SW Station House
19:12

The Cannibal was being cooperative, but the volume of his confession did not make it any more appetizing to Traask. Currently they were on a break, awaiting a dinner delivery, per the Cannibal's request. All this talk of dissecting and decapitation had worked him up some kind of appetite.

Traask exited the questioning area and returned to his desk. There were myriad messages awaiting him, none of which he cared to answer at the moment. Most had to do with upcoming court appearances in the Cop Killer trial, slated to begin the following week.

Damn inconvenient, this whole cannibal mess. Bad timing. Now the spotlight would really be focused on him. This would probably go national, and they would hook into the Cop Killer thing all over again.

His stomach started to churn.

Picking up the phone, he dialed his home number while simultaneously asking the staff sergeant what Bennie's position was.

"He's probably hiding. The Reds lost again last night. He

owes me fifty bucks now." Then, when the sergeant saw that Traask wasn't interested in the levity, he added, "But last I heard, he was on his way back in, Lieutenant. You want me to get ahold of him?"

"No, just curious if we had wrapped at the scene," Traask replied as his own cheerless message sounded in his other ear. He punched in the appropriate combination to receive a playback. It appeared he had several messages.

"Hi, Dan."

Traask closed his eyes and rubbed his temples. The sound of his ex-wife's voice made him ... well, a bit cranky.

"Just reminding you that you agreed to take Jennifer for the week that I'm in Rio on location. I thought you would have called by now to get the flight information."

Yeah, that's the way, Liz, rub it in. Traask's headache was coming on full strength now.

"If you forgot, I hope you're not going to pull a fast one on me. She's looking forward to this, you know. I've arranged for her to get to the airport and all that. So, grab a pen because here it is."

Traask fumbled across the desk for a pen and found one, flipping out his message pad from an inside pocket just in time to catch the numbers, but barely. Then she repeated the information—efficient to a fault, that woman.

"I haven't told her that you didn't call, I made something up, as usual. I don't appreciate covering for you, Dan. So do yourself a favor and don't call tonight or she'll get suspicious. And be at the airport to meet the flight, will you? I'll call in sometime during the week to say 'hi' and see how it's going. Okay, and if you need to reach me, call the production company—they've got the location schedules and all that crap. All right. Well, that's about it. I hope you find some time to be with her at least. You can't be that busy that you can't spend time with your daughter. After missing her at Christmas, it's the least you can do." The beep sounded extra loud in his ear as the message ended.

Yes, in fact, he had forgotten about Jennifer coming out. His daughter was yet another part of his life that had taken a backseat since the onset of the Cop Killer investigation.

Quickly he jotted a note down underneath her flight information to check with the cleaning service and get the apartment in order. After that call, Traask hoped there would be no more surprises.

A call from his insurance agent.

A call from some crank about the Cannibal story—although his phone number was unlisted, he figured this was the same crank who had left previous messages—all harmless. Just another comment from the peanut gallery. There were a lot of nuts out there ...

Then there was:

"Uh, hi, Dan. It's Deborah. Morrison. I was just wondering how you were, uh—doing."

Traask's hand grasped the phone tighter. His pulse raced a bit quicker. It was a long time since he'd heard her voice. A long time since he even had thought about that voice.

"Can you give me a call? I'll be home tonight—I know you have the number. Or you can just give me a call before the weekend if you're busy."

Traask rarely allowed himself to let the guard down, but Deborah's voice was so unexpected.

Was something wrong? Were her kids okay? His mind flew—when was the last time he had heard anything about Deborah? Jesus, it had been months.

Traask disconnected with his answering machine and dialed her number. It didn't surprise him that he could remember it by heart after so long. But you don't forget your partner's home phone number so easily. Not after calling it nearly every day for over five years.

"Hello?" Deborah's voice answered.

There was a moment of hesitation. Traask swallowed, self-consciously.

"Hello?" she repeated.

"Deborah, it's Dan."

"Oh. Hi ..."

There seemed to be the same uneasy feeling on both sides of the fence.

"Can you hold on a moment? I'd like to change phones."

"Sure," Traask replied.

In the background he could hear her asking John to hang up the phone when she picked up the extension.

"Who is it?" Traask heard John ask.

Evidently, Deborah didn't reply. Traask heard the receiver scrape the countertop as it was lifted to John's ear.

"Mom will be back on in just a second," John muttered. But he was clever. He wanted to know who was calling his mother and when he hadn't gotten his answer directly, he was going to get it any way he could. "Are you still there?"

"Uh . . . yes. I'm here," Traask answered.

"Dan! It's you, isn't it?" John's voice was suddenly full of Saturday afternoon basketball games in the Morrison's driveway. "God, Dan! We saw you on the TV! You should have told that Twat Leader to shove it!"

"Well, I wanted to . . ."

"Yeah, but just once I'd like to see her get what's coming . . . I mean, I think . . ."

"John, hang up now." Deborah's voice cut in on the line.

There was another uncomfortable moment. John had more to say, but he knew that there was more to his mother's conversation than he could be a part of.

"Okay." There was disappointment in his voice.

"Bye, Big J." Traask found himself half smiling. It was coming back so easily. With children it is easy. They forget—and forgive.

"Bye, Dan. Uh, see ya!"

The telltale click told both of them it was safe to continue their previously strained line of conversation.

"Sorry about that," Deborah apologized, an embarrassed laugh coming through.

"No—sounds like he's doing great! How's Chatty-Kathy?"

"Oh, fine, fine. She just had a birthday, you know, so she's certain to tell you that being ten years old makes quite a difference to her social status."

"I can imagine."

"And how's Jennifer?"

"Well . . ." Traask paused.

"Nothing wrong, is there?"

"No—no. I've just been so damn busy, you know. It's well . . . well, Liz called today to remind me that Jennifer's flying out tomorrow."

"She is!" There was sudden excitement in Deborah's voice.

"Yeah, and I can't say that it's terribly convenient."

"But it's perfect!"

"Oh? How so?"

"The reason I was calling was to invite you over for a— well, sort of a barbecue. The Morrison Blue Flamer needs a man's touch, I'm afraid. And if Jenny's along, well that's just perfect! Kathy's having some of Jenny's old friends here—we can make it a sleepover for the girls."

Traask didn't answer right away. Mention of the Morrison Blue Flamer brought memories flooding back. Building the brick enclosure for the barbecue unit was his idea, and Frank had turned it into one of the best times in their partnership.

"Would that be all right with you?"

Still, Traask hadn't found the words to express himself.

"If you have to work, I understand." Deborah's disappointment in stooping to allow him that out was showing in her voice.

"No . . . no, I don't think that would be a problem."

"Dan, I'd really like you to come." Deborah suddenly found herself blurting it all out. "I haven't invited anyone over in a long time. Not any adults, I mean. The kids have their own plans with videos and all that. I was hoping . . ."

With the wind out of her sails, she awaited the effect upon the water. But then she feared the worst and allowed her fear to carry her.

"You don't have to come, Dan. I just wanted you to be invited. You've . . . been *missed*. If Jennifer wants to come . . ."

"Deborah . . ."

The silence closed in. Dead space hung between them, but only for a moment.

"Of course I'll come."

Deborah smiled, silently.

"But you gotta promise me something. You won't be putting any raw eggs in my hamburger meat. I hate that—you know I hate that."

"Then bring your own goddamn hamburger!"

Traask let out a laugh and felt a warmth go straight through his heart. Deborah laughed with him.

Yes, it had been a long time.

"Okay, I'll do that. What time?" Traask inquired, smiling broadly now.

"Detective!" The staff sergeant called, motioning that Traask was needed.

"How about if you show your face about one o'clock Saturday?"

"Sounds good, Deb. I'll call before we come to see if there's anything else we can pick up for you."

"Great. I'm looking forward to it," Deborah replied.

"Me too. See you then."

Traask hung up the phone and shook his head with a smile. God it felt good to peel off some of the dirt from the last nine months.

"Lieutenant?"

Traask turned to see the sarge still insisting on his presence. He reluctantly left his desk to join him. As he approached, he could see the sarge was with a frumpy man, wearing a strange overcoat and hat. He almost certainly had to be a "Homey"—king of a cardboard condo somewhere on the city streets.

"This is Mr. Willem DeYoung. He claims he has spoken with you before . . ."

Mr. Willem DeYoung thrust out his hand, grasping Traask's firmly. He was a rather tall man and, as his hand was pumped up and down, Traask noticed that DeYoung carried an old-fashioned, reel-to-reel tape recorder slung over one shoulder. With all this vigorous shaking, the recorder appeared to be bouncing up and down with sheer delight on DeYoung's back.

"You may not recall, Lt. Traask—but it was about five or six months ago. I was asking you about an interview?" DeYoung's exuberance was overshadowed only by his overwhelming bad breath.

46

Traask recoiled. Retrieving his hand, he bristled, "I don't do interviews."

"No, no, no ... not with you, Lt. Traask. At that time I was trying to get an interview with Eddie Jefferson—the Cop Killer? See, I'm a writer, and I'm writing this book on serial killers ..."

"... You'd have to get ahold of his counsel ..."

"I know, I tried. Too late!" Mr. DeYoung grinned. Several teeth were missing and/or chipped. "But this time I figured, early bird catches the worm!"

All journalists were assholes to Traask these days; all of them predators, circling his turf in search of fresh carrion. It sickened him.

"Sorry. Can't help you." Traask turned, beginning to walk away.

"But has he named his counsel yet? Does he have a contact person? Hey, can I at least get a *phone number?*"

Traask left the man standing in the lobby as he passed his own desk, headed for the lunchroom. Surely the food was here by now, and Traask was starving. There had been no time for lunch since they'd opened the Cannibal's apartment door.

And then, after it was opened, several lunches had been lost. Traask wasn't easily swayed. His stomach could take a lot of punishment.

Except when it came to hamburgers.

4

Just Desserts in the Desert
June 21st—Offices of the FBI/Dallas, Texas
20:09

Special Agent Claire Randall forced the newspaper down into her lap, suddenly leaning her weight back in the chair, and closed those burning eyes. Her shapely shoulders moved this way, then that, allowing the tension to be kneaded in between ball and socket joints.

Her face turned upward, revealing an angelic, yet passionate release. The moment held ... and then she allowed her head to turn to one side. She rotated her neck and shoulder muscles in a circular motion until the telltale pops and clicks subsided. Reversing direction, she collected a few more pops for good measure, then stopped all movement, pointing her chin at the ceiling. Her lazy head lay balanced on the edge of the chair back.

After a strong exhalation, she succeeded in flooding the small room with a sensual air. Wherever she belonged, it was as far away from here as one could get.

"You should go see my bone crusher, Randall. He's good, I tell you," Joey spoke up from across the room.

Claire's eyes remained closed, resting for a few merciful

moments. She didn't care what she looked like right now. It felt good, and she needed to stretch. Sitting for so long had made her body ache down to its very core. She didn't like waiting. She hated the paperwork, and she really hated this office.

"So you keep telling me," she replied.

"So what gives?"

"I don't ..." Claire began, but couldn't finish. She really didn't want to get into this with Joey. She shook her head almost imperceptibly. "I'm all right."

"Uh-huh, right."

Claire turned her face away from this rebuttal. She could hear movement as Joey rose and crossed to her. Strong hands took ahold of her shoulders and began to massage. Claire's expression turned to rapture as she breathed in deeply. Joey worked her neck and shoulders muscles with a talent most treasured.

"You need to take it easy. Things will break in their own time. They always do. Your sheer will isn't going to force this guy to show any quicker."

"Oh *please* ..." Claire moaned.

"You want me to stop? You want these hands to go away?"

"No, no, don't stop. Just shut up."

Joey smiled and resumed the treatment. It was always hard working around a looker. Claire turned heads everywhere they went. Sometimes it worked to their advantage, and they got more than they had anticipated. But there were times, like these, when things got tempting and the contact between them became more that of a couple than just partners who worked together at the Bureau. It was comfortable. And Joey enjoyed being in her company, whether at work or play.

But this feeling wasn't something a person could explain easily. Claire was just ... well, *different.* She was one of those women that you suspected kept many secrets, and Joey knew—didn't have to guess—wore real silk underwear.

She didn't talk an awful lot. Claire was a thinker who kept to herself, didn't date and had never been married.

People often mistook her silence for arrogance and therefore did not understand her—but that didn't mean they didn't want to. She had been approached by numerous men in the field and by certain fellow agents at the Bureau, but each time she had politely refused their invitations. Joey was really the closest person to her. There was a theory that someone had once burned her in a bad relationship, but Joey wasn't the kind to kiss and tell. Partners kept each other's secrets. And between the two of them, there were years of trust.

It wasn't all physical, however. Claire was as intelligent as she was finely chiseled. Sometimes Joey was certain that her legs must be on a most wanted list of their own. No matter what she wore each day, even the final day of a five-day stakeout (which never guaranteed the freshest laundry), it was just the way she *moved* underneath those clothes, that conjured up visions of the stunning frame this woman possessed.

Claire had proved herself invaluable at research, detection, and guesswork. Someone had nicknamed her The Lucky Little Bitch. But what they didn't know was that Claire's intuition was scary to her in its accuracy. Joey didn't believe in such things, but nonetheless, it had become something that they both had learned to rely on.

Although Claire was many things, she was not patient.

Awaiting a break on their three current cases was driving her away, sending her out on a limb by herself. What was frustrating was that she performed her best in action—on the chase. Joey could literally smell the inner workings fire up when Claire's nose pointed in the right direction. It was exciting and dangerous to accompany her, but Joey felt closest to her then. So it was a little more than obvious that she was not happy being held captive behind a desk in this infrequently used office space.

Besides, since November of '63, nobody in the Bureau much liked being assigned to the Dallas office.

"Remember Mad Maxx?" Claire mumbled as Joey manipulated her head and neck muscles in soft, tender strokes.

"Who?"

"Rudolf Maxx, ax murderer, 1975 through ... '78, I think."

Joey's forehead wrinkled in thought. "Gimme more" came the request.

"Raped, then buried the women up to their waists in the desert. New Mexico, right? Then hacked off their arms ..."

"Oh, *that* Mad Maxx. What about him?"

"His remains were discovered about two weeks ago."

"I thought he got locked up."

"He was. Released on 'Goody.' After his last victim survived the bastard's sick version of "Entertainment Tonight," she testified at his trial. But he still served only fourteen years."

"Yeah, I vaguely remember the girl and her parents talking on the news. Real sad. So what happened to *him?*"

"Apparently someone took him out into the desert of New Mexico, close to the area where those girls had been found, buried the son of a bitch up to his waist and hacked off his arms."

"Hmm ... seems appropriate," Joey replied dryly.

The tension wasn't leaving Claire's shoulders. It was growing. Joey felt it rising and knew all too well that the waters might be rising.

"So, what's got you thinking about that?"

The newspaper on her desk had been pretty much ignored by Joey. Until now.

Claire held the glaring headline up to meet Joey's gaze. It read: "Richard Winert Reported Missing Only One Week After Being Released From Jail."

Joey's hands left her shoulders, taking the newspaper. Claire rubbed her neck while she watched her partner pace the room, absorbing the information. Her eyes flicked across the ceiling and walls, as she tried not to feel the queasiness rising inside. The skin on her arms rose into gooseflesh as an involuntary shudder occurred deep within her, causing her to rise. She crossed to a dying plant in the corner and absentmindedly fondled its leaves until two dropped to the floor.

Joey shifted focus from the newspaper to catch the downward flight of those leaves, then focused on the sight of Claire's shoeless feet. One stocking bore a tiny run up one side, probably caused by Claire impatiently banging her shoe against the desk. That nervous tapping was a noise Joey had learned to live with over the past few years.

"I still don't get it. What's this got to do with Mad Maxx? The guy probably just took off."

"I don't think so."

That comment commanded Joey's full attention. Claire never turned that phrase lightly, and there was too much history between them to deny this warning. The sheer weight of its impact hung out over them in the form of a pregnant pause. Joey's eyes searched Claire's. It was clear that something was tugging at Claire's brain.

Concerned, Joey began to circle the desk in an attempt to close in on Claire, but she was too quick. Claire turned away, plucking a can of Diet Coke from her desktop. She took a swig, grimacing at the flat, warm aluminum taste, then crumpled the can in her hand.

Joey's brow wrinkled in confusion. "Hey, wait a minute . . ."

"I will. I'll wait. We'll *all* wait, until this one turns up, fried to a fucking crisp, and then what?"

Joey could see the frustration and intensity of her words, but felt helpless to do anything about it.

"It's coming, Joe. There's something . . . *out there*. It's just far enough away that . . ."

Claire moved away from the wastebasket and tossed the can into a file drawer in her desk that, instead of containing files, contained about twenty other empties.

"Oooo! It's driving me crazy, I've got to get out of here." Closing the drawer with a slam, she moved to gather her things. "Page me if you hear anything."

"Hey, where you headed?"

"I dunno. I'll go for a drive or something. I just need to clear out the cobwebs, you know?"

"Maybe you need a little vacation, Randall."

"Hrmph . . ." Claire managed, a little grin appearing at the corner of her mouth as she slipped into her suit jacket.

"And leave all this excitement behind? That'll be the day. A long drive will do it, thank you."

"Need some company?" Joey asked, hopeful that the offer might be accepted and not seen as an empty offering.

It stopped her. Claire turned, and an appreciative smile graced her features. Her eyes held a mischievous glint. "Now, just how am I supposed to clean out the cobwebs with you around?"

Joey shrugged. It wasn't a denial, just the truth. Claire needed some space.

"Thanks, Joey. I'll be okay." And with that, Special Agent Claire Randall left the room.

It was suddenly pretty quiet. And lonely. Joey didn't waste a lot of time wondering what Claire's warning had meant. It meant there was work to do. If she said there was something out there, it was out there all right. Finding it, however, could be a problem.

Crossing to a seated position, Joey reread the article on Mad Maxx. About twenty minutes later, a call was made to Research requesting the file be pulled, with emphasis on any updates within the past six months.

Joey stayed up all night, covering the bases, doing research and preparing. That's all that could be done. If Claire was right.

Again.

5

A Real BBQ Weekend

June 22nd—The Morrison House
13:12

It seemed like Jennifer had talked nonstop since her flight landed. It was going on twenty-two hours since Traask had met her at the airport, and yet she continued on as if she were getting paid by the participle. There was no way he was going to survive the weekend without reinforcements. As they pulled into the Morrison driveway, he was certain he owed Deborah a gigantic thank you.

He couldn't blame Jennifer. It wasn't her fault, just bad timing. Traask's attention remained with the Cannibal and the events of the past few days. It wasn't going to be easy to pull out of it. He didn't want Jenny to feel he wasn't listening. But it was difficult to follow the cast of characters she was unraveling; all the new friends, boyfriends, and teachers . . .

Nodding, he gave her the best supportive answers he could muster.

Currently, she was telling bad "blonde" jokes.

"—So, Daddy, how can you tell when a blonde has been using the word processor? There's White-Out all over the screen!

"How can you tell when a blonde is off her diet? Just follow the trail of M&M shells!

"What do you call a blonde who dyes her hair brown?"

But right now, he was mostly concerned about being at the Morrison house again. As he switched off the ignition to the Ranger, he caught sight of something leaning against the side of the garage. It was Frank's old Harley, draped with mismatched drop cloths, like an old warhorse put out to pasture. He was barely aware when there came an abrupt end to Jennifer's incessant storytelling. His attention had drifted.

Her twelve-year-old heart sobered in the silence.

After a moment, Traask awakened from his stupor, realizing something was wrong.

"I'm sorry . . . did I miss the punch line?"

"That's okay."

"No . . . tell me again."

"It's okay, Dad."

"No, come on . . ."

"Okay. What do you call a blonde who dyes her hair brown?"

Traask thought about that one. He shook his head.

"Artificial intelligence."

Traask nodded, his eyes returning to the bike. Jennifer's forehead wrinkled as she bit down on her lip.

"You don't have to come with me, Daddy. I can tell Mrs. Morrison that something came up."

Traask smiled a genuine smile, his first in a long while. It felt good. "You're trying to provide cover for me?"

"Well . . ." Jenny shied from responding. No one had mentioned Frank or the Morrisons for a long, long time.

"Thanks, but I don't need it, Pun'kin. I want to be here. Deborah and I need to work things out. It's been awhile, so it'll be hard at first. But it's got nothing to do with you kids, so you guys have a great time, okay?"

"Okay."

As they stepped out of the Ranger, the front door swung open to emit Kathy and a screaming mob of frantically flying ponytails.

"Jennnnnifuurrrrrrrr!"

From out of nowhere, Traask was surrounded by squealing ten-year-old girls, all jumping up and down in sheer delight. Squirming hugs were exchanged in a flurry of braces, ponytails, and preadolescent perfume.

They were all of Jennifer's old friends, overjoyed to see her.

John appeared from around the side of the house and waved to Traask.

"Dan! Hey, Dan!"

Traask inched away from the writhing circle of girls and met John under the basketball net. They embraced.

"Hey, Dan . . ."

"Hey, Big J. Still working on that hook shot?"

The hug lasted a little longer than the normal embrace a thirteen-year-old boy would give, but no one was watching. When they released, John appeared mildly embarrassed. But it wasn't because of the close contact. A lot of water had gone under this bridge since they last met.

"We gonna shoot some baskets later?"

"You know it," Traask replied, trying hard not to tear up. He turned quickly back to the Ranger to avoid being caught misty-eyed, but suddenly, there was Deborah.

"Hi." She greeted him with only a hint of nervousness. Her dark features were as lovely as ever. They invited a welcome without having to speak the words.

"Hi," Traask responded, suddenly feeling the need for distraction. "Uh, where'd the girls go?" he said, pretending to look around, as he wiped the tear away with a casual motion. John headed into the house, allowing his mom a moment alone with Traask.

"Back to Kathy's room. They've got someone's boyfriend on the phone—you know."

"Oh."

There was another uncomfortable moment. Traask's attention once again returned to Frank's old Harley in the garage, but only for a second.

This was going to be harder than he had imagined.

Traask carried an armful of groceries into the Morrison kitchen, following Deborah's lead. The house remained pretty much the same, although Traask noticed a few changes here and there. For one thing, Frank's favorite gun case had been removed from the front entry.

"You didn't have to bring so much! I've got plenty, Dan."

"What's a few more chips and dip? You got a house full of mouths here."

"That we do."

A round of squeals increased in volume somewhere down the hall.

"Knock it off, will you!" John could be heard, followed by a slamming door.

Deborah touched Traask lightly on the shoulder.

"I'm glad you're here. Perhaps you can keep World War Three from breaking out over the VCR."

She reached into the refrigerator and handed him a diminutive bottle of beer—Little Kings, his favorite local brand. Frank and Dan spent many an afternoon with those Little Kings.

"Thanks."

"Your brand. It hasn't changed?"

"It hasn't changed."

Deborah finished putting the bags of potato chips into the pantry cabinet. She shut the door with a sigh.

"I think I'll take one of those."

Traask was standing closest to the fridge, so he moved quickly, retrieving a beer and opening it for her.

"Thank you."

They both drank deeply, not really knowing how to address anything but the lightest of banter. The tension was making Deborah feel physically sick. Her knees were shaking, and she couldn't take much more of it.

"Look, Dan, I don't want us to be like this. Whatever you think of me—please, can we just talk about what happened?"

Traask avoided her gaze. He studied the top of his beer bottle as if it were mesmerizing him.

"Sure," he replied, not really meaning it.

"Dan, I'm sorry. I know you wanted to be here when Frank died, but that was a really bad time for me and the kids. I guess I knew what Frank was doing, but I didn't want to face it. What I really couldn't buy was the fact that *you* didn't know, either." Deborah put the beer down and braced herself at the intersection of two countertops, hanging on for dear life. "I thought you were lying. To save yourself. I couldn't believe that you didn't know Frank was out there. Christ, you saw more of him than I did! He told you everything!"

Traask shook his head. He didn't want to be going through this. He hadn't really faced it himself.

Frank had been shot by the Cop Killer. He had been the seventeenth victim. And the last. Dan Traask had made it so.

Because he couldn't live with what he had learned about Frank Morrison that night.

Frank didn't have to take that bullet. He had been off duty. He was with other off-duty cops at the time. For Frank was an Enforcer. In fact, it turned out that Frank was the head Enforcer. It was he who'd been organizing these men, bringing them together to catch the Cop Killer with a vigilante task force of lawless professionals.

And he had never told Traask about any of it.

"I know now that you didn't know. I realize now, Dan. And I'm sorry. But it was such a shock ... such a terrible shock. I got the note you sent. But I couldn't let you be here. The others, they were already in it. They had been there and were a part of it, so if Internal Affairs came down, then you would be clear."

Tears were coming to Deborah now. She was crying openly as she continued.

"I always wanted you to know that I didn't think it was your fault. I never blamed you. I wanted to, but we both know the kind of man Frank was. When he wanted something done—well, there was no discussion."

Traask shifted, not wanting to hear any more of this. He faced the living room, where a TV had been left on.

"He didn't tell you because he wanted to protect you."

Although the sound was too soft to be heard, the images on the TV were clear enough to be understood on their own. It was the news, and there was a story running about that sicko who had set his kid on fire a couple years back. Traask recognized the name on the screen under the press photo. The asshole who had kidnapped his own daughter after a bitter divorce and driven halfway across the country, promising the kid that they were going to fly to Hawaii together for the vacation of their dreams. But instead, the jerk had set the kid on fire while she peacefully slept in a hotel room bed just outside of Vegas.

"I know you don't want to hear this. You blame yourself and that's why you went out there and got that son of a bitch like you did. It didn't surprise me at all when I saw it on TV. I knew you would find him. You did it for Frank—and for the others."

Meanwhile, on the tube, sheriffs were circling a site in the desert where a fire had taken place—but Traask could tell this was no ordinary fire. A leg was strewn out awkwardly in one direction, while what appeared to be an arm was outstretched in another. Traask strained to hear the story, but could not. Finally, he refocused on Deborah.

"I just need to know how you want to leave it, Deb. If you want me to go, I can go and we can say we've put it away."

"Oh Dan!" Deborah cried, rushing to him with an embrace. She was sobbing between words.

"I—don't—want—you—to—go—away!"

Traask stroked her hair and shoulders as she clung to him, catching her breath in sharp small breaths in order to speak again.

"We've needed you—and we've missed you."

Deborah's breaths were slowing now, not as gasping as before.

"And Jennifer too. You've left a big hole in our lives, you two."

Traask nodded, in understanding. But he saw an opportunity and took it.

"And Liz?"

Deborah's breathing stopped for a moment of confusion, but she soon realized it was a joke.

"Well, no, not Liz."

"Me neither."

Deborah laughed as she released Traask. She reached over the counter to grab a fistful of Kleenex and dabbed at her tears.

"Good thing I didn't put on mascara today."

She reached out to embrace him once more.

He hugged her tightly.

And when he released her, his attention wandered back to the TV, but the story had ended. Traask made a mental note to catch up on it later.

He had no explanation for the sudden shudder he felt, nor why the hair on his arms was standing at attention.

A doorbell was ringing.

In her slumber, Claire stirred.

Why was a doorbell ringing way out here?

She was standing on a mountainside that overlooked an unspecified city that was buried in cloud masses far below. It was smog, she guessed—and it was particularly thick today, which made it difficult to see exactly what part of the country they were in. The dense population of pine trees ahead indicated that she was about to enter a real forest. The thought of walking through the tall trees seemed refreshing—the cool air might be invigorating. But the sudden chill she experienced wasn't related to the crisp mountain air.

It was from the view below.

Freshly dug mounds of earth lay scattered about the hillside. An unidentified sheriff's department searched the shallow grave sites containing the remains of the victims. They were all young women, mostly naked. Some were horribly decomposed, some ravaged by animals, others by the elements.

Claire stood stock-still, watching the men work, their faces without expression. She was an observer here, without the right to question the goings on. This was just a dream, and she was a spirit walking among them. This investigation had ended a long time ago—but it was about to begin again.

Claire tried to meet their gaze . . . tried to warn them of things to come. But they looked straight through her.

Like she wasn't there.

And where was Joey? A feeling of panic began to course through her as she scanned the field. Dozens of small graves—dozens of young women.

Nameless and sometimes faceless, young women.

Claire shivered.

The doorbell sounded again from the surrounding hillsides.

No. Not from here. Not from this place.

Claire tossed in her sleep, her consciousness rising to greet the morning in her small upstairs apartment, conveniently located near the DFW airport. That made two things good about it. Cheap rent was the other.

She had fallen asleep on the couch, watching the eleven o'clock news. Upon waking, she squinted to read the clock on the VCR. It was incredibly early.

"Randall!" called an impatient voice from behind the front door. Someone banged loudly upon it.

It was Joey, she thought. Pull yourself together.

Claire rose too quickly from the couch in an effort to reach the clamor beyond her door. Her mind may have been awake, but her body was still at rest. It nearly brought her to her knees, the blood rushing from her senses. Grasping the arm of the couch, she breathed in deeply, involuntarily.

And the pounding continued.

"Okay, I'm coming!"

The pounding stopped.

Claire worked the knob to find Joey standing before her in traveling clothes. This could only mean one thing.

Joey headed for the dining room table with an armload of paperwork and files, noticing Claire's morning face.

"Sorry for such an informal wake-up call, hope you're alone."

Claire snorted at the remark as the front door closed. She made her way to the kitchen and searched inside the fridge for a Diet Coke. Joey started up their usual banter.

"How was your drive?"

"What drive?"

"The long drive, the cobwebs—remember?"

"Oh. Yeah. I drove around a bit but it didn't seem to help. I decided to come home and crash, instead."

"Good choice. Tell me, have you been a good girl?"

Claire appeared at the doorway with the cold soda in hand. She popped the top in the direction of the file folders scattered across her dining table.

"Not that good. What'cha got?"

Joey opened the first folder, revealing a photograph that had been sent by wire, a grainy black-and-white blow-up severely marred by the electronic translation. Claire took it, walking to a better light source—the streaky front window of her apartment. She held it up for closer examination.

Joey surveyed the room, noting the rumpled couch cushions and the remnants of a soup-and-crackers meal on the coffee table. The TV was, as usual, set to CNN—Claire's twenty-four-hour-a-day "third eye" on the world.

It was a barrel of laughs over here lately, Joey mused silently. Claire needed a man.

"Where—when?" The questions from Claire as she studied the photo.

"Yesterday morning. Phoenix. A grocery store parking lot. Some woman found it and brought it inside, going on about a white van. Local office showed her a few models, she thinks it was a Ford Econoline, maybe early eighties. Employees of the store were grilled, and we have some descriptions but nothing concrete. No one actually saw who was in that van, and there's no real evidence that the photo came from that vehicle."

Joey sighed.

"So what we really have is shit. Oh, there are descriptions of the last shoppers that were served. Local agency confiscated the register tapes and matched them to the descriptions so we have something to play with when we get there." Then Joey added with a knowing smirk, "I assume you're already packed."

Claire nodded toward the bedroom where a flight bag sat outside the doorway, waiting.

"I can never surprise you. You'll make someone a terrible wife," Joey moaned with mock disappointment.

But Claire wasn't listening. She studied the terrified expressions of the children that beckoned to her, locking into them. They sliced down to her core, and she could not look away.

"Do we have the Jewison's positive ID?"

"No."

Claire turned to Joey for an explanation.

"I was thinking that after we get through with the preliminaries in Phoenix, you could take the original photo to New Mexico with you. This"—indicating the copy she held—"doesn't help much. Local is working on some better copies and blow-ups for you."

Claire thought of the boy's mother and the first time they had met. How she had tried with such resolve to keep from crying. How would she react when presented with this horrifying photo and asked if the boy bound and tortured in the picture was her young son?

She blinked the thought away. She could not allow such images to work against her right now. There was too much at stake, and time was already against them. These assholes could be in Mexico by now. Easily. And who was to say that this photo was recent? Perhaps the lab could give them more on it so they weren't chasing their tails for answers.

"I need to take a quick shower ... change my clothes. Do we have time?"

"Sure."

As Claire crossed to the table and placed the photo back in the file, Joey touched her arm lightly.

"I'll go with you, if you want. To see the Jewisons."

As usual, Claire shook her head, denying the help.

"I've got to go alone. Two of us would just freak her out. Mrs. Jewison would think her son was gone for good."

She was right.

Claire's attention went back to the photo. She mentally outlined the face of the terrified girl whose frightened eyes seemed to cry out, *"Please—help me!"*

"Coordinate with the records group down there and get some possibilities worked up for the girl."

With that, Claire disappeared around the corner and into the bathroom. The door shut solidly behind her.

Joey closed the folder. It wasn't going to be a picnic, this trip to Phoenix. Claire's last contact with the Jewison family had left her fairly shattered. Joey figured she might appreciate some backup. But Claire had to do things her own way.

A strong woman.

Joey considered that to be one of the best things about her.

Stepping into the kitchen, Joey opened a few cabinets—hoping to come across a can of coffee. Giving up in disgust, Joey made a decision at that moment to never again take on a partner who didn't drink coffee in the morning. It just wasn't natural.

The water began running in the shower. Inside the bathroom, the shower curtain rings clacked open and closed. Something crashed to the floor. Joey smiled, hearing Claire curse, imagining her bending to pick it up, the spray against Claire's skin as she first stepped into the water. The warmth of her body, slippery with the residue of lather. The splashing and dancing of the droplets against her shoulders and back—her breasts, perfectly upturned. Oh well . . .

They were partners, not lovers.

But one could fantasize . . .

Crossing to the couch to wait, a search was conducted for the remote control, without success. On the TV was a desert scene. Several sheriffs, boots kicking up sand around a charred piece of ground. An outstretched skeleton, it seemed to be reaching . . .

Then came a photo of the victim. Richard Winert. And all at once, Claire's warning became a reality. Joey rose quickly, crossing to the television and adjusting the volume.

". . . His charred remains were discovered by a cattle rancher, approximately fifty miles north of Phoenix, late yesterday."

Phoenix!

Fuck me. That means we're flying right into the thick of it.

No. Wait a minute. Take it one piece at a time. This can't be happening. It can't be. How could Claire possibly have known?

It has to be some kind of weird coincidence because otherwise ...

If she finds out about this connection, she'll be ramrodding that investigation, as well as the kidnapping case. The local office won't know what hit it if she gets ahold of this one.

If she gets ahold of it. That's the secret now, isn't it?

You didn't see this, Joey. You don't know nothin', you understand? You're gonna turn this idiot box off now and escort Ms. Randall out of here real nicey-nicey without mentioning a thing. Keep her mind on those folders and keep her nose on track.

That was how it was going to go.

Their plane landed in Phoenix at approximately 1:17 P.M.

Waiting for Claire to come out of the ladies' room, an ache was rising in the pit of Joey's stomach. Claire had been right about something being on its way—and now it seemed like it was nearly here.

How did she know? What is it about her, anyway? It was spooky, that's what it was. Just plain weird.

Joey wasn't going to think about it anymore. But a mantra had been repeating in the back of the agent's brain ever since the plane left the ground back in Dallas.

Oh, fuck,
Oh God,
Here it comes ...
Oh fuck,
Oh God ...

6

A Dawn of Realization
June 23rd—South of Phoenix
05:52

The colors of the sunrise reflected off the canyons and hill-sides produced a vivid painting in traditional desert hues. Even the tallest cacti came to life as their shadows danced their morning dance, tracing a circle of shade around their base in the ancient chase of shadow and light. The morning sun evaporated the chill off the desert floor, exchanging its promising warmth for any memories the night had left behind on the cold, rocky terrain.

The motionless body lay down a steep embankment, approximately three hundred and fifty feet from the roadside. It was bordered by scrub and rock on one side, a sheer drop on the other. The body appeared to be dead, placed here on the side of the hill for concealment.

In search of morning condensation, a stinkbug, black as onyx, made its way around one of the hands. It left a zigzag trail, as if a zipper had mysteriously been pressed into the patch of silty sand.

A jackrabbit watched nervously from a few feet below, standing way up on his hind feet to get a better view of the body that lay so still on this early morn. The body's face was hidden from view.

So when Bobby began to stir, the jackrabbit took off like a shot in the opposite direction.

The first things Bobby could sense were the cold, sharp edges of the ground on which his body lay. Rocky daggers lay underneath his 225-pound frame, which, over the past several hours, had imbedded themselves into his bare skin and were sending painful jabs to his brain. The desert is not a good place to nap.

But Bobby had not been napping. Not voluntarily—he was sure of that. The pieces were still not all in place. He couldn't think so straight yet.

I gotta get up.

Struggling with both hands to brace himself, he appeared to be doing a partial push-up—what guys referred to in high school as a girl's push-up.

While balancing on one elbow, he tried to wipe the sand from his face and mouth. He quickly realized that his face was covered with congealed blood, probably from a head wound. The sand and tiny rocks had found a sticky purchase and by now the whole mess was as solid as glue. As he ran his hand over the caked surface, he imagined he must resemble something out of a teenage slasher movie. He grunted, pushing himself up farther to a sitting position. He needed to think.

He must have been ambushed.

Dangling his legs over the side of the rocky ledge, he realized that there was about a twenty-five-foot drop from that point. If he had not been carefully positioned far back and to the side, one good shove could have sent him over the edge and onto the floor of the ravine.

Scanning the terrain in the opposite direction, he could see this was a natural runoff wash that hadn't seen rain in quite a while. The monsoons had not yet started. They usually started in mid-July. He was lucky. One good storm could have washed his body right the hell down to some godforsaken border town.

Yeah, he was lucky. Sure.

Where the fuck am I?

He couldn't hear any noise at all, so he deduced that he wasn't close to the highway anymore. Catching the direction of the sunrise, he knew he was facing west now. That meant that those mountains ahead of him might be the backside of the Chiricahua range ... if he was still anywhere near where he had been last night.

If he were, it would put the highway behind him, toward the rising sun. A quick check of his legs and arms told him there had been a scuffle and he must have been dragged because there were a few cactus needles in his left calf. Otherwise, he was okay.

Or so he thought.

Until he tried to stand. Then he noticed that his ankle had been pretty banged up. It wasn't a break, though ... probably a bad twist.

It felt horrible, in any case.

He tried to find a walking stick, but found nothing big enough or strong enough for the job. Getting up that sandy hillside was going to be difficult on bare knees.

But he had to get moving. Someone had stolen his bike and his clothes, not to mention his gun. And he didn't figure that this particular someone was Boy Scout material.

Why didn't they just kill me?

That would have made a cleaner getaway.

They must have known that I wouldn't be out for too long. Someone had to drag me down here and lay me out on the ledge, but why be so careful about it? Why not just toss me over the side? That would have guaranteed I wouldn't be able to get back up to the road anytime soon.

No answers were forthcoming. Was it Sunday or Monday morning? Could he have been out that long?

That was when he realized his watch was missing, too.

Shit! Cindy gave me that for Christmas last year! Well, she'll be pissed. After she gets done being glad I'm not dead ...

Bobby began to edge his way slowly toward the embankment. Crawling on his knees, with his butt in the air, he wondered:

If I manage to get to the road, will any fool motorist even stop for me?

Not likely. Not on this stretch of highway.

If a road was even up there.

Out of the frying pan and into a Phoenix firestorm.

The major part of the day had been spent going over the grocery store leads from an armchair out at the Phoenix Bureau office. The transcripts of the witnesses' testimony turned out to be filled with vague connections and supposition—nothing concrete. Several of the checkers "swore" that they had the suspects at their check stand or had thought something was "funny" about a customer that morning. But no one actually saw anything in the store, the parking lot, or around the van itself.

After thoroughly covering the evidence, Claire insisted on going to the store location, although all available evidence had been gathered from the site and put in the green folders on the desk in front of her.

Standing in that parking lot.

Phoenix twilight.

Claire walked to the area where the van was reported to have been parked. She stood there for several minutes, drinking in whatever she could absorb from the spot. It might be futile, but she was trying to stave off the feeling that the trail was cold from here on out.

Right now, it felt very cold indeed.

Hunger pangs were hitting her pretty hard as she drove back to the local office. Claire had not eaten on the plane and did not grab even a sandwich at the Bureau. Now it was way past the dinner hour, and she was hungry.

She was becoming fairly bitchy. She had sent Joey out to find a hotel room and get some dinner plans together for later on. Rooms were going to be hard to come by on this holiday weekend, so they were told.

Returning to the local office, Claire was dead set on pushing hard to get something more out of the lab boys on that photo before making a determination on the day's work.

Many of the lab techs had hinted at taking Sunday off, this being a holiday weekend and all.

She expected to see the lab area dark and lifeless, with only a manila envelope left at the counter with her name on it—the results she'd requested. But the lights were still on, and the men inside were working steadily.

"Thought you were trying to wrap things up." She commented lightly as she entered their domain. "What's the deal?"

Their faces were none too cheerful. They had been at it nearly thirty-six hours straight now.

"We got shit passed on to us from the Pima County Sheriff's office—it's kind of important. A.S.A.P. type. But don't worry, we got the results on your photo."

Claire's blood pressure rose. She stepped closer to the desk and grasped the countertop with one hand, squeezing it tightly.

"It's four to six months old. Standard Polaroid film, nothing fancy. We got a fairly decent fingerprint off the back of the film, but it doesn't appear that we'll be getting a full image of it till the lab in Los Angeles comes back with it. Looks like one of the kid's prints anyway. They have a better spectro-analysis setup, and we wanted to give you the best we could give."

"When can we expect to get it back here?"

"Tuesday at the earliest. They're a bit backed up themselves. See, this is a favor they're doing for us. Our machine has been a bit buggy lately."

Claire nodded.

"The blowups are ready, if you want them. Our people already went over it pretty well. Nothing to get excited about. No identifying numbers, signs, dates, or anything that would suggest clues."

"I'll take them with me."

The lab tech went back to fetch the blowups, leaving Claire with a local agent who had entered the room and moved beside her. He gave her a typical, "So, what brings you here?" look, readying his advance, but Claire was in no mood for stale sexual innuendos from the locals. She looked away immediately.

"Dallas office?"

Claire didn't care for the approach and just nodded, pretending to watch the lab tech's movements, as if she could will him to move even faster. She hated these types, the married ones with the nowhere look in their eye. She'd dealt with enough of them to know that even making simple conversation at this point would be misleading.

So she didn't.

The tech returned with the photos, peeking in the envelope at the proofs as he approached.

"Oops," he apologized in an offhanded way. "Wrong kidnapping case."

He directed the envelope past Claire to the local agent. "Here's your weekend barbecue photos, Bill."

The local agent winced. "Very funny. Listen buddy, next time you wanna make jokes, you go out in the desert and take the pictures. This guy turned out to be one fried fajita, I can tell you."

The agent pulled a photo from its sleeve and tipped it toward Claire. He wasn't going to give up on her so easily.

"Care to take a peek? It's becoming one of the most exciting attractions Arizona has to offer these days."

She glanced at the photo only out of courtesy. Claire wanted her own photos, and she wanted to get the hell out of there. But when she saw what it was, her expression changed entirely.

"Anyone I know?" she managed.

"I'll say," the agent chuckled. "This is what's left of the late great Richard Winert."

Then he added, "You know . . . the award-winning Father of the Year?"

Okay. Now the locals had Claire's full attention.

7

Shootout at the One Stop

June 22nd—Outside Tucson, Arizona
Estimated Time, 23:00

The dim lights of the tiny gas station/convenience store barely illuminated the pump area, let alone the path to the rest rooms around the back.

The moon was hardly a sliver in the sky tonight, making the empty road ahead seem not quite worth the effort. They had kept their eyes peeled for a wide spot in the road, hoping to find a little dirt avenue that would lead somewhere private, where inquiring eyes wouldn't find them.

Where the screams would not be heard.

The old man behind the counter was getting ready to close, but he wanted to give holiday traffic a chance to bring in a few more bucks. It wouldn't be much, but it might be worth staying open an extra hour or so. He spent most of this time watching the small TV he kept up on the shelf above the liquor display. It had been a gift from his daughter on his sixty-fifth birthday.

The news was on, and he was interested. Most of it was so unbelievably bad these days! Democrats hadn't been in the White House in years now, and the economy was tend-ing to resemble something he had already lived through once and had a hard time forgetting. You don't forget eating nothing but potatoes for two weeks straight so easily.

Every night seemed to bring another horrifying story from somewhere else—and tonight it was that cannibal in Ohio. Four heads in the refrigerator, and God knows what else he had in the bedroom.

Where were these sick people coming from?

When the white van stopped for its fill of gasoline, the old man was most obliging. He apologized for the bad light by the pumps, telling the two men that he just hadn't gotten around to calling his grandson to bring the fire truck down so he could replace those damn burned-out bulbs.

"My grandson is the fire captain down here at the local station, you see. It's the only ladder that will reach."

That's okay. We don't mind.

They even bought a six pack of beer and a bottle of booze on top of the full tank of gas! That made the old man very glad he'd held out for the extra hour.

In fact, it made his whole night.

He thanked them kindly as the screen door slammed shut behind them. He watched the older one walk back to begin pumping gas, while the younger one took a tour around back to visit the "necessary."

Looks like they're camping out. Probably a father and son. Nice to get away like that. Probably got a bunch of gear in the back of that van. Maybe they're going to do some fishing.

But the old man's gaze did not remain on the small TV on the shelf. He kept watching the man as he set his groceries down on the cement by the van and inserted his key ring into the locking gas cap. The man began to unhitch the nozzle, but stopped. Raising his hands in the air slowly, he backed away from the pumps.

Something was happening out there.

The old man rose from his stool and crossed to the rickety screen door in an instant, using one hand to shield his view from the glare as he peered out. The interior lights of the store were preventing him from seeing clearly, but it appeared to him like a customer of his was being robbed!

Into the dim circle of light appeared the white helmet and black leather jacket of a highway patrolman. His gun was drawn. He was ordering the customer to the rear of the van.

The old man stepped away from the screen door. He scanned his store quickly, recalling that the other customer had gone around back.

And if these men were trouble, then there was going to be a lot more trouble before too long.

The cop ordered the man to lie on the ground, arms out to his sides. The man didn't appear to struggle as he was frisked. But he kept asking what was going on, what he had done. Loudly. The cop didn't answer any of his questions. When the cop discovered a set of handcuffs in the man's back pocket, he still didn't comment. He was quiet, this cop. Quiet and direct.

Then a shot rang out from inside the store.

The cop reacted quickly, stepping back to the van, just a foot away. He kept his gun trained on the man facedown before him.

"You're first, you understand?" The cop hissed.

"Officer?"

Peering in the direction of the store entry, the cop could make out a large hole that had been blown through the screen door.

The old man exited the store slowly. As he did, he held up his hands in surrender, waving a double-barreled sawed-off over his head.

"Koot Wilson, Officer. This here's my place." He stopped, waiting for permission to move closer. He was no fool.

A moan came from the darkness to his left.

"I winged the other one. He was drawing on 'ya from the side."

Another moan and then a cry.

"You fucker, Tom! You motherfucker!"

"Shut up, Roger," the facedown man replied.

The cop motioned to the store owner, who stepped forward, gun pointed into the darkness at the man he had just fired upon.

"Where's the gun, kid?"

"You shot both my legs, you fuck!"

"Don't give me no crap. Where's yer gun!"

The old man stepped into the darkness. The cop held his position until he saw the man return from the shadow with a small firearm silhouetted against the storefront lights. His shotgun was held clumsily to the side.

"It's okay, I got it, Officer!"

"No," the cop replied. "Don't leave him open. There might be more. Pat him down."

The newly deputized store owner took hold of his shotgun with renewed purpose and slipped into the shadows. The cop stepped from behind the van and removed the key ring from the gas tank. He tried the van's side door, but it was locked.

"Get off me, you fuck!"

"You move again son and I'll finish the job. Iff'n you'd like to keep those legs, you'll be listening to me."

The cop was examining the key ring now with interest. He moved to the man on the ground and handcuffed him.

"Don't move," he warned.

The old man was moving closer, but the cop waved him back.

"Stay there. Cover them. I have to search the van."

"Aren't you gonna call for backup?"

The question went unanswered. The cop moved to the van's side door and inserted the key.

From where the old man stood, he could not see what happened next. He heard the sliding door open and thought he saw a rocking motion inside the van itself. Nervously, he kept watching the handcuffed man on the ground for any sign of movement. He knew the other one wasn't going anywhere. Both his legs had been hit good. They were a bloody mess, that was for certain.

After a moment, there was movement again from behind the pumps. And voices.

"You okay?" the old man hollered.

A young boy appeared from the side of the gas pump. His hair was sticking to his face and **neck**. There was a big welt around his mouth, as if he'd been recently wearing clown makeup and it had stained his skin red. His clothes were filthy.

"Wait!" the cop ordered.

The boy froze when he saw the old man with the gun. New terror lit up his eyes.

"There's two children here. I want you to see them safely inside your store. You got a phone?"

"Yes sir."

"Call for help. My radio's down. I'll handle the men from here."

"Okay. All right."

But the young boy didn't want to leave the officer's side.

"Go on now," the cop ordered.

The boy stepped from the pump and stared down at the man on the ground for a moment before he stepped clear. The old man would be hard-pressed for years to come to describe the emotions he saw as the boy looked up.

The boy bolted for the store entry. The old man didn't try to stop him. The screen door banged shut behind him.

Then a girl appeared. She had bruises on her face and arms, and the same telltale welt around the mouth. Rubbing her left wrist with concern, she was having a hard time walking. The cop stood and joined her, taking her arm and leading her past the man on the ground. Unlike the boy, she didn't stop to stare. She was clearly dazed and confused by what was happening. Her eyes wandered from the store to the old man, to the parking area, and then to the lights.

The cop let go of his hold on her about twelve feet from the old man. Unsure, she lurched toward Koot. He reached for her, tenderly. Her long hair lay in stringy, unkempt knots, half covering her face. Her clothes were stained with dried blood and numerous lines of dried sweat. She wore no pants, just a pair of partially ripped panties. She fell against him, clutching his chest and shoulders, sobbing. Together, they headed for the doorway to the store.

Once inside, the old man did not let go his hold on her.

She clutched him with a death grip that suggested to him what terrible, horrible things had been done to these children. He led her to his own stool behind the front counter and sat her down.

He could see that the boy had grabbed up two cartons of milk and some doughnuts right off. On the floor of the store, the boy sat beneath the reach-in and sloppily drank from the milk carton. His shirt was wet from the overflow. He didn't stop as the old man watched him with saddened eyes. He held no shame for his thirst and did not fear repercussion for his actions. He was starved and beaten half to death. A few doughnuts and milk were nothing now.

The boy rose and took a fresh carton of milk from the door, pulled two more packages of doughnuts from the shelf and crossed to the counter. He arranged the items in front of the girl, even opened the milk for her. She loosened her grip on the old man and reached for the carton. She drank deeply.

The old man wanted to assure them, and said, "Help yourself to whatever you want, whatever you need." These kids were past needing permission. They were desperate, like starving and mistreated animals. He only wanted to stand out of their way and let them eat. He only wanted to help.

He reached for the telephone on the wall and dialed with shaking hands.

"Sheriff's office, Deputy Tyler speaking."

The old man cleared his throat. He was beginning to choke up. Tears were welling in his eyes as he watched these kids. He shifted his stance so not to face them, leaning his gun against the liquor case.

"This is Koot Wilson down here at the One Stop off the old bypass road." Then the old man began to choke for real. He barely got out the last bit. "We need some help down here."

The sound of the van starting up brought the kids' attention sharply toward the front door. The old man turned to it as well.

It only took a moment, and then ... it was gone.

"What's happening down there? Uh, Mr. Wilson?"

The old man dropped the phone and picked up his shot-gun, heading for the door. Through the blown-out screen, he tried to see what was going on out there, but all he caught were the taillights of the van driving out of sight.

Carly reached for the phone dangling at the end of its cord. She raised it to her lips. Her mouth was full of dough-nut, but she managed to choke it down. "Help us! God, please help us, they're getting away!"

Koot Wilson stood guard at the doorway, waiting for whatever was to come next. He suspected the cop had been overpowered somehow, although he didn't see a body lying by his pumps.

That cop could be laying out there in the shadows bleeding to death!

He raised the barrel of the gun protectively. One thing was perfectly clear—he wasn't going to leave these kids to find out.

8

Missing Pieces
June 23rd—FBI Headquarters, Phoenix
03:45

The door to the conference room burst open, causing Claire to jump involuntarily.

"What in the *hell* are you doing?" Joey stood in the doorway, hands on hips—clad in rumple wear and blurry-eyed.

Claire exhaled slowly. Her adrenaline was pumping from the shock. She looked up at the clock. Four forty-five A.M. and here she was, still at the Bureau. She had never left. Her gaze returned to Joey uncomfortably.

"Working."

"What happened to dinner? What happened to perhaps coming back to the hotel and acting like a human being for fourteen, fifteen minutes at a crack? Jesus, Randall, you could have *called!*"

Claire didn't flinch, didn't apologize. Instead, she held up a photo. It displayed the charred remains of the body Joey had seen on CNN in her apartment, the day before.

"They found Winert—someone toasted him in the desert about eighty miles from here."

"Oh Christ."

79

Joey began a ritual of frustration that Claire had witnessed many times before—pacing about the room, turning away from her, looking out the window, then at the tabletop, then at the door.

But there was no fooling Claire.

"You knew about this, didn't you?"

"What?" Joey replied, stalling for time.

"You knew this back in Dallas."

"No I didn't."

"Sure you did. That's why you were so quiet on the plane. Why didn't you tell me?"

"This isn't our case, Randall! This isn't our jurisdiction. You can't just hook into every case that fascinates you. We work on assignment remember? We already have three cases. We're here to follow up on the photo, that's all."

"Our other cases are dead in the water, and you know it."

"Did you even look at the information I got on the girl?" Claire held up the file. "Right here. And you're right—I think it's a match."

It squelched Joey's anger. "Good."

The two partners were back on square one.

"I called up Las Vegas for more info. It should be here tomor"—Joey stopped, then gestured to the clock on the wall—"in a couple hours."

There was silence for a moment. Claire returned her work.

"I forgive you," Claire said, under her breath.

Claire was on to the scent now. And Joey realized it would be useless to argue with her.

"All right, what's so damn interesting here that you're pulling an all-nighter? You're gonna be fucking useless tomorrow, you know."

Rubbing her eyes, Claire replied, "I'm fucking useless now."

Resigned, Joey joined her at the table. Two heads were better than one.

Claire began. "This is just a basic outline of where Winert was last seen, photos of the hotel room where he was abducted, etcetera. No prints were discovered there. There was nothing missing from his hotel room except a bedsheet. Fiber samples match those found at the burn site. Evidently he had the sheet with him when he was torched. Tire tracks show that a half-ton truck was probably used for transport. Tire marks link both the hotel parking lot and desert area. Nothing conclusive on the model of the truck yet. As usual, nobody saw anything. But look at this . . ."

She opened another file that was labeled Maxx, R. "Here is a boot print taken from Mad Maxx's site."

"I saw this back in Dallas. Maxx's killer is a fucking Neanderthal."

"Yeah." Claire's voice took on a sexy, throaty tone. "A regular Big Foot."

"So that's it. Big feet turn you on, huh? I'll remember that."

Claire ignored the comment and opened to another photo at the Winert burn site. It was another large boot print.

"Same thing was found at Winert's site. They match. Exactly."

Joey's head shook with a sarcastic, sideways glance.

"The girl's in love."

Claire's beeper went off, followed only seconds later by her partner's—the Bureau's dueling banjos.

Joey reached for the phone on the tabletop and dialed in. Claire began to put away the photos, not paying attention to the call. She was lost in thought as she considered the evidence. This was what she was waiting for. This was what she had felt back in Dallas. She knew it was out there.

She knew *he* was out there.

Joey had hung up. "You got the Jewisons' number handy?"

"Yeah, why?"

"You'll need it."

Joey headed for the door in a hurry. "Come on."

"What! What's going on?"

"We're going to Tucson. It's about a two-hour drive. I suggest you take a nap on the way. You look like hell."

"Tucson? What's in Tucson?"

Joey stood in the open doorway as Claire grabbed her

jacket. Joey's words were accompanied by a playful smile, full of promise.

"More cactus. Some sand. Might see some cowboys ... you like cowboys, don't you?"

The suspense was killing Claire. "Oh, please. Cut to the chase, will ya?"

Joey nodded. "They've found Jimmy Jewison."

Claire's eyes met Joey's. It was a revelation. Her joy exploded in an instant but just as suddenly faded.

"Is he ...?" Claire began.

"He's gonna be fine," Joey reassured. "Now saddle up."

Security at the medical center was lacking, to say the least. Joey and Claire walked right through to the pediatrics wing without being stopped and found out where the kids were being held without showing one piece of ID. Claire nodded to Joey at that point, to pull the local boys aside.

"From now on there's an invisible line at the front door to this joint. No one comes in or out without being I.D.'d, understand? And if any press shows, you know nothin'. Those lips of yours were rented, and the Bureau repo'd them last night while you were countin' sheep. There's nothin' here worth mentionin' or we'll have your badge for it."

As Joey walked away from that one-sided conversation, one of the men remarked, "God, I hate Feds."

Another one said, "Especially that kind."

"Yeah, well maybe it's cuz they never get laid. Did you get an eyeful of the other one? I wouldn't mind a minute or two with her ... Whewee! Enough to make my mouth water."

Joey heard, but didn't bother to acknowledge the remarks. There had been enough of them.

A doctor stood with Claire, outside the kids' room.

"... Dehydration is our primary concern at this time. Our initial examination revealed evidence of repeated sexual abuse in both children, foreign objects have entered their bodies—the girl will require surgery if she ever wishes to carry a child to term. The boy has repeated scarring of tissue around the genitalia but appears to be in fairly good shape on the whole—two currently fractured ribs on the girl and formerly fractured wrist and ribs on the boy. There are multiple bruises and superficial lacerations from duct tape that was used to bind the hands and mouth. They're both underweight by at least fifteen pounds, but we're doing what we can for their immediate circumstances. Uh . . . I suppose you want to question them."

"Not if they're asleep."

This response seemed to impress the doctor, and he gave Claire an appreciative glance.

"No, they aren't asleep. They told me that they usually had to sleep during the day and were forced to . . ." The doctor paused, trying to think of a nice way to put it. "Well, the captors liked to keep them up awake at night. You understand . . ."

"Then we'd like to meet with them. The parents have yet to be contacted. I have to make a confirmation on their ID first."

"Okay. They're both in here. They were assigned separate rooms, but insisted on staying together."

"Can't say that I blame them," Joey commented.

Claire thanked the doctor and paused before entering the room. Two years of hope and fear hung over her. She felt as if she were greeting her own child, abducted for that long.

Her hand trembled as she pushed the door open.

The two kids sat together on the single hospital bed, facing each other. Dual IV poles hung at their sides, providing the much needed fluids. A bedside table, cluttered with juices and soup, had been pushed aside. They had been restricted to a fluid-only intake for the first twenty-four hours.

Their private conversation suddenly cut to silence when the door opened. Claire noticed their expressions. They had not yet lost a frightened, glazed look. Fear was hard to let go. Clearly these kids were still half expecting the nightmare to reclaim them at any moment.

Claire and Joey entered slowly and carefully, allowing the kids a moment to realize they weren't "the bad guys."

"Hi. Sorry for interrupting. Can we come in?"

This obviously surprised the children. They weren't used to giving permission for anything. The kids exchanged glances between themselves nervously, then nodded.

"This is Joey and I'm Claire. We've been helping search for you for a very long time now. We just waned to say 'hi,' but we can come back later if you want us to."

The kids wanted to please and shook their heads, allowing permission for the agents to enter. Claire continued, moving closer. She could then see the horrible red welt around each of their mouths. It had been treated with a salve and now had the appearance of a bad sunburn.

"I feel like I know you, Jimmy. I've visited your mom and dad's place so many times. I even met your dog Sam!"

Jimmy's eyes lit up. "He let you in?"

Claire stood right in front of the bed now. The kids warmed up to her immediately.

"No, he tried to bite me the first time I entered the gate. But I showed him my badge and explained I was trying to find you and then he let me by. He even showed me your room."

Jimmy nodded to Carly, "See, I told you if I woulda had Sam with me that day, those guys woulda been hamburger."

Carly didn't seem to feel much better about that. Claire understood that she was more suspicious than her young companion, and sympathized.

"I bet he's been sleepin' with my sister ..."

"No, your mom said he won't budge from your bed."

Jimmy smiled, probably his first really big smile since ...

"Are you cops?" Carly interrupted.

"No, we're from the FBI. You are Carly Williams, right?"

"Yes."

"Good. That makes my job much easier." Claire's playful banter had worked. She allowed her confident, friendly manner to lead them along. "I was wondering ... would you two like to call your mom and dads?"

The kids reacted with mixed feelings. Jimmy nodded enthusiastically, but Claire saw that Carly wasn't so eager.

"Listen," Claire insisted in a maternal tone. "Your parents have worried for a long time. They just want to hear your voice. You don't have to explain anything or talk about anything you don't want to. Okay? They just want to know you're here. I do have to call them and let them know where you are, but I thought you might want to hear their voices too. Would you like that?"

The kids had tears welling up in their eyes as Claire continued to assure them that everything was going to be all right and that they didn't have to explain or defend what had happened to them. Over and over she repeated that it wasn't their fault.

But just when Claire was sure she was getting somewhere, the fearful questions resumed.

"But they're still out there, aren't they—those guys? Are you gonna get them?"

"We'll get them, don't worry. You're safe now, that's what matters."

"But I think they killed that cop. The one who helped us . . ."

Claire had been briefed only slightly on the details. All she knew was that a highway patrolman had initiated the rescue, but was missing along with the bad guys. Presumed dead.

"That's why we're here. We're gonna get those guys. And you can help us. But we're gonna start now by first calling your parents. Okay?"

The kids nodded.

Joey commandeered a private lounge in the OB wing where the kids could make their calls in relative privacy. As they shut the door behind them, Joey moved to one phone and Claire to another. While the Bureau agents dialed, the kids held each other's hands in anticipation. Carly had tears rolling down her face. Jimmy laughed nervously and put a protective arm around her. She held on to him.

"Hello, Mrs. Jewison?"

"Hello, Mr. Williams?"

"This is Special Agent Randall . . ."

". . . Special Agent Quintel of the FBI."

"Sorry it's so late, but we've got someone here who really needs to say hello."

They turned the phones over to the kids.

"Hi Mom ... Mommy. It's me, Jimmy."

"Dad? Um ... it's Carly."

Joey and Claire stood back and watched as a circular conversation took place. Snatches of conversation from Jimmy's mouth would end up in Carly's conversation and vice versa. The charged energy and emotion inside the room made Joey step outside at one point to get some air and wipe a tear.

But the kids were doing fine all by themselves. They had moved farther and farther from each other in order to better hear their parents and loved ones. Now they were standing in opposite corners of the room, listening intently to the beloved voices they had yearned to hear for so long. In doing this, they were letting go of each other and the nightmarish hell they had endured and were stepping back into their own lives. Before it all began. Back to being the kids that they had once been. Independent of each other.

They will walk away from this and manage to be all right. Somehow.

Claire knew there were still miles to go before these kids could really return home. Many unpleasant memories would never quite be erased.

And I've got to go through all of it. I've got to feel their pain and fear and relive almost every inch of that insanity with them. I've got to bring it back and make them relive it all again.

But she had hope. Somehow, these kids had beaten the odds already.

They were still alive ... and very much loved.

Claire and Joey let the kids rest after the calls had been made and later followed the sheriff's department over to where efforts were being coordinated on the search for the white van.

Luckily, there were doughnuts set out when they arrived. Claire munched away on her favorite, a chocolate long john, before they went over the evidence, piece by piece. The room was filled with officers and standbys, all there for the briefing. They eyed Joey and Claire suspiciously, discussing the presence of the Feds in hushed tones and making them feel uncomfortable.

Then Koot Wilson appeared, bringing more questions.

"How are the children? What did the doctors say? Have their parents been contacted? Where are they now? The wife and I wanted to send them a little something . . ."

Due to a fluke of timing and circumstance, the old man was going to be connected to those kids for the rest of his life.

"Let's get started here. I got a missing man out there, and I can't say that I like it," Sheriff Andrew Levy complained, standing behind the podium of the watch command room.

Joey settled in right beside Claire as papers were passed around.

"You got there a photo of Officer Robert Koplowski. He started his patrol on Saturday afternoon shortly before four. Last contact with him was logged shortly before nine P.M. The suspects at the One Stop were encountered at approximately ten P.M. Now he might have been following this van with plans for an ambush, but Officer Koplowski isn't the shoot-em-up type. He's not stupid. He would have called for backup long before that."

"But he told me his radio was out," Koot explained.

"Yeah, well, we found his bike parked down the hill from your place, way out of sight. There was nothing wrong with his radio."

A murmur started among the observers.

Claire spoke up. "Had Officer Koplowski any knowledge of the suspects? Had he been made aware of the van or the photo found in Phoenix?"

"If he had run across the van, he would have certainly called in for a plate check and then he might have known. But he didn't call, so how could he know?" The sheriff sounded pained in his response. Claire guessed he didn't appreciate having to work with the Bureau on this one either.

"Maybe he saw them the night before. Maybe he'd been following them," an unidentified deputy suggested.

"And *kept* following them? I don't think so. That's where it gets too weird. He worked by the book."

Claire shifted her attention to the old man. "How close did you get to the cop—the one at your store?"

"Oh ... I dunno. Maybe ten or fifteen feet. There was a lot going on, you know, so if you're gonna ask me if I got a good look at his face, the answer's ..."

"... Not his face. His feet. Did you notice his boots?"

Joey yanked on Claire's arm, and she shrugged it away.

The old man thought about it a moment. The room grew quiet, awaiting his response.

"Ya know ... I can't say that I recall his boots ..."

"Can we get the missing officer's boot size?" Claire addressed the sheriff.

"His what? Has the FBI got something going on that we don't know about, Miss Randall?" the sheriff asked.

Claire cringed. Using the "Miss" was meant as an insult, and it was taken as one. But no one was going to stop her, especially not a bunch of hicks.

"Is it safe to say that the missing officer doesn't have large feet?"

A chorus of chuckles went up around the room, breaking up any semblance of organized discussion. But one man stood. He alone seemed to be taking this line of questioning seriously.

"Uh ... Bobby borrowed my runnin' shoes once. We're about the same size."

All eyes went to the floor. The officer stepped forward. His feet were neither large nor small. Just ... well, *regular*.

The deputy shrugged in a helpful sort of way, then sat back down.

"Sheriff, I'd like to go out to the scene and check the area where the bike was parked," Claire requested.

"For what, pray tell?"

"Boot marks."

"Boot marks?" The sheriff echoed her. Then he let out another small chuckle. "That bike was parked on a small patch of dirt, just off the side of the road. You know how many of my men have walked around that bike since last night? No one was checking for boot marks. We were busy trying to figure out why Officer Koplowski would report his radio dead for no reason."

Claire's cork was beginning to blow. Joey saw it and watched warily. "So you're admitting your men destroyed valuable evidence," Claire retorted.

"My men were doing their jobs."

The sheriff was now openly challenging her, and Claire was about to accept.

"Hold on now, let's wait a minute here ..." Joey stood, hands out, in peacemaker fashion. But Joey didn't get a chance to finish.

All eyes had shifted.

At the door, a man was standing. He clutched a Mexican blanket about him and hobbled on one good foot. His face was streaked with dirt and blood, wiped at hastily, without benefit of a mirror.

It was Officer Bobby Koplowski.

9

A Private Piece of Hell

June 23rd—The Sonoran Desert
13:10

It was a scorcher.

A bitch of a day.

Hotter than hell outside.

This valley floor had indeed turned out to be a private piece of hell. Champ had made sure of it. And he didn't mind the heat one bit.

Stripped of the officer's uniform, he munched on the groceries bought by Roger and Tom at the market in Phoenix. He even drank down the beers that they had purchased at Koot Wilson's store.

He had some time to kill, so he was making himself quite comfortable. As comfortable as one could get out in the desert in 114-degree heat. Lucky for him, he had found a small outcropping of rock that provided shelter from the heat and had pulled out his blue rabbit's foot key chain, toying with it for a moment.

There was a pocketknife attached to the bundle. He held it up, looking at the inscription on the grip that was nicked and worn from years of service. It read simply *Michael*.

His expression changed to sadness for a moment, as if he were recalling another place and time. He turned the knife over in his hand, feeling the weight of it while he waited.

From his wallet, he produced an old photo. It featured a young girl at her high school graduation. She was standing next to a young man who was smiling proudly at her in the cap and gown, and she was laughing.

He wore a policeman's uniform.

It seemed a lifetime ago.

No chance of bringing them back.

After a while, he pocketed the key chain and knife because the noises inside the van had stopped. Champ knew it was time to open her up again and make the animals beg for their lives. Since he had found the other photographs, he had been making the men relive those special Kodak moments. He especially liked the one where the victim (in the photo it had been Carly) had the barrel of a shotgun shoved up her ass while a rifle was being inserted into her vagina.

That photo had given him ideas. Just like the one in the grocery store had allowed him to head in the right direction, faster than anyone else was prepared to move. That's the way it was meant to be.

Champ wasn't believing in luck anymore. He was on a mission now. And someone was helping him . . . guiding him toward these kinds of outcomes. He felt he was becoming empowered. And he liked it.

But the plain truth was, he was just lucky enough to have headed down I-10 in the right direction. After all, it was a fifty-fifty shot—north or south.

Sweat ran down his chest in rivulets. The juice from the peach he sucked on had spilled there as well. He tossed the stone away and wiped his hand on his pants, glancing at his newly acquired watch as he did so. He liked this sleek, shiny timepiece. It made him feel the part.

It was one o'clock in the afternoon. These guys were not going to last much longer.

Hmmm . . .

91

And they had tortured those kids for how many months now?

When he'd seen the cop up on the overpass that night, he knew he had found an easy solution. There wasn't much to do. He only had to weave a bit, pretending to be drunk. As he disappeared behind a small rise in the highway, he was sure the cop had seen him.

And he had, of course.

Then Champ went to work. Once again, he relied on help from a blue tip. By the time the cop had passed over the small rise between them, he was greeted with the spectacle of a truck on fire and no driver in sight. As the cop reached for his radio, Champ appeared—waving. After that, it was only a matter of minutes until Champ was dressed for the part and cruising at over one hundred miles per hour to catch up to the van.

Fate had brought them together at Koot Wilson's place. The old man had provided good backup. And he was sure that the kids were being well taken care of. Champ owed Koot one. And he grinned, considering how he could pay back the old man.

But for now, there was still the question of Roger and Tom. Tom had been bleeding pretty badly for a while after the last game of "Tow Truck." Champ had to stop the game because the rope kept breaking, and he was getting tired of having to stop and retie it.

After reading aloud the litany of their crimes, Champ had questioned the two men thoroughly. And were they willing to talk! They became downright chatty after Champ brought out the photos and the guns from under the front seat. They talked a blue streak until Champ indicated he wanted to give them a taste of their own medicine.

Then they didn't seem to have a lot to say.

Champ pointed out how the kids had been dragged through an ordeal that would stay with them for the rest of their lives.

He wanted these two men to know firsthand, just how it felt.

But for right now, dragging them across the desert floor would suffice.

The rocky, cactus-laden terrain was perfect for it. He handcuffed their ankles and tied their hands with the duct tape. Then he tied rope under the armpits of just one of them, fixing the other end of the rope to the trailer hitch under the van's bumper. With the second man locked inside the van, Champ put the vehicle in gear and drove slowly over the rugged terrain of the desert, stopping every now and then when his load got weary so he could continue his tour with a fresh man in tow.

This routine continued until dawn, when Champ realized he would need the rest of the van's gasoline to get them the hell out of there.

With most of their clothes and much of the skin shredded from their bodies, Champ allowed the men to rest—inside the locked van, as he had found the children. The van's interior temperature had to be over 150 degrees. Every once in a while he opened the side door to check on them.

They weren't quite done yet.

As the sun began to set, Champ gathered the paper, bottles, and other trash from where he was sitting and stuffed it into a grocery bag. Removing another blue tip match from his pocket, he lit the bag on fire and threw the cop's shirt, jacket, and helmet on it as well.

He kept the pants.

Reaching for the shotguns at his side, he headed to the van. As the side door opened, he could smell the rancid odor of stale vomit and could see some evidence of it on Roger's chin. The men did not move as Champ climbed in. He stopped, noticing that their chests still rose and fell in repeated motion. They were alive all right.

"Anyone want a drink?" Champ offered, holding up the liquor bottle purchased at Koot's store the night before.

Roger's eyes opened. His left eye was swollen shut, but with his right, he managed to get a good look at Champ.

"Why don't you just *do it?*"

"Do it?" Champ asked, bemused.

"Kill us."

Champ chuckled as he loosened the pants of the unconscious Tom. He pulled the shredded, bloodstained jeans off his motionless body.

"What's your hurry?" Champ replied.

"The old man saw it. They're looking for you. They know you have us."

"No. They probably think you have me."

"You're a cop! You can't do this! You're just supposed to turn us in, man!"

"Oh ... so you can get a fair trial. Is that the idea?"

Champ slapped Tom's face back and forth, which elicited a grunting sound. Then he rolled Tom over on his stomach, which put his face smack into Roger's drying pile of vomit. The strong scent of bile brought Tom around. He grunted and groaned loudly, unable to speak clearly because his tongue was swollen for lack of water.

Champ pointed the barrel of the shotgun at Tom's scrotum and pushed, hard.

One good jolt.

Tom screamed, his knees rising involuntarily; a reflex to get away. The movement brought his ass up to Champ's eye level.

Perfect.

"You're gonna lose your badge for this," Roger warned.

"I got news for you," Champ replied as he jammed the single barrel of the gun up inside Tom's anal cavity with one swift motion. Tom strained against the metal, struggling to get loose of it. But only for only a moment.

"I'm not a cop," Champ replied.

He pulled the trigger.

"Lt. Traask! Just a moment please!"

Traask turned, and his whole day went down the drain.

Holly North and her cameraman crossed the length of the parking lot in less time than it would have taken Traask to run for cover, if he had warning. He was only a few feet from the entry to the jail.

How the hell did she get in here?

"Start rolling, Pat," she commanded.

"Ms. North ..." Traask's terse greeting was unaccompanied by his trademark grin.

"Just a few comments on the Cannibal case." As she spoke, she arranged herself in front of him, clutching a microphone; the umbilical cord to her profession.

"Didn't you receive a copy of the statement we issued on Friday, Ms. North?"

"Yes, but that wasn't exactly *news,* Lieutenant. It's been two days. Tell me, why all the secrecy on this case?"

"There's no secrecy intended. We just don't need any more press interference on this one. Now, if you'll excuse me ..."

Holly had not received such off-camera attitude from Traask in months. She had expected his charming, public face to give her something she could take back to the station. Anything, really.

"Uh ... yes, well—we understand your position, Lieutenant, but it would be helpful to get some kind of comment from Cincinnati's top cop. After all, the public is horrified by what has been discovered in its backyard."

"I feel the same way. And when there is something new to report, you can be assured that I will be available for comment. But right at this moment, I have an appointment inside, and I don't intend to keep anyone waiting."

Traask managed to get a handle on the door, and pulled it open before Holly could fire any more missiles in his direction. He left her outside, angry and unappeased.

He was going to get it for that.

But for now, it was back to work for Traask. Another body had been discovered in an abandoned lot just across the street from the apartment they searched on Friday. The Cannibal's apartment. The suspicion was that it was his handiwork. Traask was there to find out if that was true.

As Traask stepped up to the front desk, his attention was drawn to a strange man sitting in the corner of the lobby. He was grasping a Styrofoam cup in one grubby hand, clutching a notepad in the other. When he saw Traask, he smiled broadly.

"Hey there, Lt. Traask!"

Traask realized that the friendly greeting came from none other than Willem DeYoung, the wanna-be writer who appeared to be in even worse shape than at their former meeting.

Traask leaned in to the sergeant on duty. "What is he doing here?"

The sergeant leaned back, shrugging. "He's on the visitor list."

"He's what?!" Traask was working that one over when he was approached from behind. The smell hit him first.

"I got this one! Got it by the friggin' toe! Yup! Good old early-bird logic for you. So, whaddya think?"

"What do I think?"

"Yeah! What do you think about that!"

Traask really didn't have time for this. "That's great, pal." Then to the sergeant he asked, "Uh ... are they ready back there?"

The man behind the desk buzzed Traask through the security gate. Traask nodded sympathetically to Mr. DeYoung as he exited the lobby and headed into the back rooms. DeYoung waved happily as Traask left.

"Well, see 'ya around!"

Traask hoped not. Actually, Traask hoped into that life some cleansing rain would fall. Jesus, even the Cannibal himself wouldn't sit still for being locked in a room with that kind of stench!

As he crossed through the front offices, Traask noticed that most of the men were at lunch, away from their desks. An abandoned newspaper was lying open across a desk in his wake. As he got closer, a headline caught his eye.

Two Worst Cases in Cincinnati History!
Cannibal in Custody While Cop Killer Trial Begins

Before Traask could read more, Bennie crossed to him. "Hey, man ..."

Distracted, Traask nodded a greeting.

Bennie noted his attention to the paper. "Hey, this went national, you know."

Traask observed that it was, indeed, the colorized national rag. That meant the entire United States was reading about him today.

He went back to scanning the article, but a photo below it caught his eye.

Arizona is Home to Crimes in the Desert

A picture of Richard Winert's burned body was featured next to a photo of a boy and girl, bound and gagged. Traask's finger wandered through the copy.

"Pretty wild, what's been going on out there, huh?"

"I haven't had a chance to catch all of it. Jennifer's been keeping me busy."

"Oh yeah? Where is she today?"

"She's at Deb and Fr—" Traask's habitual reference to the Morrison's house had yet to be revised. He tried again. "Deb Morrison's. Kids wanted her to stay."

Traask continued reading. Bennie followed Traask's lead.

"I would have liked to be present when they opened that van, let me tell you."

Traask glanced up from the paper as Bennie continued.

"They found it, you know. It just came through on the news channel. It showed up last night, back in the parking lot of the gas station where the shoot-out took place. The FBI opened that sucker up and found themselves one hell of a mess."

"The cop's dead?"

"There weren't no cop! The real cop showed up over the weekend. He'd been bushwhacked and left at the side of some cliff. He's okay. Nothing bad. Whoever it was stole his motorcycle, uniform, and gun, and got away without a hitch. What they found inside the van was the remains of the kidnappers! The perverts who took those kids and tortured them for over a year. You know those kids were barely alive when they were found?"

Bennie was seething underneath. "But I must say, it had to have been quite a sight when they cracked open those doors."

"Why?"

Bennie struggled to answer. "Well, let's just put it this way. It's gonna be hard as hell to make a made-for-TV movie with a climax like that!"

"What happened to them?"

Bennie stopped, seeing that Traask wanted an answer. The real answer. Bennie leaned into him and spoke quietly.

"Someone stuck a shotgun up both their asses and let the shit fly."

"Christ . . ." Traask replied. His mouth dried up. He returned the newspaper to the desktop, feeling suddenly drained.

"Yeah," Bennie agreed.

Traask was being called to the entrance to the interrogation room. Bennie cleared his throat. It was showtime once more. But just for that moment, the two of them stood together eye to eye.

Both men had children. Both men were sworn to uphold the law. But both men had the same gut reaction.

Good for you, Mister.

10

Big Foot Becomes A Reality
June 24th—The One Stop
12:37

Now he was *real*.

No longer a ghost to be chased through vague corridors and listless hours spent in the waiting game.

The sheriff's department didn't laugh this time when Claire insisted they search and recover any oversize boot marks in the area surrounding the One Stop. And they found them, all right. One particularly good heel mark was found on the adjoining property where their man had obviously made his exit from the scene after depositing the van back at the One Stop.

Now the lab boys from the Bureau were sent out. Not only did the van evidence require the most professional handling possible, but when the sheriffs saw the mess inside the Ford Econoline, they were downright relieved to hear that the case was no longer their problem.

Bobby Koplowski showed up sometime later that morning in plain clothes. He limped over to the van, took notice of its contents, and turned a lighter shade of pale. There was no mistaking the fact he was a lucky man to walk away from that mess with only a limp.

Claire had questioned him extensively the day he showed up at the sheriff's station, but his information was altogether lacking. Together they had traveled out to the site where he had been attacked, and they found the burned-out truck and a scuffling of dust where he had been hit from behind and dragged down the embankment. No other clues were present. Bobby's boots came back from the Phoenix lab without yielding any prints or additional evidence. The burned vehicle was designated as incendiary fire, because it had clearly been set to bring the officer running to the scene. And since Bobby admitted to having been within full view of the underpass at the time, obviously the suspect had observed him as he passed underneath and had then pulled over and set the fire.

Everyone was coming up with the right pieces to the puzzle, but that puzzle was already in the past.

Claire was concerned with future events now.

Identification on the kidnappers didn't take long. They were brothers who had priors for indecent exposure and solicitation of minors. They didn't really matter anymore. They were dead. And by the looks of it, they were probably grateful.

But there was someone out there who did matter. And the burned-up truck was registered as stolen, so the police still had no description on the guy. The kids were the ones who had gotten the closest to the suspect, and they still had no idea what he looked like. He was wearing a helmet that covered his hair and most of his face. The rest was hidden behind sunglasses.

Sunglasses at night. That should have clued them all in from the beginning. But it hadn't. He was their knight in shining armor come to rescue them!

Local authorities had managed to keep the "Big Foot" information from leaking to the press, per Claire's request. For the time being, it would have to be their little secret. But they couldn't keep the parents of the kidnap victims from talking about the case.

"They got what they deserved," Carly Williams's father told

one reporter just outside the hospital. The interview appeared on the Sunday night news. "I just wish I could have been there to help the son of a bitch. I'd like to shake his hand."

The Jewisons held their tongues the longest, but it was Mrs. Jewison who finally commented briefly to the press with a mother's words that would soon be printed around the world.

"The man who rescued my son is not a criminal. Those men in the van were the criminals."

She later added, "As far as I'm concerned, it's over with. I don't care if they ever find the man who did it. As a matter of fact, I hope they don't."

So now Claire was saddled with an investigative nightmare; the description of the suspect was weak, and public support was building by the moment. All she knew was their suspect was a white, 6'4" male, roughly 250 pounds, wearing man's size sixteen custom-made boots.

What the press had built up in only twenty-four hours was an Arnold Schwarzenegger-type hero. Big Foot was well on his way to becoming an American institution.

Heroes like this guy belonged to the likes of Dirty Harry—not to a 114-pound brunette FBI agent. But out here in the real world, real people were responsible for finding them. And stopping them.

Easier said than done. Claire stopped paying attention to numerous so-called related reports coming in on the case. She was busy trying to figure out where he was going to next. She wanted to be there when he surfaced.

This didn't surprise Joey at all.

There were thousands of creeps out there to choose from. Like lottery numbers. And the combinations seemed as endless. Claire still had no idea how Big Foot had stumbled upon the kidnappers in the first place. Perhaps he had seen them at an earlier stop and followed them until the moment was right.

As for the rest ... well, she'd have to work on it. There had to be a pattern or a clue in there somewhere. Something to tell them who this guy was and why he was on this vigilante spree.

Claire had called out the big guns, sending everything she had to the Behavioral Sciences Division in Washington. She had some friends there she hoped might be cooperative in providing her a fast turnaround on the information she needed. She was hoping it would be able to give her some insight into Big Foot's motivation. His actions might indicate that he was a victim's relative or loved one. Or perhaps he personally knew one of the girls Maxx had taken care of in the desert. Claire set Joey on that case.

So far, the media had not linked the three crimes together. She wanted to keep it that way. With popular support so strong over the subsequent outcome of the van kidnapping, it could be dangerous to admit there was a successful vigilante out there. After all, his string of accomplishments was growing.

Shit, he'd be booked on talk shows for months. Or, he might disappear for good. Or worse. Copycats were likely to come out of the woodwork and destroy any trail that might lead to the true killer.

Right now things were calm. With luck, Claire could keep it that way until her man was in custody and behind bars. After that, she didn't care if they made him into a fucking hero.

Ah . . . Southern California. The beaches, the smog . . . So many assholes, so little time.

Champ was doing well for himself. He stumbled on a brand-new 4 × 4 parked outside a Tucson convenience store early Monday morning and stepped up to it without hesitation. The engine had been left running. No problem. He clipped the keys to his rabbit's foot and away they flew. There was some money in the tray between the seats, so he treated himself to a burger and fries before leaving town.

He headed toward the coast with an itch to put his feet in the sand of the Pacific and take a long, fast ride up Highway One.

There was business to attend to in California. Big business. Something he had wanted to do for quite a while. And as he listened to the reports of his handiwork in Arizona, he became increasingly aware that now was the time to see it through.

The man who rescued my son is not a criminal. Those men in the van were the criminals.

Damn straight. And they died like criminals should die. Not with a whimper, but with a bang. Straight up the old wazoo.

The crumbling steps of the Cincinnati courthouse were awash with reporters from both the local stations and the networks. Fresh batteries filled their video cams, running shoes adorned their feet. It was a textbook display of media activity as the reporters pushed and shoved their way toward each new star that arrived for the Cop Killer show.

Daniel Traask watched from high above. He patted himself on the back for escaping at least this portion of the media madness. He was fortunate enough to have a neighbor who was working for the reconstruction project on the rotunda and law library in the east wing of the courthouse. On his advice, Traask slipped through the door of the construction site and up the back stairs, avoiding detection by the front-door press.

As he gazed down upon them now, he felt the raw edge of his distaste once again. This wasn't the place for them. They had told their story months ago. Now it was the lawyer's turn to take over. The press were just there for the ride—to keep the public's interest up until there was an outcome. And by Traask's estimation, they could be waiting for quite a while.

Today, the curtain would rise on the Cop Killer trial in Cincinnati.

"So what do we do? Wait until someone else turns up missing and go after that one too?"

Joey was getting frustrated. Nothing useful was coming via the regular channels—this guy was still a ghost. No clear ID, no clear prints to match . . . just some fucking boot mark in the sand.

As far as taking sides, Joey didn't know how to feel about

that. The "Caped Crusader" who rescued the Van Kids was being talked about everywhere in Phoenix. Joey guessed it was happening all around the country. This guy's actions raised questions of morality and the law, questions that weren't so easy to answer when you stood and stared into the bruised and tortured faces of Carly Williams and Jimmy Jewison, listening to them tell about the horrors they'd endured.

And for what? The men who did this to them were now dead. Big Foot had seen to that. There could be no purpose in gathering such information except for the record. Joey felt terrible having to ask such questions, but procedure must be followed. And perhaps Jimmy or Carly might remember something on their own. Had they seen their rescuer before? Could Big Foot have known the men and tracked them down?

But they were following any lead they could come up with. At least Joey was. Smart money said that something would show up if enough clues were available.

Claire remained stationary. She was holding out for the psychological profile. She needed to know more about this guy. So far she wasn't getting much, and she was damn hungry for something . . . anything.

What was Washington up to? Why was a response taking so long?

In the meantime, she was throwing together a listing of possibles—new victims for Big Foot. There were a lot of them, but Claire had managed to narrow them down to a handful of notorious crimes against women and children. These were what the guy seemed to have been targeting so far, so she was going to run with it, try to anticipate his next move.

When the preliminary psych profile came back on Tuesday afternoon, she was relieved to see she was headed in the right direction. It supported her hunch about the connection between the three killings and suggested that the killer would be likely to strike again soon.

"He's probably feeding off of all this public support like a leech. The report says there are two possibilities. Either this was an ex-cop or a cop wanna-be that couldn't make the force for some reason, or he was related to a victim somewhere down the line—perhaps one of Mad Maxx's victims."

"Bingo." Joey's excitement made Claire smile.

If this killer started with Mad Maxx, the report had cautioned. Claire let this idea go unvoiced as she continued.

"He might have gotten a taste for it on the first blood . . . revenge for a loved one who was hurt by that particular person. Thus he felt relieved of guilt, and then, afterward, he convinced himself he had done something worthwhile. Something we, as law enforcement, could not and dare not do. So he was proud of himself, and then he wanted to do it again."

Claire was fascinated that she had come so close to their theory on her own. But she had begun to doubt her intuition after she and Joey had arrived in Phoenix. It was the coldness of the trail that had her confused.

This killer was leaving no surprises behind—no handholds, nothing to reach out and take ahold of. Claire's mind had been working, searching for his trail, anything that might make an impression and seem familiar to her. She had found nothing she could identify.

Nothing that gave her an edge over this damn report.

"However, this guy does break the mold of the traditional serial killer." Claire mused. "Serials don't personalize their victims. They don't want to know anything that would make them seem human. This guy knows who his victims are, and he picks them in advance. He also doesn't seem to take any trophies or mementos from the victims. Even that cop's watch was found back inside the van. On the dashboard."

Joey nodded, lost in thought as Claire continued.

"His killing methods are not professional by any means, which tells us he has little or no training and background in this area. So any professional mercenaries or veterans can be dismissed. I would guess he is probably a regular Joe from a working-class background."

"Yeah, but is it Ozzie or Harriet?" Joey joked, of the

opinion that any and all theories were mere supposition until the creep was in the bag.

"This is important!" Claire said. "This means he could possibly be a local from around here or New Mexico, where he started."

"Are you sure that's where he started?"

"No. I'm not. But it could take weeks to dig up more cases like these. My preliminary check of the national computer database shows nothing else out there so far with a Big Foot marker quite like his. But that doesn't mean shit. For now I'm going to concentrate on Maxx and see if something doesn't surface."

"I already got you most of the Maxx information."

Claire patted a set of files at her side. "Right here. You and I are going to go through every inch of it. There's got to be something in here that tells us who he is." Claire passed a few files across the table to her partner.

Joey didn't react.

"What's wrong?" Claire asked.

"So what's *your* guess?"

"About what?"

"Don't play games with *me,* Randall," Joey began, using a tone that a third-grade teacher might find effective. "I see that look in your eye. You're light-years ahead of the rest of us. Stop with this psychological profile mumbo jumbo and tell me what's going on inside that wild child brain of yours. Where is the bastard? Where's he headed? C'mon, who's next on the list?"

Claire blushed slightly, smiling. She suddenly couldn't meet her partner's gaze. "I thought you didn't believe in that sort of thing."

"I don't," Joey replied with a pained sigh. "I don't believe in the tooth fairy either, but I'll go along with it. If you've got something extra up your sleeve, then let's use it."

The statement was not meant to hurt Claire's feelings, but it had. Joey hastened to explain the remark. "I believe in *you.* I know you, Randall. You've got something in that head of yours that makes you a natural-born hide-and-seek expert with guys like this. You've been batting a thousand lately. Now let's see if you can beat him to third base."

"And if I don't?"

"There's always the next inning. Come on. What does the 'Amazing Randall' predict?"

Claire glanced down at her list of possibles. There were so many. She had begun crossing a few off the list already, in a process of elimination. And at the bottom of the list she had recently added the Cincinnati Cannibal.

"I'm not sure. He's begun to make headlines. I think he'll try for something bigger—you know, fan the fire—pick someone that will make this story go national."

"Who?"

"He's thinking . . ." Claire stared at the list now with full concentration. Her sentence had dropped off into thought. She worked the names.

Joey watched as she studied the list, growing increasingly uncomfortable. *Jesus, she's getting inside of him right now. Right here.*

". . . he's thinking, 'Now I have a chance to really say something and be heard. Everybody's watching.' So it's got to be big."

Claire paused over the list of names. Seeking out her natural instinct, the unseen force whispered to her, letting her know which of the headline-making criminals might be next. Her pen struck the paper several times as she crossed out names, narrowing it down to only a few.

Claire's stream-of-consciousness narration continued. She wasn't talking to Joey or for Joey's benefit. It was clearly just the way she worked all this out in her head.

Right. Like receiving radio broadcasts with your fillings, Joey thought.

"He's not doing this one for himself. He's not doing it for revenge. The others might have been for a revenge of some sort, but he's doing this one because . . . because *it needs doing.*"

"Randall," Joey warned, getting a little spooked. Standing now, Joey crossed to Claire's side and looked over her shoulder as she narrowed down the list.

"He's not going to go far. He's going to head to the closest possible location to make his statement and then get the hell out of there."

She crossed out The Cannibal from Cincinnati. Too far for now.

"Okay. So where's that?"

Four names remained on her list. Their common denominator was Arizona's next-door neighbor.

California.

11

On the Hill, Looking Down
June 25th—Hollywood, California
13:52

It was a winding, sprawling, hopelessly switch-backed road that led up the hill into the exclusive neighborhood. There were too many twists and turns, too many narrow roads with dead ends. Directions were nearly impossible. People who lived up here drew detailed maps and faxed them. Their unsuspecting dinner guests inevitably showed up late, but not from lack of trying.

It was pizza delivery hell.

Film legends of long ago had been the first to settle the auspicious hillside. Many of the old homes were still owned by people in the trade, but more were being purchased by reclusive sorts, who hoped to find some privacy on the vertical landscape known as the Hollywood Hills. And they paid for that privacy in cash.

The exposed-beam ceiling of the Camerons' home suggested a friendly, open home. It spoke of a happy couple living the good life. The decor was nearing very well-to-do, with little reminders scattered here and there that revealed there might have been a struggle along the way to reach this lofty plateau.

The fortunate homeowners were currently outside, near the Jacuzzi on a deck that faced the southwest end of the Hollywood Hills. There was usually an incredible view of the city, but not this afternoon. Heavy smog inhibited the daytime visibility. First-stage smog alerts were called for in the inland valley areas.

It seemed a perfect afternoon to add some souls to the list, Champ thought. In a city full of angels.

It was a great afternoon for Eric Cameron as well. His wife, Caroline, stood at his side, wrapped in a full-length terry cloth robe. Her attire contrasted with his business suit and tie. His hair was perfectly groomed. Not a speck under his fingernails. He looked squeaky clean, as if he had just come from a lunch at the Vatican.

"It's over now, Eric. It's all over." She raised her champagne glass to his, and they both drank it down.

He nodded afterward, a satisfied smile filling his features. He studied the view for a moment in silent thought. *Thank God, it's over.*

The wife moved away. She crossed back toward the house and flipped the stereo switch mounted on the wall. Loud music flooded the hillside.

Every breath you take,
Every move you make,
Every bond you break,
Every step you take,
I'll be watching you ...

Eric watched as she reached for the next switch, activating the Jacuzzi jets. Slowly moving toward the stairs and the water, she dropped her robe, revealing her fully naked body. Eric sighed, appreciatively. Those breasts were worth waiting for. A seductive smile played upon her lips as she motioned him toward the whirlpool.

Eric abandoned his glass on the railing.

Now standing upon the stairs to the Jacuzzi, she reached out to take him, holding his head in her hands and kissing him deeply. She used her tongue to arouse him, playfully pulling on his bottom lip with her teeth.

The softness of her cascading hair brushed against his cheek as she cradled his head—drawing his mouth closer to her breasts. Led by her perfume, his nose moved downward in sensual pursuit along her bare skin. He grasped at her breasts, using his palms to raise the nipples to his mouth, gently kissing each of them in single, exaggerated turns.

Her head arched back, and she let out a laughing sigh. "Oh, Eric ..."

Her empty glass grazed his left earlobe. He noticed. Continuing this kind of activity called for a refill. Maybe two. He wanted to slow the pace and enjoy himself for as long as he could

"I'll get some more of this," he volunteered, removing the glass from her hand and starting for the house.

She moaned her disappointment.

"I'll be right back. I'll just get out of these clothes and get us a refill."

Her pouting expression lasted only a moment.

"Bring the bottle!" she demanded, heading into the water.

Every breath you take,
Every vow you break,
Every smile you fake,
Every claim you stake
I'll be watching you ...

The music was not playing inside the house. So as soon as he entered, Eric could hear a phone ringing somewhere in the back. He moved toward it, then changed his mind. *Aw, let the fucking machine pick it up.*

He continued into the kitchen with his wife's glass. After another two rings, the machine did pick it up.

He set down his wife's glass on the countertop and realized he had forgotten his own. Stepping back, he glanced out at the glass sitting on the rail. Caroline was still in the Jacuzzi, luxuriating in the steam bubbling around her. Music blared from the speakers. He abandoned the idea of reclaiming his glass.

No offense, darling. But right now, I need a real drink.

He opened a cabinet near the kitchen sink and removed a rocks glass. Expensive crystal. Eric vaguely recalled that it had been a wedding present. Someone from Caroline's side of the family, wasn't it?

Reaching into another cabinet, he pulled forth a fifth of Johnny Walker Red Label. The seal had not yet been cracked. Good. He planned to drink most of it before nightfall.

The ice maker made noisy turns as it strained and rotated, finally filling his rocks glass to the rim. He licked his lips in anticipation. But a cube bounced off the top and skittered across the linoleum, coming to rest in the kitchen corner. Eric swore a string of obscenities under his breath and bent over to pick it up, before it puddled.

He never saw it coming.

Out on the deck, Caroline relaxed in the waiting. Her eyes remained closed against the music as she swayed to the song.

Every move you make,
Every step you take,
I'll be watching you . . .

And then it was over.

Another song played. Then another.

At first she called for him, but figured he couldn't hear her over the music.

Rising from the tub, finally, she sought out the terry robe and wrapped it about her. She could just imagine that he was talking on the phone or making a sandwich, leaving her there to wait. Well, not this time, buster. She'd waited long enough.

Inside, she found quite a mystery.

A cracked glass, Sunday's paper strewn across the kitchen floor, and the front door . . .

It was wide-open.

"What we got is a missing man, Agent Randall. That's all. The son of a bitch panicked and decided to split."

"Leaving the wife in the Jacuzzi, naked and waiting? Come on . . ."

"It's a setup! He wants it to seem suspicious. He wants it to appear as if he's been abducted."

Aging and unimpressed, Agent Weis of the Los Angeles Bureau was unfamiliar with Claire and Joey's credentials, so the attitude began to surface the moment the three of them pulled away from the curb and into the clogged Los Angeles traffic.

"So the place was pretty well trashed? I love those types. The ego of man never will allow it to be said that he went without putting up a really good fight."

Weis didn't respond to Joey's comment.

"I know he was being tried for the Hillside Murders—but can you fill us in?"

"Pieces of twenty-seven separate bodies were found in shallow graves on a hillside in the Angeles Forest. And this son of a bitch did it," Weis stated with an assuredness that unnerved Claire.

"And they called a mistrial?"

"Yeah . . ." Weis snorted, shifting uneasily. "Some kind of 'discovery' thing. It was a fuckin' technicality! But that's it. Screw the law! The son of a bitch was guilty as sin, I tell you. He deserves the fuckin' chair."

"What happened to innocent until proven guilty?" Joey reminded him.

"Explain that to the families of those girls. Tell it to the one who barely escaped from his car and was so terrified of testifying at the trial that she slashed her wrists the night before! He's a satanic son of a bitch, I tell you!"

"Did you know the families personally, or are you going on pure assumption here?" Joey couldn't resist the temptation.

Claire's hand flew to her mouth, concealing an amused grin. Both had been operating on so little sleep that they were slightly punchy.

Joey shrugged back at her, miming wide-eyed innocence.

"Go ahead, make jokes. You guys didn't have to deal with him . . . you weren't there."

"No, we weren't. But we have to deal with him now. So enlighten us." Claire steered the conversation back into safe territory. "Start at the beginning."

"Christ!" Weis shrugged and threw his hands up in the air. "What am I, a walking case file?"

"You'll have to be. We didn't have time to pull anything ourselves before leaving Phoenix. We had our hands full over there."

"Jesus . . ." Weis was begrudging, but coming around. "All right. Nineteen eight-eight: Eric Thomas Cameron, age thirty-two, married. Wife is Caroline Cameron. She's twenty-something, used to being taken care of. He's a lawyer, works in the mid-Wilshire area, takes on the Beverly Hills crowd—divorces mostly. Only Eric has this problem, see. He likes to rape teenage girls, cut up their bodies, and dump them up on a certain hillside in the Angeles Forest. Sort of a quiet little hobby of his.

"But *damn,* he's good at it! In fact, he's so good that for the first couple of years, no one even finds a connection between the missing girls until a hiker discovers their bodies up there on the hill. A whole shitload of used parts, so to speak. So many, in fact, that we still haven't made an accurate determination on just how many he really took up there.

"Once the story goes public—hits the newsstands—the trail stops cold. No new murders for over five months. But then he slips. He gets drunk at a Christmas party and tries to pick up an underage prostitute. She's a smart one, though, and before he can pull anything really rough, she sinks her

114

teeth into his thigh, opens the car door, and bails out onto the northbound 405, going about seventy miles per hour."

"Brave kid," Joey commended.

"She's the one who slit her wrists later," Weis replied, loading on as much sarcasm as the words could carry.

"The cops catch up to him a few days later and turn him over to us. What we've got is a man who perfectly matches the description of the suspect in the Hillside Murders and is subsequently ID'd by three eyewitnesses. Except suddenly we got a 'Mr. Clean' from Beverly Hills who knows the law and is gonna play it for every inch it will give, and then some. Did you know he was out on bail within twenty hours? We had surveillance on him, but he was way ahead of us. He kept his nose clean, even managed to raise some public sympathy, before we could gather enough evidence to go to trial.

"The first thing he did was totally destroy the prostitute's case. Cameron claimed she tried to rob him as they were driving. The girl had priors, so it wasn't much of a reach. He had even called in with a report of missing credit cards late that evening, if you can beat that for smarts. He claimed he didn't go to the police because it was 'the first time he'd ever done anything like that'—meaning, pick up a prostitute. Yeah ... right!

"So once those charges were out of the way, his legal beagles took over, tearing the eyewitness testimony to shreds. But lemme tell you, we talked to those witnesses and knew they had it right-on-the-nose. Of course, after three years, memories are not as reliable and because it was such a high-profile case, people testifying tended to be more intimidated by all the press, you know."

Unfortunately, Claire and Joey did.

"So, despite all the evidence to the contrary, you're convinced he was guilty," Joey stated flatly, not caring for this agent's attitude. "Why?"

"Hey, I went over a lot more evidence than what got presented in that courtroom. I saw things and heard things that eventually were declared inadmissible. Inadmissible, my fat ass!" Weis grunted like a rutting hog, then continued.

"That guy was never once concerned about his situation. He never once looked worried, not even that first night we brought him in. That kind of confidence is rare. You would think an innocent guy would be worried about the publicity hurting his practice or upsetting his wife and family. But this guy was an ice man. He never even blinked when they described the murders during questioning. Pretty grisly stuff too. Again, you would think a Beverly Hills-type would be fairly put off by that kind of thing. At least show some compassion when he saw pictures of the remains. This asshole acted like he had a hard-on the whole time. He knew he was going to get away with it.

"He made sure we couldn't find any evidence to link him. There were different cars used in each abduction, murder weapons varied—even cause of death. But the women all ended up on the same hillside."

"So how do you think he did it?" Claire asked.

"Well, there's several theories. Personally, I think he stole some of the cars in question, sort of a pregame thing, you know? A car matching one description was stolen across the street from his offices the night victim number twenty-one was taken. A month later, he was getting his Mercedes repaired, so he was driving a loaner from the dealership that matched number twenty-two's eyewitness report. But that's still all circumstantial, right?

"Perhaps sometimes it was the girl's car, like it was in number fourteen's case. We recovered that one at least. So let's just say he had ways of getting transportation, okay?

"He probably picked up the girls however he could, and then reached behind the seat and knocked them out with a tire iron, like he was trying to do with that poor kid after the Christmas party. Once they're out, he drives them up into the mountains. And that's where my own pet theory comes in."

"Oh?" Joey raised an inquiring eyebrow. Joey didn't like Weis, or any law enforcement official of his kind. His know-it-all attitude was irritating and offensive. But it had to be endured. "Pray tell, let us have it."

"I think the son of a bitch has a cabin or some sort of

116

shelter up there. Perhaps it belongs to someone he killed early on, and he's been using it ever since. At any rate, he takes them there, has his way with them, and then slices and dices until he's got them just the way he likes 'em, loads them up in the stolen vehicle, and dumps them alongside the hill on his way back to the city. He then leaves the car in East L.A., doors open and engine running, so it's sure to get stolen again—that way it's not his problem anymore. He walks away clean."

"That would make it difficult to trace. Anything found on the hillside? Anything on the girls themselves?" Claire continued the questions.

"No. Nothing. That was the kicker. This guy was the luckiest guy in the world; not a thread, not a hair. Now bear in mind that it took two years to discover the cache of remains—so animals and weather helped him out a lot in terms of evidence."

Claire pounced on him. "Then what you're saying is that this guy could be innocent."

"In a pig's eye." Weis was resolute in his conviction.

"If you don't have anything material tying Cameron to the killings, then I'd say that's reasonable doubt," Joey affirmed.

"I told you, we had solid stuff on him! But folks, I'm here to tell you, with money comes privilege. His Beverly Hills counsel saw to it nothing incriminating made it to the courtroom. They managed to hide plenty, believe me. That guy was as guilty as they come."

Joey took the dare. "It seems to me the prosecution could have done something, if there was as much on him as you say."

"Hey, I agree. Everyone who worked on the case said the same thing. He was one lucky fuck. To this day, I don't know how he managed it. His marriage didn't fall apart—his law practice remained rock solid. His life went on like nothing at all had happened."

"What about psychological testing?" Joey asked.

"Inconclusive. He was better than that. This man was educated. He was brilliant at what he did! The charm of the devil and threads of Rodeo Drive. What woman wouldn't go out searching for this type?!"

Joey didn't comment on that one.

"What have you got on the wife?" Claire asked before her partner could respond.

"A dead end, if you'll pardon the pun. She's stone-fucking convinced of his innocence. Of course, she wasn't around most of the time when the murders were taking place. She goes out of the country a lot. But she seemed just as cool as he was about it all. He ordered takeout when it came to his sexual appetite, and I'm sure she knew. Most of those Rodeo Drive bitches do."

"Maybe she knows more," Joey suggested.

"Maybe. Maybe she's just scared shitless. I think she's helping him to stage this little scenario so they can escape the country together before some real evidence turns up against him."

"Then this would be a waste of our time," Claire announced firmly.

She knew that if Cameron was serious about leaving the country, then Big Foot would have found the cupboard bare over here and would begin searching somewhere else for a victim. They could be chasing Cameron's shadow, if he was simply hiding out.

Well, Claire wasn't here to catch Cameron.

Weis turned to her, "Yeah, I heard you have some sort of a theory going yourself. You requested we search for boot marks or unusually large prints?"

"Any found?"

"No."

Claire nodded to Joey. "We could be chasing our tails."

"Well, what do you think?" Joey replied.

Claire knew what her partner meant. Not, what do you think? It was, what do you feel, what does your gut tell you about this?

The space reserved in her head for such matters was growing cloudy from all the recent activity. She didn't use this area often, so she never knew what to expect. Should she sense by now that this Cameron case was a dead end?

Nothing was clear.

She was going to need some time with this. She decided to reserve judgment until they reached the Cameron house.

Weis leaned forward to speak with the driver. Claire shrugged at Joey. Their eyes connected in a short volley of secret messages. A toss of the head told Claire that Joey felt Weis was full of himself and that they shouldn't take his opinions as gospel. But something told Claire that at least part of what Weis was getting at had been on track.

It was just like when they first got to Phoenix. There wasn't much out there to grasp in terms of Big Foot. It was as if it were all well taken care of—as if they'd been anticipated and outsmarted.

And if that were true, it would mean they weren't wasting their time ... It would mean they were right behind him.

"I ... I wouldn't let anyone touch anything. I wanted them to leave it just the way I found it so that you could get everything you could. But they said they had to run tests ..."

The wife was not bearing up well, and it showed. Her long, bottle-blond hair was mussed and fastened back to keep it off her face. Her clothes appeared to be fresh, but there were remnants of tear-streaked mascara that indicated she'd been awake most of the night. Two other FBI agents stood by her side.

Claire sensed immediately that this woman wasn't covering for her husband. This wasn't merely a smoke screen so Cameron could flee the country. Caroline circled about the room, her movements as disconnected as her thoughts, while trying desperately to appear calm and hopeful.

But the bottom line was that she was filled with doubt. She had been abandoned. And with his disappearance went her belief in him as well. Her husband was a murderer and only now did she believe it.

Claire's heart sank. If she was reading this right, they were wasting their time. Still, it wouldn't hurt to go through the motions. So she and Joey moved slowly toward the kitchen area, noting the taped outline on the floor where the newspaper had been found. A few more paces brought them to where the glass had been recovered.

"This is all?" Joey asked. Expectations of seeing evidence of a male ego in full flight went down the drain.

"The room's clean, right?" Claire asked.

Weis replied affirmatively, admitting to being present during the sweep that lasted over twelve hours.

Claire's attention shifted back to the wife.

"Mrs. Cameron, what do you think happened to your husband?"

"What do you mean?"

"You know there are only two possibilities. Well, actually there are three, but I'm relieving you of any involvement with his disappearance when I say there are only two possibilities."

Apparently one of the men accompanying Caroline that morning was not an FBI agent, but Eric's defense attorney. He wasn't going to stand for this kind of implication.

"Now wait just a goddamn minute . . ."

Claire ignored him. "The first possibility is that your husband was forcibly removed from your home against his will and kidnapped. The second possibility is that your husband left under his own volition. Now, which, in your opinion, is what happened here?"

The lawyer immediately advised Caroline not to answer.

Weis liked Claire's direct approach. He smiled broadly, arms crossed on his chest like an amused spectator.

Claire pointed to the spot on the floor in front of her. "This was a . . ."

"A newspaper. I got it."

Weis pulled forth a plastic-wrapped newspaper, handing it to Claire.

"It was clean at the lab. Just the Camerons' prints."

Claire opened the package and removed the paper, spreading it across the kitchen table.

"There's only a few pages here."

"Yes," Weis said. "That was all that was on the floor."

"Where's the rest of it?" Claire asked Caroline.

"I don't know."

Weis stepped in. "It's probably around the house somewhere."

"No," Caroline interceded. "Eric was a neat freak. He wouldn't even let me cut so much as a recipe out of a paper. He had to have everything in order. Nothing was ever left lying around."

"Just the same, why don't you look around for it."

Caroline excused herself and moved in the direction of the bedroom. Her lawyer stayed, on guard.

"Agent Weis, can you position the paper exactly as it was recovered?"

Weis stepped over and removed a small notebook from his jacket pocket—documentation on the evidence in question. He found his scribblings and removed the newsprint from Claire's grasp, placing it on the floor, at the proper angle as indicated in his notes.

Claire backed up and crossed to the champagne bottle and full glass on the counter. In pantomime she raised the bottle and poured, then moved to the fridge for ice. Dropping the glass in a brief struggle, Claire continued her charade, moving backward in staggering steps. Then, in a sweeping motion, she turned and her arm grazed the top of the counter. Claire froze at that moment as she followed the trajectory of the imaginary paper in mute fascination.

Clearly, the paper landed here in the scuffle. Stepping forward to the marks on the floor, Claire concluded that it would be difficult to get past the newspaper without stepping on it, if one wished to exit the kitchen.

As Claire had moved through her scenario, Joey watched intently from the sidelines.

"What's up?"

"I'd say the rest of this section is missing," Claire replied, taking note of its date and which section it was.

"Obviously," Weis retorted.

"No, I mean gone, as in it's not going to be found. He took it."

"Who took it? Cameron?" Weis queried.

"Can we get our hands on another copy? I'd like to check out this section myself."

"Way ahead of you," Weis signaled to the driver, who then exited the house. "I brought one from the office. That is, if you don't mind a few coffee rings on the sports pages."

"Just be sure there's no chocolate doughnut smudges. Randall might just have a conflict of interest," Joey commented with a smirk.

Claire slapped Joey playfully on the shoulder, as Weis chuckled.

"I suppose you two are pretty tired."

"Exhausted," Claire affirmed. "If we can't find a tie-in here, we're back to Phoenix this afternoon."

The driver stepped forward with the paper in hand. Claire took it over to the table, next to the partial section and laid the missing layer inside, completing it.

"There," Claire announced, taking it over to the countertop.

Caroline had returned from the bedroom.

"The rest of the newspaper is right by the desk where he left it. The sections weren't separated—he doesn't like them separated."

"That's okay. Tell me . . . can you remember how this paper was lying on the counter at the time?"

Caroline crossed to Claire, unsure where this was leading.

"I was the one going through it. I was reading that article about the Cannibal."

"Cannibal?" Joey echoed.

"Yeah, I haven't been watching much news since . . . well, since Eric's trial . . . you know. . . . But my mom's from Ohio, so I notice when I see things like that Cannibal guy. See?"

Caroline opened the paper to the headline.

Two Worst Cases in Cincinnati History!
Cannibal in Custody While Cop Killer Trial Begins

And below it were the twin stories of Big Foot's handiwork.

It hit Claire like a mallet in the face. Her heart skipped.

Her throat constricted into a knot. She stepped away from Caroline.

Here it was.

And suddenly she remembered the dream. It seemed like a million years ago—standing there on the hillside, wondering where Joey was. The turned-out graves. The great Angeles Forest behind, the metropolis hidden in smog below . . .

She moved farther away, struggling to open the sliding door to gain access to the deck. She needed air.

Joey joined her, standing close by her side . . . waiting. Lending whatever comfort and calm there could be to the moment.

Weis wasn't so patient. "What the hell's wrong with her?"

When Claire spoke, it was in hushed tones, facing away from them.

"Take Weis, check the hillside. Cameron'll be there. This was no coincidence."

Weis was confused. "What's going on?"

Joey nodded in understanding. Together they reentered the house. Claire lifted out the page with the articles and folded it.

Joey refused to answer Weis's questions. "Cincinnati then?"

"Yes," Claire responded vaguely. Everything had gone a bit numb. She left the kitchen with the article in hand, motioning to the driver who'd brought them here.

"Hey!" Weis snapped, stomping his foot in protest. Things were getting out of his control.

Joey reached out, gently touching Caroline's shoulder for a moment. "I'm really sorry, Mrs. Cameron."

Caroline's nerves were going. "What! What's happened? Where is she going?"

They watched Claire cross through the entry and disappear from sight. Joey took over.

"Weis. Let's go."

"Where? Look, you guys, just what the hell is happening here?"

"We know where Cameron is."

"What?" came the simultaneous response from Caroline and Weis.

"I'm not going to explain it all now. Besides, we won't really know for sure till we get there."

"Get *where?!*" Weis had had enough of being toyed with.

"Up on the hill. Where the victims were found."

"But my husband ... what about my husband?" Caroline pleaded.

Poor thing, Joey thought, *she still wasn't giving up on him. Could she love him that much?*

Joey studied her face, so full of new hope, and somehow found a comforting tone. "Don't worry, Mrs. Cameron. I'm sure we'll find him up there."

12

Cameron's Killing Field
June 25th—Angeles National Forest
19:21

The dirt road threw up on them. Indiscriminate bits of dust and gravel were unleashed in the wake of the caravan. Two FBI vehicles led the way, producing a cloudy curtain. They were followed by a canine unit and several local sheriffs' cars, as they snaked cautiously along the mountainside. The long shadows near sunset caused distortions, so that nothing appeared to be in its place.

Los Angeles County was still in the throes of the five-year drought that had withered just about every living thing that didn't have a pool parked behind it. So the dry earth lent itself to the munching of their tires. The scrubby trees and tall dry grasses waited for them, listening for the approach. The whole mountainside paused for them to pass.

Fire Danger HIGH Today

read one sign as the procession continued. A cautious forty miles an hour made their progress slow, but any faster and they might miss something important.

They rounded a turn and could see the helicopter hovering up ahead over a pullout on the side of the road.

"Looks to me like you definitely got something over here." The radio crackled and spit. The announcement came from the chopper pilot himself.

Weis reached for the radio. "Can you tell if it's Cameron? Is he alive?"

There was a pause in the conversation as Weis waited for the reply. "Negative. Negative. Whatever's down there is in pieces, that's for sure. Little pieces. Lots of them."

Weis stomped on the gas, closing the distance in a hurry. "Give another look-see around, let me know if there's anything else we should check out," Weis ordered as he approached.

The helicopter lifted from its position and moved off over the hill.

Weis advanced and then pulled to the side of the road, jamming on his brakes at the last moment.

Joey gingerly exited the passenger seat and approached the downward slope to get a glimpse of the famous killing field. This was the area that once belonged to Eric Cameron's Dead. It resembled the rest of the scrubby mountainside they had previously passed. But on this terrain there lay several scattered mounds of dirt that had been exhumed in the previous investigation and then replaced, appropriately marked with identifying stakes.

And lying atop each meticulously replaced mound of earth was a deeply disturbed piece of Eric Cameron.

"Jesus . . ." Weis muttered at the sight.

He stepped from the car onto the incline and tripped into stumbling, uncontrolled movements, his expensive leather shoes quickly filling with sand. Gravity was working to pull him closer to the gruesome display below. Weis struggled frantically against the downward momentum as the other vehicles pulled to a halt behind him, but the dirt crumbled under his weight. Closer and closer he stumbled, in an unwilling plunge toward the nearest grave. Finally, Weis forced his weight back and plopped himself down quite unceremoniously in the dirt—butt first.

There he sat, staring in horror at the severed foot and ankle directly in front of him.

Joey watched from above, without comment. The canine unit unloaded as a small gathering of sheriffs appeared at the top of the hill.

"Don't ya'll be disturbing that evidence down there, Agent Weis," one sheriff hollered at him. Nervous chuckles went around the group.

"Guess you found your man all right," another commented loudly.

Joey studied the German shepherd and his handler. The dog was already working the area, even from a distance. He leaned into the wind, sniffing at all the hidden clues that his human counterparts could not discern.

But then his attention was diverted by some invisible message in the air. The nose of the dog swerved in another direction, followed by his body. The handler was more concerned with the view over the side of the hill than he was with his animal. He yanked the dog back to face front, patting the animal's head without ever looking down.

But the German shepherd was intrigued with the new signals he was receiving. He was on to something. He pulled away again, testing the air with his sensitive nose. Joey followed his gaze to see what was drawing his attention. All that could be seen was more scrub, a few pines in the distance, and a sign that indicated the start of the Angeles Forest.

Something was fluttering, under the sign—a piece of paper there.

Joey tapped the shoulder of the canine handler and pointed to the dog, who by now had turned himself completely around and was tugging powerfully at his leash.

"What is it, boy?" the handler asked. "You got something?"

Finally, the handler moved away with the dog, allowing him to lead. Joey followed close behind.

The dog began to jump and rear, whining and yapping. He had stopped, just short of the sign. Now the handler was having difficulty holding him back. Joey advanced on them.

Below the sign lay a full length of arm. Shoulder joint to fingertip. It was still fully clad in the steel gray dress jacket and expensive, Italian silk that Eric Cameron was last seen wearing. The shoulder end had been bloodied and torn jagged in the separation effort, while the hand itself still clearly bore a thin band of gold on its fourth finger. It was unmistakable that the hand had been positioned so as to be pointing, directing them up the road and into the woods.

Pinned to the disassociated appendage was a piece of paper. As it fluttered in the breeze again, Joey could see that it was a map—but not a regular road map. This was a topographical map, a map that within its pale green and brown concentric circles could outline the hidden secrets of the Angeles Forest with frightening accuracy.

And someone had gone to the trouble of circling a particular point of interest for them.

13

The Cannibal Gets Catered
June 26th—Cincinnati SW Station
11:06

"You wanted to see me?"

Traask entered the jail's small visitation room, followed by Bennie Sarkissian. He tried not to allow his resentment at being summoned cloud his responses, but it felt as if his back was breaking from the emotional baggage he carried around with him these days.

It was the nature of this baggage that concerned the Cannibal. He had no choice but to call upon the one cop he knew to have proven himself to be bound to the public interest; the one guy in Cincinnati who had demonstrated an unwavering commitment to defending the law and keeping the order, no matter what personal bullshit might get in the way.

The Cannibal watched Traask closely. Traask was a real trustworthy sort. He wasn't a hard-ass like some of the others. He was approachable. You could really talk to him. The Cannibal somehow knew that Traask would tell the truth, no matter how bad it might get. He had a million questions.

129

A million concerns. And it frightened him to see bad news painted so clearly on Traask's face as he entered.

Bennie closed the door, and Traask moved to the table.

Kenneth P. Marlovich, a.k.a. the Cincinnati Cannibal, was a slight man—barely 145 pounds. He rather resembled a redheaded Opie Taylor from "The Andy Griffith Show," hardly someone you would run from. His delicate features and effeminate movements had unnerved Traask in various degrees over the past week. It was difficult to imagine that this redheaded, almost frail-looking man had somehow overpowered and then carved up at least eleven different people.

But Traask had uncharacteristically tried to steer clear of the messier details in this case. He had not assumed the reins. He felt it would be best if the B-string boys took over on the interrogation and the paperwork so he could stay loose during the Cop Killer trial. The Cannibal's case history might make interesting reading, but at this time Traask had other murky waters to wade through.

The media circus this monster succeeded in attracting to Cincinnati these past four days had transformed Traask's life once again into the fishbowl nightmare he had hoped was left behind after the Cop Killer had first been arraigned. He had been fighting off reporters day and night, ditching them whenever he could, but only finding refuge inside the station house itself. So once again, his personal life, or what was left of it, had been put to the test, and he couldn't say that he was enjoying the situation. Not one bit.

But here was the eye of the newest cyclone, staring Traask in the face, summoning him to this small white room with a tiny table and two chairs. The Cannibal had urgently requested his presence, which had Traask wondering, rather wearily, just what this guy had to say that was so goddamned important? What could he possibly want? Did he want to deal? Then why talk to him? He wasn't the DA.

"You know, this is all new to me. I ... I'm not used to this; so I don't know if they're just trying to freak me out or what. But if that's what they're trying to do, it's working." The Cannibal moved in uncomfortable, nervous twitches, shifting around in his chair as if it were sending low-voltage shocks to his backside every few seconds.

In an attempt to make the man feel comfortable, Traask sat down opposite him and gave a comforting smile. "What's wrong, Kenny?"

"There's been a lot of talk, you know. A lot of talk back there. I know they don't like being around me. I know that they don't like it. But I'm here, and they're talking right in front of me, like I don't exist."

"Who's talking?" Bennie asked from the corner of the room.

"Guards, the guys in the cells. Everybody. They're all talking about what happened out there. You know ... in Arizona."

"What about it?" Traask jumped in, shooting a warning glance over at Bennie. He wanted Bennie to play stupid, but the Sarkissian sarcasm was showing through as usual. It had the potential of making this visit interminable.

"You know what happened, right?"

"Well, if you're talking about those guys in the van, then I guess I know as much as anyone else who reads the papers."

"Not just them. There were others too."

Traask played as dumb as he could manage. "Others?"

"The guys in here, they follow that kind of shit. They know when someone's gonna get it. One guy was telling me that there's been others, just like what they found in that van."

"Was this a guard who's been talking to you?"

The Cannibal refused to answer Bennie's inquiry.

"Some say he might be an ex-cop, you know? And they say—"the Cannibal swallowed involuntarily—"they say he's got a list."

"So what, you think you're on this list?" Bennie interjected with a tone that was getting more condescending by the minute.

But the Cannibal was serious. "You gotta help me."

The sheer preposterousness of this plea, the paranoid delusion, was making it hard for Traask to take him seriously.

He bit down on his tongue until it smarted, seeing that the poor little prick was really scared shitless.

"It sounds like you know a lot about this. Maybe you should be talking to the FBI, not us," Bennie intoned, winking discreetly at Traask.

The Cannibal stared at Bennie for a moment. It was a long enough moment to unnerve the experienced cop, who dropped his gaze down and away, almost apologetically. The anxiety the Cannibal was experiencing was causing him to grip the table tightly. He was getting angry now.

He didn't trust Bennie.

He *did* trust Traask.

"No one's coming to get you, Kenny," Traask tried to reassure him.

"Some guy in California just bought it. It was that guy who was accused of killing all those teenage girls—the Hillside Murders? I heard two guards talking this morning. He didn't even get to finish his trial! He could have been innocent, man!"

Not likely. Not after what they found.

That story had replaced even the Cannibal's own headlines, thank god. It was one of the few things that Traask had kept current on during the mess of the trial and the demands of the public.

As it turned out, Eric Cameron had been far from innocent. The story that was printed in the national newspapers stated that evidence was uncovered during the investigation of his disappearance that led the FBI to a remote cabin where Cameron's victims had taken their last breath before being dismembered. He'd been using the tumble-down shack as his personal slaughterhouse. Once that was revealed, all the evidence they had ever needed to convict the son of a bitch came all too easily.

Whoever abducted Cameron had made him talk before they killed him. In less than twenty-four hours after the Cameron case had been closed, there was at least one person who had managed to accomplish what the most civilized criminal justice system in the world had failed to deliver.

And now it was crystal clear—the man had been a monster all along.

This had posed several disturbing questions in Traask's mind. *We had let this monster out! We had let him loose on a technicality. He would have gone on killing until someone stopped him.* Luckily, someone did.

On the other hand ... *we had an obligation to protect Cameron's rights. He could have been innocent. Could have been* ...

The Cannibal was waiting for his response.

"Yes, he could have been innocent. But as it turns out, he wasn't. And the guy who did that, probably knew it. He was probably in on it and was scared to death that Cameron would tell. So he exposed Cameron."

"And what about Arizona?"

Traask was genuinely puzzled. "What makes you think the two are related?"

"But they were saying ..."

Traask rose from the table. "Look, Kenny, someone in here is just trying to scare you. Don't let them."

Traask headed for the door. Bennie had his hand on the knob already. But the Cannibal rose quickly, becoming agitated.

"You don't care! You don't care if I get it or not, do you? I'm just another headline ... just another psycho to you."

"Hey, don't start with that kind of shit, asshole. We've kept them off you plenty already ..."

"Knock it off, Bennie," Traask warned, putting himself between the two men. Bennie backed down and swore under his breath.

"We're doing everything we can to make sure you're safe, Kenny. Nobody's getting in here unless you invite them in. Okay?"

Resigned, the Cannibal shook his head, knowing that he was being placated with words of assurance. Nothing was going to change. If anything, he'd made it worse for himself.

"Okay?" Traask reiterated. He thrust his hand out to shake.

There was something in this simple act ... something that

133

made the prisoner feel better about his fears. This was Traask's special gift. He was, at the core, a true arbitrator. There was a sense of fairness about him that came through, no matter what the circumstance. The Cannibal nodded and shook Traask's hand gratefully.

"Thanks man. I'm s-s-sorry about that."

"It's okay."

Bennie opened the door for Traask, and together they exited the room. Traask nodded to the two guards outside that they were finished.

As they moved down the hall, Bennie wasn't content to let it lie.

"That sorry little shit. I hope he is scared. I hope he's scared shitless."

Shaking his head, Traask knew that his partner would never be very understanding about the human rights aspect of the job. Yes, they were despicable, loathsome, and sometimes sickening individuals, and they caused a lot of grief and harm. But Traask had always managed to keep in mind that underneath it all, there was a level of humanity here. To him, maintaining an awareness of that humanity was part of their job.

It was a waste of effort to try and explain his philosophy to Bennie. Bennie would think he was going soft. Traask wasn't going soft, he'd always been this way. It was his nature.

"Can you believe that he thinks these murders are related? Next he's gonna be telling us it's all a political conspiracy," Bennie said, letting go a big sigh of complaint. "Yup, the Democrats are finally cleaning up America!"

Traask had his mind on coffee. He was tired and needed something to get his motor running. He let Bennie ramble on without objection until they nearly collided with Detective Carlisle, who was leaning against the wall, scanning the morning paper with interest.

"Yes sir! Didn't you know, Carlisle, it's all a plot!"

The detective was engrossed and reluctant to tear his attention from the article he was reading. Bennie faked a punch, disturbing Carlisle's paper, and that made him mad.

"Hey, knock it off, Sarkissian! Jesus!"

Traask and Sarkissian continued down the corridor, barely breaking stride.

"Hey, that the sports page? Reds play the Cubs tonight, right?" Bennie asked as he shot a glance over his shoulder. Carlisle angrily refolded the paper. The article that had the detective's interest so piqued, was, for a moment, in clear view.

It wasn't the sports page.

Bennie cleared his throat. It was a nervous habit he had developed. It signaled to Traask that something serious was coming, and under his breath he tried to sound casual. "Have you heard the public support that's been stirred up over that van killing?"

Unfortunately, Traask had. He had been allowing the media attention over the van killing to get under his skin. He had undergone a similar media frenzy himself. The night the Cop Killer had been taken into custody had been one of the worst nights of Traask's life, so even observing the onslaught of TV and newspaper coverage secondhand made him feel like he was reliving his own experience with the media in exhausting, emotional detail. The circumstances behind Frank's death and the events that followed had remained in the forefront of his mind lately, probably because of the impending trial, but he still wasn't ready to come to grips with it yet, not on a personal level. And especially not with Bennie, who continued to rattle on.

"You know, he ought to go on *Nightline.* They had two whole shows this week dedicated to nothing but discussion about the criminal justice system and what those two guys would have faced—if they had lived. Did you know that they probably only would have gotten ten to fifteen years?"

Traask was trying not to listen, so he just nodded when it seemed appropriate. His stomach was tying itself into knots now, and he desperately needed that cup of coffee. As he rounded the last doorway into the office area, he could see that there were several people waiting in front of the visitor's desk. One had a familiar kind of rumpled-raincoat appearance about him. It was that homeless writer again. Traask turned away quickly, nearly slamming Bennie into a chair.

"Hey!"

"Sorry, Bennie."

Glancing back, Traask could see that the homeless man's attention had not yet been alerted. He was facing the other way, head down, busily fooling with the ever-present tape recorder that was strapped to his side.

Traask began to move in the opposite direction.

"Traask!" Someone yelled from the corner.

He cringed, knowing that DeYoung had to have heard. It could only be a matter of moments before he was saddled with another confrontation with the King of Halitosis.

But it was the captain's voice, and not to be ignored.

"Traask! Come over here."

Traask moved with his automatic defense shield at full tilt and managed to cross to Cappy's office without being snared by DeYoung.

"There you are. Come in. And, uh—close the door."

There was another person in the office with Cappy.

As Traask entered, he sensed something was afoot, and his first instinct was to be on guard. But he had a surprise coming . . . and it completely disarmed him.

His eyes met hers.

Deep browns that went right into him . . . and landed on a place that Traask had not realized, until this moment, had been entirely too empty. He was at a loss to explain their instant connection.

He smiled involuntarily, in tacit admission that he didn't understand his own reaction. It had been so immediate, so overpowering. Her presence here seemed almost familiar to him, as if this stranger should be reaching out at this moment in a passionate embrace, reassuring, "There you are! I've been searching all over for you, where have you been?!"

Wait a minute, Traask thought. *What is this? Am I completely crazy? What's happening to me?*

Traask's fantasy quickly melted away, but the vision before him remained. She was real, and she was standing right in front of him. There was nothing to fight against, nothing to hold him back.

No excuses this time, she seemed to admonish.

She rose from the chair, setting an oversize attaché on the floor by her feet. He could see then that her skirt and jacket were badly wrinkled, as if she'd been sitting far too long, traveling maybe, or waiting for something or someone to show. Her features seemed tired and flushed, as if she hadn't slept for a couple of days, but it didn't count against her. The legs, the body, even the hair, comprised a package that surpassed Traask's expectations. He instantly sensed that this woman was a professional, but one that brought a great deal of heart to her performance—another common denominator they shared.

"Lieutenant Traask?" she asked, reaching for his hand.

Out of habit—after all, he was part detective—Traask's eyes wandered to her left-handed ring finger.

There was no band of gold.

A spike of relief went through him, and his smile grew larger. He reached out and shook her hand, but Cappy's voice brought them back to earth.

"Dan Traask, this is Special Agent Randall."

"Claire Randall," she clarified, releasing her hold on him.

"FBI?" Traask found he still had a voice.

"Yes," she replied.

The captain suggested that they set up in the conference room. Claire had a lot to show Traask, and the captain was late for a meeting downtown.

As Traask got to his long-awaited cup of coffee, Claire pulled files from her attaché and arranged them on the table.

"You're sure I can't get you some coffee?" Traask offered. Claire just shook her head, absorbed in thought as she assembled her work.

He joined her. "I assume this has to do with Kenneth Marlovich?"

"Yes," she replied. "Your captain tells me he's being held here."

"Yeah. I was just talking to him. But why are the Feds interested? We were pretty sure he was keeping local."

Both seated themselves at the table. Claire shifted to business. "We have reason to believe he's connected to another case."

"You've found another victim?"

"No, not exactly." Claire lifted from her files the photo of Richard Winert's charred remains. "You might have seen this one on the news."

"Uh, yeah ... I did." Traask was starting to get worried.

Her quiet, deliberate approach might have been considered distant by some, but Traask felt as if he understood her perfectly. What she had to say was serious. She had come a long way and didn't have time to waste with pleasantries. Being professional meant having to put aside what had sparked between them. For the time being.

"I was assigned to another case in the area where he was found. You've probably heard about it, too."

Traask's attention focused on her intently as she pulled forth a section of newspaper that was folded into a neat quarter. As she presented it to him, she unfolded it once, revealing the article headlined: "Arizona is Home to Crimes in the Desert." Traask recognized it immediately as it hit him.

Jesus, the van kidnapping ... that horrible mess was her case? Suddenly he had a new respect for this woman.

"You're not serious. These cases were all related to each other? I thought that was just some bullshit rumor."

"Not this time. There is a link between these two. And while I was following that link, Eric Cameron disappeared."

"I was reading about it in the paper this morning. Whoever did it sure had that guy pegged," Traask commented. Part of him didn't want to realize where this all was leading.

Claire's eyes locked on to Traask—as a warning, out of respect. With a single motion, she flipped the section of newspaper over to reveal the other headlines.

Two Worst Cases in Cincinnati History!
Cannibal in Custody While Cop Killer Trial Begins

"Whoever did it is on his way here," Claire stated.

This was a joke ... surely. The headline stared Traask in the face. The sick feeling was returning to his stomach, and it would take more than coffee to settle it if she was right. Claire continued to explain.

"What we have is a man with a mission. Someone who goes by signs. When he took Cameron, he saw this article and took it with him. I think he believes this is a message, telling him where to strike next."

Traask rose from the chair and moved behind her, nervously pacing.

"Wait a minute ... wait a minute. You mean to tell me that this thing is for real? C'mon, you really believe someone out there is going to go after these guys, even though they're in jail already? This is all just supposition, isn't it? I mean, what makes you so sure he's headed for Cincinnati—just this little piece of newspaper? You've gotta have more than that!"

Claire wasn't fazed by his protests.

"He may pick someplace in between—and do something we find later—but this is where he wants to make his next statement."

"Why? I mean, why do you say it like that '... make his statement'?"

"He's message-motivated. What I get from him is that he's fed up with the way law works—or, in his mind, doesn't work. He wants to take care of business, and he wants the rest of America to be watching."

"How many do you think he's responsible for?"

"Five ... that we are aware of. I think it started with Rudolf Maxx, three months ago."

"Jesus."

Traask was having a hard time thinking straight.

"So far we've kept this from going public—the connection between the killings. But it won't hold."

Traask nodded. "Just wait till the press finds out."

"It's going to get worse before it gets better, believe me," Claire agreed.

"How does this guy think he's gonna get past the front desk of the Cincinnati police department?"

"I did," Claire replied flatly.

Traask stared at her for a moment. This woman knew how to unsettle him.

"No one's getting within a hundred yards of Kenny."

"I'd like to meet him."

"Why?"

"He should know what's going on."

"I don't think that's such a good idea."

Traask would have explained more, but a movement outside their window drew their attention. Some kind of commotion. They watched as several members of Traask's team moved quickly toward it.

'What's that all about?" Claire demanded. She was rising.

Nearest to the door, Traask opened it and headed out. Claire was close behind. Together they moved toward the back offices and holding area where the disturbance seemed to be centered. As they approached, the confusion seemed to envelop them. Voices had no faces, as frantic messages were shouted.

". . . Get an ambulance."

"Is he all right?"

"Secure the building! Call for black and whites! Shut down the block. We gotta find that guy!"

"Get Traask back here!" Bennie yelled at full bore.

"I'm here!" Traask replied.

He was fighting his way back toward Bennie's voice, past the number of officers in his wake. The narrow hall was suddenly crowded with bodies. Some moved with single-minded direction, searching the room for signs.

One officer grabbed Claire's arm. "Hey, who are you?"

Claire unhanded herself easily with a mere change of positioning. It was an Aikido move, so subtly effective that it surprised the officer and made him feel foolish. As he reached again for her, Traask stopped him.

"She's with me."

The implications of the statement lingered between them. *Yes, I am . . . aren't I,* the wrinkle in her forehead seemed to say.

"Traask!" Bennie shouted once more.

"I'm coming!"

"Make a hole, will 'ya? Let the man pass!" Bennie commanded.

The officers complied, and suddenly there was a tunnel ahead and the open door to the visitation room. Bennie stood in front of it, propping it ajar. His expression was grim. He motioned to Traask.

Traask's first thought was that the Cannibal had committed suicide somehow. The man's paranoid fears had been taken pretty lightly, and if Claire was right, maybe he had had something to worry about after all.

As Traask neared, his stomach tightened.

"Ambulance is on the way," someone yelled from down the hall.

Bennie nodded. His eyes were cold, blue, serious.

Traask didn't like that response from Bennie, so he moved into the room, relieved to see his answer.

The Cannibal sat in the chair he'd been on when they had been with him only moments before, slumped over the tabletop, arms protectively encircling his head, for all the world as if he were a grade school child, caught napping. His face was hidden from view.

As Traask stepped farther into the room, he became aware of the guard lying on the floor being tended to for severe head lacerations. He was groggy and confused. The surprise blow had come from the side. He had no chance to fight off his attacker. The attending officer nodded to Traask that the downed man was going to be all right.

Bennie stopped Claire at the door, preventing her from entering. She paused, watching Traask continue toward the table. The Cannibal still wasn't moving.

"The floor," Claire warned.

Traask followed her gaze as she nodded toward the floor under the table. Traask had circled behind the man, but now knelt to inspect the area beneath his chair. A large puddle of bright red blood had gathered there. More was draining over the edge of the chair seat and cascading to the floor, as a leaky bathtub faucet might continue to trickle well after the shower was finished.

Traask shook his head in anger. Security had obviously been nowhere near tight enough for this individual.

So the Cannibal had been successful in finding a way to

take his own life. A rather messy way, but successful nonetheless. He had not considered the Cannibal to be depressed enough to warrant special consideration. But obviously, he had been wrong.

Traask rose and gently lifted Kenny Marlovich's head. Lacking muscular control, the head flopped backward lazily, his shock of red hair fringing the chair back. The bloodshot eyes stared out blankly against the fear that had consumed them, the lashes and cheeks still wet from tears of pleading.

Only when he upturned the face did Traask notice that something was jammed into the man's mouth. His jaw was dropped, fully open, but still the contents of his mouth overflowed. The object inside was obviously much too large to be contained by it. And bloody.

A red ribbon of fluid continued to drain down the side of his neck and over his chest, on down into his lap, where his pants lay bunched in disarray, a hole cut into the crotch where the zipper had once been. Traask involuntarily recoiled at the sight ... and the realization that followed.

The Cannibal's genitalia had been removed from his body— cut away by the slash of a knife, and shoved down his own throat. He had choked to death on it. It was obvious that he had tried to bite through the organ in an attempt to cough it out, but someone had made sure he hadn't the time or strength to do so. Red marks around his nose indicated that perhaps someone had pinched his nostrils shut while holding his head in position.

One fleshy pocket of fleshy matter that dangled over his chin appeared to be the remains of a testicle.

Thipp Thipp Thipp Thipp Thipp Thipp Thipp.
The strange repetitive noise caught Traask's attention.
"On the chair, man," Bennie indicated.

At this, Claire entered the room. She seemed to be the only one unfazed by the scene. She crossed to the chair that had been so neatly pushed in and yanked it from the table.

Upon the seat lay DeYoung's reel-to-reel, gyrating spastically in a frenzy of loose tape. It had run out.

14

Close Encounters
June 26th—Cincinnati SW Station
18:27

"We were too late."

Claire summed up the day's events for Joey with a rueful shrug.

Using the phone in the conference room to report in with her partner, she had been watching Traask through the window.

With only some glass and louvers separating them, he sensed her unwavering attention. He had been holding a hushed conversation with some of his men, but all at once became momentarily distracted. Her eyes held his, forming an oasis of understanding in the midst of the chaos. Things had turned serious in a hurry.

Then, consciously breaking the connection, Claire blinked and sauntered to the open door, closing it against Traask and the activity around him. Traask distracted her, and she didn't need any more distractions today.

Joey listened intently to every word on the other end of the phone, trying to absorb every nuance of Claire's voice.

The trouble had already come to Cincinnati, and Joey had not even booked a flight out of L.A. yet.

"Evidently, our man got past the front desk under the guise of being the writer who had contracted with Marlovich to write his story. The real writer was found about a block away, locked in the trunk of a Chrysler New Yorker. He's okay. We ran the plates. The car was stolen right from the curb of the airport."

"He's one quick motherfucker," said Joey.

"Too quick. We've got the vehicle in now for a workup— but it's a rental. God only knows the kind of shit we'll come up with."

"Did he see anything? Can he ID the attacker?"

"The writer? No. Not really. All he kept saying was, 'big guy—he was a really big guy.' "

"Tell us something we don't know."

"I want you to pull everything we can get our hands on from the Winert investigation, the kidnappers, and the latest from California. Bring it with you. I'll set up base camp here."

"I gotta wait on the tests from Los Angeles. They're expected tomorrow morning."

"Wait for them, but then get here as soon as you can," said Claire.

"Aw . . . you miss me?"

"I can use all the help I can get. It's getting a little close for comfort. You know what I mean?"

"I know what you mean, jelly bean. Say, what's the reception been like out there, anyway? We got some cooperation, at least?"

Claire peeked out at Traask between the louvered shades that covered the windows of the conference room. She thought about Traask before answering her partner. Her first impressions of him had been quite positive. She'd surprised herself, stepping outside the stoic professionalism that cloaked her working environment and allowed herself to see the man, not the cop.

For one thing, he *moved*. His body was well trained physically. And you trusted him right away. He had a kind face, she felt, open to everyone, including those in need. It was those eyes of his. They spoke to her so clearly, as if the two of them had been holding entire conversations without words.

But he also held a few cards tight to the chest. There was some kind of secret there that clouded him. And yet, somehow, she suspected he wasn't as impenetrable as most men. He intrigued her, she had to admit.

"Randall ..."

"Sorry," Claire replied, blushing. She shifted her attention back to the phone. "Someone came in. I was ... interrupted."

"Are they cooperative?"

"I haven't had much of a chance to find out. It seems like they're going to be fairly helpful."

"Good. Can I pick up something for you? Anything at the office or your apartment?"

"No ... no, I had a layover in Dallas and packed a bag."

"You're sure ... ?"

"I'm fine."

"I'll see you soon, then."

"Right."

There was an uncomfortable pause. Joey said, "Take care of yourself ..."

"Don't worry."

"Hey, I listen to your crazy shit. Now you listen to mine. I don't like this one. He's too close."

"I know. I can feel him."

"Oh? And how does he feel?"

"With his hands, like the rest of us."

Traask rapped lightly on the door just after Claire hung up. He had been watching through the glass. He poked his head inside the door.

"Just thought you'd like to know, the room was clean."

Claire nodded, running a trembling hand over her hair. Suddenly she wasn't feeling so well. The letdown after the adrenaline rush caused by recent events had zapped her remaining energy. Shit ... she had been running on fumes all day.

When she didn't acknowledge him, Traask crossed in front of her. "Hey," his voice was concerned as he noticed the pale color of her face. He moved close, fixing on her. "Hey, you don't look so hot."

Claire sat down abruptly—practically an involuntary movement. She put a hand to her temple. Her stomach groaned. Her mouth dried up. "I don't feel so hot."

"I'll get some water," he volunteered, heading for the door.

"No."

He took a few steps back to her, studying her face, her body. It appeared that she might be sick any moment. "Coffee?" he offered, desperate to help.

She shook her head.

Traask paused, unsure what to do next. "I'm sure we've got some Tylenol or something."

"No. No aspirin."

Traask had run out of offerings. He was just about to head out the door to call emergency services when she spoke up.

"I think ... I think I'd better eat something."

Traask smiled. Now this was too easy.

The restaurant was a little Italian place. It had only a couple of tables against the wall and one in the corner, which is where they sat, eating. Most of the business was carryout, but it was the closest food to the station house that Traask could vouch for.

This woman definitely had an appetite. She devoured the antipasto and fettucine appetizers, pausing only briefly before diving into the sausage lasagna and seconds on garlic bread.

"Doesn't the FBI feed you people?"

Claire's face changed with the simple upturn of her lips. She was smiling at him.

Traask liked this woman. It was all coming too easily. Too *naturally*.

"Not like this. This is terrific!"

"What ... no Italian food in ... uh ...?"

"Dallas."

"Oh, well, that explains it!"

Her laughter wiped away the last of Traask's defenses. He hadn't been his normal, preoccupied self with her. He should be thinking about what happened today. He should be concentrated and focused. But as he reached for his beer, he felt quite relaxed and at ease. This woman was relieving him of duty, and he didn't need to fight it. For a moment, at least, the horror could wait.

"Actually, I frequent a fairly good Chinese place for take-out," Claire volunteered. "But I don't get out a lot socially, so I don't know many other places."

"Me neither. It's enough to just get home at night."

"Yeah, well, I don't have a wife at home to take care of me," Claire replied, indicating that she had noticed his wedding ring. The band around his finger came to her attention earlier in the evening while they both were reading the menus. She tried to tell herself that it didn't matter, but it did.

"Me neither," he announced.

Claire tried to act casual, but her heart quickened at the revelation. Her throat had constricted momentarily as she struggled to swallow the last bit of garlic bread, unable to voice her questions.

Traask saw the furrowing in her brow and raised his left hand so she could see. "I can't get it off. I've tried." Traask tugged against the band, but it wasn't budging. He tried a bit harder, to make the attempt seem more realistic. And, to his surprise, the ring let go its grip, forcefully separating from his finger. Dumbfounded, Traask froze for a second, taking in this momentous occasion with mixed emotions.

Claire guessed that he had never really tried taking the ring off, probably feeling more comfortable with it on. She would have felt the same way. But now that it came off so easily . . .

They both began to laugh. Perhaps it was fate. It certainly seemed like a sign. But sharing this uncomfortable situation with Claire made Traask realize something about himself. He was able to move on with his life now. And meeting this woman had made him want to, more than ever.

After a moment, Traask found the words to explain. "I got married young. After fifteen years, I guess, I got used to having it there. Well, that's all ancient history."

Claire watched Traask make his decision. Unwilling to put the ring back on, he opted to pocket it. But she could tell that the emotions he was trying to sweep away during this act were not simple ones. She felt suddenly as if she were intruding on his privacy.

"And you?" Traask inquired, turning the spotlight away from himself. "Don't tell me ... you're married, but you don't wear a ring."

Claire laughed politely. "No. Never been married. The only person I see regularly is my partner. Talking to Joey, you'd think we were an old married couple."

Traask's hopes fell. Could the signs have been wrong? Or were there really no signs here at all, just a ring that was ready to be removed? Things had started up so beautifully between them. It had seemed too good to be true. There had to be a catch somewhere.

Tentatively, he asked, "You two been seeing each other awhile?"

Claire understood what he was really asking. As she took a mouthful of pasta, she shook her head and waved her hands negatively as she hurried to swallow.

"Nuh ... no. Not like that. You don't understand. Joey's ..." then Claire paused, her feminist side taking over. Why did she need to explain? Would Joey want her to? Probably not. Was it really necessary to go into detail with someone she barely knew?

"We've worked together, yes. But I don't ..." Claire didn't know how to put it, without giving Traask the wrong impression. She swallowed down hard. "No. It's not like that."

The light returned to his face. Her flustered response obviously meant this was a misunderstanding on his part. This Joey character must be a fat old fart or something. He leaned in again, smiling.

"Well, a good partner is better than a hot date any day."

A sudden, faraway expression told her that his own words

had some hidden resonance. He finished his wine while she studied him. Maybe this was the source of his pain. This was his secret. Here was the wall she sensed.

"You're referring to . . . what's his name—Uh, Bennie?"

"No. Not Bennie." Traask's response was distant.

Claire stared down at her plate, suddenly feeling quite full. She looked away, out the window, down at the floor—anywhere but at Traask.

He watched this reaction with interest. He tried to engage her, with no luck, and finally stifled his own amusement with boxed frustration. "What?"

"I learned a long time ago that I talk too much. I'm . . . just trying to shut up."

Her directness was enough to change the mood. Traask's laughter filled the small room. Claire watched him in confusion as he let his laugh build and release all the tension of the past months of work and fatigue. Suddenly, she was the funniest thing he had ever encountered. It took several minutes for him to gain control. When he did, there were tears rolling down his cheeks.

"I don't know what I did, but I think it was good for you at least." She was still confused at the humor he had found in her last comment.

"I'm sorry. I'm sorry. It's just . . . you're just—different."

"I'm not so different." Her toss-away glance told him she might have construed this as an insult.

Traask's beeper went off. Remembering his promise, he suddenly sobered. "Oh, man . . ."

"What?"

"Someone's reminding me it was my turn to take a couple of young ladies to dinner tonight."

Claire glanced at her watch. It was after nine.

"I'll have to call." Over his shoulder, he could see the pay phone in the back had a big OUT OF ORDER sign on it. Claire was gathering her things to leave.

"Can I drop you somewhere?"

"I was going to go back to the station and start . . ."

"Oh no . . . everybody's gonna take a break here. It's nearly ten. You were ready to fall over before we ate. Tomorrow we can all start on the new stuff. You need to rest just like us locals do." Traask threw a couple of bills onto the table.

"Oh, I was going to get this," Claire began, fumbling with her bag.

"I've got it. Come on."

Normally, Claire would have put up a fight. But she didn't even try to contradict Traask. She sensed it would be futile and that her acceptance would be a compliment to him. And before she knew it, he was already at the door. She hurried to follow.

It seemed so natural to be by his side. Even as he reached for her hand when they crossed just a few blocks down, it was as if they were old friends who had been apart for a while but were picking up where they had left off. Old friends. But good friends.

They approached Traask's car and he opened her door, assisting her inside. During all of this, she had neglected to ask where they were going and he had never volunteered, even when they entered his own parking garage, went up in the elevator, and through the front door of his apartment. There was simply a trust there, and neither one seemed to have much of an inclination for small talk.

Traask picked up the phone and dialed while Claire set her things down. The place was dimly lit, but Claire could make out the room quite well. She noticed it was neatly kept and sparsely decorated. This was a man's place, but a woman had been here first. And she'd had good taste, too.

Claire was studying Traask from where she stood, listening to him on the phone just inside the kitchen. She could hear apologies being made, she guessed it was the ex. But in the one-way conversation, his tone was honest, apologetic, and filled with warmth. That made Claire rule out the ex.

Traask hung up and joined her in the kitchen. "Well, I'm off the hook. For now. She made me promise two movies and a lunch to make up for it."

Claire didn't say anything. She just nodded. Then it dawned on Traask that she might not understand what all this was about.

"My daughter. She's supposed to be visiting me, but she's been staying at a friend's while things have been a bit ... well, messed up. Bad timing. Real bad."

"She understands?"

"They saw the news tonight, so she knows what happened. I don't know if she understands so much as she ... well, she tries to support what I do." Traask shrugged, trying to get through the explanation without feeling defensive and on trial. "It gets old for her, I know. As my ex always reminds me, she's not a cat or a dog. You can't set out food, leave for days, and expect her to be happy to see you when you finally come home."

"Hmmm," Claire nodded.

She understood completely. Nothing more needed to be said about that one.

"Well"—Traask shifted gears—"can I offer you something to drink? Or do you have to ... ?"

"What have you got?" Claire cut in on him, anticipating.

". . . But of course, not all of them agreed with me."

Traask laughed at this remark. He found himself observing the sultry creature who sat cross-legged on his living room floor with the kind of respect and wonder one might accord a favorite college professor. Her stories had been amusing, and although she took great care not to reveal certain confidential information about each case, Traask felt he recognized one or two from the news stories he had followed over the years.

Her way of perceiving a case was complementary to his own. She had a sense of direction that he could follow, and as she talked, he often felt like interjecting, "I know, I've been there."

They had begun on one bottle of Cabernet and had just uncorked a second. Traask was lying stretched out on the carpet at her side, listening to her talk, taking it all in with a growing sense of need. But he tried to keep their exchanges limited to business, picking at her experiences and comparing notes as much as she would allow.

"I ... I have to ask. What was it like, out there on the mountain when you found Cameron's remains?"

"I had already left for Dallas when they actually found Cameron."

"You're kidding! You missed that?"

This drift in the conversation brought Claire back from her comfortable respite. She knew the scene. Every last piece of dirt on the ground—every leaf on every bush—was as vivid to her as the room in which she now sat. However, she had never been on that hill—not physically.

"I ... I knew that's where they would find Cameron ... and how they would find him. But I had to leave. I needed to beat the killer to his next appointment." She lifted her glass. "And I was too late."

Traask felt her self-condemnation. Remembering, she was full of remorse and was twisting it, like a knife inside herself, lest she repeat the mistake. He didn't want to see this kind of pain. Not tonight. It might even touch on his own.

"Hey," Traask disagreed. He reached out to her and took her chin in his grasp. Her face flushed, full of the animation that a full-bodied red wine can lend to an evening. What had started as a friendly move, had made his desires known. His touch was delicate, tender. But the wine was working its way into his system, and he was afraid he was unable to deny his feelings much longer.

She glanced up at that moment. Smiling at his attempt to comfort her, she nonetheless betrayed a hurt, rarely shown. Traask was beginning to understand her, and he could not believe how much they were alike. Down to the core.

His nearness to her was a request to be let inside, begging for an explanation of her pain, but she would never attempt that with anyone other than Joey. Joey had the privilege of sharing these kind of private moments with Claire over the years, but Claire had only known Dan Traask for twelve hours.

It was something intensely personal. Just how she knew so much about that hillside of death was a secret part of Claire, a part she wanted to keep hidden, like an embarrassing birthmark. She considered it to be a grotesque disfigurement—not a gift. To her, it was a burden to be endured.

But Traask couldn't know this. Not yet. He lifted himself up from the floor on one elbow and let his hand rest on her shoulder, silently imploring her to reveal herself. In that moment, a million unspoken messages were exchanged. It was becoming a mutual understanding of the way things were to work between them.

He wanted to kiss her then, to tell her that it was all right, but he knew if he were to close in too quickly, he might be added to the bottom of a long list of rejected lovers. So he stalled for time, watching her reactions carefully for any hint of encouragement. He offered her a smile—an invitation for her to stay with him—to play this out.

But she would not.

"I really should be calling myself a cab." She set her glass down, starting to unwind her legs from their twisted position.

"You don't have to."

She gave him a raised eyebrow, as if to remark how predictable he sounded.

But Traask was ready for her. "Jenny's not here. I have a spare bedroom."

He waited for her reaction. She didn't object. But to stave off any attempt to do so, a commanding tone rose in his voice.

"You don't want to try and find something now—it's really late. Come on, I won't bite."

She ignored her instinctive, on-guard response and allowed the wine to work through her. What were her insides telling her?

That this was safe.

This man was safe. Still, she reproached herself, she should be following up on the events of the day, poring over the latest information, not allowing herself the time to breathe.

But here, with him, she felt all the nervous energy and excess drive slipping away. She wasn't going to argue. The

153

weight was heavy on her to just follow his lead. And that weight was winning.

Traask picked up her flight bag and led the way back to Jenny's room. Once illuminated, she could see it was fairly sparse as well. Only a couple of stuffed animals decorated the bureau and empty bookshelves. The bed was a white four-poster canopy, done up in typical eleven-year-old eyelet fashion.

Yes. It was full of the most harmless intentions . . .

Traask left the flight bag on the bed, gesturing as he talked.

"The bathroom's right through there. Feel free to use anything you need. I have my own. Bathroom, that is."

He nodded toward the partially closed door to his room, adjacent to hers. Claire took note of it.

"Are you sure . . . ?" Claire started to ask, but Traask squelched her question.

"I'm a light sleeper, so if there's anything . . . just . . ."

Traask stepped in front of her for an unsettling moment. It would have been easy, almost expected of him, to reach for her now, to hold her against him. He was aching to feel her against him. Just being close enough to smell her perfume had become a test of his willpower. He longed for an excuse to express what he had been feeling since the moment that they had met. But he wanted her to be sure. And right now, she didn't appear to be certain of anything except that she needed to sleep.

Claire nodded and he backed away, returning to the living room before retiring. She viewed his retreat with amusement, then shut the door between them.

From the other room, Traask moved to the kitchen with the wine and glasses. He placed the glasses in the sink and set the bottle on the counter, recorking it. He checked the front door and extinguished the lights, pausing at the light peeking out from under her door. He knew she was comfortable with her decision to stay.

As comfortable as he had been in inviting her to be there with him.

Now, it was off to sleep ... if he could. There would be a lot to go over in the morning.

Traask awoke with a start. There was someone in the apartment. Jenny ... his sleepy head reminded him. No. It wasn't.

Traask faced his clock, which revealed only a few hours had passed since he had fallen asleep. He rose from the bed and stood near his door, listening, but couldn't make out any further movements. He reached for the bathrobe hanging nearby and headed into the hall. The lighting was dim; just the way he left it. It appeared that he was mistaken. No one was moving around now.

He entered the living room. Again, it was just as he had left it. Out of curiosity, he glanced back at Claire's door. It was closed. Her light was off. *I must have imagined it.*

Traask entered the dark kitchen and reached into a cabinet for a cup. He got some water from the refrigerator door dispenser. Sitting back at the table for a moment, he drank the cool water and enjoyed the refreshing feeling it gave him.

A door opened. Cautiously, Claire made her way into the living room. When she rounded the corner and found no one there, she relaxed.

It was the gun she was toting that had Traask worried. It was a big one. From the size of it, he guessed it was a .45.

But his gaze just couldn't stay on the gun long enough. From this angle, he could see her outline quite clearly. She was wearing only a tank top and panties, and her form was *phenomenal*. It was the kind of picture someone might work for hours to set up for a magazine shoot and here all it was, in his own living room. For a split moment, he wondered if this was part of a dream.

Well, if so, it was a very good dream.

The bare skin of her thighs shone in the dim triangle of light that filtered through the front curtains. Obviously relieved to find no one there, she allowed the gun to drop to her side. The light splashed across her stomach, chest, and left shoulder. He caught the silvery outline of her breast underneath her now-transparent Fruit of the Looms and knew in that instant that he could not be dreaming. His dreams were never this good.

Traask felt suddenly like a peeper in his own apartment. Not that he wasn't enjoying every moment, but it was obvious that she didn't see him sitting there. He cleared his throat to let her know he was present.

Claire turned toward the kitchen, her weapon rising with her attention level. It was dark in there, but she knew it was Traask. She peered though the darkness, trying to figure out if he was standing or sitting or what. It didn't matter that she was wearing next to nothing at this point.

"Expecting someone?" Traask grinned, trying to ease the tension out of the situation.

The placement of his voice allowed her to figure out that he was sitting down. Probably at the kitchen table, which was completely cloaked from her view. "I must have heard you. I sleep pretty light."

"And you carry a big stick," Traask added, indicating the gun.

Claire allowed herself a small laugh. She was laughing at herself, really. How do you carry off confronting your host with a .45? She waved the gun away.

"It's nothing personal."

"Yeah, I hope not," Traask replied. Her laughter had loosened them both. "I got up to get some water. You like some?"

"No" came her reply, a bit too quickly. So she followed it up with, "But thanks. I'll . . . just . . . I'm sorry."

"No, it's okay."

"No, it's not. It's pretty ridiculous, actually. I get these . . . I guess you might call them . . . anxiety attacks. I lie there in bed for hours sometimes, thinking I hear something."

"And you come out packing?"

"I'm certain someone's there, wherever I am at the time. But it's never really happened. Just nerves, I guess."

"It's because you're in a strange place. It's hard to feel comfortable—every little sound must . . ."

"I should be used to it by now."

"Well, I promise I won't break in. Just don't blow a hole in my water bed. They don't know I have one. I'd like to keep it that way."

"It's a deal. I'll um ... I'll see you in the morning."

Traask nodded, but then realized she couldn't see that so he blurted out, "Okay. G'night."

She had already started back down the hall, which gave him a glimpse of the back of her panties and the arch of her shapely behind. It was all he could do to keep from leaping up to follow her. Just watching from behind was tempting enough. Then Traask heard her door close with some finality and realized that any opportunity he might have had was now gone.

And for a moment, he felt excruciatingly alone.

Abandoning his cup to the table, he rose from his chair. Good thing she didn't want to have a glass of water after all. It would have been difficult to hide the fact that, in that brief moment in which she was silhouetted against the light, she had managed to get his full attention. And now he had to take himself, and his full attention, back to bed. Sweet dreams.

15

Partners & Crime

June 27th—Outside Cincinnati SW Station House 08:22

"**I** guess you're used to this," Traask commented as he parked the car outside of the station house.

Claire separated her attention from her laptop to see a mob of reporters gathering in front of the station's front door. "The press? You never quite get used to them. Especially the climbers, the ones who want to get somewhere, like on national news? They're the absolute worst."

"Yes, we have one of those, all right. She's the one in the checkered suit, headed for us now."

Holly North's trademark blond ponytail bobbed up and down as she ran toward them, leading the pack. Her determined look and heavy makeup drew a disapproving cluck of the tongue from Claire.

"You have a history with *that?*"

"Yes. A very unpleasant one. She has a nickname with the guys, but I don't care to repeat it."

As Traask watched, Holly performed on cue with her usual head start, which was how she earned her nickname.

The rest of the reporters were at least a hundred feet behind her.

"Come on, set up the shot! We can get something—a statement from here," she instructed her cameraman.

"How do you usually handle this?" Claire inquired, watching the circus descending upon them. She closed the flip-top of the computer.

"Well, first I have to fight the urge to put my fist through her face. Once I get over that, I usually put on my best shit-eating grin and treat her like a five-year-old who keeps asking for candy before dinner."

"I see." Claire spoke with a wide, understanding grin. "Well, she doesn't know me. How 'bout if I handle her this time?"

Traask snorted at the suggestion, grinning broadly. "You don't have to do this."

"No, I want to."

Traask turned the key, shutting off the engine. "Then by all means, be my guest."

Claire and Traask got out of the car.

Holly advanced on Traask without hesitation, seizing the few seconds she had before the hoards would catch up with her. "Lt. Traask . . ." Holly began, but was stopped short.

"Pardon me."

Holly faced this . . . this *interruption*, and an interesting moment passed between Claire and the reporter.

Claire flashed her FBI credentials in the reporter's face.

"Claire Randall, FBI. Lieutenant Traask has no comment at this time. You'll excuse us."

It wasn't a comment, or a statement. It was a command—so direct, in fact, that the reporter had no time to react, no opportunity to speak. She had been, quite effectively, cut off.

Claire pressed forward, and Traask fell in behind her. Miraculously, they left Holly North speechless. She didn't even attempt to follow them. She had been left no room for manipulation. Flop sweat appeared on her upper lip for the first time in years. There they were, running on dead air, while the Twat Leader tried to recover from the unexpected development.

"A statement, a statement, please!" the rest of the press clamored, as Traask and Claire made their way quickly into the station house. It was quite a show of force—they had to be outnumbered ten to one, at least. But it didn't seem to matter. They were aiming at Traask, but were being deflected by Claire—and damn it—it was *working!*

Once inside, Traask paused to watch the throng of press outside the doors, still begging for a word. He reached out and caught Claire's elbow, confused. "What did you *do* to her?"

"What do you mean?"

"She didn't even try to follow us. You shut her up!"

"She's used to manipulating you guys. She's not used to someone manipulating her. I've got news for you . . . she'll never make it to the networks."

Bennie met them a few feet ahead. "You two all right?"

"Fine, fine," Claire replied, all business once again.

"The captain is gonna issue a statement in a couple minutes about what happened yesterday. But first, he wants to talk to you, Ms."—Bennie felt the mistake before it even crossed his lips, so he put full steam to the reverse thrusters and pulled out of it, with an apologetic grin—"*Agent* Randall."

Claire shot a glance to Traask, which Bennie took in. Traask winked, then nodded, encouraging her to move along. Together, he and Bennie escorted Claire to the captain's office and left her behind closed doors.

Bennie followed Traask as he leisurely made his way to the coffee table and fixed himself a cup. His eyes kept wandering back to the captain's door.

"Uh . . . I gotta wake up." He drank deeply, then turned back toward the captain's office. Again.

"Long night, huh?" Bennie guessed with an insinuating tone.

"Yeah." Then Traask caught the meaning. "I mean, *no,* not really."

Bennie's eyebrow lifted, questioning his partner in the

usual, scrutinizing manner. "If I didn't know you better, I'd say you were on a hook—my friend."

Traask didn't reply right away. He felt rather like a teenager, caught in the act by the early homecoming of Mom and Dad. He shuffled his feet, deciding what to say next. "Come on, Bennie."

"You had this look about you yesterday, but I was hopin' it was somethin' you ate. Now I see it could be serious."

"Get outta here ..."

"Nope ... you definitely have it bad. Let's hope it's just the twenty-four hour kind or this week is gonna be *history*."

Traask shrugged as he finished his coffee and then disappeared to his office, leaving Bennie behind.

Claire appeared in Traask's doorway before too long. She was ... preoccupied.

"Your captain has agreed to let me set up in the conference room for the time being. My office sent over some equipment. At least now I can hook into the central files." She indicated the laptop slung over her shoulder.

"You need some help?" asked Traask.

"No." The answer came short and sweet.

Her reservation remained, but she soon realized that he was only trying to offer her a hand. She smiled, as an apology. It was accepted.

"I mean, yeah. We need to go over this anyway."

Traask nodded, waving a folder in her direction. "Yeah, the transcription of that audiotape just arrived. I suppose we should listen to it together."

She hesitated, knowing that wouldn't be a pleasant task, even done together. She tried not to sigh, but it came out anyway.

"Wanna doughnut first?" he joked.

"No," she replied firmly. "But you know, I'd kill for a Diet Coke."

"What's going on here, you're not ... ohhhhhh, you're *him*—you're the one!" That startled exclamation had been the Cannibal's last.

By now, the conference room was teeming with life. Several pop cans littered the table among the take-out lunch boxes.

Claire was pacing the room while she listened, head down—the intensity was all there. Traask sat at the table, tapping a pencil about on his pad, trying not be terribly obvious in his boredom. This was the ninth time in a row they had listened to the tape. Traask exchanged glances with Bennie as Claire crossed behind them. Bennie felt the same way. He lifted up his hands silently, as if to say, "What the hell are we doing?"

"Listen . . . listen," she urged them.

"Poor little rabbit." A new voice on the tape.

"What?" came the Cannibals' startled response.

"You've been waiting in your cage . . . waiting for me."

"No . . NO!"

A scuffling of chairs and shuffling of bodies, feet—the noises blended together to reveal the initial struggle.

"Please . . . I'm, I'm . . ."

"Try not to speak. Yes, I know, I know . . ." The voice was soothing, almost paternal.

The Cannibal was crying now. Probably because he was realizing that this time he was to be the victim. The sniffling quickly reduced to sobbing. Traask's eyes turned downcast, hating to hear it again.

"You know, they let me in here because they want me to do this . . ."

Traask tossed his pencil in disgust. Claire stopped short, a warning glare fired off in his direction. Bennie reached over and switched off the recording.

"Okay, all right, we've listened to this enough already. What is the point?"

"He calls him a rabbit. What do you think that means?" Claire asked Bennie, then Traask.

"Rabbit? I'm not sure. Maybe he's a Bugs Bunny fan."

"Bennie," Traask warned.

"Where were you born and raised?"

"Jersey," Bennie replied, proud of it.

Claire's attention moved to Traask.

"Uh . . . um . . . Chicago area. The suburbs. Why?"

"I was raised in farmland. People who were raised around farms know that rabbits are treated pretty badly. As a result, they tend to be a bit cannibalistic. They'll chew off a foot of a mate, or sometimes just gnaw on their own."

"Oh God . . ." Bennie muttered, making a face. Then he burped.

"That's terrific," Traask murmured, glaring in his partner's direction.

"It's someone from a small community. Perhaps the Midwest, but not necessarily."

"Why the Midwest?" Traask inquired.

"His accent. It's definitely midwest, but he could be disguising his voice. We can't assume . . ." Claire moved to the recorder. "I'm gonna send this to our offices, see what they can make of it."

On the table in front of her was an 8 × 10 black-and-white photo of the killer who had successfully disguised himself and gained access to the Cannibal. "It's too bad that your surveillance cameras didn't get a better shot of him. What kind are you using, anyway?"

"He was disguised. He knew he'd be filmed if he came in here," Traask retorted, not at all comfortable with how things were proceeding.

"He's a tall fuck, isn't he?" Bennie commented.

"He could be wearing lifts," Traask warned.

"No. He's that tall," Claire replied casually. She busied herself at the computer terminal for a moment.

"Oh, you two dating?"

Claire's head popped up from the screen. "His shoe size supports the fact he's a tall guy. Besides, there were witnesses in Arizona." Then, when she saw that he didn't follow, she clarified. "The store owner and the two kids?"

"Oh," Traask mumbled, tired of all the supposition.

Bennie was now studying the photo. "Well, this makes him . . . about six-six."

"Yeah, that's right."

"Wouldn't wanna piss that one off. He's built like a brick shit house." Bennie tossed the photo down and then rose,

163

stretching. He was in need of a break. "Oh Christ . . . I'm going for coffee. Anybody want some?"

Both Claire and Traask shook their heads as Bennie moved past them and out the door. He closed it behind him.

Claire continued at the computer for a moment while Traask watched Bennie disappear down the hall. Claire had transformed herself in the last six hours into an FBI agent, through and through. Traask didn't like this hard exterior she was presenting. He wanted the woman who stepped into the light last night to at least raise her hand and be accounted for.

"So, what are you doing for dinner?" he asked.

She didn't look up. "I dunno yet. Any suggestions? It's your town."

"Well, I can cook us up something . . . that is, if you want to . . ."

Claire stopped. He had managed to break her concentration quite effectively. Her face appeared beside the terminal. The woman, not the Federal Agent, had returned.

"That would be nice. I'd . . ."

The door to the conference room opened. Claire's expression altogether changed. Her smile became unguarded, broader and full of warmth. All at once, she was yet *another* person. She rose from the table, forgetting all about Traask.

"It's about time!" Claire exclaimed.

The woman who entered the room was someone who commanded one's attention. She was taller than Claire—in fact, she was taller than most women Traask knew—and built in a muscular fashion. She sported a fresh appearance, with short brown hair, simply worn, and no makeup. This was clearly a no-nonsense person who moved with a sense of purpose. And right now, that purpose was to reach Claire, without delay.

Crossing to the table, she let loose several flight bags, a clutch of files, and an over-stuffed briefcase. Claire moved in quickly to assist. Traask watched with keen interest how they reacted to each other.

"I went to your place anyhow, got some stuff I thought you could use." The woman handed Claire a red flight bag.

These two were close friends, Traask could tell. He almost expected them to embrace, and later supposed they would have if he hadn't been standing there.

"Thanks," Claire replied, taking the bag and inspecting it.

"Just some more clothes, shoes ..." The woman's nose wrinkled, and she shrugged, as if to say, I know you didn't want me to, but I did anyway ...

She was already heading back out the door. "The news out of L.A. isn't great. I'll get to it in a minute. First I gotta use the john."

"Sure." Claire had begun to follow, then realized that she had forgotten all about Traask. "Oh ... hey, just a second." Claire caught the woman by the arm. "There's someone I want you to meet first."

The two women stood in the doorway, side by side, which emphasized their differences. This woman made Claire appear ... well, petite. The Amazon noticed Traask for the first time.

Claire began, "Detective Daniel Traask, Cincinnati Homicide."

The woman nodded in a professional, if curt, manner and then turned back to Claire, intent on continuing into the hall. "Which way?"

"Down there." Claire pointed while she spoke. "It's a few doors past communications ... on the ... uh ..."

She turned to him for assistance.

"Ladies' to the right," Traask assured her. But he was confused. There was something more masculine than feminine about this new arrival. It wasn't just the physical attributes. She moved with a certain raw-boned determination, like a man. And she didn't apologize for it, either.

She took off down the hallway without hesitation and no thank you, which is what Bennie might have done, Traask told himself, had the situation been reversed. Claire paused for a moment, watching the woman's progress with concern. Then she shrugged.

"She has a tendency to be a little ... brief. I think she's really shy, but won't ever admit it. Once you get to know her, she loosens up."

Traask nodded, trying to follow. "Dallas sending you some extra help?"

It was Claire's turn to be confused. "No ..." Then, upon realizing her omission, she became flustered. "Ohhhh! I'm sorry, didn't I ...?" She frowned, annoyed with herself for losing track of her manners, and corrected her mistake. "No, no ... Dallas isn't sending in relief. That was Joey—*my partner.*"

16

A Little Misunderstanding
June 27th—Cincinnati SW Station
14:45

"Your partner!"

"Yes. Jo Ann."

"Oh." Traask looked away—up, down, and around—anywhere but at Claire, trying to keep the questions inside. It was a perfect, if unconscious, imitation of her performance the night before.

"What is it?" she asked, noting his quandary.

The other night ... had he just imagined her response, or had he simply misconstrued it?

Traask weighed the consequences of his next comment carefully, understanding the possible ramifications. Still, he decided that he couldn't just let it lie. "Last night ..." He struggled with it, trying to put it tactfully. "Well, we were talking about your partner, and I had the distinct impression that your partner ... was a guy."

Claire flushed a moment. Of course, she recalled what he was referring to, but she was not prepared at this moment to explain it. "Yeah, well ..."

"Were you just trying to choke my chain?"

"No!" Her voice rose angrily.

"Then what? Why all the . . . why didn't you tell me she was a woman?"

Claire's cheeks flushed hotly as she sought an answer. Her eyes searched the windows to the hall for any sign of Joey's return. "Because . . ." she started, then faltered. What came out of her next was angry and defensive. "Look, I don't expect you to understand. In fact, I don't know why you even asked!"

Traask's mind was finally putting things together from the bits and pieces she was offering. He replayed her response to his questions the night before to himself, with careful deliberation, and found there to be many possible answers . . . perhaps too many.

In the silence, walls had appeared. All at once, the cord between them was broken.

"Hey, there's cookies out here from Laramie's wife. Should I grab a few and bring them in?" Bennie's reappearance in the doorway couldn't have been more timely. He immediately noticed the tension in the air. It was underlined when Claire breezed past him without a word and marched down the hall toward the Ladies.

"Did I interrupt somethin'?" he asked, noting the solemn expression on Traask's face. "You two aren't having lovers' quarrels already, are ya? Jesus, Traask . . . we ain't never gonna get through this week!"

For the next several hours, the FBI team sat behind closed doors. Traask tried his best to wrap a professional attitude around his demeanor, trying to push off the personal feelings that might have clouded his vision. But that's what had been happening. He was wrapped up in something and someone he hardly knew. And now it seemed he had a mystery on his hands.

The Cincinnati boys had been asked to step aside so that Jo Ann could properly brief Claire on the events that had been investigated in California. But from his desk, Traask had a clear view of the conference room. He could watch the two women as they discussed the case behind open louvers. He studied Claire as she listened intently to every word her partner uttered—only occasionally glancing outside the walls of their domain. Together, they poured over documents like they were photos from a long-lost family album. And what was even more disturbing was that this woman made Claire light up in a most amazing way. They appeared as two halves of one whole as they worked together, the one working off the other as a team. A good team.

Joey had assumed Traask's chair—he noted, as a curious coincidence—and she kept looking outside the conference room distractedly, as if she were uncomfortable in these surroundings. More than once, he caught her gaze and found himself unable to sustain it. He immediately disliked this Jo Ann.

His eyes returned to his own desk and the discovery reports, but his mind was just not going to follow. He tried to lasso his thoughts, but they kept returning to Claire, as did his eyes. He observed her body language while he tried to get a handle on just what the hell had been going on between them since they first saw each other.

Was he losing it? Hadn't there been signals between them last night? Hell, it'd been that way since the moment they met. Then what's this? A partner who is clearly . . . Could Claire be a . . . ?

No. Traask wasn't prepared to accept that Claire wasn't interested in men.

She had rejected him, although politely. But she had stated quite clearly that she and her partner were not involved outside of work.

Traask ran over all of it and came to the conclusion that this was all one big misunderstanding. It had to be. He was getting the distinct impression that an apology was in order. An apology from him.

So when they were called back into the conference room at 6:15 P.M., he was itching to get her alone and clear up everything. He could hardly think of anything else as Claire closed the door to the room and Bennie joined Traask at the far end of the table.

She had not looked at Traask when he entered. She stared

at the floor, deep in thought. Joey only looked at Claire and the reports she was studying. She ignored Bennie and Traask's entrance completely—almost as if they annoyed her.

He noticed that Claire appeared to be quite wrung out. Her color had faded again. He couldn't recall how much she had eaten at lunch, if anything. The news from California must not have been good.

As she began to speak, she remained standing—grasping the back of her chair and holding on to it, as if she could physically alter the facts of the case by molding its frame into something they could use to their advantage.

"Although I can't discuss all the findings from the Los Angeles and Phoenix investigations, it seems that we're no further ahead now with the preliminary results than we were before the Cameron case."

"But you've got a photo of him now!" Bennie reminded her.

Joey snorted, "Yeah, I could have drawn you a better picture than *this*."

She tossed over the 8 × 10 that had been lifted from the station's surveillance cameras. Traask sighed and shifted in his chair, avoiding the temptation to react to her insulting tone. Bennie reached out and took the photo, only then fully realizing the weight of her words.

Claire was right. No progress had been made.

"He knew he was under surveillance and he was careful to hide himself. This is too grainy for any adequate interpretation. We've been hoping for something a little more solid. Prints, hair, blood—something to tell us more."

"What about those guys in that van? I can't believe you couldn't find anything in there after what he did to them." Bennie said.

Traask smiled. If this was going to be a pissing party, then so be it.

"We have found evidence inside the van. That doesn't mean it directly connects it to any findings at the other sites," Claire stated. "We're going to sweep your lobby and the holding room again to try and get something you've missed."

Traask looked up, objecting. But she continued.

"What I'm really calling you in for is to let you know that this may get ugly. We're going to need your full cooperation. Cincinnati isn't prepared for what has blown into town."

Traask was confused again. The men from Cincinnati exchanged bewildered glances.

"I've spoken with your captain, and he agrees that certain precautions need to be taken from this point on."

"Wait a minute. Precautions? What in the hell are you talking about? You think we wanted this to happen to Marlovich?" Bennie hotly countered. He turned to Traask, who deeply wished to add to the outburst but said nothing. "This guy has to be on the inside! He knew where to find the Cannibal and exactly how to get to him. He's got to be a cop. How were we supposed to protect the son of a bitch from a cop?"

Traask's hand grazed Bennie's arm, quieting him before he spoke himself. "You're working from the assumption he's still here, in Cincinnati. I mean ... wouldn't he have left by now?"

The two women stared at Traask stonily—like he was s-l-o-w.

"He's not gone?" Traask asked, confused. "What makes you so sure?"

Claire broke the eye contact and dropped her gaze to the tabletop.

"When I first came to Cincinnati, I told you of a newspaper clipping that was recovered in California—at the Cameron house."

"Yeah, so?"

Claire fished for the clipping, finally pulling it from her files. She pushed it toward Traask. As he took it from her, their eyes connected. Hers seemed ... sad. Apologetic. But still, they were professional. And cold.

Traask's gaze fell after she let go of her lock on him. As he looked at the article, she spoke.

"I thought I made it clear. We didn't know which one he would go for *first*."

Bennie shook his head. "I don't get it. The Cop Killer?

171

Why? That would be stupid! He knows you're here. It was on the news."

This got Traask's attention.

Bennie shrugged, apologizing. "Guess the Twat Leader didn't care for the reception she got from you this morning. She let everyone know the Feds were here."

"Great," Traask mumbled.

"He'll wait for the right moment. But he's staying here," Claire explained, with a tired, angry sigh. "Because America and the whole damn world is going to be watching this time. And that's what he wants. He wants the public to anticipate his handiwork. He needs their endorsement. It's part of his plan."

"So, gentlemen, you're stuck with us. At least until we can get our hands on this guy," Joey added.

"Hey now, couldn't you be wrong? I mean, aren't you putting all your eggs in one basket with this kind of theory?" Bennie asked.

Joey and Claire exchanged knowing glances. They seemed to be pitying Bennie for his shortsightedness.

"We didn't choose this basket," Claire reminded him.

"... Local authorities say. And still there is very little information being released on the investigation into the murder of Kenneth P. Marlovich, which took place inside the station house itself only yesterday afternoon."

The familiar face of Holly North appeared on the television screen inside the Morrison home. John, Kathy, Deborah, and Daniel Traask's daughter, Jennifer, watched the proceedings, eagerly awaiting any new word on the case—and about Traask.

"Captain John Sawyer made a brief statement this morning, which summed up the events that took place yesterday inside the room where Marlovich was being held, but no one has explained the sudden appearance of FBI Agent Claire Randall, who now appears to be working closely with the department on this investigation."

As Holly droned on, footage from earlier that morning was shown: Claire approaching Holly and flashing her badge.

The image held. Claire's face filled the screen as a moment frozen in time.

"News Thirteen has learned that Agent Randall was last connected to the celebrated 'Hillside Murders' in California, in which the former defendant, Eric Cameron, was found only a few days ago, brutally dismembered and strewn on top of the burial sites of the alleged victims in the Hillside Murder case."

Some stock footage from the network affiliates was shown of the infamous hillside. Police and FBI personnel swarmed over the terrain.

"Agent Randall has *also* been involved with the much celebrated van kidnappings in Arizona . . ." Holly continued, now flipping to the parking lot of the One Stop where Koot Wilson was standing in the doorway of his store, pointing out the hole in the screen where he first blasted his shotgun.

". . . Where two minors had been tortured and held hostage until they were rescued by a mysterious man, dressed as a police officer, who reportedly turned the tables on the two kidnappers, leaving their bodies inside the van to be discovered by the authorities."

There were more shots of the van, and then the image returned to that of Claire Randall, the same freeze-frame that now jarred loose and followed Claire moving past Holly, her hand reaching for Traask's arm as she pushed on ahead, leading the way through the crowd and into the station house.

"Gosh," Jennifer told the Morrisons, "she sure is a pretty FBI agent."

"Yeah, she's cool," Kathy agreed.

"For real . . ." John added.

Deborah had to agree with all of them.

The image on the screen returned to a live broadcast outside the brightly lit station house, with Holly's face predominantly on the screen.

"At this time, there has been no confirmation as to whether these cases are related. News Thirteen is attempting to get a statement from the FBI on this matter, but so far, authorities are being very tight-lipped. As soon as we receive word on this, or any new word on the murder of the Cincinnati Cannibal, we will pass that along to you. In the meantime, we've taken this case to the people to see just what their reaction to this remarkable series of events might be."

Again the scene changed to earlier in the day on a sidewalk, just outside a grocery store. A small crowd was gathered around Holly as she interviewed an elderly black man.

"I heard about 'dem kids in that van. I tell you, I wouldda done the same thing to those bastards iff'n I caught up 'wit 'em. If 'ya ask me, he shouldda never turned 'em back in. He shoulda left 'em out there for the buzzards to get 'em."

Another interview.

A pretty blonde, girl-next-door type. "I don't know. I guess if all the murders *are* related, that'd be pretty wild. But I thought it was really creepy to think that the guy in California murdered all those girls and then got off because of a technicality. I mean, it's obvious now that he did it— isn't it? What if you had to work with this guy? I mean, I'm a secretary. God, I don't know what I'd do if my boss turned out to be a . . . a real live serial killer!"

Another interview.

A black woman, holding her small child. "I don't know. It's like, I wondered about that guy—the Cannibal? And I was thinking, how do you rehabilitate a person like that? I mean, we're suppose to pay for his problems? Hey, now we don't have to worry about it, do we?"

And another. A preppie white guy in a suit and tie was hesitant. "Well, you know—it's sort of a renegade-type of thing—real Charles Bronson material. But I gotta admit that I don't agree with the way things are being done right now. I mean, if this guy is going out and killing these creeps— well, they *are* creeps who were really guilty. I think . . . I think at least we need to stop being so permissive in the system. I mean, it's one thing to not agree with the death penalty, but if you've got enough money, like Cameron did . . . you can get off from anything! I heard it cost over a million and a half dollars to conduct his trial over there. But along comes a guy who isn't part of the system, and he finds out the truth in a couple of hours. If he would have come along a little sooner, he could have saved California taxpayers a hell of a lot of money." He was grinning as he said it, as if it were a joke.

But Deborah was not laughing. This man could have easily been Frank. That is ... a few months ago. That's when the Cop Killer was out there picking off the men he worked with, and there wasn't a damn thing they could do about it. It's a hard thing to face—knowing that the system you're working for doesn't tow the line. And you're powerless to help unless ... unless you take things into your own hands.

Another man was on the screen. He looked a bit redneck. "Well hell, I think this guy's just doing us all a little favor. I mean, no one else is out there doin' it. Puts a little fear into those psychos out there, don'tcha think? Makes 'em think twice about eatin' people, or choppin' up young girls or ... or takin' someone's kid on the way home from school. These guys aren't normal, for Christ's sake. They deserve to be chased through the woods like a bunch of rabid dogs. It's about time, too."

Deborah left the TV behind, walking into the kitchen. She felt sick.

Traask startled her. He was standing at the sliding glass door, peering in. Evidently he had knocked, but no one had heard him.

"Jesus, Dan. You nearly gave me a heart attack," she admonished him as she quietly opened the door. He gave her a tired smile.

"Sorry."

"The kids are watching the late news—to see if they could catch you."

"Not tonight. I managed to dodge them again. That's a record, twice in one day."

"Good for you. They'll be much happier to see you in person. It's pretty hard to hug the TV screen." She moved quickly. "Need some dinner? We got plenty of leftovers."

"Well, I ..."

"Dad!" Jennifer raced into the room and threw her arms around him. She squeezed tightly around his waist.

"Hi there. How's my girl?" He held her to him, his eyes closing. Deborah watched approvingly.

"I missed you. You weren't even on the news tonight!"

"I know."

"I like it when you're on the news. At least I can see what's going on!"

Traask frowned. "Why don't you go get your things rounded up so we can relieve Deborah of baby-sitting duty. I think she's probably had enough for one week."

"Do you have to call it *baby-sitting?* God, Dad, get real. I'm practically a teenager."

"Which makes you twice as much trouble. Go on, get going."

Jennifer raced back to the bedrooms, hooting with delight.

Deborah tried to correct him. "It hasn't been a problem, Dan. Not in the least. She's been wonderful. She can stay ..."

"At this point, I think she's really overstayed her welcome. You've been a lifesaver, Deb."

"Any time. Any time. You want a beer or something? I've got some leftover pot roast in there ..."

"You don't have to ..."

"Sit down," Deborah ordered. She was already at the fridge, removing the casserole dish. She handed him a bottle of beer. "You look like hell."

"Thanks."

She started the microwave. There was a moment of silence as he popped the top and took a swig of the brew. "I didn't get much sleep last night."

"Yeah? So ... tell me about her."

Traask nearly choked on the lager. "Who?"

"The one you rode in with this morning."

"How in the hell did you know about *that?*"

"You can thank the Twat Leader. She's got it all on tape. I'm sure if you had already slept with her, she would have reported that too. But you know her, she's not interested in safe sex."

With his face bright red, Traask looked away.

"Oh my God!" Deborah kidded him with mock horror in her voice. "You ... you haven't, have you?"

"No. No." Traask smiled, enjoying Deborah's ribbing, "She was at the apartment last night, though."

"Really!"

"It's . . . a long story, Deb. Nothing to get terribly excited about. I don't think this is . . . that I'm . . . her type."

"What?! You gotta be kidding."

"No. I'm not."

"Jesus Christ, is she blind or just stupid?"

Deborah expected to see Dan smiling at this, but instead she saw the hurt behind his sad expression. She toned down her reactions.

"Oh . . . well, she *looked* real . . . interesting."

"She is . . . believe me."

The microwave sounded. Deborah pulled out the plate and dished out some pot roast.

"Can you believe it? Tonight Holly was trying to prove there's a connection between our Cincinnati Cannibal and those killings in Arizona—even the one in L.A. She was asking people's opinions, trying to get them to believe that there's some sort of vigilante out there going after these guys on purpose. I mean, just who does she think she is, anyway—scaring people like that?"

Startled, Traask looked up at her. His eyes were stony. But there was fear there, too. Real fear. And Deborah got the message.

"Oh my God . . ." she whispered, backing away from him.

"You mean there really is a guy out there?" John jumped in. He'd been standing in the doorway to the living room, openly listening the whole time. "Cool! You mean we got our very own Terminator?"

John danced around for a moment, then snatched up some sunglasses that were lying on the counter, assuming an Arnold Schwarzenegger position, taking charge with an imaginary machine gun. "I'll be back."

Traask looked from John's parody back to Deborah, who could only stare at him.

But it was no joke.

Traask softened his gaze, but she was now realizing just why he looked so haggard when he came through the door tonight. There were many more things at stake here than just the Cannibal.

"Okay, all right ... take that, Cannibal. Take that, you kidnappers. Now, lemme see, who's next ..."

Deborah and Daniel Traask both wanted revenge for Frank's death. They were hoping that would come at Eddie Jefferson's trial. But here was the Devil, knocking on their door, offering them everything they had been afraid to wish for. Hearing those men on TV talking about an eye-for-an-eye only made it more real.

Secretly, she wanted it. She wanted the Cop Killer to suffer like the families of all the cops he killed had suffered. But now, in front of Traask, she couldn't say that. She couldn't even think it.

Traask could only nod to let her know that allowing themselves to get carried away was wrong. They were all on the same bridge now. They could stand at the edge and view together the remains of Frank's memory. And the man who made him one.

"God, Dan" was all that she could manage, realizing that the Cop Killer could well be the next victim.

A moment of silence passed between Deborah and Traask.

Kathy came bulleting down the hall and entered the kitchen. "Mommie, Jennifer needs to know where that blue jacket is. I think you washed it ..."

Beep Beep Beep Beep Beep Beep Beep.

Traask's beeper was sounding. Reluctantly, he reached for it.

Deborah reached out to hug Kathy lovingly. Her voice cracked. "Come on, I'll get it for you, baby." She led Kathy out to the laundry room, and John followed them, shooting up everything in sight with his finger.

Traask moved to the phone on the kitchen counter. He studied the number with a puzzled expression as he dialed.

"Hello?" came an unfamiliar voice.

"Hello, this is Lt. Daniel Traask. I just received a beep ..."

"Dan, it's me ..."

The left hook nearly knocked him to the floor. It was

Claire's voice that greeted him. She sounded human again . . . almost friendly.

"Oh . . . hi."

"Hi. I, uh . . . tried to find you, but I guess you left in a hurry. Bennie suggested I beep you."

"What is it?" He tried to maintain the professionalism she had exuded all afternoon. But his effort resulted in a colder and more brusque return than intended.

There was a definite pause at the other end of the line. "Well, I thought you had invited me to dinner. . . ."

Embarrassed, Traask tried to recover, keeping the professional tone to a minimum. "Oh, well . . . you looked pretty involved there with your partner and all."

He closed his eyes hard and bit his lip. What an ass! What a jerk! What was he saying?

"Look, I'm sorry about earlier. It's a very long story, and I . . . I shouldn't have snapped like that. I'm sorry, it's just that . . ."

"Dad! Look, look what Mrs. Morrison gave me! Isn't it great?"

Jennifer was standing before him now wearing a blue hat-and-jacket combination. She twirled around, so he could get a good view.

Traask covered the mouthpiece. "That's terrific, hon, I'm on the phone . . . okay? Just one minute, all right?"

Jennifer was put off, but understood. She backed out of the room slowly, and then flew down the hall to find Kathy again.

Into the phone, he said, "Sorry."

"You're busy," Claire noted.

"Uh . . . well, yeah. I'm kinda busy. I'm picking up my daughter. I haven't seen her in a couple of days."

"Oh." Her acknowledgment was tinged with disappointment.

"I wanted to talk to you, though. There wasn't any time today."

"Yeah, I know," Claire replied.

"How about breakfast?"

"Uh . . . what time?"

"You name it. I'm flexible."

"Well, I wanted to get an early start tomorrow. There's a lot ..."

"... How early is early?" Traask insisted.

When Traask arrived at the diner, Claire had been waiting in the booth for half an hour. He glanced up at the clock above the restroom entry.

Five-thirty-three.

So he was a little late. But five o'clock in the morning was asking a lot.

As he approached her table, he could see that she had already ordered a hefty breakfast, and her early morning diet Coke was nearly drained. The waitress had just appeared.

"Would you like another one, honey?"

Claire nodded, her mouth full, but she was really nodding a greeting to Dan. A big grin appeared on the waitress's face when she recognized him.

"Well, Lieutenant! It's been quite awhile since I've seen you 'round the ass-end of my shift! What the hell brings you out so ..." The wise table-tender looked back to Claire, with a wry smile. "Say no more ... say no more."

Claire blushed, between swallows.

"You remember my usual, Gwen?" Traask inquired with a grin.

"Did Liz forget Dick? So nice, she did him twice." Her enthusiasm lit up the fluorescent lighting in the diner. "Of course I remember. For you, there'll be extra cheese on that Denver."

She moved away from the table as she spoke. "Still drinking the hard stuff?"

"You know it," he said, sitting down. He knew it was a reference to Claire's cola and smiled broadly one last time toward the friendly waitress.

"I used to come here a lot," he admitted to Claire.

"So I gather." She smiled. "I can see why."

She offered him some of her English muffin, but he refused it. Gwen returned to the table with coffee for Dan and another Coke for Claire.

"Just holler if you need help. I'm gonna be in the back for a minute."

Traask waited until she reached the swinging-door entry of the kitchen.

"Oh, hey, Gwen?"

She turned and saw that Traask's eyes were twinkling with a mischievous glint.

"You put your little finger in my coffee?"

For a moment, it sounded like a complaint. Claire was confused.

"Come on now. Be honest. Did you put your little finger in my cup of coffee?"

But suddenly Gwen broke out in a huge smile, remembering the joke. Together, Dan and the waitress recited the all-too-familiar punch line, " 'Cuz you's so sweet, I don't need no sugar.' "

She blew him a kiss as she entered the kitchen.

Full of nostalgia, Traask chuckled softly. His attention shifted back to Claire. Her expression was one of mild surprise.

"I've missed coming here. I used to be in here all the time. My regular table was right over there." Traask pointed to a corner booth.

"Oh. Should we move?"

The dark cloud inhabited Daniel Traask's brow. "No . . . no. Here's just fine."

"So, why'd you stop coming in?"

"No need for the all-nighters, anymore," Traask informed her. His gaze fell to the tabletop. "The case is over."

Claire watched Traask grow somber. Here was that same pain, that same agony, he was defending only the other night. It lived in here, in this diner where they'd spent so many nights, tracking the Cop Killer. It came alive for him every day, but in here—it *breathed*.

"We caught him," he added. There was a pause before he went on. "It was the Cop Killer."

Claire nodded in understanding. "Look, I'm sorry if I was interrupting you last night. I didn't realize that ..."

"No, I'm glad you called. I ... I don't know if I could have gotten through today if I didn't get some kind of a chance to clear things up with you."

A moment followed where neither of them knew how to begin. Traask decided to jump into it, headfirst.

"I didn't mean to insult you. It's none of my business—you were right about that. I just thought ... I thought ..." Traask struggled for the words to make it right. "Well, I thought you were trying to *make* it my business ... you know?"

Claire stared at her plate. She was suddenly not so hungry for breakfast as she was for emotional substance. "I was. I ... I do ..."

Traask tried to give her encouragement.

"I've had to fight this kind of thing a lot. Usually from my own people, in my own office. Joey is ... well, what she is. So when you started in on it, I went off a little 'half-cocked.'" Then she grimaced. "I didn't intend to use any puns today."

He nodded patiently, giving her ample room to clear the air, so she continued. "I guess I get tired of being labeled a dyke all the time. It's pretty well-known that I don't sleep around and I don't have an ex-husband or a boyfriend, so people assume that because Joey and I are as close as we are that we're involved, or something. Well ... we're not."

Traask looked at her as she spoke, seeing how difficult this was for her to explain. She caught his gaze and immediately became even more uncomfortable.

"Dan, I'm not gay." Then her demeanor changed completely. She let down her guard and almost laughed at herself. "Jesus, I've never had to explain this kind of thing to anyone before. I've always just delivered a quick comeback and walked away."

But then, her serious side emerged once more. "I have no desires to get physical with Joey. She's never even tried to come on to me. We've joked about it, but ..." She trailed off, taking on more conviction. "If she were a man ... well,

I couldn't tell you if I would be thinking differently, because she's not a man. Maybe that's my problem. I never thought of myself as a homophobic sort. I hope saying that doesn't make me a bad person. She's my partner and my very good friend. My very best friend. We're very tight. We care about each other . . ."

She paused, taking in a deep breath. "But with you . . ."

Her soft brown eyes bored into his. "I can't tell you what's been going through me since we met. Jesus, it feels like weeks have gone by since then. But it's like something inside me knows you from somewhere else, and it keeps trying to remind me that we should just—"

Bammmmm!

The kitchen doors slammed open, admitting Gwen—grinning ear to ear. In her arms she toted Dan's breakfast. It didn't take a sixth sense for her to notice they had stopped talking upon her reentry. She gave them a suspicious once-over as she set the plate down in front of Dan.

"All right, what's wrong?"

"Nothing!" They both chimed in together, wide-eyed and innocent as could be.

That cinched it. Gwen's wide-mouthed laughter filled the small diner. She turned on her heel and shook her head as she headed back into the kitchen. "Yup, like I always say, if it ain't broke, don't fix it. You two need to be left alone. You're gonna do fine together . . . just fine . . ." The double doors swung shut behind her.

Traask's Denver omelet and side of blueberry pancakes stared up at him. He smiled at Claire, whose eyebrow lifted. "You know what's spooky about that woman?"

"What?" she asked.

"She's always right."

"She is?"

"Yeah. Guys from the track come by all the time just to get her word. There's no use arguing with her. Don't even try."

"If you say so."

"I say so."

Traask viewed his breakfast with renewed interest. He

183

picked up his fork and knife and was just about to dig in when he noticed Claire was eyeing his blueberries, amorously.

"Hold it," he commanded, reaching for his napkin.

She studied him as he leaned forward, napkin in hand. "What is it?" she asked suspiciously.

"Nothing, just hold still."

He advanced on her, coming around the table to her side. He slid in beside her, attempting to take her face in his hands. She fought him off in mock combat.

"What is it?" she repeated.

Traask moved slowly, pretending to wipe away something from her chin, but as he did, he leaned closer.

"Hold still, just a minute—will you!" he scolded.

She held her pose, the concern on her face growing.

But Traask erased it when he closed the gap between them, putting his lips on hers. His arms reached around her small waist and brought her closer. It was a sneak attack, but delivered with tenderness as he told her with a touch what she had been trying to make clear in her words.

They should just be together.

She reached out, stroking his hair, drawing him near. She pressed closer, feeling a wave of overpowering need for him—the closeness of him—running through her. It rose in intensity when she found herself in his arms.

After the kiss, they continued to hold each other. Her head rested on his shoulder, her eyes closed for the moment—thanking God, or whoever was orchestrating this incredible scenario in her life. It was a moment she was not going to easily forget.

Traask's chin grazed her back as he nestled his head closer to her neck. "You know, I thought I was gonna go insane the other night, seeing you in that . . . in my living room."

"Well, I didn't want you to think I was easy," she kidded, smiling at the memory.

"Easy?" Traask pulled her away from him, and as he did, his arm connected with the glass and Coke spilled across the table and into their laps. They both jumped up and a cascade of brown liquid poured over the table edge. Their clothes were soaked.

"Aw, shit, I'm sorry."

Claire laughed. "It's okay. It's okay."

"Gwen!" Traask hollered. He shook off the cola from his hands, helplessly.

The kitchen door opened, and a couple of dish towels came flying out in their direction. Along with some words from the wise one herself.

"You's way outta practice, Lieutenant."

"What in the hell happened to you?"

Joey stared at Claire full on as she entered the conference room. Her suit was now dry, but it bore a messy brown stain.

"Had a little accident."

"Mmmm ..." Joey nodded, watching her curiously. "I went to get you for breakfast and you'd left already."

"Yeah, well—I thought I'd get a head start."

"It's almost eight o'clock, Claire."

"So, I got some breakfast on my own!"

From inside the conference room, Joey could see Traask entering the station. As he moved past the front desk and closer to them, he removed his jacket, revealing a stain similar to Claire's so-called "little accident." Bennie met him half-way and was already ribbing him about it.

Joey bristled. "I see."

Claire sensed her objections and had hoped to avoid them.

But what Joey said next, made them both forget. "Well, good. Then you won't be tempted to trust the food on the plane."

Claire didn't understand.

"We've been recalled," Joey announced without fanfare.

Claire remained stock still, unable or unwilling to fathom what was being told to her.

So Joey tried again. "We're going home."

17

The Catch of the Century
June 28th—Cincinnati SW Station
07:59

"They're crazy! Did you tell them ..."

"Tell them what, Randall? Not everyone is as convinced as you are that this guy is gonna strike again in Cincinnati. At least they are willing to make the statement confirming your findings up to now. After that bitch leaked everything on the air last night, all hell's breaking loose out there. You should hear the gun lobbyists ..."

Joey continued as she moved about, methodically packing up. "The head is assigning more agents. Some brain from the Washington office is there waiting for us. I think you know him. You've mentioned him before ..."

"Who?"

"Portman."

"Adam Portman?"

"Yeah."

Joey was watching her reaction closely. Claire had turned away from the conference room table, stunned by this revelation. The mention of this ghost from her past had brought something forward with it.

"You *do* know this guy."

"Yeah. Yeah, I do," Claire finally replied, sinking into the nearest chair.

Joey moved closer, attempting to lend her support. She knew some of the history behind the name—but not all of it. It was part of a painful past that Claire had kept mostly to herself. Joey had always hoped that someday she would hear the story in its entirety. Maybe it would be today.

Claire shook her head with some regret. "Adam Portman. Jesus."

"Wanna talk about it?" Joey offered.

Claire shook her head, like a shiver—shaking off the ghosts.

"Well, he's not the one recalling us, these orders came from the home office." Joey tried to reassure her.

"Doesn't matter. It's him. He's the one pulling the string."

Claire was staring at the tabletop, internalizing. Joey could tell she was starting to lose it, and she didn't want that to happen, so she continued.

"Well, he's in L.A. right now. He wants to see your list."

"He already has my list." Claire sighed.

"Then I guess he wants to see your new list."

"The lists are old news," Claire snapped, suddenly unwilling to go any further into it. The gears were turning, and the territory was clouding over. Something was about to break.

"Yes, well, perhaps he just wants to get another look at your legs, my dear."

Claire shot her partner a glance that warned her to back off. Joey complied but was getting tired of this game. She knew that Claire had a few people from her past that she could live quite happily without ever seeing again. Joey supposed Adam Portman headed up that list in big red letters. But until this moment, Joey had not been sure just how fresh that wound had remained.

Claire had been lost in thought for several moments. She was aware that Joey had been talking, but she had not heard a word. She was recalling her past with vivid accuracy, and it was scaring her.

"I mean, they could be right. I'm not one hundred percent sure that this guy's targeting the Cop Killer next. Are you?"

Claire didn't respond. She was busy searching her intuition on this one and wasn't getting much feedback. There hadn't been time to concentrate. She'd been distracted.

Adam Portman . . .

Her mind turned on a dime as she desperately reached inward for something to grab on to. She needed some kind of confirmation that Cincinnati was still vulnerable—that *he* was still here.

She had to be positive if she was going up against Portman.

But nothing was coming.

"He has to be here . . ." she whispered.

"Well, don't waste your breath on me then. Tell it to *him*."

Claire was determined. "Where're the reports from the lobby sweep? Did they come in yet? Wasn't anything . . ."

"Clean. This guy is some kind of chameleon. He's too perfect. Or he's got a hell of a lot of luck on his side. And you know me . . . I don't believe in luck."

"There's got to be something." Claire's desperate edge was uncharacteristic of her nature, and Joey knew it.

"Randall," Joey insisted with a tone of finality, "we've been recalled! We have to regroup. Now, I've booked us on the eleven o'clock flight to L.A. I even managed to get us a nonstop so you wouldn't get your panties in a wad. They're expecting us at the downtown office this afternoon."

"He's not in L.A."

"But your pal Portman is. Now we have orders to move it. Are you coming?"

Joey was busily closing down the computer now, gathering the last of their things together. But Claire wasn't moving.

Her gaze wandered to the offices beyond the window, searching for . . . what? A reason to stay? A reason . . .

"What's with you?" Joey sounded exasperated.

Claire's mind was racing. Was she getting confused here? What was her real motivation to stay?"

Could Traask be clouding her frequencies?

Where was the killer—now, at this very moment?

"I have to think. Give me a minute. Just a minute ..."

"Think? We've got a meeting in less than thirty minutes with the local office. Then we've gotta beat our ass back to the motel, pick up our shit, and get out to the airport. Think in the car, will 'ya?"

"No."

"What?" Joey asked, turning on her.

"I'm not going. Not now."

Joey moved in to object just as Traask's face appeared in the doorway.

"Hi!" He greeted them cheerily. His jaunty, unsuspecting grin made Joey snap.

"Excuse us." Joey marched over to the door without warning, allowing it to swing shut in his face with a bang.

She then turned back to Claire as if the insult didn't matter a damn.

"All right, what's been going on here?"

Claire didn't reply. Instead, her eyes searched out Traask as he stood at the window for a moment, puzzled and embarrassed.

Joey could see she still didn't have Claire's complete attention, so in one swift motion she lowered the mini-blind. It bounced off the window as it crashed down, completely blocking Traask's view and cutting off Claire's contact with him.

"Randall!"

Claire's attention finally settled on her partner.

"Is it Portman you don't want to face or is it this one you can't get enough of?" Joey asked, thumbing in Traask's direction.

Claire's expression changed to one of focus. Her anger was now building, and Joey could see it.

"Don't try and bullshit me," Joey continued, "you're making it with that guy, aren't you?"

"I can't believe you're asking me this."

"Oh fuck. Okay—if you wanna play games, fine. But don't mess with me. I know you, Randall. I can tell when something's going on. You're—you're not even here! You're somewhere else! Now, where is it?"

Joey's words hung for a moment in the air above them until her plea turned a bit more emotional. "Let me in, damn it!"

Claire's gaze fell down and away. She couldn't lie to Joey.

"Okay . . . so, I've met someone."

"Really?" Joey allowed her full resentment to be unleashed. "We should all get together sometime! Have a few drinks . . . then maybe you could introduce us."

"Joey, don't . . ."

"Damn it Randall! We're on a case here. We came to Cincinnati on some pretty weak leads, and now the real reason you want to stay is standing outside that door, isn't it?"

"All right, that's enough." Claire flared, abruptly standing. Her anger was clear. "Traask doesn't concern you."

"He does when you disobey orders, trying to find excuses to stay."

"I'm not . . . I'm . . ." Claire tried to correct her.

"Yes, you *are*."

A silence fell between them. Their eyes locked up in an angry hold, they continued to stare each other down for several moments. It was broken by Joey.

"So what are we going to do about Portman? He's waiting for you in L.A."

Adam Portman sat in the American terminal of LAX, recalling another time and place. He could be waiting back at the ranch, poring over the latest fax from Cincinnati, getting ahead of the game, but he couldn't wait—he couldn't sit still. He wanted to see her.

He had left the office early, returning to the hotel room for a fresh change of clothes. He wanted to impress her. And didn't he look the part. He chose the slate gray suit with matching silk tie and a starched white, spread collar designer shirt. He looked smart. He looked good.

But he felt desperate.

He had a good forty minutes or so to wait. While he

waited, he found himself playing a familiar game. *What it would be like if time had zigged instead of zagged—if the cards of fortune had fallen a bit more to the left?*

Once upon a time, Claire Randall would have rushed from the jet way of this arriving plane in order to see his face. All smiles, she would jump into his arms for a warm embrace.

But that was a million miles away from the here and now.

He had not heard from Claire Randall in eight years. Not until he received her fax two days ago, describing her recommendations on the "Big Foot" case out of Arizona and California. When he saw her name on the report, something inside him moved for the first time in years.

Now he had to see her in person.

Adam came to know Claire through a mutual friend, Bernardi—James Bernardi, who was on special assignment to the Washington Bureau during Claire's time at the academy. Bernardi was a top-notch agent and had been in the organization for close to fifteen years. And although Adam had been a part of the Behavioral Science Division there for only a few months, they had taken an instant liking to one another's quick wit—and there it all began.

A likable guy, Bernardi had no trouble with women. He had a charisma that was infectious. During their down times, the two of them would frequent a local pub they affectionately dubbed "The Fishin' Hole" and hoist a few, watch a game, and practice picking up women.

That's where Bernardi taught Adam how to fish.

Adam was a fast learner. He was a good enough looking guy, but he lacked the charm that in Bernardi seemed to runneth over. Adam was self-assured, but many women merely saw it as egotistical. It took awhile for Adam to catch on how Bernardi made the male ego seem irresistible to women. It took a special knack and a special person to get it right for you. Bernardi had it all.

One particular day, Bernardi was running late for a meeting with Adam. Adam waited back at the office, thinking that perhaps Bernardi had run into a snag and would call any moment—but he never did.

The next day, he told Adam he'd run into the most beautiful girl he'd ever seen, and he just couldn't let her go. He had spent the entire day with her. He went on to say that she was everything he had ever dreamed a female could be—and that was a lot.

"She's a second-year cadet at the academy," Bernardi said.

"The academy! What—you were actually fishin' over there?"

"No ... no, no, no. This one knows all about fishing. She knows all about everything. She can see straight through crap. No, this is the kind you don't let get away, my friend. She's the catch of the century."

And he was right.

The first time she had wandered back into their offices, Adam felt his pulse quicken. He knew in an instant that this was the girl Bernardi was describing. How do they put it? It was like seeing Alaska for the first time ...

A breath of incredibly fresh but freezing cold air races into your lungs and gives you this healthy, burning sensation—reminding you that you're amazingly alive, but you're too paralyzed by what stands before you to acknowledge it in any intelligible fashion.

She possessed the kind of beauty that usually gets too dressed up in other trappings for you to believe it is genuine, but she really had it right. Little makeup, naturally bouncy chestnut hair worn simply over her shoulders, drawing your attention to her "just right" figure. It was quite a package.

Adam had formerly maintained that striking women had to do without intelligence, but Claire only need open her mouth to tear that one to shreds. She was educated, intuitive, witty, charming, entertaining ...

It seemed that Bernardi's first assessment was, albeit chauvinistic—all too true.

She was the catch of the century.

Adam couldn't help but wonder ... what if he had met her first?

Would he have stood a chance? Bernardi was ten years her senior. If he had tried, could Adam have caught her? Would she have been attracted to him instead of Bernardi?

Or was it simply that little something extra that all the girls seemed to see in Bernardi?

The three of them had gotten on splendidly. There had been some double dates—but Adam never seemed to find the right addition to the group. Claire's playfully strong sense of humor made her the perfect addition to Bernardi and Adam's friendship, disallowing the usual triangular problems to exist. The three of them were simply together, period, and there was no need for second thoughts.

Their discussions always held a magic spark that were capable of igniting the three of them into passionate arguments. It wasn't a teacher-student relationship, no—it was more of a battle of the minds. Adam found he had influenced her more than he cared to realize. Their long discussions about the field of psychology had turned Claire's studies toward specializing in that area. He hoped that someday she would request to join his department. In fact, he was counting on it.

Over the next two years, talk of marriage would surface but Bernardi's standard line was, "I've been married," and that always brought any sort of discussion to a quick end. It was his way of saying, "That's enough, Claire." Still, Adam clung to the hope that this would not discourage her and that when she graduated, Claire would remain in Washington where she, Adam, and Bernardi could all stay happily together.

Claire wanted this too. It was a realistic dream. She had been bitterly honest with herself about Bernardi. He was divorced, had no children, and traveled extensively. Weeks would go by without much more than an occasional phone call. She knew he had to be seeing other women—how could he not? But she also knew Bernardi loved her and wanted to make their relationship more permanent. But how? A ring wouldn't make things any better—any closer—than they already were. Claire was free to live her life while Bernardi was living his. But when they got together, it was more than special to all of them. Things weren't meant to get better than that.

And he was right. Bernardi was always right.

Then the dreams started.

It was her final year at the academy. Things were getting tough, but they had been tough before. Bernardi had been gone on assignment again, and they were spending less and less time together as a group. Studying had become a full-time job, and she was determined to make the top percent of her class.

But the dreams started coming nearly every night. And although Bernardi had called several times to ask her what was wrong, she felt sure that telling him long-distance would be a mistake.

Finally, one Friday night, with Bernardi and Adam back in town, they got together for the first time in weeks at their favorite corner pub. It was pretty crowded, but they managed to snag their usual corner booth anyway. That's when the two of them got Claire to confess what had been going on.

When she had finished telling them all about her dream, the two men stared at her with an unyielding silence that made her feel suddenly trapped inside of a soundproof box. Bernardi then went berserk—stood up and began shouting, accusing her of going through his private papers. Adam tried to calm him, but this was a side neither one of them had ever seen before.

Claire was mortified. While Bernardi continued to make a scene, she excused herself from the table and left the pub in tears, making her way back to the campus as fast as she could.

But Adam caught up with her a few blocks away. Adam had become someone Claire felt she could trust. He had always made her feel welcome when she came by the offices. He was also closer to her age, which made their relationship more comfortable than with most of Bernardi's friends in the Bureau, who were considerably older.

Adam usually stayed in Washington while Bernardi was away on assignment. He and Claire would catch an occasional movie or dinner together, and it was time well spent. It was as if parts of Bernardi spilled over into Adam—making him, in some small way, an extension of Bernardi. She felt safe with him.

So when Adam pulled her to a stop and held her at an arm's length, she wanted to fall into his arms and cry on his shoulder. Similarly, Adam wanted nothing more than to comfort her. He saw the look in her eyes, such a tortured, haunted look that he wanted to gather her up and soothe it all away. But right this minute, his need to know was stronger than that.

"How did you know about this, Claire?" he demanded.

"I don't know what you mean," she replied angrily, unleashing herself from his hold. She was offended at his cold, uncharacteristic manner.

He was unsure whether she was telling the truth or not. The anger she held now was directed right at him, making it difficult to tell what was beneath the surface.

"Tell me the truth. Have you been in the case files?"

"Case files?! What are you talking about? You asked me what was wrong, and I told you. Jesus, just ... just leave me alone!" She began to walk away.

"It's not just a dream, Claire. It's the case. *Our* case. It's what has kept Bernardi here for the past two years."

Claire turned back to him.

"It was classified. We weren't supposed to talk about it— not even with you. I'm sorry."

Claire shook her head, unable to fathom what he was saying. "What about those other cases ..."

"Old files. Dead files. We needed something to discuss around you. You always got such a kick out of trying to help us ..." he explained. Then he turned serious again. "Come on, Claire. How did you find out? Did Bernardi tell you?"

"Jim didn't tell me anything."

"It's all right if he has."

Claire grew tired of the accusations and began walking away again.

"Another girl is missing, Claire. Your description of her— the girl in your dream—matches the missing girl *exactly.*"

Claire stopped.

And when she turned, the look of realization on her face was something that ripped right through him.

For years Adam tried to forget that moment—that look. But he could not. More than anything, he hoped that someday they would be able to sit down and discuss everything that had happened after that night.

But she had left Washington two days before the funeral, and there had been no time to talk. Clearly, she blamed herself for what had happened—the death of the girl ... and losing Bernardi.

Adam accepted that somewhere within that blame, she held him responsible for their deaths too. So he strongly suspected that when she disembarked today, she would not be rushing into his arms.

By the time Claire's plane landed, he bore a permanent crease in one flap of his suit jacket.

He spotted her instantly. She looked good—better than he had imagined. She wasn't expecting to see him, however, and when their eyes met, she looked away quickly. She wasn't prepared for this. As she made her way to him, he closed the distance out of courtesy.

Adam began, hoping his smile would break the ice. "I hope you don't mind, I volunteered to meet your plane."

Claire nodded in grudging recognition. She was uncomfortable standing next to him—so she adjusted the flight bag on her shoulder and nervously scanned the terminal waiting area for other agents. She didn't notice anyone else approaching and concluded that he had come alone.

"What time is the meeting?" Claire managed, refusing to meet his gaze. She pressed forward into the crowd, leading the way out of the gate and toward the escalators.

"I already called in and told them your flight was running late."

Claire glanced at her watch. "But it wasn't late."

"I know ... I thought it might give us some time to talk." Adam explained hopefully.

Then he suddenly realized something was missing. "Where's your partner?"

"Sick."

"What?" Adam was taken slightly by surprise.

"Flu," she amplified. "We figured she'd better not try to fly until it passes."

"But I spoke with her this morning, and she ..."

"She puts on a brave face. It was my call. You have a problem with that?"

Adam could see that she was not going to let him in. Not one inch.

As she paused momentarily on the escalator, waiting for the slow-moving stairs to carry them downward, Adam noticed that she sported what appeared to be a large coffee stain across her midsection.

"Jesus, what happened to you?"

"Turbulence," she replied with the secret knowledge that her answer, at least in part, had been truthful.

"Randall's gonna be pissed she missed good Chinese." Joey sat around the table with Bennie and Traask, several opened take-out cartons between them.

"Don't you mean they're gonna be pissed when you're missed?" Bennie interjected, taking in a spoonful of lo mein.

"Hey, you see me ... I'm sick. I can't fly right now. Excuse me while I race for the john, will you?" Joey joked, not moving a muscle from her chair.

The men were growing to appreciate this one. She had certainly surprised them. Over the past few hours, she had released her Feds versus Locals attitude and actually let her hair down. But above all, she had proved herself to be a highly competent professional, and they respected her for it.

"Hey, I learned a long time ago, when Randall tells you to lie, you lie. She doesn't do it often, so I have some tolerance for it. She said stay. I'm staying."

"Aren't they gonna want you to see a doctor or report back in or something?" Traask inquired.

"I told you. I just raced to the john. Wanna see me do it again?"

"No, that's okay. I'll vouch for you," Bennie hastily conceded.

"I'm surprised she hasn't called yet. Her plane was supposed to land ..." The phone on the table rang, as if on cue. Joey punched up the speaker phone.

"Yo?"

"Hey, how'ya feeling?" Claire asked, her voice sounding suddenly very far away.

"Like shit, and yourself?"

"I'm not the one racing to the bathroom."

The men exchanged humorous glances while Joey nodded with the realization that Claire didn't necessarily have to be in the room to keep up with the conversation. Hell, she didn't have to be in the same state.

"Exactly. So, have you seen Portman yet?"

"Yeah, he met me at the airport."

"Everything okay?" Joey's voice suddenly turned soft. Traask eyed her, knowing something strange was going on.

"Yeah ... it's okay. Don't worry about that. How are things going? Are we secure over there?"

Joey began munching on a clump of Kung Pao chicken. "Don't be such a worry wart. Everything's under control."

"Hey, is that Chinese?"

Joey grinned at the two men. "We're busted, guys."

"Please tell me it's bad Chinese."

"The worst."

"You bitch."

Joey chuckled warmly. Traask took note of their special rapport with some envy.

"So tell me, what's happening over there?" Claire insisted.

"The captain's cool. He put a special detail on surveillance. They moved our guy into a back room with lots of camera coverage. Our cameras, may I add. Nothing's gonna happen to him."

"Good."

"So, you got them convinced that Cincinnati is the place to be?"

"I'm working on it. Where's Traask?"

Joey pushed the phone across the table. "She wants you." The line was delivered in pure monotone, but it was clearly intended as a double entendre. Traask flushed for a moment, wiping his face with a napkin before responding.

"Thanks."

"No problem."

With that, Joey was content to return to her Kung Pao chicken.

"Hi," Traask said into the speaker.

"So how come you can't have Chinese when I'm around? How come I only get the Italian?"

"Next time, I promise."

"I bet you tell that to all the Feds."

"Joey says you plan to be back in less than twenty-four hours. Are you sure about that? I'll make reservations."

"I'll be back before you know it. Just don't let anything happen while I'm away."

"I won't. I mean, I'm still not entirely convinced something will happen."

"I'm gonna persuade my people to leak the story and put the pressure back on our man. With all of America watching, he's gonna step into the spotlight. People will be counting on him. He won't let them down."

Joey's head rose as she searched Traask's face. She seemed keenly interested in his line of questioning. Just how much had she told this cop?

"Yeah, but aren't there other, more exciting fish to fry?" Traask argued.

"Not for this guy. Trust me," Claire replied firmly.

"Well, how can you be so sure?" he asked.

There was a pause on the other end of the phone, but only for a moment. "Ask me some other time" was all she could say.

"I've gotta go," Claire insisted, "there's someone knocking on my door."

She stood by the bed in the hotel room with a towel wrapped around her, still dripping from a shower. She had been patting her hair dry with her free hand while holding the phone with the other.

"I'll call later and page you," Claire reassured him.

"Okay." Traask's voice on the other end of the phone sounded worried. "But we'll see you tomorrow, right?"

"You got it." Claire promised.

She hung up the phone and started for the door just as a second knock began.

"Who is it?" She asked, irritated at their insistence.

"Housekeeping," a female Hispanic voice announced from the other side.

Claire crossed for the door, then suddenly stopped short. "I didn't call for housekeeping."

"Turn-down service, ma'am. I can come back later . . ."

Claire took a quick survey of the room, noting her gun holster was visible next to her carry-on bag. It was reassuring, but she made her decision and reached for the knob.

"No, that's okay . . ."

And as the door swung open, she saw the maid was not alone.

Adam was resting against the far wall, waiting.

Surprised, Claire hesitated. Finally, she nodded to the confused maid, who entered past her to carry out her duty.

Claire turned on Adam. "What are you doing? You were going to wait in the lobby."

"Claire, we need to talk."

His voice was full of good intention. He moved toward the open door with purpose, only to be met with resistance. Claire half closed it against him.

"We can talk *later.*"

"Claire . . ." Adam paused in protest, "why are you making this so difficult?"

"You expect this is easy?"

"It's not easy for me either."

Claire noted the genuine emotion he struggled to keep in check. His eyes met hers.

"Look, I asked to be on this case, Claire."

The maid appeared again, and Claire allowed her to exit. The workingwoman shot Adam a nasty glare as she passed, demonstrating her disapproval. Adam moved closer to Claire, so not to be overheard.

"We have to talk about it, Claire."

"No."

Adam let out a sigh. It was full of sadness and years of stifled questions. There wasn't much else to be said.

Claire made her final move. "I'll meet you in the lobby in ten minutes." And she shut the door against him.

Adam paused at the door for a moment, then half-heartedly banged his fist against it in frustration.

"You're doing it again, aren't you? With this guy ... you're seeing something, aren't you? Why don't you just admit it?"

Cursing under his breath, Adam waited by the door, but it didn't open. "Damn it, Claire! Talk to me!" There was no response. Full of anger, Adam made his way to the elevator and continued to the lobby—where he waited, his questions unanswered.

Claire remained on the other side of the door for a few minutes more, clutching the towel to her naked frame. Drops of cool water dripped down over her shoulder, causing a chill to shiver through her from inside the air-conditioned room.

Adam had been referring to the killer, of course ... but for the first time, Claire made the connection. She could be putting someone in danger again. And that someone was Traask.

There were ten of them. All suits and ties. She was the only woman in the room.

And what a room it was! Everything was gray except for the one long black marble tabletop. No windows, only one door, and each wall was carpeted in a soft gray material for sound attenuation. The L.A. Bureau maintained a sterile, stark environment.

Claire liked it even less when the lights went down and dim circles of light remained at each man's spot on the table, enabling them to take notes. This made them into faceless as well as nameless individuals, working against her and making her feel even less welcome than she knew she already was.

Besides, their machine was out of Diet Coke.

On the projection screen behind her was the photo taken in the Cincinnati station house. It was the image of a man who left no clues.

"We're wasting time here. We should be concentrating on the Cincinnati cases—trying to catch him by protecting the next target."

"We're not convinced there was a target in Cincinnati."

"Oh? Then who catered the Cannibal?" Claire insisted.

Silence descended upon the faceless crowd.

A man at the head of the table spoke.

"We know you are advising that we continue the surveillance in Cincinnati, Agent Randall. What we particularly want to know is, from this latest killing, did we gather any more evidence to prove that the killer was or is now, a police officer."

Another voice added, "We'd like to start with a profile, Randall. It's standard procedure."

Claire rose from her seat. "Okay. You want a name? Here it is. His name is Brad Hallenbeck. He lives at 322 Livermore Lane in Oakland, California. His sister was killed in a car wreck in 1979 . . ." She couldn't believe it. Some of them were actually reaching for pens to write this drivel down. Her mischievous expression caught Adam's attention. He was not amused. But she continued.

". . . He occasionally does cocaine and listens to old Beatles tunes—especially anything from the Abbey Road album—because he likes to masturbate in rhythm to the songs on side one."

"Jesus, Randall . . . sit down," Adam stammered, visibly embarrassed.

"I'm not kidding when I say you've got to stop listening to all this 'by the book' crap. This guy is not standard. He's not going to materialize for you, just because you have his name."

"Agent Randall!" the head voice reprimanded. "Take your seat."

Claire conceded, sitting in her chair. Adam watched her as she wiped a strand of loose hair from her forehead. She glanced over at him, trying to contain her anger.

"Mr. . . . Portman," the head voice started, "you have something for us?"

Standing, Adam gathered his materials and took them with him to the end of the table, near Claire. She refused to look in his direction, although he tried several times to catch her eye. He felt uncomfortable starting this speech without speaking with her first, but she had refused to talk to him.

"I have three hypotheses regarding this particular profile. They have a few things in common, so I'll cover the commonalties first. We know from the physical evidence brought to us so far that he is a large man—larger than average. A height of six feet four inches, and a boot size thirteen wide. Approximately two hundred and fifty pounds. A healthy white male, perhaps in his late twenties, early thirties.

"Agent Randall is correct, however, when she states that he deviates from the normal serial killer in several ways, making his profile highly unpredictable and hard to analyze. He doesn't keep trophies from his kills, and he derives no sexual satisfaction from this scenario, that we are aware of. So the motivating factor here is not release, or compulsory need. This man is in control at all times. Which leads us to one conclusion—he is operating out of revenge."

Claire felt uncomfortable listening to Adam's calm words. Although she would agree with most of his assessment, she was having a hard time sitting still.

"The three theories I have come up with stand together in a cross section. One is that he is a relative of a victim. Two is that he is a police officer who has walked away from the line of duty for what he sees as a higher calling. And three is that he is a cop wanna-be, a frustrated young man searching for his place in the scheme of things. This third person is one who has a deep need to be appreciated by society and so he tries to validate himself through vigilante acts."

"And which theory would you lean toward at this point, Mr. Portman?" the head voice asked.

"Well, I have a personal theory, a fourth composite theory, if you will. I think that perhaps all three of these factors have somehow rolled into one situation. Lack of physical evidence at the scenes tells us that this man understands security procedures better than the average John Doe. That, along with his remarkable success in his use of disguises, tells us that he is taking elaborate precautions not to be recognized."

Adam turned to Claire for her reaction, and when he saw none, he drew in a deep breath and continued, gaining strength. He understood this killer better than anyone in the room right now, unless Claire wanted to open her mouth and admit that she knew more. So he pushed on.

"So ... what I'd say you got here is a cop who found himself stonewalled when it came to protecting his own family or a family member, so he went outside the law and used his own resources to seek justice. First time out, it worked. And then he heard what people said about his handiwork while they read their morning paper.

" 'Gee, that creep got what he deserved.' So he thinks that the people want this ... that they need this and just don't know it ...

"So he continues. And gets a little carried away. The Jewison case—the boy and girl inside the van—now either our guy is the luckiest son of a bitch alive to simply stumble on these guys, or that was something he had to be on the inside to know about. The news about the Polaroid only broke that same morning. So he goes after them. Once that mission was complete, he became a missing person himself—because he had to."

"But what about the thing in New Mexico—Mad Maxx? If this cop is from Arizona ..." someone interjected.

Claire peered across the table, trying to discern where the question had originated. At least one person in the room had been paying attention.

"That could easily have been handled in a half-day drive each way on a couple of days off."

"So why did he have to attack a police officer and assume his identity if he is a police officer?" another voice asked.

This one had his ears open too. Claire observed Adam's recovery with interest. "Not very smart to keep moving on in something as high-profile as a cop car from a different county. It wasn't his jurisdiction anymore." Adam used a map on the overhead to demonstrate his point.

"If you'll recall, the van moved from some point here, stopping at the Phoenix grocery store, then continued past Tucson, and was nearly to the Mexican border when our man caught up with them. He's crossed several county lines by then. Perhaps our man was off duty, spotted the van somewhere north of Phoenix, and followed it until he was sure. It would explain why that officer, Koplowski, was attacked—but not killed. He realized he needed the clothes to make the stop look good. And remember, the owner of the convenience store noticed that this man assumed correct police procedures at the gas station, to the letter."

"He probably just watches a lot of TV," someone joked.

"So why go after Cameron?" another inquired.

"Cameron was his breakthrough mission," Adam continued.

Although his words rang true to Claire, she wouldn't allow him the satisfaction of seeing her interest, so she kept her eyes forward while she listened.

"He realized the publicity generated by the van kidnappers had brought about a lot of support for his new vocation."

"And that is . . .?" someone asked.

"Enacting the punishment instead of enforcing the law."

"So are there any megalomaniacs conveniently missing from the Phoenix police department to fit your theory, Mr. Portman?" Claire interjected sarcastically.

"Well, no . . ." he had to admit.

Claire smiled victoriously, as Adam pulled forth a piece of paper from his collection of files and held it up so he could read it clearly.

"But Co-co-nee-no County," he pronounced with difficulty, "now they've got a missing man."

"What is that? An Indian reservation?" someone asked.

"No. That particular county is very large. It covers the northern third of the state. The man who's missing there, his name is Michael Corbett. He ... he could fit the description of our man in the photo here, with a little imagination."

A new image spread across the screen.

Claire saw the face of a clean-cut, all-American who had sometime not-so-long-ago graduated into manhood. His piercing blue eyes, the shock of darker brown, buzz-cut hair, appeared to be neatly packaged within his Arizona sheriff's uniform. He was smiling.

It was hardly the face of evil.

"Michael Corbett is six feet two inches and at his last physical, he weighed two-hundred-and-thirty-five pounds."

There was a pause in his delivery. The men shifted in their chairs.

"The shoe size, Mr. Portman?"

"Uh ... yes ... well, that's the part of the puzzle that might need some work, but it's still not completely out of the question."

"What is his shoe size?"

"Well, he's an eleven regular. But that can be masked. He's been attentive enough to detail to tell me that this piece could be a red herring to throw us all off the trail. There's too many other correlations," Adam reflected. Then, for Claire's benefit, he added, "You see, he did have a sister."

Claire waited, wondering where this was leading.

"She was beaten up and raped—then left for dead a couple years ago. But she lived. They never caught the guy who did it. She killed herself a month before Corbett disappeared."

The men in the room murmured in hushed tones, exchanging possible scenarios. Claire surveyed the committee members and then settled on Adam.

"The majority of this investigation now needs to be focused on isolating who and where the next target will be. Wherever the next big scene-stealing crime has taken place would be my guess. He needs the headlines to keep him going."

"Exactly." Claire spoke almost to herself.

"... Which at this time, appears to be here in Los Angeles."

Claire's head snapped from the velocity of her turn.

"The AIDS Rapist was caught only last night," Adam continued. "This particular rapist has eluded the authorities for over a year and has infected at least ten of his victims with the virus. And we don't know how many women slept with him voluntarily. At any rate, the media coverage went national last night. Our man should be heading out here in no time."

"So, do you think we should even try to lure him here and set a trap?" a voice from the dark challenged.

Claire could stay still no longer. "Wait a minute, wait a minute. What is this guy? A Ping-Pong ball? A coast-to-coast yo-yo? I don't believe he's going to give up on Cincinnati that easily. It's two balls in the corner pocket for him. That's the way he likes it."

"But why would he stay in the same area when he knows we're right behind him? That doesn't make sense," a voice from the dark countered.

"He knows we're right behind him, and that's the way he wants it. He's been leading us along now for the past three murders, and now he's ready for the big finish."

"Finish?!" Adam countered. "What do you mean?"

"This guy's not stupid, he knows his ride is almost over. He's only got one card left to play, and that's why he chose Cincinnati."

"And what qualifies you as the expert here, Randall?" Adam's temper finally flared.

"I'm not claiming to be the expert, Mr. Portman, you are. But I've been tracking him since Mad Maxx, and I think I have some insight into what he's ..."

"Insight?" Adam interrupted. "Now that's interesting. Let's elaborate on that for a moment."

Claire began to sweat. All eyes were on her, and the pit of her stomach started to churn.

"You seem to know this guy pretty well. Tell us, do you have some new information you're not sharing?"

"Everything's in my report." Claire backed down.

"Nothing new from Cincinnati?" Adam baited, waiting for her to snap.

"You have the latest."

"And you think this guy is just hanging around, waiting for you to return? That's pretty egotistical. Tell me, who could be the next possible—and according to you, final high-profile victim?"

"You know the answer to that. It's the Cop Killer, Eddie Jefferson."

A murmur went up around the room. It was obvious her case was weak. There was nothing more she could say. The sensational headlines the AIDS Rapist was getting had blown her chances to the moon.

"Randall, the Cop Killer—that's old news!" The paternalistic sound in Adam's voice was making Claire angry.

It was supposed to.

"Come on, there must be something more. Why don't you just go ahead and enlighten everyone here as to the real reason why you're recommending we continue with the Cincinnati leads."

Silence descended as Adam locked eyes with Claire. They were cold and forceful. He was going to push her over the edge, and there was little she could do to stop it.

"Unless, of course, you'd like me to explain it to them."

Claire rose from her chair so forcefully, it fell backward onto the floor. "All right, Portman, that's it. Out in the hall!"

The men at the table all sat in silence, shocked at her outburst.

"Agent Randall!" The head voice countered.

"Excuse us, gentlemen. We need to take this outside, it's personal," she told them.

Adam headed for the door ahead of her, his grin half-hidden from them. It had worked! Finally, she would have to talk to him.

"This should only take a second. Just . . . talk among yourselves—you're good at it." Claire added.

"Agent Randall!" The head voice commanded, full of outrage.

The outside door shut behind the two of them forcefully, leaving the gentlemen inside to draw their own conclusions.

Adam and Claire stood opposite each other in the hall.

"Boy, you still know how to throw a party, Randall. I mean ... *Jesus!*" His nervous appreciation of her ballsy exit made him suddenly resemble the Adam she used to know. Inside, it softened her for a moment, but she wouldn't let it slip to the exterior.

"Shut up!" she spat at him. "Just what were you trying to do in there?"

"You wouldn't talk to me."

"I don't *have* to talk to you. If we work the same case, that's one thing. But you can't force me to ..."

"You're *wrong* about Cincinnati. Why don't you just admit it?"

"I'm not wrong," she insisted.

"Then tell them what's going on."

"No."

"Tell them!"

"No!"

"Then tell *me.*" Adam offered, his voice taking on a softer tone. For the first time, their eyes met without the ice forming. For the first time ... they were talking.

"Claire, what are you so afraid of?"

Claire wouldn't answer.

"Claire, it's me. Just me. Come on."

"I can lose my job, Adam."

"For what? For being good at what you do?"

Claire shook her head, mildly embarrassed.

"Or for being psychic?"

The mere mention of the word was all it took to flip her switch. She flushed with anger, her voice booming down the corridor loudly. "I am *not* ..." and then she lowered the tone to barely a whisper, "... psychic. I'm wrong just as much as I'm right."

"You are not. I've been watching your work, Claire. You're lying to me. You use it plenty. You've had three promotions in two years."

"So what in the hell were you doing in there? You quoted my initial report almost word for fucking word!"

209

"Maybe. But you didn't know about the missing officer, now did you?"

Claire was silent. Her cheeks were hot, and her head was pounding.

"Why are you so hell-bent on Cincinnati? Is it something you've ... felt?"

With a tilt of her head, Claire decided to come clean.

"It led me to Arizona—and on to Cameron. That's all. I found some bits and pieces he left behind there."

"So he's still there, then."

Claire didn't reply. The uncertainty she now felt was growing every minute. On the plane she had begun to doubt herself more than she ever had before. And after listening to what Adam had put together about the cop in Arizona, she hated to admit that she could be completely wrong.

"What's the matter?"

"You act like I have such control over it. Like I've got X-ray vision or something. It's not that easy. It's not that focused."

"Why not?" It was more of an accusation than a question. "You've done it before."

Claire's eyes rose to meet his. "And someone I loved died because of it."

Adam took her shoulders roughly. The command in his voice was certain and strong. "You had nothing to do with Bernardi's death. He was ahead of himself and got sloppy. It could have happened on a hundred other cases, Claire."

But Claire wasn't prepared to admit that. "What I saw did no good. The girl was already dead, and Jim—he was shot and killed."

"But we got him, Claire. We got Levers! He might have gone out that very night and gotten another girl, but you helped stop it. You told us right where to find him."

Claire's silence brought her near to tears. Adam could see she was vulnerable, so he took the last shot. "Look, I can get you back to Cincinnati."

Claire looked suddenly hopeful but still wary of the cost.

"When I saw your name on this case, I knew there was going to be more to it. I knew you could get to him faster than anyone else. But when you missed in Cincinnati ..."

They exchanged an uneasy moment between them.

"This is a big one and I want him, Claire. Now I know you can help."

Claire stared at the floor and shifted her foot inside her shoe.

"If this guy moves like I think he does, then I would have called Cincinnati a pretty dry well after last night." He paused. "Well, is it?"

Her gaze remained on the floor for a moment longer. When she lifted them, there were tears in the corners.

"I'm ... not sure ..."

He nervously indicated the door behind them.

"So, what do I say to them? Can we work together on this, or do I pull the plug on Cincinnati completely? They'll go with whatever I recommend."

Claire looked Adam in the eye and studied his expression. This used to be someone she could trust—someone she knew. Could she still trust him?

Did she have a choice?

For a moment, Traask thought Jennifer must be having a bad dream. He sat bolt upright in bed, holding his breath, waiting for another sound to come to his ears. She must have cried out. He waited. And waited some more.

Nothing.

He lay his head back down on the pillow, uneasy with the certainty that he had heard something. But he had been sound asleep only moments before and had awakened with such a start that he was having a hard time telling the difference between his reality and any dream he might have been hosting.

He closed his eyes, taking a few cleansing breaths in an effort to calm his nerves. After all, it had been a long day, full of surprises, and he wasn't going to be worth two pounds of dog poop in the morning if he didn't relax and get some sleep.

The warmth gathered around him, and the quiet permeated his breathing. His chest rose and fell in an even rhythm again and a hazy cloud of sleep began to envelope his brain once more.

His eyes snapped open. That cry hadn't been for "Daddy." That voice cried out for "Dan." It was Claire's voice. And she was screaming.

18

'Ere Be Dragons
June 29th—Cincinnati Courthouse
08:12

"I understand what she sees in you, Traask. You're all right."

Joey's vote of approval was delivered as Traask led her along the construction site, past the men working and the stacks of materials piled up in giant looming masses, left there for later use. Clearing the rotunda entrance, they were soon swallowed up by the unfinished building. It was a fortress in the making. The roof was eight stories high at the apex. A full-length balcony capped a circular staircase that rounded down to end on the marble floor, which they crossed in hurried but measured steps.

The workmen paid them no mind.

"When did I change?" Traask inquired curiously.

"When you stopped being the enemy."

"When was that?"

"When I realized that Claire really needs someone like you."

Traask paused briefly before a curtain of large plastic

212

sheeting that separated the construction area from the rest of the facility. "Well ... thank you."

"We should be thanking Claire," she responded wryly. "If I hadn't been forced to stay behind here, I would never have faced you head-on. Not while Claire was around." Then she added, "You're really not so bad, after all."

Traask held up the plastic sheet for her to pass under. "You're not as formidable as I first thought, either."

"Oh?"

"No. When I first met you, I thought ... well, I thought ..."

"Thought what? Come on, I can take it."

"Okay. I thought you were a real bull-dyke bitch."

"What changed?"

"Nothing," he said. "Me, I guess. I was just plain wrong."

The compliment hit Joey hard. She struggled with it for a moment before surfacing with a snappy comeback. "Well, don't let anyone else in on it. I got a rep to protect."

The two of them walked in silence for a while until they entered the hallway that ran into the security desk. Traask checked them both in, and they passed through with little delay.

"Cappy tells me Jefferson is nervous. He doesn't like being away from the other inmates. He doesn't get anything this way." Traask told her.

"Any ... any what? Drugs?"

"Information."

Together they entered the secured area. There were two men at each end of the hallway and at every possible exit. Traask knocked on the door ahead of them, and it opened from inside.

"Oh, Traask. C'mon in."

Joey and Dan entered the observation room. With all the wizard electronics jammed into the small square footage, the room was hot and cramped. It had been built and operated solely to protect the Cop Killer—Eddie Jefferson—from the man the media had dubbed, "the Vigilante Killer."

Bennie Sarkissian and two other men had been assigned to oversee the installation of this little dungeon of electronics. And now they sat, waited, and watched—all to ensure the well-being of the Cop Killer.

He had been moved, per instructions by the FBI office, and was to be held in a special section of the courthouse during his trial. Meanwhile, the entire courthouse had become a secured area, from outside in. Hand-selected cops and FBI personnel stood armed, at every possible entry. There was no getting in or out without their authorization.

"Playing Nintendo again, huh?" Traask greeted them.

"Trying to beat your high score," Bennie retorted. "You haven't missed much. They haven't even started yet. Shouldn't you be gettin' around front by now?" Bennie asked.

Traask nodded. His testimony was scheduled for the morning docket.

"I was just sneaking in the back way," he told Bennie. "A little less tight a squeeze back there. It's hell getting past the front door."

"Hey, pal ... there ain't no sneakin' into this joint."

Bennie tapped lightly on the bank of security monitors before them. One displayed the back entrance Traask had been using to avoid the press. Bennie touched a button on the panel that activated the camera. It began to close in on the vehicles parked beyond.

"See? We even watched you pull in." Then he added once the car was in focus, "And that car needs a bath."

Traask shrugged apologetically, but he was impressed.

"So you've got everything under control in here, I see. How is our boy?" Traask inquired.

The group's attention shifted to the left-center monitor, on which they could clearly see Eddie Jefferson sitting in his room at a small desk, an officer standing at either side of him. Two small speaker boxes were visible in the background.

"He's okay. He's nervous. He liked it better back in the cell block."

"I know. But this is infinitely safer."

"Tell *him* that," Bennie instructed, pushing the microphone toward Traask.

"What does he do in there all day?" Joey asked.

"Well, he's supposed to be listening to his own trial. He can hear everything that's going on in there with the new sound system."

Traask excused himself, making his way out of the small room. "You'll meet us at the break?"

Bennie nodded. "We gotcha covered."

Joey and Traask exited the room and made their way past the double security detail outside the door to Jefferson's chamber. The faces there were somber and all business. Nothing could be more serious.

Once past that corridor, security was less conspicuous, and by the time they reached the lobby area, it was nearly absent.

"Where is everyone?" Joey asked.

As they rounded the last corner, they could see what had happened. Officers lined the front entrance of the building, shoulder to shoulder, effectively sealing off the building. Only special escort officers were allowed to transport the necessary people in or out of the building.

The insanity was outside, on the steps of the courthouse. Television, radio, and newspaper reporters pressed up against the glass to catch sight of any activity inside. From this distance, the mob seemed nearly silent as they fought and argued among themselves for position. It was a class act, all right.

Traask and Joey exchanged humorous glances. "Jesus, they're like a bunch of sardines!" He pointed her toward the door to the courtroom, and they entered.

It was late afternoon, and the Hall of Justice was beginning to heat up. It was practically on overload. Huge portable fans whirled to help circulate the air, since the air-conditioning system had been shut down during the renovation project. Humidity was high, and people were beginning to feel uncomfortable.

Dan Traask was one of them. He had been enduring a difficult cross-examination from the defense since after the lunch break. This attorney was tough on procedure. He continually forced Dan to restate his actions and elaborate on his intentions. As the arresting officer, Dan had to explain with pinpoint accuracy everything that had taken place that night—hoping that this son of a bitch would realize just which side his badge was buttered on.

But as he was finishing the grueling ordeal, Dan's attention was distracted. Something in the courtroom caught his attention, and he stopped talking altogether. It was Deborah Morrison.

She was sitting on the far side of one of the benches in the gallery. Her face was somber. When she saw that Dan had lost his train of thought, she looked away, embarrassed that his attention had been diverted by her presence.

He knew why she was there. This was as much Frank's trial as it was the Cop Killer's. If things had been different, it could have been Frank up there giving testimony.

Somehow . . . Frank was with them all today.

"Lt. Traask," the prosecutor prodded him, jarring Dan back to reality.

Traask continued with the testimony.

Finally, the prosecutor closed his questioning, and Dan was excused from the stand. As he rose to leave, he saw the double doors at the back of the courtroom open, and two figures entered. One was a man he didn't recognize. The other was Claire Randall.

She appeared pale and worn. From this distance, she seemed to move differently. Although he couldn't yet explain it, he felt that she had changed. She smiled a tired, yet genuine, smile, unable to let him know what she had been through since they had been apart. She stopped just inside the courtroom and waited for him to come to her.

Deborah had caught Dan's change in expression and followed his gaze to the back of the room. She could catch only a glimpse of Claire from this angle. But Deborah watched as Dan crossed quickly to her and took her arm in his. The way he held on to her, the way he seemed to take her to him, confirmed to Deborah they had something between them. This kind of possessiveness was not easily demonstrated by the man she knew, so she could tell that whatever he had complained about earlier regarding Claire was by now in the past.

Another, taller woman now moved to Traask's side and ushered the small group into the hallway.

Deborah again faced forward. As she did so, she took into account that she was glad that Dan Traask's attentions had finally been engaged by another woman.

And she couldn't help but be curious about this new influence in his life.

"I'm parked in the back. This way. We can avoid the press."

Once out in the lobby, Traask led them away from the front doors, away from the mob outside. They headed down the corridor toward the security area. They moved quickly as a group—working from a common understanding that they needed to get the hell out of there, quickly.

The stranger at Claire's side was already barking out orders as they moved along. "We'll want to make a statement, though. As soon as possible."

"I see you brought more reinforcements," Traask commented, indicating the man at Claire's side who seemed overly concerned about obtaining media coverage.

He was taller than Traask, and he dressed well. Too well.

Claire exchanged glances with the new guy. With a glance, she warned him, *Later.*

And it was not negotiable.

"Adam Portman, Washington Bureau, Behavioral Sciences Division," Claire introduced, without much fanfare. "He's here to ... to supervise."

The group stopped on a dime.

"You're Adam?!" Joey's shock was not easily hidden.

Claire sighed, reluctant to get into a lengthy explanation, but Joey was already sizing Adam up. Eight years had made Adam formidable. He was well trained. His confidence was high and his charm impeccable. He held out his hand to Joey, and they shook, much to Claire's surprise.

"Good to finally meet you," Adam said, hoping the diversionary move would break the ice that was threatening to crash down on them all. "I've followed your career with interest. I consider it a pleasure to have you on our team." He was clearly going to assume control from the very beginning.

He turned to Traask. "You must be Lt. Traask. Claire has told me a lot about you on the plane, but I remember reading about you last year. You've had your hands full over here, I see."

Traask found himself wishing he knew what the hell was going on here. He saw the quizzical looks being exchanged between Joey and Claire, and suddenly felt like an outsider to some sort of privileged information. Why was this guy suddenly in charge?

"We've got some new information I'd like to go over as soon as possible. Do you think we could arrange to get some space set aside here in the courthouse? I'd like to be as close to the action as possible while we're ..." Adam began, then trailed off.

Claire's attention wasn't with them any longer.

Off Adam's lead, the group turned to watch as Claire had walked away, looking back down the corridor from which they had just come. She locked on to an image no one else saw.

Frozen with a trancelike stare, she was completely focused on the lobby area now, and something there seemed to be guiding her toward it. She followed images that seemed to be moving past, although nothing was visible to the others.

"Claire?" Traask called to her. "What's wrong?"

The color had drained from her face, appearing panicked and ill. She was unable to speak.

"You okay?" Adam queried. He stepped out of the group to her side.

Suddenly the two men were both vying for her attention like two beaux at a school dance. They surrounded her, demanding answers. And she didn't want to face either one of them. Joey moved in, brushing past the men and hooked her arm protectively through Claire's.

"Hey, back off you two." Joey commanded, leading her

partner away toward the restrooms. "Come on, let's take a little time-out."

As the two girls moved on, Traask turned to Adam.

Both had realized from the moment of their meeting that there was much more here than a working relationship—on either side of the coin—and that it might get a bit uncomfortable from here on out. Claire was their common ground. Without her, they had little to say to one another.

Inside the restroom, Claire splashed some cold water on her face and wiped it dry. Joey waited for her by the door.

"You all right?"

"Yes, yes, I'm fine," Claire mumbled.

Joey flashed a menacing glare toward the door of the bathroom, as if to ward off Adam. She handed Claire some more paper toweling. Claire took it, thankfully, wiping her mouth with a shaky hand.

"Tell me this is the result of bad airline food."

"I didn't eat on the plane," Claire replied, checking herself out in the mirror.

"What's going on here, Claire?" Joey asked seriously. She hovered about, trying to find a way to get through to her partner. "What is it with him and you? What's the connection?"

"I can't explain it, Joey. It's—something happened in L.A. Something big."

"What?"

Claire didn't want to go into an explanation here. Joey didn't believe in hocus-pocus. She didn't believe in luck or insight. She definitely wouldn't believe that Claire allowed Adam to hypnotize her in her hotel room last night. So she avoided it all by hitting it head-on.

"I know how we're going to catch him, Jo."

19

All This, Inside of One Kiss
June 29th—Regency Hotel, Cincinnati, Suite 2117
17:30

"It'll take a few days to get everything set up the way I want it, but it appears I'm getting the cooperation I need out here," Adam said.

They had gone directly to the hotel where Joey had been staying, and made arrangements to procure adjacent suites, with a main living area that would double as their office and base camp.

Adam finished his call and sat down at the small desk in the corner where Claire's laptop was waiting. Clearly, he didn't need permission to move in and take over, he just did it. He began flipping through files and activating the modem link to the central office.

There was a couch and two casual chairs, a small wet bar and an entertainment center where the TV was tuned to CNN, volume off. Traask stood nearby, occasionally glancing up at the door to the bedroom where Joey had disappeared with Claire. The door had closed behind them, and they hadn't come out for a while now.

"You're really sure this guy's still here—in Cincinnati . . ."

Traask began, wanting some reassurance. Nobody had been doing much talking.

Adam cocked his head at Traask as he peered over the laptop. "You're not?"

"No, I'm not convinced. And I was told you didn't think so either."

Adam had resumed typing, but couldn't dismiss that remark so easily. He paused at the keyboard, irritated. "Well, let's just say that I wasn't completely convinced . . ."

"So what changed your mind?"

Adam stopped. If he didn't try to explain, his greatest adversary could turn out to be Traask. It would be so much simpler if everyone understood.

"I've worked with Claire before. In Washington, a few years ago. There was a case there, locally. She had a few . . . ideas about it. With her help, we were able to find him—and stop him.

"He was something, real leading-edge slime. Somebody wrote a book about him, and I think there was a movie of the week . . . you know, the Levers case?" Adam tossed out the information casually.

But there wasn't anything casual about it. It was intentional. Adam had an agenda.

Traask didn't like it. "You don't mean Barry Levers—the satanic guy with the dogs, and the girls in the basement?"

"Yeah . . ." Adam continued without any fanfare. "I take it she hasn't told you much about it."

Adam was staking out his territory, clearly marking out his prior history with Claire so there was no mistaking which man had been in her life first.

"No. She hasn't." Traask admitted. Then he thought about it. "Wasn't an FBI agent killed in the arrest?"

"Yeah," Adam stated flatly. His eyes didn't meet with Traask's. "He was a friend of ours—mine and Claire's. More a good friend of hers . . . if you get my meaning."

"Oh. I'm sorry," Traask offered, diplomatically. He understood all too well. Claire's lover had died. Traask shot a glance over to the bedroom door where she had disappeared for sanctuary.

"Don't feel bad. We haven't talked about it, either." Adam tapped the laptop twice and sighed, clearing his memory. "But, anyway—she's good, you know—at what she does? We have to trust her. If she thinks the guy we're looking for is still here, then . . ."

His glance wandered to the television for a moment. On the screen was a report on Ramone Mendez, the AIDS Rapist.

Both their attentions were immediately diverted. Work came first for both of them.

Traask pointed to it as he spoke, "Now there's someone to go after. His last victim was a fourteen-year-old girl."

"I know," Adam said, watching the screen for a moment. He was still clearly torn. His gut instinct was the same as Traask's. But Claire had been able to change all that in a matter of minutes.

"I would think you guys would be preparing over there as well . . ." Traask commented.

"We are. Turn it up . . . I think this is it," Adam instructed, indicating the TV.

Traask worked the remote to bring up the volume. The picture had changed, and what was now on the screen was the image of the Cincinnati courthouse from earlier in the day. The face of a network correspondent appeared in the corner.

"Startling events are unfolding here in Cincinnati this week. Only four days ago, police entered the apartment of Kenneth Marlovich to discover the unspeakable house of horrors within. On Wednesday, Marlovich was found murdered in a holding room inside the Northside Precinct. Evidently, the killer entered the precinct in disguise—claiming to be the writer who was preparing research material on Marlovich—and killed him in cold blood, escaping the precinct without a clue. Today, the FBI released a statement indicating they believe that the man who dismembered Eric Cameron, and the man who rescued the children south of Tucson, Arizona, by disguising himself as a motorcycle police officer is, indeed, the same man that murdered Kenneth Marlovich only two days ago.

"In the written statement, FBI officials admitted to having information that suggests that the killer had been headed for Cincinnati, but were unable to ensure that adequate security was provided for Marlovich in time.

"The real question is, will he strike again in Cincinnati? Public opinion locally was mixed."

The picture changed to a sidewalk interview session. A man with a newspaper in his hand was commenting.

"You know this guy is going for the real sickos, so why waste his time here? I mean there's plenty of them out there . . ."

The reporter countered, "Yes, but what about the fact that he's been attacking the accused before they've been brought to trial . . . before they've had due process?"

The man shrugged, "Hey, that Cameron guy got his due process. That should only go so far, you know? We probably never would have known about the cabin in the woods—so that's another guy who would have just walked away."

The reporter continued, "So you think it's a good thing, what he's doing?"

"Oh, yeah . . . definitely."

Another interview. A workingwoman on her way back to the office. The reporter filled her in. "And what do you think of the fact that one man has been reported to have committed all these murders?"

"Well, they're not exactly murders, now, are they? I mean, when you use the term 'murder'—you never refer to 'capital punishment,' do you? I think that's how he's thinking."

"Do you agree with it? What's he's doing?

"Well, I don't know . . . I don't think we should have people out there just running around killing people at random. But it is what the police do sometimes, isn't it? At least he just kills the guilty ones, the ones who deserve it."

"What about his next target? What if the Cop Killer, Eddie Jefferson, is the next to go?"

"Well, he is guilty. He confessed, didn't he? That's a lot different than someone about whom there's some doubt.

How many people does a man have to kill to deserve being put to death?"

The reporter came back on the screen.

"And earlier today, one of the local affiliates was able to get a brief interview with the wife of one of the Cop Killer's victims."

The face of Deborah Morrison appeared before them. She was moving away from the camera in a hurry, but it pursued her.

Traask froze, his expression changing to one of concern. It was undeniably Holly North's voice calling after her.

"Jesus Christ . . ." he murmured.

Deborah's name appeared, in the standard white letters below her face on the screen. Adam's attention was briefly torn from the set as he observed Traask's worried expression.

"Mrs. Morrison, Mrs. Morrison, what do you say about the allegations that your husband's murderer might be the next target of the Vigilante Killer?"

Deborah tried to wave her off.

"Do you know that public support for this kind of action is running quite high? How do you feel about people calling this man a hero?"

Deborah finally turned to comment. She was clearly trying to control her emotions. She knew what Holly North was implying. Frank Morrison had never been called a hero. He had been considered an outlaw by most. He had not followed orders. Now here comes another man that isn't following orders, and he is everybody's hero?

She approached Holly, carefully choosing her words. She did not want the anger inside to take control of her.

"This man . . . this hero you all are going on about, he's not what you think he is. He's not doing you a favor. My husband died because of Eddie Jefferson. There's no question about that. A lot of good men died by his hand. But my husband believed in the system."

"Is that why he joined the group known as the 'Enforcers'—because he believed in the system?"

"Frank Morrison was being ripped to pieces by this Cop

Killer. He lost good friends to that maniac's bullets. He couldn't eat, he couldn't sleep ... all he wanted to do was stop this man so no other cop would get hurt. But he would not have assumed the role of the judge and the jury. He knew where his part in it ended and where the court system began. He just wanted to do his job and catch the man. That's all."

"Your husband was a police officer, but he went out to track a killer and bring him to justice on his own. Isn't that strikingly similar to what this man is doing?"

"This man is murdering people in cold blood. Some of them, he's torturing. Are you implying my husband would have done that, or endorsed that?"

"What would your husband have said about a man like that?"

Holly was pumped with adrenaline, goading Deborah to continue. This was hot stuff. She could hardly believe her luck.

"My husband would have thought ... my husband felt that there are many gray areas within the law. He knew that playing by the rules didn't always work, and that some of the time, some of the time you had to bend them to help the good side to win. But this vigilante ... he's not bending, he's breaking. If we truly wanted to endorse this kind of thing, then we'd say, 'Screw the system,' and we'd be a nation of Dirty Harrys. Where would it end—your neighbor plays his music too loud, so you shoot him?!"

Deborah paused and took a deep breath. *Slow down. Don't lose control here.* "I've been on both sides now. I've been the wife of a victim, and the wife of an Enforcer. And as a victim, I'm telling you—it's very tempting to want to see Eddie Jefferson get what he deserves. He killed my husband—he has confessed that it was premeditated murder. But as the wife of an Enforcer ... I've seen what can happen. This madness has to be stopped."

Deborah broke from Holly's reach and stepped quickly away. Holly did not attempt to pursue her. She had gotten what she wanted.

Traask turned from the television and scanned the room

for a phone. Moving quickly toward it, he didn't notice that Adam had been watching his response to the broadcast with keen interest.

The bedroom door opened, and Joey stepped into the room quietly, pulling it shut as she entered. She seemed concerned.

It made Traask stop just inches from the table that held the phone. He pointed the remote to the set and muted the sound, cutting off Holly.

"How is she?" he asked.

"Oh, she's okay. A bit tired. She needs some rest."

"She didn't get much sleep last night," Adam remarked casually.

This comment hit both Traask and Joey. It appeared they were supposed to assume that Claire had slept with him.

Both Traask and Joey didn't care for his insinuation, their combined stare let Adam know it.

But Adam wasn't paying attention to them. He was already on-line with the Washington mainframe and was wasting valuable computer time.

Traask broke the moment. "Well, I need to be going."

Objecting, Joey moved with him, "You're leaving?"

Her eyes shot over to Adam accusingly. Traask understood and cocked his head apologetically.

"I have to get my kid to the airport by seven. She's flying back to California tonight."

"Oh," Joey mumbled, rather disappointedly. Her distaste at the thought of being left alone with Adam had been made clear to Traask.

"I can come back after . . ." he offered.

He was beginning to wonder if he should warn Joey to leave Adam in identifiable pieces, at least.

"No, no need. We can regroup in the morning. Everyone ought to get a good night's sleep. It may be our last for a while." She gave him one of her rare smiles.

He nodded in return. She pushed him gently toward the suite's double-door entry, walking with him. Her voice lowered as she spoke. "I don't trust this asshole."

"I know. There's something both of them aren't telling us."

The look on Joey's face betrayed the fact that she still knew more than he did and was not at liberty to discuss it.

"Yeah, well, don't worry about that. I'll call you if anything comes up."

"Tell Claire I was planning to take her to Chinese tonight, but . . ."

"No way. Then she'll never get to sleep."

Traask needed to get going. He shot one last glance at Adam, who didn't bother to look up from the computer, even when the door opened.

Traask paused, looking Joey in the eye. "Go easy on him."

"Who . . . me?"

They both broke out in a smile.

Traffic was heavy as Traask threaded his way back from the airport by himself. A drizzly summer rain had just begun falling as he pulled onto the loop that would take him off the highway and onto a shortcut of busy side streets. The highway was a nightmare, and he was in no mood for stop and go tonight.

His mind was wandering. He was thinking about Adam and the Levers case—about Claire's involvement. His first thought was to pull some strings here locally and get ahold of the file on the case—if he could. He wanted to know more about it.

More about Claire's dead lover, you mean.

He shook it off for a moment. Did it matter so much? No, not really. But there was something else within the framework of this question—something else in her past, in this case that was nagging at him now, and he wasn't going to let it rest. He made a mental note to speak to his FBI liaison tomorrow morning. Maybe he could get them to whistle down a few particulars for him to browse through.

Meanwhile, traffic was going to be a bitch. He turned his air-conditioning to maximum cold. He switched radio stations five times. He hummed along with a song he hated.

But his thoughts kept returning to Claire.

*   *   *

Sleep was not coming easy to her. She was exhausted. Beyond exhausted, actually. But Claire never had been the type to nap during the day. Not even as a child. She had been an insomniac since birth.

Joey entered the room as quietly as she could, only to find Claire sitting up on the edge of the bed. "What are you doing awake?" Joey admonished in a whisper.

"What time is it?" Claire asked, reaching halfheartedly across the bed for her watch on the table.

"It's just after seven."

"P.M.?" She inquired, making sure.

There were heavy drapes on the windows in the suite. It could very well be the next morning for all she knew.

"Yes, P.M." Joey confirmed.

Claire held her watch in her hands, not yet ready to put it on. She appeared deep in thought.

"You're not going to rest, are you?" It was more of a statement than a question. Joey was getting testy. "Look, I don't do this mother hen bit very well. I'm more likely to slap you upside the head than sing you a lullaby. Why are you getting up?"

"It's okay, I'll be fine. What's going on out there?"

"Portman is jacking off the computer again. He wants to call a meeting for six A.M. I let him know that we could all use a good night's sleep, so he switched it to seven."

"Generous to a fault, that one," Claire murmured, dropping the watch in her lap and running her hands through her hair. She paused, massaging her temples for a moment. "What about Traask?"

"He had to go the airport—something about putting his kid on a plane?"

Claire nodded, remembering he had mentioned it earlier. She flexed the muscles in her shoulders and back to try to loosen up.

Joey moved closer. "You gonna talk to me about this or do I just have to keep on guessing?"

Their eyes met for an instant, and then Joey sat down next to Claire on the bed. Claire was unused to this kind of request. Usually her partner was all business. She had never demanded to be let in on the personal side. Claire appreciated this. It made them a good team. Neither one of them had had much of a personal life to speak of anyway.

But now . . . that was changing.

Claire shook her head in denial. "I'm not sure I can answer that. What specifically do you need to know?"

Joey took offense. "I'm not asking you if you've slept with him, for Christ's sake. I don't care about the details. I'm not asking for that, and you know it."

"Then what do yo want to hear?"

Joey sighed loudly. "You can really be one cold, stone bitch sometimes, Randall. It's the part about you I love and hate the most, I think. What in the hell do you think I want to know?! Are you going to be coming home with me to Dallas when this is over or is a reassignment request to Cincinnati in your future? Not that it matters after so many years, but I've gotten pretty used to seein' your face in the morning, if you know what I mean."

"You really think it's that serious?" Claire asked with a bemused tone, but her eyes refused to rise to meet her partner's.

"Hey, when someone's been on the love wagon as long as you have, they don't just fall off one night when nobody's looking then get back on and pretend nothing happened. Usually, when they fall off—they fall for good," Joey surmised, trying to make the conversation easier. "If you ask me, you've fallen pretty far and pretty hard."

"How can you tell?" Claire asked with genuine interest, a smile playing about her lips as if she were testing her friend.

"I can tell," Joey said with a note of finality. "I know you—maybe too well. And . . . I've been waiting for this."

For the first time since Dan's name had been mentioned, Claire met her partner's eyes. "Waiting for this? Waiting for *what?*"

"Waiting for you to find someone. To let someone in. Your walls are so high sometimes, I think nobody's gonna have the strength to climb them. And what are they gonna find on the other side, huh? Just a bunch of rabbit trails where you've retreated back down that hole."

Claire was astonished at Joey's assessment. Her partner was shooting now with pinpoint accuracy, and she knew it.

"Then I see this guy come along, and I think, is he the one? Can he do it? Does he have what it takes to keep this girl from running? And I see Traask and I think, *damn!* If she lets this one get away, she's fucking nuts!"

An involuntary chuckle overtook both of them from the sheer comedy within her words. But they were true, and Claire knew it.

"He wanted to take you out to that Chinese place tonight, but I told him you'd take a rain check."

"Is their food really that good?"

"Brings me to tears to tell you, but it's one I had to write down in my book."

Joey had a listing of restaurants that she kept in a little black book she always brought along on out-of-town trips. She kept a "Good" list and a "Bad" list on every town they'd ever been in. She also kept a list of "recommended places," but she rarely had to refer to it. If she wrote it down, that meant that it was well worth going back to.

Joey groaned in protest as she crossed to her jacket, carelessly tossed across a chair from earlier in the day, and pulled forth the little black book. She flipped to the appropriate page and thrust it at Claire.

"Go on, take it. I can see you're not going to do us any good moping around here. If I can't talk some sense into you, then maybe he can. But you might want to reconsider any big seduction scenes until you've had a chance to catch a shower and some shut-eye. You look like hell, you know."

"I know."

Claire reached up for the tiny book and eyed the scrawled address warily. She gave Joey a long appreciative look.

"Thanks, Jo."

"Aw, what the hell," she mused. "I'll go make conversation with dickless out there so you can make a clean break of it. No sense in him asking a lot of stupid questions about what you do with your personal time."

Joey approached the door, then returned with concern.

230

"But if he sees you, he's gonna wanna keep you here, you know. That means no time to clean yourself up ..."

"It's okay, I'll manage," Claire reassured.

"And in the morning, I'll tell him you, uh—you got up early and must have gone out to get some breakfast, eh?" Joey added with a wink. "I bet you left me a note that said you'd meet us at the courthouse."

Claire smiled at her. "However did you know?"

"I got this thing in my head. It tells me things sometimes," Joey mused. "See, hanging out with you for so long has kind of rubbed off on me. Now *I'm* predicting things."

Claire flushed hotly. Joey patted her shoulder. "It's okay. Don't get your knickers in a twist. I'm just joking."

"Thanks," Claire said sullenly.

"No problem," Joey replied, then lowered her voice as she once again approached the door. "But you owe me big time for having to be nice to the jerk-off in the next room."

"I'll make it up to you," Claire promised in a low tone.

"Yeah, and I'll dance at your wedding," Joey whispered sarcastically as she opened the door. And then she was gone.

Claire rose wearily to claim her flight bag, stuffing a few items of clean clothes inside it. Fastening her watch to her wrist, she knew that Traask should be back from the airport soon and would more than likely be headed straight home. So the plan was to surprise him there with the food.

But what if he didn't show? What if he went somewhere else? She had his pager number. She could call and set it all up ...

No. It was going to be more fun this way. She wanted to surprise him. She wanted to make the effort. She used the telephone to call in a take-out order, and then she was ready to go.

Pausing at the bedroom door, she listened for Joey's voice to let her know Portman was sufficiently distracted, and then she silently crept out of the suite's double doors and into the hallway beyond.

It was raining. The clouds had opened over Cincinnati, and the drizzle came down upon her. She hailed a cab.

If the Fates were with her at all, she told herself, then Dan Traask would be at his apartment, waiting for her.

The cabby knew the name of the restaurant and didn't need the address. Within minutes the car was parked outside the storefront, and Claire was running through the rain in search of her take-out order.

If the Fates were with her at all ... she assured herself, she would be able to trace the route to Traask's apartment from the station house, just as they had the night they first met.

If the Fates were with her, she'd spend the night in Dan's embrace.

As the cabby pulled up in front of his apartment house, she wondered what she would say to him when he asked about their relationship.

If the Fates were with her, she would find the words.

If the Fates were with her.

Traask was surprised to see Deborah Morrison's car sitting in the garage of his apartment building when he returned from the airport.

Climbing out of his own vehicle, he saw her reach over and unlock the passenger door of the family station wagon and wave for him to climb in.

"I thought I could catch Jennifer before she left. I had a present for her."

She handed over a brightly wrapped package.

"That's sweet of you, Deb."

"Maybe ... maybe you could sent it to her."

"I will."

The silence that enveloped the car made them realize that this wouldn't be easy.

"I ... I saw the news," he stated, rather tentatively. "I'm sorry I didn't wait for you. Maybe I could have helped you today."

He was searching for the right words to make his feelings known.

"I've avoided them all enough this past year. Someone had to tell them."

Traask knew what she meant, but knew it was probably the hardest thing she had ever done. "I'm sorry, Deb."

"So am I ... because after all that, I still didn't really tell them the truth."

She seemed to want to get this off her chest. He knew she was filled with the pent-up emotions she had been suppressing, and he anticipated that what she'd have to say would not be easy for him or for her.

"Not really. Not how I truly feel. I want that son of a bitch Jefferson to rot in hell. I want that guy, whoever he is, to come in here and drag Jefferson off into the desert, light him on fire, chop his arms off—all of it. I want Eddie Jefferson to know what it's like to feel real pain."

Traask watched as a tear ran down her cheek. She was gripping the steering wheel in front of her tightly.

"I said all that other stuff for Frank. And ... for you."

"Deborah ..."

Deborah's defenses began to disintegrate. Tears welled up, and she made no attempt to hide them.

"Oh Dan, I hate him! I want him dead, I want him dead!"

Traask reached out, taking Deborah into his arms. She was sobbing uncontrollably now, her angry fists pounding Traask's shoulders, powerless to change what had happened.

"Oh Deborah, don't ... shhh, don't. Hey, I loved Frank. He was family to me. But you know, he did what he needed to do. I'll never understand it. Part of me wants to ... but it's the same part of me that is glad he never asked me to join him. And I gotta respect him for that decision, no matter what."

Deborah nodded, bravely. She was gathering courage from his words. Her sobbing had slowed, and she was just crying softly now.

"As much as I hated to see it, Holly North made the networks tonight. But in doing so, she made your words go national. It'll help, Deb ... it will help."

"But Dan, what if ..." she cried.

"It doesn't matter," he reassured her. "Shhh, everything's gonna be okay. I promise."

It was quiet here. The parking garage was dimly lit, so

sitting there together in the shadows, they held hands in silence for several minutes.

"Thank you," she said.

"Anytime," he replied.

"You are a good man, Daniel Traask. Sometimes ... I think, too good." She paused before finishing. "And I hope she can appreciate it."

Traask was not following her. "Huh?"

Deborah nodded toward the entrance to the elevators. Traask's head turned to follow.

There stood Claire Randall, with two large take-out bags of what he could only assume was the Chinese food he had promised her. She entered the elevator without seeing them.

Now it was his turn to sigh. A long one.

Deborah shrugged. "Go on. I'll be okay." And she meant it.

Claire was waiting at his door, just about to knock, when Traask came bounding down the hall toward her.

"Claire!" he called out.

She was startled. But when she saw it was him, she recovered quickly, holding out the two take-out bags like a trophy.

"How did you ... ?"

"Joey told me the name of the place. I couldn't let you duck out of this one."

He nodded at her determination, then fished out his keys, opening the door.

"I thought you weren't feeling well. I was told you needed some rest."

"So I rested."

They entered the apartment and hoisted the bags to his kitchen counter.

Later, the two of them were sitting on the floor of his living room, between the coffee table and the couch, using the low table's surface as a serving tray. Their appetites had been voracious, and they were surprised to find they had devoured most all the food without difficulty—and without stopping.

"I hope this was okay for you. I didn't know what you liked, so I ordered all my favorites."

"You did good. You did all right. I'm a Mongolian beef kind of guy . . . and their egg rolls are the best in Cincinnati. Well, I'd say that at least in the eating category, we've proven ourselves fairly compatible. My ex-wife hated Chinese."

"Oooo . . . too bad."

There was a quiet interlude. Traask pushed his empty cartons forward on the coffee table and rested his weight against the couch. He was feeling full and a bit drained from the day's events.

Claire was finishing her last two bites of pork fried rice. She twisted her fork into the rest, thoughtfully. "I'm sorry about today."

"Sorry . . . for what?"

"I didn't mean to cause such a scene."

"You didn't. It wasn't a big deal. Just forget about it."

Claire wished she could. She sighed and joined him. Side by side, they rested against the couch, allowing their necks to be supported by the edge of its seat cushion. They shared one of those "oh-so-good" feelings as they sat profile to profile.

"So. You okay now?"

Claire sighed again. Her reluctance to answer immediately told him she wasn't. "I'll get over it."

"That's what Adam said."

"Well, he's right."

"I get the feeling he likes to be right."

"Yes. Yes he does." She replied, clearly amused.

"So . . . what is it with him? He acts so . . ." Traask hedged, knowing full well he was headed into uncharted waters. "Pardon me for asking, but were you and he ever . . . ?"

"Romantically involved? Whatever gave you that impression?" She asked, her voice suddenly carrying an undertone of indignation. Then she jumped to conclusions with the smolder of a growing fire. "Did he tell you that?"

"No . . . no, he didn't say that," Traask admitted, "not in so many words. He'd like me to think it, though."

"That little shit," she fumed, gathering her energies to rise and stand beside the couch. Her hands automatically found their way to her hips as she stood—accused.

Traask felt as if he'd blown it. He shouldn't have pressured her, but he wanted to know more about everything. Joey knew her, Adam knew her. He needed to know, too.

"Hey—hey!" Traask approached from his still-seated position on the floor. In a soothing manner, he reached up to take her hand in his. "We don't have to talk about him. It's not important."

"Yes it is. Day by day you seem to be getting the wrong impression about me, and I . . . I'm tired of defending myself to you. You need to . . . I want you to . . ."

She faltered and withdrew from his grasp, feeling a wave of emotion overcome her. She turned away from him and started for the kitchen.

Then she stopped. With her back to him, she paused, unable to go farther, unwilling to step back. A silence enveloped the room as they both waited for her to speak. When she did, her voice was unsure and shaking.

"I—I want you to know. I want you to know . . . about me."

Traask wanted to cross to her, take her in his arms, and tell her to forget it. He wanted to make her forget it—erase whatever unpleasantness was seated in her mind and replace it with only thoughts of the two of them.

But instead, he sat—unmoving. Because he understood her. He had to give her what she wanted—what she needed right now. And what she needed more than anything was his understanding and patience, and these things he was only too glad to give her. He had private things of his own—things that reared their heads now and then and reminded him that in an instant, things can change. Terrible things. And change is often the hardest thing to live with.

If this was about her lover—the one that died back in Washington so many years ago, he wanted to hear it. Somehow . . . somehow he knew she needed to work this through. Whatever it was—it wasn't quite buried yet. Perhaps, with some patience, he could be the one to help her walk through it, move past it, and on to a new beginning.

Patience was paying off. She had moved to the kitchen counter, her hands resting on top of her briefcase, as if she had a purpose standing over there. But she didn't. She simply needed room for the emotion to wash over her and be done with it.

"First—Adam Portman is about as far from my type as they come. I never have, nor will I ever be interested in him. We were friends—once. A long time ago. That's all. He's got a lot of gall saying something like that to you."

Traask nodded, "I think I know how he feels."

"Well, it's not how I feel," she snapped. Her anger was building. This was not how she expected to spend her evening with Traask.

"Well, now we've ruled out that I'm not a lesbian and that I haven't been sleeping with Portman. So I guess that just leaves who have I slept with?"

"We don't have to go into this if—"

"Just tell me, what else did Portman say?" She demanded with a grinding, punishing edge, as if she were regretting the answer to the question in advance.

"He told me about the Levers case ... how you worked together in Washington on that one, awhile back. Tough case. I didn't know you were a part of it."

Claire's face clouded with her subtle nod, affirming her involvement. She did not expect this. She was surprised that Adam had time to be so forthcoming with Traask about their past.

"He said that you had a friend that was killed in the arrest." He waited for her response, and when it didn't come, he added, "He said it was a close friend. I'm sorry." When again she didn't respond, he let down the ropes and allowed her an escape route. "If this is too personal ... if you don't want to tell me about it, I'll understand."

"It's ... it's not that," she replied, trying to find the words. But she could not find a way to describe the guilt she felt over losing James Bernardi the way they did. She shook it off. She had to finish. "He had no right to tell you about that," she started, her strength gathering again. Her face became impassive for a moment, then fixed and determined.

"There hasn't been anyone in my life for years, Dan. Just . . . the work." She admitted with a sigh.

And he could tell that she was admitting it painfully. Perhaps regretfully.

"There's been no 'Adams,' no 'Jo Anns,' just the work. I've been burying myself in it, trying to escape something, something I blame myself for. It's my own form of punishment, I guess. But when I met you . . . for the first time, I felt like all that wasn't going to be necessary anymore."

Their eyes met, and she attempted to smile.

"I may be difficult and demanding—secretive at times, but with reason. I think you know what I mean. It comes with the job."

He nodded.

"But I want you to know that . . . I haven't been with anyone because . . . because . . ." Her eyes sought out a distraction to the tears that invaded them. She turned to the countertop for the strength to finish. ". . . Because I won't lose anyone else the way I lost him." The wetness escaped her lashes and trailed down her cheek. She wiped at it with a brush of her hand.

"I'm . . . I'm falling in love with you, I think. I think it happened the first day when we met. I don't know. I don't know what it is, really. And I . . . I don't want it to—I don't want the work to . . ." The tears were coming faster now, and she couldn't go on.

Traask was on his feet and within two strides had encircled her in his embrace. There was simply no denying it now.

The wind going from inside her, she collapsed against his frame in an anguished sigh as she pressed herself closer to him. Her forehead grazed his cheek as he planted a kiss there and she rested her chin on his shoulder. He was soothing her with a loving stroke, down the length of her brown hair that caught itself up in the tangle of his arms. Her breath had the raspy sound of silent tears, which were indeed collecting on his shirtsleeve as she bobbed her head to relieve them.

After a moment, he turned and raised her head to his,

kissing her on the lips with the same tenderness one might use in greeting a newborn. There was a slow softness in his touch, the warmth of his lips caressing the air above her skin before the contact, and afterward that same warmth hanging in the space between them like a magnetic link, assuring them both that this tie was more than sensual.

It wasn't lust. It was love.

It was not the kiss of an impassioned lover. It was the touch of the heart—of the soul—it was there upon his lips, and she knew it had always been there and was waiting for her even still.

But she could not wait.

As he pulled back, she sensed his withdrawal and instinctively closed the gap between them, reaching up, hungry for this moment—more than she ever knew was possible.

Dan felt her change position in his arms as her lips opened on his. But his surprise at her response melted into his own response and ultimately into the shared passions that had been locked between them for several days.

As the kiss ended, Claire withdrew, and he allowed it. Her desire had been stated, and he understood, but there was still something else. Wiping at the corners of her eyes, she moved into the hall toward the bathroom. The door closed with some finality behind her.

Looking around the room, Dan suddenly felt like a guest in his own apartment. He couldn't stand still. He felt the need to be busy—to clean in order to distract himself. He gathered the plates and cartons of Chinese food and carried them to the kitchen.

In the hall the bathroom door opened. "Dan?"

He moved to the hall to see the door was ajar and the light was on inside. Just outside the door he asked, "Yeah?"

There was no answer. He pushed it open gently, giving her time to refuse his entry. The water suddenly started in the shower. It was an unexpected sound, and it startled him.

But what was more startling was the sight of Claire, standing by the shower door in just her bra and panties.

"I need to get cleaned up," she said rather apologetically. "I'm ... I'm a mess."

Traask shook his head, correcting her. "Not from here, you're not."

She smiled faintly, any sign of tears in her eyes nearly gone now. Turning away from him to test the water, she arched her back in a graceful motion as she reached for the controls. Her breasts swayed with this movement, and her smooth and shapely hips rounded down in an unforgettable view. Her dark chestnut hair flowed down her back and across her bare skin, making it impossible for Traask to contain himself any longer.

"Mind if I join you?" he asked, moving into the room. He was going to make her glad that he had some control left underneath all these clothes.

She didn't wait for him. Unfastening her bra and letting it fall, she then stepped out of her panties and turned to him. He let her unbutton his shirt as he reached for her, touching the bare skin of her waist and back, finally coming to rest his hands on the roundness of her buttocks.

Her skin was smooth as silk and lovely to the touch. The rounded flesh of her backside fit into his cupped hand like a glove. He had mentally undressed her from this angle many times in the station house, but never with such stunning detail.

Without letting her finish with his shirt, he drew her closer, nuzzling her hair and breathing in deeply all the perfumes that came with it. He allowed his head to dip down, into her rich mane, finally reaching deep into her neck, kissing the arcs and valleys that lay waiting there for him.

She pressed against him, and he could feel her nipples against his shirt, contacting his skin and exciting him all the more.

Now she came alive in his hands. She pulled his wrists together, bringing his hands up to her breasts and leaving them there while she reached for his shirt once again and caught his mouth with hers.

They kissed, long and deeply, as she finished disrobing him and together they climbed into the cascading water. She used the soap over all of his frame, sudsing his front and then scrubbing his back, his legs and everything in between.

She was purposeful in her reach and when she slid full-against him from behind, he thought that he might explode right then. The contact from that angle was unexpected and amazing, heightening him sexually to a point he could no longer endure.

She released her hold then, as if to command, "Your turn."

And he obeyed.

Reaching between her legs, he cupped both of her buttocks in his hands. This brought him to his knees and his mouth moved against her stomach gently, in small but widening circles toward her mound. When he found his mark, she opened her mouth and gasped, reaching out to take hold of the glass enclosure . . .

. . . Thanking God this building had an industrial size water heater.

They continued with more of the same later on, in the bedroom and then again on the living room floor.

They ordered a pizza at four A.M. from an all-night spot he knew. Double cheese with everything. Even the little fishies.

And by then, any more questions Traask had about her or her past had completely slipped his mind.

Joey and Bennie waited until nine o'clock the next morning for them to arrive at the courthouse with plenty of questions of their own. And when they finally showed up, Adam was nowhere to be seen.

They offered only embarrassed—but not too embarrassed—grins when they finally entered the observation room. Traask shot Joey a thankful nod, and she chuckled into her morning coffee, which was, by now, quite cold.

"Anything happening?"

"Adam's setting up things in the antechamber of the courtroom. You have to go around front to get there. You ought to take a peek, though. It's something else. That guy has a serious erector-set complex," Joey warned.

Claire and Traask shared a curious exchange. "Okay . . ." Traask mused.

Bennie was acting like a burr had found its way up his ass overnight. Bennie wouldn't meet his eye, so Traask guessed that there was something afoot. But that would have to wait.

Traask led Claire out the door and down the hallway, leading the way past the front doors, to a small, unmarked entrance.

Inside, was a large conference-room table and several chairs, a large dry-erase board, and a perfect reproduction of the courthouse in one-tenth scale. Traask regarded it with some curiosity. The model had been hastily thrown together, but expertly finished. Even the newly constructed areas were represented.

Adam sat at the far end of the executive table, hiding behind Claire's laptop computer. He was dressed in an expensive suit, as usual. His hair was combed in perfect strokes, not one out of place. He looked too good to be an agent. He belonged on the cover of *GQ*.

"Oh ... hi there," he muttered distractedly.

Traask nodded in greeting, and Claire crossed to the model on the table.

"What is this?" she inquired.

"We'll get a better handle on things if we can see them clearly." Adam's answer was brusque as he took in the implications of their late arrival together.

"What is this supposed to prove?"

Adam looked up from the keyboard. "Nothing. I just thought it might help."

Claire rolled her eyes at Traask, who shrugged, preferring to stay out of a conversation so filled with subtext.

"I need to check in with my troops. I'll be back in a few, okay?" Traask told her, moving toward the door. There was no response from either of them, so he exited without further comment.

"So ... you get some rest?" Adam tossed out in a tone heavy with implication.

"What the fuck did you mean by telling Traask about Bernardi?"

Adam pushed away from the laptop, prepared for the

fight. "He asked me some questions about how we knew each other, so I told him."

"Told him what?"

"Claire, calm down."

"This is calm. You wanna see upset?"

Adam couldn't help but let go a small, uncontrollable chuckle.

"No . . . no, that's okay. Look, he was asking about you, so I told him that we worked together on the Levers case . . ."

"I wasn't on the Levers case."

"But we did work together on it."

"Why are you doing this? Why are you trying to make me look bad?"

"Look bad? What are you talking about?"

"What part of this don't you understand? I don't want people knowing about my part in the Levers case. And if you talk about it anymore, I'll deny I had anything to do with it."

"Claire, what's wrong with you?"

"What does it take to get through your head? This whole thing could be very embarrassing. They'll all end up thinking I'm a nutcase or something."

"For the last time, I wish you'd get off of this. You really don't understand what we've got here. Do you know how many psychics I've worked with in the past eight years? There's a woman in Montana that is amazing. You should really meet her."

"And what kind of jokes do they tell about her when she's not around?"

"Nobody was joking when she helped us locate a missing eight-year-old last year. They were practically kissing her feet. My God, Claire, they call her in at least twice a year now. She's been invaluable to us."

"Good. Go put the moves on her."

"Can't. She's married. Besides, she's in her sixties."

Claire stared at the floor, studying the carpeting.

"What? Are you so happy with your life, hiding from everything? Who's putting these things in your head, anyway?"

Claire didn't respond.

Adam tossed his pen down with resignation. "Fine. Have it your way. I won't mention it again. I just think you could do a lot of good. But if you're happy ... oh, how shall I put this ... staying in the closet—"

That was the final straw. She could take all the insults about herself, but when he started in on Joey, that was something she just wouldn't stand for. Her cheeks flushed hot as she turned to address him.

"You son of a bitch, who the hell do you think you ..."

But the shouts from the hallways cut her short. A muffled commotion could be heard just beyond their closed-off room. Claire made it to the door first. Adam was right behind her.

In the lobby, several officers were attempting to restrain a man in a dark green raincoat. He had a pockmarked face and was quite slight, perhaps five feet eight inches, but packed with wiry muscle. He was struggling ferociously with the officers, shouting all the while—"He's a fucking cop killer! A killer! Don't you want justice? You are justice! Just shoot him! Go on!"

He tried to overpower the two, and in the process, knocked a third to the ground. He then tried to rush the security barricade.

Several officers had their guns trained on this assailant. Adam and Claire stood motionless in the doorway, watching the scenario unfolding in front of them.

Traask entered the scene from the sidelines, as if in slow motion, pulling his weapon and taking command.

"Okay buddy, hold it right there—don't move."

The man stopped. He saw Traask's determination and seemed to realize at that point that there wasn't much hope for his plan of attack. He waffled for a moment, but finally he put his hands in the air and stepped back from the security men.

Several officers moved together, and all at once the attacker was on the floor, facedown. The whole episode had taken maybe thirty seconds from beginning to end—but a cold sweat had already broken out on Traask's forehead.

All the right instincts had come into play, but they hadn't secured the situation fast enough for his taste.

He recoiled, holstered his weapon, and caught sight of Claire at her doorway. An odd feeling ran through him.

As an incredible package of FBI smarts and tactical training, Claire, it seemed, had better access to this attacker than Traask did—and yet, she stood calmly in the doorway with Adam's head at her shoulder.

Her shoulder holster was clearly visible under her jacket, yet she had not made any move to arm herself when every other officer in the room had.

Adam stood close behind her as Claire watched the situation. Somehow, they knew this was not what they were here for. They knew it was a false alarm.

Adam nodded, putting a hand on her shoulder.

"You see Claire? It's just like you said. He's using them."

Her gaze connected with Traask after a moment and then flicked away almost apologetically while she listened to Adam's words.

"He's probably here right now ... right in front of us—watching."

They both scanned the crowd for a clue, a hint of what they could expect when the time came.

"He's laughing at us, Claire. Now it's your call. Right now. Do you see him? Is he here—is he?"

She knew Adam didn't mean that she could find his face—but she could probably pick him out of a crowd.

She tried ... but it wasn't coming.

The faces, the noise ... the activity in front of them blurred her visions. There wasn't anything Claire could see that would make a difference right now. And the pressure was getting to her.

Claire broke from Adam's hold and disappeared back into the conference room.

Traask watched as Adam held a small smile of—of what? Triumph? It was hard to tell.

Adam nodded to Traask, knowing that his card had been well played. Well played indeed.

The ghosts were getting closer. But Traask had no clue they were even there.

It took a few moments for the police to finish securing the lobby. Despite all their precautions, the madman in the dark green raincoat had still taken most of them by surprise. Cincinnati's finest had begun pushing all nonessential personnel out the front doors, leaving the press corps none too happy.

Champ didn't mind. He was enjoying the show. This was a far better turnout than he had expected. Standing there, just inside the lobby doors, with the rest of the reporters and cameramen, he grinned at their enthusiasm as they began to realize what they had.

"Did you get it? Did you get any of it?"

"I got it, I think I got all of it," a harassed soundman replied against the pressures of a network exclusive. "Just give me a second."

"Cliff, did you get the shot—did we get to see his face? Network won't take a bunch of ears and necks you know . . ."

The truth was, the network would take anything at this point. They were running dry for news on this mysterious serial killer that was rumored to be trapped in Cincinnati. America wanted to see him perform as predicted.

Now this poor schmuck in the raincoat was going to hold the spotlight.

Champ smiled. Hell, he grinned from ear to ear. Everything was just as he knew it would be. The copycats and fanatics were crawling out of the woodwork, trying to steal some of his spotlight. He didn't mind, as long as they were willing to help. Every time one of them showed up, it made Champ stronger. He was learning more about their line of defense every day.

It wouldn't be much longer now. He had to be ready.

As he walked down the steps of the courthouse unnoticed, he figured a cop uniform would be easy enough to come by. After all, he'd already proven himself quite resourceful when it came to costuming and disguises.

He stood at the bottom of the stairs and surveyed the street, pondering his next move.

A fire truck was backing into its station. He watched as the chrome on the vehicle caught the sunlight, winking at him. *Hey Champ,* it seemed to say. *I got something for you.*

Time was on his side. And he intended this to be his last—his greatest—performance.

20

Revelations
June 30th—Cincinnati Courthouse
11:27

The conference room was empty. Traask stepped inside tentatively, Bennie right behind him.

"They musta taken off ..." Bennie assessed, crossing around the table to view Adam's chair, his notes and files. "Ain't that just like the Feds, when we finally got something real brewing, they've sent their people looking in the other direction."

Traask shot him a warning glance.

"You know, I have a strong dislike for this FBI fuck," Bennie stated, poking through Adam's scattered paperwork.

"I know what you mean," Traask replied, studying the meticulously constructed paper model of the courthouse. It was such a curious item, sitting there, so ... out of place.

On the table was a newspaper. Traask hadn't seen it yet, and the headline made him groan.

"What?" Bennie asked.

He held the newspaper up for Bennie to see. The headline read: "Beefed-Up Security at Cop Killer Trial Costs Taxpayers $$$."

"Oops . . ." Bennie muttered.

And then a voice started up from somewhere—muffled, almost . . . yes, sounding almost recorded.

Traask put down the paper as Bennie lifted Adam's jacket from the floor, where it had lain since falling from the back of the chair this morning. He had stepped on it by accident.

The plump lieutenant fished around in the side pocket and pulled forth a miniature recorder that had been activated under the pressure of Bennie's foot. It was playing back a previous recording.

It was Adam on the tape all right, but his voice was so soft it was nearly indistinguishable. It droned on for a moment.

Bennie's eyebrows arched quizzically.

"Bennie . . ." Traask warned.

Bennie was toying with him . . . tempting him. He nodded at the recorder. "Maybe there's something on here we can . . ."

"Bennie!" Traask commanded without humor.

Sighing, Bennie moved to replace the small machine in Adam's jacket pocket.

Adam's droning voice suddenly segued into Claire's own. "What is *that* for?"

This caught Traask's attention, holding it fast and firm.

"Well, what do you think?" Adam's voice clearly responded, sounding very matter-of-fact. "It's a tape recorder. I'm not going to trust myself to remember everything you say. I'm going to record this."

"Like hell you are!"

Claire's strong objection brought an unconscious smile to Traask's lips. Then he caught himself and managed to stifle it.

"What's wrong with recording it?"

"I just . . . I don't. I don't want it."

Bennie interrupted with, "What in the hell . . ?"

Traask turned to him, realizing this was more than just some minor dictation notes and correspondence. Their gaze didn't waver for several seconds as they debated their actions in silence. Traask glanced toward the closed door, unsure, knowing they shouldn't . . . understanding they mustn't. They continued to listen anyway.

"All right, okay. No problem. I'll put it away." Adam continued, sounding a bit rejected.

The small device erupted with new sounds of shuffling about, and the voices grew weaker, less clear. But it was still recording. Adam had not shut it off, as promised.

"That son of a bitch!" Bennie hissed under his breath. "That sneaky son of a bitch!"

"Probably concealed it in his jacket pocket," Traask guessed.

"So you just wanna sit like that?" Adam's muffled voice inquired.

Bennie adjusted the volume to hear better.

"Yeah, I suppose so. Why?" Claire asked.

"Well, last time—you were lying down," Adam replied.

Bennie shot a glance to Traask. "What in the hell is this, anyway?"

"Shhh," Traask warned.

"So?" Claire sounded irritated.

"So, I believe in tradition," Adam urged.

"Tradition?" Bennie interjected.

Traask seized the tape recorder from his grasp and took a step away, desperate to hear what this was all about.

"Maybe we should call in an expert. You don't trust me— after what happened last time," Adam wondered aloud.

"I trust you," Claire promised.

"Really?" There was a hope in Adam's voice that was genuine.

Then the recording became garbled and Traask frantically adjusted the volume to hear every word. But he couldn't make it all out.

"I'm just . . . I'm afraid of (muffled) that way again. Of being, (muffled). It's that sickness . . . I can feel it (muffled) my own (muffled) like it's part of me. So . . . uncontrollable."

Traask looked at the small machine and considered rewinding it, just to hear this part again. But then Adam's voice returned at full volume.

"This was a bad idea. I never would have asked you to do this if I knew how hard it was going to be on you."

Claire sounded like she was appeasing him. "It's okay," she whispered. "I want to do this."

"Okay then," Adam announced, as if he were speaking to an audience. "Listen to my voice, Claire. Use my voice as an anchor. Hold on to my voice, and then allow yourself to move away from here and out ... out to wherever you need to go. Think of it like a safety line, Claire. I'm holding on to you. I won't let you fall. I'm holding on tight."

"Christ!" Bennie swore out loud. "It sounds like he's hypnotizing her."

Traask nodded, his brows knitting together. They listened for several moments as Adam walked her through a series of relaxation exercises and finally into a state of semiconsciousness.

"Claire?" Adam asked.

No response.

"She must be under," Bennie stated, listening to the whole thing without saying a word. Traask only nodded, too fascinated with the whole thing to break his concentration.

"Claire? Can you hear me?" Adam asked.

From the sounds on the tape, it was clear that Adam had pulled the recorder out of his pocket and had it close by.

"Claire, listen to me." His voice was calm and ready for her. "Listen to my voice. Focus on my voice and let it guide you along. You need to find someone for me. Claire, are you there? I need you to answer me."

Her voice was very small. "Dan?"

Traask's eyes closed involuntarily, a small blush creeping into his cheeks.

"This is Adam," he corrected, sounding slightly distracted. "You need to go to work now, Claire. You need to find someone. Do you know who I mean? Do you know who we're trying to find?"

"This is unbelievable!" Bennie huffed, nervously glancing toward the door.

"Good, Claire. Now look for him. Look sharp. He's going to be there. We've got to find him before he can do it again." There was a pause. "Do you see him?"

Without even seeing her, Traask could imagine the way

she looked as the wheels began to turn. His heart began to beat faster. His brow was beginning to sweat.

"Do you *see* him ..."

Suddenly, Adam wasn't the "good friend" anymore. His voice had turned. He was taking command.

And it was upsetting Traask. His heart was pounding in anticipation of her answer. He was uncomfortable. His body was on fire with the need to know what this was all about.

Was this what Adam had meant when he spoke so cryptically about the Levers case? Had they gotten information from Claire? This was all too bizarre.

"Claire, do you *see him!*" Adam insisted for the last time.

A few precious moments passed until suddenly, Claire let out a frightened gasp that struggled in her throat to be let loose. It was obvious that she had found him.

Traask listened to the recording until it was through. His gut wrenched with hers.

It was amazing. And strange. And it wasn't until Adam walked into the room that they stopped the tape.

It was all over anyway.

The five of them had gathered in the conference room.

Or six, if you included the pocket-size recorder sitting on the tabletop in front of Traask.

Adam stood quietly in the far corner of the room, his back to them. The rest of them filed in and sat at their respective places—Bennie and Traask on one side of the table, and Joey and Claire on the other.

The lines were now clearly drawn. Traask and Bennie had listened to the tape recording in its entirety. They now knew what had happened in Los Angeles and just why Claire was so certain the killer would be walking among them soon.

The secret that Adam and Claire had shared for so long was now out in full view. The tape recording had revealed the session in which Adam had hypnotized Claire in L.A. in order for her to search her feelings and tap into the same resources she had used eight years previous.

It revealed without a doubt that Claire had more than just a hunch about the case.

Joey reached under the table, taking Claire's hand and gripping it tightly. Claire was avoiding direct eye contact with anyone—especially Traask.

But Traask couldn't tear his attention away. She was no longer a minor mystery. She was a complete one. What he had listened to had not just moved him—it had blown him completely away. He didn't know what to say. But moreover, he felt betrayed.

This was what everyone knew about her. This was her secret they had all been protecting. Why?

Adam approached the table. When he spoke, it was with a reasoned, level inflection. He was doing his best to diffuse the situation.

"All right, you've got some explanations coming. But first, I need you to . . . I mean, I think Claire would appreciate it if you would consider this information strictly confidential."

The group did not respond.

Adam continued. "It was never intended for anyone to hear that tape. And now, well, this could hurt our investigation, not help it."

Bennie looked to Traask, who only nodded in agreement. It was clear that Bennie did not agree.

"Claire has been able to give us some information on this case, information we couldn't get without her help. Don't ask me to explain it. I couldn't. I wouldn't know what to call it. I only know that the last time we did this sort of thing . . . well, we got the son of a bitch."

Traask shifted in his chair, "You mean the Levers case?"

Adam froze, unable to answer. He looked over to Claire for confirmation, but she wasn't talking. "Yes. That's right," Adam took the chance, and Claire let him have it. "I assume you two listened to the whole thing."

Bennie and Traask nodded.

"Then you know that we're expecting the man to walk right through the front door, very much like what happened this morning."

"Excuse me," Bennie interceded. "But how did you know that that guy this morning wasn't the guy—*our* guy?"

Adam nodded over to Claire. *"She knew."*

Bennie was not satisfied with that explanation.

Traask stood up from his chair. He cleared his throat, self-consciously. "Would you all mind if Claire and I spoke privately for a moment?"

Bennie was the first to stand. He gave Traask a heavy nod and headed for the door. Joey whispered something into Claire's ear and gave her shoulder a squeeze before joining Bennie at the door.

Adam clearly didn't want to abandon his post.

He held his spot for what seemed like an eternity, then apologetically headed for the exit.

Traask moved closer to Claire, over to her side of the table. It wasn't a direct, voluntary movement, but more of a gravitational pull.

"Are you all right?" The voice was caring and full of quiet tenderness.

She nodded.

Traask strained for words but found none. He exhaled, long and hard, struggling for something . . . anything to make the moment right.

Traask had a million questions. His mind was exploding with them. He had to start somewhere. He nodded and cleared his throat.

"So, does the FBI—"

"No. They don't know. Nobody knows."

"Well, Adam—"

"*Only* Adam," she replied tersely. "And that's because—" She froze, deciding she wasn't up to a lengthy explanation. "Adam promised not to use this—publicly."

Another awkward silence followed. Then she suddenly stood up and began gathering her things together.

"Look," she started up again, pulling herself slowly together. "There's really no reason for you to consider anything that I have speculated. Why don't you just forget this whole thing."

"Whoa . . . wait a minute . . . hold on," he interrupted. He reached out to her shoulders and stopped her busy work.

"I'm not the enemy. We're supposed to be on the same side . . . I mean, aren't we? Haven't we?" Claire softened at his encouragement. Traask could tell he was gaining ground, so he continued.

"Believe it or not, our department has used physics in the past."

"I'm not a *psychic*," Claire emphasized with anger, again reaching to gather the files on the tabletop.

"Well, whatever you want to call it. But this AIDS Rapist in L.A.—"

"Our guy's not interested in L.A. He wants Jefferson. It's his last mark. He's out to prove something. If he succeeds, he'll move on into obscurity. We'll never see him again."

"And you know this because of what you and Adam did in L.A. together?"

"You don't have to believe me."

"I'm not saying I don't believe you. I'm trying to understand."

Claire met him face-to-face. Her belief was evident. "He's gonna walk through that door, Dan, and we'll have one moment, one instant, when he will be right in front of us. Either we get him then or we lose."

Traask studied her face, and the strength of her conviction ran straight through him. He knew she was right.

"I'm telling 'ya, if I were a few years younger, I'd be making a stink about it too. They'd all best be glad it ain't an election year, I can tell you that much."

The man standing behind Champ held the scissors like an instrument—wielding them with years of experience.

"There's only so much this nation is gonna take, you know? And this guy—well, let's face it. He's doing us all a big favor."

Champ's attention shifted to the mirror, taking in the barber with interest. Then he refocused on the magazine in his lap. He had seized this moment to catch up on his reading. But the man wouldn't keep his editorial to himself.

"There used to be a time when a man knew the basics— he knew when it was necessary to separate the wheat from the chaff. What's wrong with us now is we've gone soft, I tell you. The whole goddamn system's gone soft. Why, it's come down to the point that you can't even fry a bad egg around here no more."

"I hear 'ya, Jackie. I hear 'ya," a regular at the door echoed, giving up on suppressing the man's opinions. Nothing was gonna stop him.

In his lap, Champ held the current edition of *Time* magazine. Emblazoned across the cover was a headline festooned with blood-toned streaks.

"Vigilantism—Could this be the next Man of the Year?"

Champ realized he wasn't going to be able to escape so easily from this debate.

"I'm only saying we've stopped paying attention here, and I think that's exactly what he's trying to point out. He's as fed up as the rest of us. He's just, well, he's just better prepared to do something about it, that's all."

In the back of the barber shop, a fat guy with a New York accent peered over the top of his newspaper with contempt. "Aw, what do you guys know? This guy—he's just some sick fuck. A psycho killer sicko who gets his rocks off by attacking these other psycho killer sickos. Wake up! He ain't no goddamn hero. That's just his *angle*. When he's caught, he's gonna use that to get the jury to go easy on him, that's all . . . Am I right?"

"Whattya talkin' about, Arno?! Even the FBI knows this guy's doing it for a reason. They know he's making a statement and they're afraid. Because that statement is—this system don't work," Jackie rebutted, growing angry at the opposition. He was especially angry, because the person in opposition was someone who drank up all the free coffee.

But the New York accent continued.

"You think this guy has a plan? Who do you think he is, Einstein? He's got no fuckin' plan. He's a psycho like the rest of 'em. Hey, no normal guy—a guy like you or me, with a family and a job—could do things like this guy has done and not be fuckin' *de*ranged."

"You's full o'shit, Arno. You're no expert."

"Okay, okay. You try it. You go home and hack the arms off the old lady and dance around the apartment—see if you don't feel a bit *de*ranged afterward."

Arno began to chuckle at himself, shifting his newspaper.

"But he didn't hack up his old lady. That's the whole point," the regular at the door chimed in.

Arno had a pained expression on his face.

"Oh yeah? Well, maybe he likes little boys. Maybe this superhero of yours picks up hookers and leaves them in the river when he's not lighting bad guys on fire. You don't know anything about that, see? And maybe, just maybe, one of them hookers isn't a hooker but a nice girl—like the Patterson kid who was found in the dumpster, back of Marvin's Meat Packing last year."

"He's picking on the guys who deserve it. Not the wife, not the innocent kids," Jackie defended, flatly.

"Yeah, he saved those kids in the desert, remember?" the regular agreed.

"He's a man with a conscience. And I don't think he's dancing around afterward, neither," Jackie huffed.

Arnold crushed the newspaper into his knees. "Oh, what? You think that sick fuck's out there somewhere crying about all this right now? Think he's sorry for what he done? Give me a fuckin' break. He's nothin' but a sick psycho, you'll see. When they catch him, you'll see—he's just as bad as the rest of them he killed, maybe worse."

This final statement caused Jackie to lose his control. "So what if he is? So what?! Not everyone's a fuckin' flying superhero—heart of gold and all that. He's not some cartoon character, Arno! He's just a man, a man doing the right thing. He's just doing the right thing since we can't. I'm not saying it's easy ... I'm not saying that. I'm saying maybe he's got something in him that can. That's the point. That's the *whole point*," Jackie argued.

Jackie reached down and removed the plastic bib from Champ's collar. With a soft brush, he scattered the last bit of hair from the nape of Champ's neck.

Champ studied his new face in the mirror. The blond dye job he had done on himself back in the motel was doing him a world of good. The long, pale locks were gone, though. Now he sported a buzz cut. As he examined his new look, he noticed that his features seemed to stand out in high relief, a finely chiseled vision of justice, in his estimation. He liked it.

Champ stood up from the chair and nodded to Jackie, who backed away, grabbing a broom and beginning to sweep the hair from the floor in broad angry strokes, barely cognizant of the big man's gaze.

"Yeah . . . like some guys, they can't take to huntin' on their own," the regular at the door began again. "My brother Jerry's got two boys. One cries and kicks and screams all the way— even when we take him fishin'! But the other, well—he just got a thing for it. And he ain't no weirdo psycho killer. He's just able to take care of business. He ain't squeamish about it."

Champ turned to the man in the doorway, who had so eloquently stated the argument, and grinned. It was warm and welcoming, not what you might expect from such a large, muscular, and now quite blond, package. The regular straightened up a bit, growing uncomfortable with the stranger's attention, and shifted self-consciously.

Champ peeled a ten-dollar bill back from a bundle of cash and handed it to Jackie. As Jackie pocketed it, he noticed the key chain with the blue rabbit's foot dangling from the big guy's grasp. It was something you didn't see much of anymore. It drew his attention.

There was a lull in the conversation.

Champ moved forward to the door where the regular had politely separated himself from the doorjamb he'd grown so attached to, unblocking the path of Champ's exit. As he did, he shot a glance back at Arnold, who had raised the newspaper again, as if he could shut out the argument with the wrinkled walls of newsprint.

Champ paused, with his hand on the doorknob. But he didn't leave. The big man was suspended in time. Jackie and the regular behind him were exchanging puzzled glances as seconds ticked away, creating an uncomfortable moment.

Finally, words came from the stranger in their midst. Words that were barely audible, except to the regular, standing closest to him.

"Tell that guy back there . . . he's *wrong*."

*   *   *

Dinner had been a total disaster. But when Claire said she didn't want to go back to her hotel, he really didn't know what to do, so they sat in Traask's apartment until two A.M.—with virtually nothing to say to one another.

It was Traask who made the leap, deciding he would have to risk losing her, because he just couldn't sit there in silence any longer.

Out of the quiet he blurted, "Why didn't you . . ."

Then he stopped, the presumption of what he was going to ask, mocking him. They had just met a few days ago—their relationship was in its teetering, first stages. Why should she tell him? This was clearly something so personal, so delicate and controversial, that under normal circumstances, it might have taken years for her to confess, if she would have at all.

Traask shook his head, then began pacing the floor. He then cocked his head, and drew in a deep breath, letting it out painfully. "Look, I know this isn't something you wanted me to know—but I do know about it now, and I'm trying not to let it change things between us."

Claire didn't have much left to give at this point. She wasn't going to fight, if that's what he expected.

As Traask moved closer, he knelt in front of her. His shoulder gently brushed against her knee as he studied her features with determination. "Hey . . . I'm not going anywhere." He reached for her hand. She allowed him to take it. "So don't do this. Don't shut me out."

Slowly, she began to believe that he really wasn't going to give up. Her unrealized fear of losing whatever it was that they had was just that—unrealized.

He waited. Patiently.

And she drew him to her, her breath shuddering as she felt despair fall from her shoulders. They held each other for a long, lingering moment.

"It's okay," he whispered. "It's all right."

Her breath began to come in short, quick gasps. A small, tortured cry was building inside her, and she wouldn't allow it to break free. Not yet. Instead, she held on and waited until her need to explode subsided, which it finally did.

That was when she realized he was holding her in his arms, and they were headed for his bedroom. The intensity of his touch was overwhelming. It made the ugliness and tension of the day wash away in a flood that carried with it the fears Claire had locked away for many, many years.

"I don't have control over it. It comes and goes, and sometimes I can use it and sometimes I can't."

"But this time you could."

"This time, Adam did it."

"Like with Levers ..."

"Yes."

"And no one knows about that?"

They lay in bed after lovemaking, feeling the comfortable closeness that prompted this dialogue.

"Joey knows," Claire admitted. She paused, feeling the pain and anxiety beginning to build again. "What happened in Washington was a nightmare. I never wanted to feel that way again. But Joey has sort of a problem with this ... putting your money on a 'feeling.' "

"Claire?"

She turned to face him.

"Tell me what happened with the Levers case. I need to know."

There was a moment there when he thought he might have lost her again—that perhaps this was the step too far.

Then she drew in a deep breath and began. "It was during my last few months in the academy. I had been dating an agent named James Bernardi. We had been seeing each other for about two years. Adam was his best friend.

"Ten girls had been missing over those two years—all from the same general vicinity. They were all about eighteen or nineteen and, according to the families, the trusting sort. Real innocents. I didn't know it, but it was Jim's case.

"So one night, I told him I was having these weird dreams about it. I don't know why he believed me, but he told me that I shouldn't ignore it. He volunteered to hypnotize me, make me remember more about the dreams."

In the dark, Traask could tell she was struggling to break the spell this had on her.

"The next day, I didn't go to classes—just slept all day. I figured it had all been a big waste of time."

She shifted under the covers, and Traask could feel the tension rising through her body. He reached beneath the sheet and took her hand in his, but she pushed it aside.

"But it wasn't. Adam had taken the information he got from me and turned it over to Jim Bernardi's team—calling it an anonymous tip. As it turned out, Levers's place was incredibly easy to find. There were dogs—lots of dogs barking. I had described a chain-link fence that was like a cage and lots of high-tension wires. When it was quiet, you could hear them hum. The street was a cul-de-sac that dead-ended at one end, and there was a two-story house—the only two-story around for miles—directly across the street."

She shook off the recollection. Her voice turned steely with it. "So—they found it. Adam and his team staked it out all day long until they had seen and heard enough to tell Jim where to find his man."

A brief silence followed.

"When they stormed the place, several of the men were wounded. Levers had long since decided he was not going to be taken alive. He had booby-trapped the place with dozens of homemade contraptions—guns, explosives. Jim—" Claire drew in a breath before continuing "—was the only one killed. Levers shot himself in the head before they could get to him. Afterward, they found the bodies of three girls in the basement—all of them, dead. He had starved them, and when they were nearly dead from starvation, he had let the dogs . . ."

"I know . . . I know . . ." Traask interrupted. He caressed her shoulder reassuringly.

Then she added, "The irony is, the neighbors had called the cops several times because of the barking. They had been out there to fine him several times. The complaints even made it to a local court. Unfortunately, while the authorities were around writing out tickets, they never paid much attention to the bones. The report said the dog run was littered with smaller bone chips and pieces. They found a femur in the bushes."

Traask turned away for a moment, his head reeling.

Claire's voice fell. "When Adam came to tell me what had happened, I thought—this can't be happening. It can't be true. But he took me to the house, and I saw all of it for myself."

She reached for a glass of water on the bedside table. She was shaken but determined to finish.

"Two days later, I finished my finals and took the next plane out. I haven't spoken to Adam since."

Traask needed something encouraging to say. "But you pointed them to the bastard. In using whatever you could, you helped to stop him."

"And in doing that, I helped kill James Bernardi. And that's something I just can't live with."

"Claire . . ." Traask insisted, pulling her closer. But she wouldn't accept it. He understood all too well. "Then I guess we have something in common."

She turned, demanding a clarification.

"I had a partner. The one I told you about in the coffee shop?"

Claire nodded.

"He was . . . he and I were close. We used to joke about being brothers separated at birth—you know—but that was the joke. He was black, you see." His voice wavered as he continued. "He was Frank Morrison—the Cop Killer's last victim."

Claire blanched. She had suspected that the pain she'd sensed in him had something to do with the Cop Killer— but she had no idea of this . . . none.

"I can't forgive Frank. I haven't been able to forgive him for going out there. You know what happened with this case . . . with our men . . ." In the darkness beside him, she nodded. "Well, Frank Morrison was leading them. But he knew me well enough to know I would never agree to what they were doing. So he never told me. The day I found out was the day he died."

Claire shuddered back a sigh. "Dan . . ."

"To this day I think there are men out there I'm working with who think I knew about Frank all along."

"But you didn't."

"Any more than you could have known that Bernardi was stepping into a trap—see? You didn't send him in there ... it's what he had to do. And Frank did what he felt he had to do."

Claire considered this, her emotions rising. Tears began to spill over.

"How do you let it go, Dan? How do you just let it go?"

"The big secret is, I can't. I don't. I walk in there every day with this huge invisible chip on my shoulder that I can't afford to let anyone else see. I can't let them know my feelings, because they aren't important. We have a job to do, and right or wrong—it's what I've been sworn to do."

Then his voice changed. "You may hate me for saying this, but I feel I owe you something for telling me, for trusting me—so here it is. What I'm about to say, I've never said out loud and I never thought I would."

Claire did her best to understand as Traask shifted gears.

"Being out there—it changes people like us. Nobody sees what we do every day. They just see the headlines. They are shocked at the horror of it when it's in their face. And that's their job—to be shocked and horrified. But they don't live with it. They can turn it off or walk away. We can't. We've got to get up the next morning and face it again. The same old song and dance. We're the ones they trust to bring in the bastards so they can be sanitized and martinized and stuck into their little boxes for life. We're supposed to keep society safe from all those big bad public enemies. But this guy—your guy, he knows what the real public enemy is all about."

Claire was mesmerized by his passion and his words. She waited for him to continue.

"It's the *sickness!* The violence against women and defenseless children—against innocent men doing their jobs. These people—these faces we seek on the wanted poster, that's just packaging! It's the sickness we need to address! And how do you do that? The same bastard who steals someone's child and sexually mutilates them before dropping the body in a dumpster probably considers life in prison some sort of sick reward! Jesus, we just don't think the same way they do. We're too civilized for that. But I've been thinking about it lately, and your guy is smart. He knows this won't work, so he gets down on their level. He says, 'If you're gonna play, you're gonna have to pay the band' and what they are beginning to understand is that he *means it!*

"Jefferson's scared out of his mind—thinking that any moment he's next on the list. And you know what? He deserves every bit of it. Jesus Christ, it's exactly what we went through for two years while he was out there picking us off like pop bottles on a fence post. It's about time he gets a dose of his own medicine."

"Dan, I—" Claire warned.

"I'm sorry, Claire, but you don't know what it's been like. I've lost friends as well as my credibility to this bastard. I can't help it. Part of me wants to see him pay—and not in a nice warm cozy jail cell, either. Part of me wants to take him out in the desert and do what this guy is doing."

"So what are you suggesting? We change overnight to an eye-for-an-eye mentality instead of the justice system we have now?"

"No ... I don't mean that. I don't have any fast and easy answers. But since this whole thing began, crime has been down in Cincinnati, citywide. I wouldn't be surprised if the same thing is beginning to happen all over. It's making the sickos think, Claire. It's doing something we can't."

He waited for her to respond, and when she didn't, he added, "It's wrong I know, but it's how I feel."

"God, Dan, suddenly I wonder—whose side are you on?"

"You know what side I'm on, don't get me wrong! I told you—I'm sworn to uphold the law, and I've kept my promise every step of the way. That's not gonna stop. I've made my choice. If I was gonna get Jefferson, I wouldda done it the night I brought him in. A clean shot in the back, and there wouldn't have been any questions asked. But that's not my job. That's not the way I do things.

"We'll get your guy, and we'll put him away with the

others. Ol' Jefferson won't have a hair on his head out of place, I promise you. But I owed you the truth, Claire. The deep-down truth."

"Which is . . . ?"

Traask paused before his final confession. "God help me, Claire . . . it goes against everything I've ever believed in . . . but a part of me wants Jefferson to pay more than your guy does."

21

The Cop Killer—*Revisited*
July 1st—Cincinnati Courthouse
09:02

"What's this?"

"You'll need it from now on to get in."

Joey inserted her ID badge into the electronic monitor, allowing the magnetic strip on the back to work the lock. The door clicked open, and she and Claire entered the Hall of Justice, flashing their FBI tags at the two officers at the door.

Security was being beefed up all along the entry corridor, Claire could tell. Good. They would need it.

"So, how we doin'?"

Joey's curiosity was up as they walked down the hallway toward the back entry and the observation room for Jefferson, beyond. They hadn't spent much time together over the past few days. Claire had slept at the hotel only once since Joey's arrival. The distance between them was taking its toll.

"I'm okay," Claire replied. "How're you doin'?"

"I'm hanging in there ... you know."

Claire noticed her friend was only responding as a good sport. But she understood that Joey's patience was running thin. Concerned, Claire grabbed her elbow and pulled her into a corner.

"Hey, I'm sorry I haven't been around ..."

"It's okay."

"No it's not. I haven't been—here. I'm sorry."

"Look, Randall, I understand." Joey gave her one of those husband-to-wife, "I know you better than you think I do" expressions, with an additional smirk for emphasis. "You finally got laid. It was bound to happen sometime this century."

Claire blushed, her color rising. Joey enjoyed the effect she was creating. Turning on her heel and continuing down the hall, she toyed with her partner some more.

"Now remember, Randall, it's just like riding a bike. You never quite forget ... no matter how long it's been."

A warm smile spread over Claire's face.

"And you can tell the son of a bitch that I'm happy for him too." Joey stopped in mid-stride, "Come *on*, Randall! I may not have a dick, but you can still walk with me."

The observation room was full that morning. Traask had just finished making his daily rounds when Claire and Joey entered.

"How's it hanging, boys?" Joey asked, breezing into the room and heading for the coffee machine.

The response to this was decidedly mixed.

Traask noticed Claire's sly expression and high color, which caused him to wonder what had been going on between the partners.

"Well, they busted another lunatic last night. This one didn't even make it as far as the parking lot. These guys have got to start getting more inventive. Third one that claimed God appeared in a tortilla or something with instructions to shoot Jefferson," Sarkissian barked.

"Damn Mexican food," Joey replied.

"We figured it musta been a take-out order," Abrams added. "Get it, Dan? A 'take-out' order?"

Traask nodded.

"Jesus, everybody wants their fifteen minutes, I'm telling

'ya! We're looking for one guy ... *One*—and all we got is a bunch of pathetic wanna-bes." Sarkissian fumed.

"And they're not very good at it," Abrams added. "Did you see that guy, Dan? He didn't even try to sneak in, he just drove up to the back gate and announced his intentions."

Claire moved closer to the glass, attempting to get a view down into the room where Jefferson sat, waiting. She wanted to see the face of Daniel Traask's secret nightmare—the thing that tore his soul apart last night.

The tall black man sat at his desk, hands clasped nervously in front of him. He sported a good build on a broad muscular frame; might even be considered a handsome man in other circumstances. In the background, the proceedings of the trial droned on but did not engage his attention. His head moved this way and that, in impatient motions. Then his eyes roamed up to the mirrors, and finally, directly at Claire.

Just for a second, the two of them were looking directly at each other—although she doubted Jefferson was even aware of it. The one-way glass made it impossible to detect any activity inside the observation room.

She expected his eyes to be cold and heartless, devoid of emotion. But what she observed today was ... well ...

Dan's wish was coming true. Jefferson looked like a hunted man, living in a constant state of fear. He knew he was the target, and it was taking its toll. If Big Foot had a hunger for rabbits, he certainly knew how to pick them.

This one was nearly ripe.

"Detective," Adam greeted Dan with a nod.

Dan entered the room and eyed the model of the courthouse with apprehension, reminding himself he had some questions to ask.

Claire was already busy studying some materials in the files before her. She had switched gears, now showing her purely professional demeanor. She didn't even glance up as Traask entered and sat down. Something had her engaged.

Upon seeing Claire so absorbed, he switched gears as well and joined them at the table.

"Agent Randall has decided to listen to reason and actually review some of the backgrounds I've been working up."

Finally released, Claire looked up, connecting with Traask.

"I wasn't able to find anything I really agreed with. None of these men ... none of them felt right. Until now."

Adam nodded to Traask once again, commanding a lead in the proceedings. "Catch the lights, will you?"

The lights in the room were dimmed, and Adam activated a slide projector. What appeared on the screen was a photo of a crime scene. Somewhere in a woody area, a cop car sat between two trees, the doors wide-open. Several officers stood around in the shot, caught in what comprised a still-life portrait of the investigation. Traask thought he could make out the word "Arizona" on their uniforms.

"On February second of last year, this abandoned sheriff's car was found off a dirt road on Mount Elden. That's in Northern Arizona, just above Flagstaff."

"Hey, that's Groundhog Day," Sarkissian observed.

Adam didn't appreciate the humor. "The vehicle had been missing for about a week, and the officer assigned to it had simply vanished without a trace."

The next slide was a newspaper clipping of the story. The headline read: "Missing Officer a Mystery."

"Just like the motorcycle cop near Phoenix," Traask commented.

"Yes and no," Adam corrected, prompting Claire for assistance.

She finally spoke. "We think this missing sheriff might be our man."

Adam activated the slides, and another photo appeared on the screen. It was the same photo, the same man that Adam had been touting in Los Angeles. A clean-cut, all-American-looking fresh face in uniform.

This cut through Traask like a knife. His spine grated against the chair back as he sat to attention.

"The guy we're looking for is a cop?!" he exclaimed.

Suddenly his words from the night before were ringing in his ears.

But don't you think that by being out there it changes people like us. Nobody sees what we do everyday ...

They had rung in Claire's all night long. She now had the pieces of the puzzle coming together.

Rising from her seated position, Claire paced as she spoke. "When Adam first presented this information in Los Angeles, I'm afraid I wasn't giving it my full attention."

"You've known about this guy since Los Angeles?" Traask interjected, with an edge.

"I had taken the psychological profile Claire had submitted to me in Washington and put it through the computers, pulling various names as I went. When this one popped up—well, it seemed too good to be true," Adam explained.

Traask was demanding an explanation from Claire, but she wasn't about to get into it here.

"I'm still not positive. There's something not quite right about all of this—I'm not sure what it is," Claire admitted.

Adam continued. "His name is Michael Weston Corbett, born 1/14/66 in Butte, Montana. He was the youngest in the family for several years before his sister Julie was born in '73."

Adam changed the photo on the screen to show a pretty young girl—a school photo, supposedly.

"Pretty girl," Adam noted for them before continuing. "The family moved in '81 from Montana to a small town in nothern Arizona, and from there, Michael entered the sheriff's department of Coconino County in '87."

The photo changed again to show another girl, a blonde who looked a bit too happy and carefree.

"Michael was married in '90 to Trina Davis, who was nineteen at the time. They had a reportedly rocky romance that ended in an ugly separation and divorce. Michael's performance left a lot to be desired over the last few months before his disappearance. He'd been passed up for a promotion two weeks before, and many men who worked closely with him commented that he took it hard. Especially after what happened to his little sister."

All eyes were on Adam, except Claire's. Hers were waxing the floor.

A new slide bore the headline: "Local Girl's Tragic Ordeal."

"Julie was eighteen when she was beaten up and raped outside the café where she worked as a waitress. She was then left for dead on the side of the road. She survived, but they never convicted the guy who did it."

Traask shook his head in silent regret.

"So she killed herself. Two weeks before Corbett was denied the promotion—one month before his disappearance. This could be what triggered all this."

"And you've got nothing on this guy since?" Sarkissian grumbled. "He's just thin air to you?"

"It can be pretty easy to disappear in this country if you really want to," Adam retorted. "We did a follow-up up on the alleged rapist, Vanderhoff—Alan J. Vanderhoff. Figured Corbett might have gone after him. Seems we can't seem to find anything on him."

"So this Vanderhoff might have been Corbett's first victim," Traask assumed, filling in the blank.

"Very well could be. There's no trace of Michael Corbett after February second at seven A.M. roll call. He took off in his squad car, and that was that. The weird thing is, he didn't take anything with him."

"What do you mean?" Traask was curious.

"He didn't take money, clothes—nothing. He just left with the uniform on his back and whatever was in his wallet. That's why they thought he'd been abducted or something. The sheriff's department doesn't want to believe he's a killer."

"Can you blame them?" Bennie said.

"You've talked to the wife—any kids?" Traask inquired.

"The wife's pregnant now. Not his. She's been seeing someone else for quite a while. Michael hasn't been around. We've had a phone tap on her since last week, but there's nothing going on there."

Traask was persistent. "What about the rest of the family?"

"Father's dead, mother is just barely hanging on in a nursing home. Extended family had the usual things to say—didn't know there was anything wrong. There's an older half brother from a former marriage, but he's way out of the picture."

"How's that?" Traask wanted to know.

"Stepfather kicked him out when Mike and Julie were still young. No word from him since then. Arizona authorities caught up with him in Washington State shortly after Mike's disappearance, but he claims he's had nothing to do with them since the day he was asked to leave. Didn't even know they had moved to Arizona. Had no idea his brother turned out to be a cop. He checked out pretty solidly—been working as a day laborer, heavy construction mostly. Not so much as a speeding ticket in the past twelve years. We think he's telling the truth. He doesn't know anything. Was pretty upset to find out his momma had been stuck in a nursing home."

"So this cop just up and disappeared without a trace?" Sarkissian summarized.

There was a pause as everyone considered the options.

"So what's next?" Traask asked, posing the question to Claire. "It's pretty hard chasing a shadow."

"Even if the shadow has a name," Joey agreed.

"Yeah, but this shadow also has a face now. It could make all the difference," Adam suggested hopefully.

Claire was nibbling her bottom lip. There was something . . . something about this that just wasn't right. Traask could see it in her. Adam, too.

Bennie rose from his chair. "Well, this is just great," he muttered. "I assume we can distribute some photos of this guy?"

Adam responded. "I'll have some for you this afternoon."

Bennie nudged Traask, "We're supposed to meet the security guys. The installation was finished last night—they want to start using it this morning."

"Use what?" Adam asked.

"We're installing metal detectors at the entrances and exits—you know, first the ID cards, now this. We're beefing up the security, per your request. As if anyone but a cop could get back there anyway ..."

Adam's response was to change the slide. Michael Corbett, in full sheriff's uniform, grinned back at them as if he'd heard that challenge.

Bennie didn't like that. In retaliation, he flipped on the lights as he walked over to Traask. "You coming?"

"In a bit."

Bennie nodded and gave his partner a soft punch on the shoulder on his way out.

Silence took over as the three of them sat there, the dimmed image of Corbett facing them on the wall.

Traask realized that, although they were desperately searching for an answer—there was no way to narrow it down. They could be staring at his picture right now or they could be light-years off the mark. There was no way to be sure. But wait ... there was a way ... wasn't there? "So what do you think?" he asked Claire.

Suddenly both men were focused on her, quite intently. Adam had been waiting behind to ask the very same thing. Here they were, the two men in the world who knew her better than anyone, and she didn't want to let ... them down. From one to the other, she paused, then finally, after a moment of indecision, simply shook her head.

"I don't know."

"What exactly do you mean?" Adam asked.

"I mean just that, Adam. Jesus, what do you think I am? A fucking fortune-teller?" Claire retorted hotly.

"No. You're not a fortune-teller. You're our Geiger counter. And right now, we need to know. Are we hot or cold?"

Claire looked at the face on the wall, trying to get something she could use. It wasn't coming.

"Claire ..." Traask started, rising from his chair. "Is there something we could do. Something that might help?"

Adam nodded in agreement.

Claire looked at the two men accusingly. Suddenly she was being backed into a corner, with her lover on one hand and one of her former best friends on the other.

And yet she knew they were right. There was something she could do. She wasn't trying hard enough. And they were running out of time.

"Not right now," she protested, moving to gather her things. "Maybe later, but not right now."

"Claire ..." Traask said, moving in on her.

"Dan, leave me alone. I can't do it right now, okay? I just can't."

She began moving past him just as the door to the conference room opened and Joey appeared beside it.

"Hey, anyone need lunch?" she inquired.

Claire breezed past her and out the door, tears forming. She was halfway down the hall before Joey could respond.

It was evident that they were pushing her too hard. Joey took a moment, shooting an eviscerating glare at Adam and a less lethal glance at Traask before hurrying after her.

Traask turned to Adam, who tried hard not to look guilty, but failed. He tossed down the remote changer to the table-top, and as he did, the slide changed automatically.

But neither man looked at it.

It was Michael in his sheriff's uniform, towering over his young sister, Julie. He was smiling proudly, and she was laughing at him, still dressed in her high school graduation cap and gown.

The same one in Champ's wallet.

The water felt good on her face. She doused her skin several times with it, letting the shock of the cold wetness bring her back to earth.

A can of Diet Coke appeared on the sink ledge.

"Thanks," Claire murmured, reaching for some paper toweling. As she dabbed her face dry, she avoided Joey's questioning stare.

"You gonna tell me, or do I have to drag it out of you?"

"Just nerves. I'm okay."

Dubious, Joey moaned, "Oh, yeah, right."

Claire tossed the toweling in the receptacle and reached for the soda.

"Maybe we should go see if this town knows the meaning

of 'greasy spoon.' I haven't had a lunch out in Cincinnati yet. What do you say we get out of here?"

Claire didn't respond.

"Come on ..." Joey demanded, linking her arm with Claire's and heading for the door. "They can live without you for an hour or two."

In the hall, the two women paused as their attention was drawn to the new sounds coming from the entry down the way. The metal detectors were now in use. As people moved past, an alarm would sound momentarily, then there would be silence as they tried again to pass after dumping their keys—sometimes their entire pocket contents—out for inspection.

The court was getting ready to break for lunch, and some of the people were getting a head start. There was a bit of confusion here with the new procedure, and people were not being patient.

"Look, I'm the deputy district attorney, you moron. You've seen me every day for two weeks! Let me through!"

"I don't care if you're the tooth fairy, you asshole! Now back it up and wait your turn."

Thinking quickly, Joey tugged Claire's elbow. "Let's take the escape route, shall we?"

The metal detector sounded once again. Joey attempted to pull away, but Claire held fast. Not only were the bells going off on the metal detector, but they were going off in her head as well. Warning bells.

She was there.

She was here.

This was ... it. The moment she had been waiting for.

She pulled free of Joey's grasp and in slow motion, dropped her briefcase to the floor, drawing her gun from beneath her jacket.

Confused by Claire's actions, Joey paused. The detector chimed on. Stumbling against Claire's briefcase, Joey realized her partner was taking position ...

The monotonous tone seemed to grow in intensity, but Claire was focused on the man in the booth.

Joey's attention shifted from Claire to the security booths.

No one was reacting yet. The man in the booth was standing there ... frozen in time.

Something inside Claire had known. There was no time to question.

Without hesitation, Joey drew her weapon—throwing her body sideways across the hallway and taking position behind another pillar—directly opposite Claire.

It was at that point that everything began to happen at once.

The man in the metal detection booth lunged forward, past the guards, latching on to the first thing he could get his hands on.

It happened to be blond.

It happened to be the Twat Leader.

22

A Piece of Cake
July 1st—Cincinnati Courthouse
11:43

"Everybody freeze!"

Within seconds, the man had moved about twenty feet down the hallway using Holly North as a human shield. This put him twenty feet closer to Eddie Jefferson.

From their positions, Claire and Joey could see everything clearly. The man had darted from the metal detection booth, grabbing Holly just as she was filming some coverage on the beefed-up security at the trial.

He dragged her with him, moving away from the rest of the crowd, his back to Claire and Joey.

Holly's cameraman, with visions of Emmy-making footage dancing in his head, kept his focus tightly on them. Holly's shocked and breathless gasp was front and center.

About twenty cops surrounded the entry, but the man and his hostage weren't headed in that direction. Claire and Joey were the only ones who could get this guy ... and no one knew they were there.

"Nobody move. Nobody! Or I'll blow her away, you hear me?" He was inching his way backward, tugging at Holly's

277

perfect hair with each motion as his arm clenched tighter about her throat.

"Drop her, man. Drop her now, or you're both history," a tough young cop ordered, moving in. No one else was taking the lead.

"No. I mean it, stay back. Stay back or I'll kill her."

The man seemed to be nervous more than anything else. His dark complexion and scruffy hair made him the picture of a desperate individual, but the appearance was deceptive.

Claire peeked between the cold marble column and the wall. This was not their man. Not tall, not big enough and definitely not his style. The guy holding Holly was a copycat; another sick individual who needed attention in the worst sort of way. And now he would receive it.

She lowered her gun for a moment while considering this. Doubt filled her face. What was going on? Here she was, smack in the middle of her premonition, the same one that Dan had heard on tape.

It was real. It was happening.

Right now.

She swung back around to the other side of the pillar, facing her partner.

Joey was there, waiting. Claire shook her head exaggeratedly—"Not the guy."

Joey nodded, continuing to assess the situation. Even if he wasn't the guy, he had a hostage, and they were the only ones between him and a headline.

He had to be stopped. Joey knew she couldn't fire from this angle. If she missed, there was a good chance someone in the crowd would get hit. And if she did take the shot, Holly would certainly be injured as well. They had to wait until he moved closer and hope the cops didn't inflame him further.

Joey stepped out from the pillar, just enough so that the cops ahead could see she was there. She motioned for them to let the cop continue to allow the madman to move backward until there was a clean shot.

The tough cop lowered his gun somewhat. "Okay ... okay ... take it easy. We don't want anybody hurt." He said this for Joey's benefit, not for the man holding Holly North. He could see there was an immediate danger of cross fire into the crowd, and he wanted Joey to be aware of it as well.

Holly was struggling weakly, panic setting in.

If she's to live through this, she's got to fucking relax, Joey thought.

The man continued to move backward, but not fast enough for Joey. Something had to give. She stood, positioning herself to shoot as soon as there was an opening.

"I'm the guy ... I saved those kids in Arizona. I killed Cameron. I killed the Cannibal too. And now I'm gonna get Jefferson ... just like you said."

He was hissing his threats to Holly, but everyone could hear him. Claire wrinkled up her nose at this. She stepped from behind the security of the marble, completely disgusted with his performance.

"No, you didn't."

The man's focus pivoted and his body followed, as he tried to figure out which way to protect his back. He grappled with Holly, whose eyes bulged when she recognized Claire. She gurgled a plea for help, but it was unintelligible.

"Let her go," Claire demanded.

"No!" The man insisted.

Claire stepped forward, lowering her gun. "Then take me instead."

The man stepped backward, sneering and choking Holly harder. "Fuck you. You think I'm stupid?"

Claire took his full attention by forcing him to watch as she lowered her gun to the floor in a slow, exaggerated bend. It gave Joey the time necessary to move into the hall and take the right position.

As she rose, she held the man's gaze straight and level, delivering her response with a cold hard punch. "No, I don't think you're stupid. I *know* you are."

And with that, Joey could find him in the crosshairs.

"... And with that, I believe we will adjourn until ..."
BAM!
BAM!

The muffled gunshots could be heard over the speakers in the containment room as clearly as they had been able to hear paper rattle or shoes shuffling on the floorboards over the past few weeks. Clear enough to tell that the gunshots weren't emanating from the courtroom itself, but somewhere just beyond it.

Eddie Jefferson went wild. All at once he rose from the desk and kicked his chair backward, listening to the confusion of screams that followed.

"He's down! All clear, he's down!"

"Ambulance. Call for paramedics!"

"Clear the area . . . stay back—please."

Jefferson threw himself against the nearest guard, screaming, "He's here! Jesus Christ! He's here, man—right here!"

The guards struggled with Jefferson. The man who had been waiting to meet his fate could wait no more. Suddenly, he had the strength of ten men, and with this strength, he clawed at the cell door, throwing the guards off as they attempted to restrain him.

"Goddamn it, let me outta here . . . let me out. *Let me out!*"

When the shot rang out, Bennie Sarkissian had a face full of doughnut.

"Fuch . . ." was the sound that came out.

Bennie extricated himself from the observation room and made his way down to the containment area in record time for a fat man. The guards outside the door were confused, wondering if they should open it and assist.

"Go get backup," he instructed one guard. His voice was hard and commanding, although the powdered sugar on his chin didn't help his image any. "I don't care what you hear on the other side of that door, you don't open it until I tell you to," he told the other.

"Yes, sir," replied the guard, standing back at attention.

Suddenly they were all very alert. Adrenaline had kicked in. Bennie nodded and surveyed the hall for any sign of Traask. He had left to use the john before lunch, but the regular ones were out of order again—because of the construction. No telling where he had to go to take a piss.

Abrams approached out of breath. "Here, you left it in the booth." He handed over the walkie-talkie, adding, "It's FBI."

Bennie took the transmitter from him. "Randall?"

The hallway was awash with panicked confusion.

Most of the press had rushed the security barricade. A mob of bodies made it impossible to ensure anyone's safety with a degree of effectiveness. In the rush, several people had been shoved to the floor and were being stepped on. Clothes were torn. The cops shouted orders, but were powerless to stop the proceedings.

In the center of the hall, the copycat's body lay before the two FBI agents in an ugly, crumpled mess. Most of his head was gone, the bullet's impact having shattered his skull completely. It had exploded onto Holly North, spewing brain matter and bloody bone fragments all over her.

She had managed to stand for a moment afterward, shaking and stammering—then had passed out into the arms of the first cop to reach her. Shouting for paramedics, they had carried her to the side of the hall and laid her down, uncertain whether she had been hit herself.

Joey crossed to her partner with unsure steps. She was questioning the use of deadly force in a simple nutcase, but Claire gave her a cool nod, reassuring that they had done the right thing. Joey looked again to the body of the wannabe killer and heaved a large sigh of regret.

Claire grabbed ahold of Joey's walkie-talkie from her belt. "Traask, Traask!" But what she finally got was Bennie. "Where's Dan?" she asked.

"Not here. What happened?"

"We had to take down a nutcase. He grabbed a hostage. She's all right ... but this is a mess. We can't secure this area! It's a madhouse. Get Jefferson out of here."

"I've sent for backup. We'll be outta here in a minute."

Claire handed the receiver back to Joey and glanced around the room.

Cops were running this way and that, people were shoving and pushing—yelling to each other. All three metal detectors were clanging away. Reporters were jockeying for coverage, and several court personnel were crouched on the floor, still in shock.

It was total chaos.

One cop close to them began yelling at the crowd. "Back up now—back up. We've got paramedics on the way. Back up now, we'll need an opening here."

Claire shook her head over the copycat, thinking this was all so unnecessary ... An *opening!*

Suddenly her neck stiffened with the realization. The hair on her arms stood up, and her head snapped back, surveying the room. She reached out to Joey and pulled them both from the center of the room.

"He's here, Jo," she warned in a low voice. "He's right here. One of them is *him.*"

Joey and Claire simultaneously began to scan the crowd. They met each face, taking in each frame that passed before them. They measured, they compared. They searched for someone they'd never really seen, but knew by heart. He was right in front of them ... He had to be.

The cops had moved in quickly, attempting to contain the horrified crowd—but there was nothing they could do about the situation.

While attempting to assist in the skirmish of people being trampled and thrown aside, one officer failed to notice when he was relieved of his clip-on ID badge.

The adroit recipient was Champ, of course, who brushed past him without hesitation, casually fastening the ID to his own uniform.

Two big cops forced their way through the crowd, and Champ stepped in behind them. They had moved down the hall before Claire had a chance to put it all together. And then he was gone from view, his heavy footsteps echoed together with the others.

But separated from them at the first intersection.

* * *

"Backup, I told you, I need backup before we can move!" Sarkissian shouted into the transmitter. The van operator kept calling for them. Bennie was having a hard time holding tight as the minutes eased past.

Finally, he spotted some new men heading for them down the hall.

"Come on—move it, move it! We gotta get him out of here."

Bennie nodded to the guard who had been waiting with him.

"Here we go. Just hold him. We're gonna cuff him and take him out to the van."

The cell door opened. Shoulders and heads poured into the room. They fell onto Eddie Jefferson and attempted to pin him to the floor. There was a struggle as Jefferson cried out and kicked, screaming at them—blind with fear.

When Champ finally arrived at the open door, Bennie was not so enthusiastic.

"Oh terrific! Now they send me the big guys ... Jesus!"

When Champ saw the four men struggling to hold Jefferson down, he cocked his head at Bennie.

"Ah ..." Champ commented wryly, "a piece of cake."

They began escorting Eddie Jefferson down the hall, toward the back of the building. The Cop Killer had been both hobbled and cuffed against his protests, so it made for slow going.

There were four men in uniform, including Champ: one cop to lead the way, while a cop on either side of Jefferson held him up, and then Champ, flagging the procession, adding extra security.

He watched carefully for any opportunity.

They were all walking on the edge, ready to jump at the slightest movement. Their eyes checking the halls, forward and back—they couldn't move fast enough.

"Hold on, boys, what's happenin' here?"

Daniel Traask had appeared behind them, as if by magic.

"Where are you taking him?"

Champ bent down, seizing the opportunity to check the hobbles on Jefferson and avoiding Traask's close inspection.

"We've gotta get him out. There's been a shooting, Lieutenant," one of the men replied.

Traask's face clouded over. He reached for his walkie-talkie and realized he didn't have it on him.

"Shit. Gimme the phone," he demanded of the nearest guard.

The guard handed over his walkie-talkie with an unspoken protest, as another man assured him it was all right. Traask tried listening to the transmitter, but the interference was overpowering. All he got was static.

"Transmissions break up back here, Lieutenant. Try around the containment room—it's better over there."

Traask moved away from the men, his legs moving before his mind caught up with them. "Wait for me," he ordered, moving away down the hall. The men remained in position. "Don't leave the building!" Traask added before rounding the corner and disappearing from sight.

"Seal the building," Claire instructed. She knew he was here. Something was coursing through her now. She knew they had missed their opportunity, and if they weren't careful, it just might be too late.

Sarkissian joined in the shouting. "Seal the perimeter and get those goddamn reporters off the steps!"

The crowd was thinning now, and people had moved back from the security area. Paramedics had arrived and had begun working on Holly, who was in a state of shock, but otherwise unharmed.

"Bennie, Randall—come in."

Traask's voice on the receiver came as a surprise to them all.

Bennie grinned in relief. Into the radio he greeted, "Welcome to the party, Captain Ahab ... drained the white whale, have we?"

Traask was in no mood for jokes about his inconvenient visit to the restroom. "What the hell happened?"

"We've got a problem here. Another copycat. But he's

out of the picture now. We—I mean, Agent Randall thinks this might have been some sort of diversion ... you know, that the real one is here—somewhere."

Claire seized the receiver from Bennie. "Dan, we've got to secure the place. Shut it down, shut it down now!"

"It's being done."

"We've sent Jefferson back ..." she added.

"I know, I'm going with him. They're waiting for me."

This hit Claire like a punch in the stomach. "He's not gone yet?"

Bennie shrugged.

Claire's voice was urgent, "What the hell are you waiting for? Get him out of here!"

Traask ran all the way back to the hall where he had left Jefferson waiting with the guards.

But they weren't there. They weren't at the van, either. No one had seen them.

Attempts to hail them by walkie-talkie had failed.

"Oh man ... stop ... I gotta make the can."

"Shut up," one of the guards replied.

"Please, oh man ... I'm gonna shit my drawers if I don't make the can. Please?"

"Knock it off, Jefferson. We're leaving. Hold tight."

"I can't, man ... I just can't ..." Jefferson whimpered as the cops held onto him.

"His bowels have gone to water. He's freaked. Think about it," Champ said with authority, nodding in the direction that Traask had taken. "The man's gotta go."

The cops exchanged nervous glances, but soon conceded.

"Hurry man ... uh, hurry—will ya?" Jefferson pleaded.

Swiftly, the group headed back toward the intersection and found the only available men's room in the back half of the courthouse that was still working.

"You two wait here," the lead cop said, instructing Champ and one other man to remain outside in the hall while he and the other cop entered the bathroom door with

Jefferson in tow. "If you see Traask, tell him what's happening."

Champ nodded, not at all happy to be separated from Jefferson. His eyes roamed the hall, his displeasure showing.

"Hey ... I don't mind waiting out here," the other cop joked, letting out a nervous chuckle.

Champ didn't even acknowledge him.

"I don't know about you, but I'm fucking hungry, man. I just want to get this guy back to lock up and catch some lunch, you know? I started this morning five-thirty. What time did you come on?"

Champ suddenly became all business. Casually, he reached into his pocket to pull something out.

The other cop took in his silent partner somewhat curiously. What was his problem, anyway?

When Champ turned to him, the cop was completely unprepared for what was coming. It was stick of gum. Champ offered it out to the man.

The cop smiled, pleasantly surprised and a little relieved. "Hey, thanks, man!"

"No problem."

The cop took the stick of gum and unwrapped it, popping it in his mouth eagerly, talking all the while. "You know ... my wife said I shoulda ..." The man was having a hard time chewing, suddenly. "I shoulda ..."

He began to choke and cough. His hands rose to his mouth in alarm. He tried to swallow, but his muscles contracted and closed his throat.

"Urggh, mmrf!" he sputtered and gurgled. With his last good intake of air, he let out a holler. Then, clutching his throat and choking for more air, he collided with the door in an attempt to reach Champ.

Champ moved backward, causing the man to sink to the floor, helplessly gesturing. He croaked out a few more syllables, but Champ wasn't listening.

The lead cop came through the door, right on cue.

"What's going on out here?" Then he saw the man lying on the floor, having what appeared to be a seizure.

"Jesus! Jake ..."

As the lead cop bent down to assit, Champ took him from behind.

All was going according to plan.

The Cop Killer's bowels had indeed been affected.

The one cop left inside the bathroom had the glorious duty of assisting the fully cuffed Jefferson with his pants.

So he didn't notice when his partner was replaced.

He was too busy with the grateful Jefferson.

At the other side of the men's room, the last cop reached out for the handle of the faucet, pretending to be busy washing his hands. He was politely trying to avoid the watchful eye of his partner. But as he leaned over the sink to rinse off ...

Thunk. His head was shoved forward, smacking the porcelain sink. His limp body then slid to the floor. The water kept on running.

Jefferson saw boots appear under his stall door. He knew who it was. And there was nowhere for this rabbit to run.

23

Waltzing into the Quick Fire

July 1st—Cincinnati Courthouse
12:38

Everyone talked at once.

"Where is he?"

"Did you see him?"

"Was anyone hurt?"

Joey, Bennie, and Claire converged on Traask in the hall by the observation room.

"Are you okay?" Traask wanted to know, touching Claire's shoulder.

She nodded, cutting right to the point. "Where the hell is Jefferson?"

"I don't know. He was with the armed escort. I told them to wait. They didn't make it to the van."

Claire did not take the news lightly.

"But we've sealed the perimeter. Nobody is getting out," Traask reassured. "We'll get him."

"He doesn't want to get out—he's gonna do him right here," Claire snapped. She pulled her gun, checking it as she moved. She was leading them.

"We'll split up, assign sections. Keep in radio contact."

"There's a lot of interference back there. Something having to do with the renovation of the library wing. It's impossible to use the radios."

Claire nodded to Joey. "You and Bennie take the first intersection we come to. Traask and I will work from the back."

Joey didn't want to split up. In any other situation, Claire would not have gone with someone else. It was always the two of them. Always. But this wasn't personal. It was professional. And Joey had to remain objective. She was smart enough to see what her partner was doing.

For some reason, she just didn't trust Traask enough to let him go on his own.

"Look sharp, Jo," Claire warned. Claire had stopped trusting the Cincinnati police department. She wasn't going to risk losing Jefferson.

The man was there, right there in their midst, and still no one knew what he looked like.

Was he really Michael Corbett? Would studying that face pay off for them? Was he going to be that recognizable?

As Claire considered her options, Traask was shouting orders over the walkie-talkie. He sent his men down to the loading dock, instructing them to check every door along the way.

The question floated before her. Was Jefferson already dead? Or, on the other hand, could this all be just a mistake? Had the guards just been overcautious? Could they turn up around the next corner? What was happening?

Claire reached out with everything she had to get a grasp on the situation. Somehow, it came to her.

"Over here," Claire called to Traask.

She led him to a stairwell and propped the door open with her foot so Traask could follow.

On the floor just inside, were two of the guards. As they bent to inspect the unconscious men, Traask had time to realize that their greatest fear was indeed being realized.

"They're not dead," Claire announced, grimly. "Although ... there is something ... this one seems paralyzed."

The gum chewer's body was rigid, not limp. He stared

straight up into space, as if he were frozen in time. His hands kept clutching in spasmodic grasps at the air. The other man groaned and tried to raise himself on his elbow.

Traask leaned down to him. "What happened?"

The man attempted to respond as best he could. "Don't know. Jake . . . was havin' a seizure on the floor. I tried to help him . . . he musta got me."

"Who? Did you see who hit you?"

"Yeah." The man nodded, struggling to sit up. "He was one of ours."

"All right . . . come on, you wiseacres . . ." Bennie Sarkissian spoke softly as he and Joey crept down the hallway.

"Jefferson probably decided to take a leak," Joey fumed half-humorously.

She was nodding toward the bathroom door clearly marked, "MEN."

Bennie didn't rebut her. "Why the hell not? Everybody else was . . ."

"Whew . . . something die in there or what?"

Bennie and Joey exchanged glances. Yes, something could have died in there. But who wanted to go in and find out?

Joey kicked in the door, Bennie right behind her.

Crumpled on the floor, blood on the sink from the impact, was the last cop. He was motionless.

At first, the Cincinnati courthouse seemed small, so Claire was only beginning to realize the enormity of the problem. From the stairwell, the group that had been assigned to Jefferson could have gone up or down—or anywhere.

"This way," Claire murmured, allowing her instincts to guide her.

A giant swath of plastic draped a doorway to the next section. It barred their entry like a gigantic diaphragm. Claire noticed that it moved with a draft, as if there were an outside exit behind it somewhere.

"What's this?" Claire asked.

"Construction zone—the renovation, remember?"

Claire nodded, unsure.

"Randall!" Joey's voice reached them from the stairwell, her footsteps echoing on the concrete incline.

"Here, Joey."

She ran up to them. "He's got Jefferson."

"I know," Claire replied, her jaw set in the grim reality that they had already failed.

"He's dressed like one of the cops," Traask added. "Be careful."

"He musta taken them down in the bathroom—we found one there, he's gonna be okay."

Traask and Claire nodded in recognition.

"He's consistent all right—keeping with tradition," Joey added.

"What do you mean?" Traask snapped irritatedly. Joey and Claire were suddenly talking in shorthand, and he just wanted to get on with it.

Claire made it clear for him. "He doesn't want to kill your men. He just got them out of his way. Now he doesn't want to just *kill* Jefferson. He wants to make a statement. Otherwise we would have found all them dead in the bathroom already. He's had plenty of time now to get in and out."

Joey smirked. "He's got something special in mind for your boy."

Traask wasn't expecting to hear such sharp command in her voice. It was ominous, like a threat. He was beginning to feel like Claire was blaming him for this slip-up—as if he was letting Jefferson go on purpose.

After his words the other night, he could understand her assumption. But he had nothing to do with the turn of events.

Claire didn't wait for it to sink in. She parted the plastic sheets with one hand and motioned to Joey. "Come on."

Once inside the entry, the surrealistic appearance of the hall took both Joey and Claire by surprise. Gigantic lengths of clear plastic tarp draped the doorways, swaying with invisible breezes. All this movement was playing havoc with their concentration—each new billow was treated as a possible target.

The workmen had been painting in here. The fumes were still strong. Several portable scaffolds were parked in the space with open paint cans and brushes left on them. It was, after all, lunchtime, so the workmen had left their tools scattered out in the open.

Where was that draft coming from?

Some of the rooms were darkened, making it difficult to determine in which direction to begin. Without a word, Joey moved away from them, across the hall, and into another room. As she disappeared from sight, Traask objected, but Claire didn't seem to care. She was focusing on what was ahead ... what was out there.

Suddenly, uniformed officers burst into the room from an outside door. Adam was with them.

Claire's hand shot up, in a motion to stop them, waving them back. She was listening ... stretching ... reaching out with all her senses.

The small group of officers turned to Traask for confirmation. He also waved them back until they eventually exited completely. He knew the more uniforms in the area, the more targets there would be.

But Adam stayed behind. He was relying on Claire's instincts to guide them. And he was going to follow her lead.

But she wasn't going to include him on this. "Get out," she ordered quietly.

Adam shook his head.

"Adam!" she hissed, her whisper carrying to him. "Do it!"

Adam reluctantly moved back inside the doorway, keeping his eye on her.

Meanwhile, Claire turned her attention forward. He was there, all right. She could feel it. He was one step ahead, but he was also right in front of them. Her confidence was growing with each passing moment of the chase. Her heart raced with her senses. She was suddenly in her element.

She was living the dream.

Champ had them right where he wanted them.

* * *

On her own, Joey continued into the next room. She wanted this guy pretty bad, now that she had been forced to fire and kill a wrong number. Wrong numbers stuck with agents for a long time. This had been Joey's first. The questions running through her mind were putting her at a severe disadvantage. She couldn't afford to think about it right now.

She stopped, folding back against the hallway, and listened.

Mr. Right was here. And his hostage was still alive.

Something itched at Joey just below the surface. Something . . . was trying to tell her the right answer—how to get this guy. But she just couldn't stop to listen now.

She was close—deadly close.

She had to be careful. She didn't want to shoot the . . .

That was it!

Quickly, she listened for any sign of Claire, but she had moved too far away by now.

Jesus, this guy was brilliant. Fucking psychopathic brilliant! He was luring them in for the kill. The Cop Killer.

He wanted *them* to kill the Cop Killer, so just desserts would again be served in Cincinnati.

BAM!

Shots fired.

Claire surged forward, Dan Traask in tight at her side as they scurried quickly toward the deadly sound.

"You're supposed to be a fucking cop! Cops don't kill cops, you know."

Claire paused to listen. Joey's voice sounded strained . . . and tough.

Something was wrong.

Claire ran toward the sound of her partner's voice, pushing aside the flowing tarps in her way, cutting through ladders and scaffolds. Finally, she stopped—listening. She could hear Joey's breathing close by.

Claire stepped out of the darkness and circled a huge pillar of granite, entering the main room of the law library. The rotunda. Above them was a balcony area, circling the room, and above that, a tiled mosaic ceiling extending up into the dome itself.

Across the magnificent design of the marble floor, stretched against one of the pillars, lay Joey. She had been shot in the chest, just below the shoulder. A dark red patch of blood was expanding there. The bullet must have punctured a lung—she was having a hard time breathing.

Joey saw Claire on the other side of the room. Weakly, she nodded to the balcony level, indicating he was above them. Silent. And above them.

Joey was unarmed. Her gun had skittered across the floor and lay in the shadows, location unknown. But Joey remained out in the open.

Claire motioned to Traask with her gun that the man they sought was above. Adam appeared in the next room, holding the men back as he watched Claire and Traask in silent pantomime.

Traask nodded to Claire, searching for a stairway while she started circling behind the row of pillars in an attempt to reach Joey.

Joey could see Claire's intention and shook her head feebly. She didn't want Claire to ruin this chance.

"So why are you fucking around? Just kill the asshole and let's go home! You know we all want Jefferson dead." Joey's attempt to shout was a bit breathless, but her intention was to cover so the others could have time to move in.

"No ... no!" came the moaning response from Eddie Jefferson.

Good. At least they now knew he was still alive.

There was no answer from the balcony. Their man had yet to speak.

In the near-dark where she stood, Claire could make out a set of steps—a circular staircase—only a few feet from her. She took off her shoes and started to climb.

Traask moved forward in a hurry, motioning in silent pantomime for her to stop. She waved him back and gestured toward the other side of the hall. She wanted him to try to nab the killer from below, if she could flush him out above.

He nodded, only because he knew she wouldn't let it happen any other way. He slowly made his way toward Joey and the opposite side of the rotunda, craning his neck every few feet to see if there was anything moving up there.

On the stair, Claire found she had to maneuver around still more plastic, which made noise—something she wanted to avoid. She carefully nudged at it with her toes and stepped gingerly around it where she could, but in doing so, her progress was painstakingly slow.

"I know what you want ... You want us to do it, don't you ..." Joey was continuing to try for a distraction.

Good. Claire needed to be invisible right now. She was almost at the top of the stairs. Countless rows of boxes were spread out here, housing the vast volumes that normally filled the shelves on the upper level. The tall maple bookshelves rose up from the back wall, encircling them.

Claire sought cover behind a tall stack of boxes, peering around to see what might be there.

She could hear someone moving, all right—but it was dark up here, shadowy. The area was crowded with boxes and benches, confusing her.

Claire crept around the side, determined to find his position, even at the risk of revealing her location. It didn't take long. Almost at once, she caught sight of the uniformed man, his dark frame silhouetted against the lighter background beyond. She couldn't see his face, but his shoulders were broad atop his rugged frame. He was tall and built like a powerhouse. He was just standing there ...

"FBI, hold it right there!" she warned. "Don't move."

But he moved. He lunged for her, his arms reaching. His movement strange and erratic.

And somebody else was there in the darkness ... probably Jefferson.

There was a commotion. "No ... no don't!" It was Jefferson's voice.

Claire took the shot. The impact shoved him back against the railing, face forward.

From below, Traask was ready. He saw the flash of uniform, and took the shot.

"No!" Joey ordered. But no one was listening.

With two bullets in him, the man was still standing. He was about to turn on Claire again.

And she couldn't take that chance. She shot again. So did Traask.

"Claire, damn it—no! It's Jefferson! It's Jefferson!" Joey screamed.

The body toppled over the banister, gravity taking charge. Last over the rail was the chain and hobbles the man still wore. The body hit the floor with a hollow smack. Traask couldn't believe his eyes. It was Eddie Jefferson.

Champ had switched clothes with him, dressing Jefferson in the stolen Cincinnati police uniform. And now, the Cop Killer was as dead as he was gonna get.

Above them, Claire was dazed with the realization of what she had done. Good intentions kill more men than perfect aim. But she couldn't retrieve a bullet from midair. Attempting to take cover, she pulled back from the banister, but she encountered a puddle. The liquid soaked through the bottom of her stockings. It was paint thinner. Its strong odor began to permeate the air.

Moving away from it, she proceeded to conceal herself as best she could. But in the darkness of the upper level, she could not see that a chisel had been left behind by one of the carpenters. Its razor-sharp steel blade sliced into her foot, cutting straight to the bone.

She made an attempt to stifle her cry of pain, but it was too late. She stumbled out of control, blindly reaching out for something to take hold of.

What she found was a solid block of flesh and bone. Champ took her gun, tossing it aside like a candy cane. He grabbed her in a firm, steadying embrace. His large hand clamped over her mouth as he pulled her backward.

Strangely, there was no need to struggle. She had sensed his protectiveness immediately. He wasn't going to hurt her. He was shielding her from gunfire. He had lifted her up— steering her away from her harm—away from the edge of the balcony and into the safety of the shadows.

Claire got the impression he didn't even have a weapon on him. And hers was gone.

They came to a stop along the back wall. Claire moaned softly against the pain, closing her eyes for only a moment. With Champ's hand over her mouth, it was hard to breathe. She needed time to think, to consider her alternatives.

"Claire!!" Traask yelled frantically from below.

He fired off a warning shot. She heard a muffled argument, probably between Adam and Traask.

Claire flinched as the ricocheting bullet passed dangerously close by.

Unable to balance on only one foot, she was forced to rest her weight fully against Champ. Her foot was bleeding, copiously, going numb. She knew that soon her entire leg would be useless.

Several seconds went by as she waited for him to break the silence. Her heart pounded rapidly against Champ's chest. She couldn't help but notice how tightly he was holding her against his broad frame. They had been right. He was a very big guy.

She was surprised at how gently he removed his hand from her mouth and motioned for her to remain silent.

Footsteps and shouts could be heard from the lower level. Adam had entered, complete with all the fanfare and a bevy of reinforcements.

Being held from behind, Claire could not see Champ's face. This made it impossible to identify her captor. Time was ticking away, so she took a chance.

"Michael?" she whispered.

He separated his concentration from the activity below, in response to her inquiry.

Claire began to tremble with the adrenaline that was coursing through her at that moment. So Adam had been right after all ... it was the cop from Arizona.

"Michael, listen to me," she pleaded.

But he had begun to move. Once again, he covered her mouth as he dragged her with him toward the stairs.

Attempting to hobble alongside him, Claire inadvertently stepped back into the puddle with her bad foot. She cried out, stiffening in his arms, unable to free herself of the burning sensation.

This brought Champ to a halt. Realizing what had happened, he scooped her up in his arms.

Claire drew in a breath, too startled with the sudden motion to react defensively. She tried not to let the pain overcome her. She had to think, goddamn it!

He had begun to carry her toward the stairs.

I'm the hostage, she feared, trying desperately to calculate his next move.

But he was way ahead of her.

Traask had crossed to the nearest route leading up and found it blocked by construction materials. He then waved his men over to the circular staircase that Claire had taken. Her shoes were right where she had left them.

Champ had paused at the top of the stairs.

Her mouth now free of restraint, she tried again.

"No, Michael, don't . . ."

Sensing Traask's movement below, Champ quickly retreated back into the shadows. He seemed to be trying to decipher how many men had gathered below them in the past few moments.

And if they had heard Claire's warning.

"Michael?" Someone had.

Champ plotted the direction of Traask's voice. It was coming from the stairwell. "This is the Cincinnati police."

Claire realized there was going to be no escape for him.

Champ set her down, allowing her to take refuge on some dry floorboards. But he would not relinquish his tight hold around her waist.

"Michael, Michael, listen." Claire spoke quietly, trying not to let her voice waver. "Let me talk to them. I'll get them to back off."

It was too dark. She strained to get a reference point, but could find none. She knew he had turned toward her. Their noses could only be inches apart because she could feel his breath against her cheek. She desperately wanted to see his face at this moment. Because she sensed he was smiling.

"All right," he whispered.

Traask was tensely waiting for a reply. He had paused halfway up the stairs when Claire's voice filtered down to them.

"Back off, Dan."

Traask exchanged a glance with Adam, who nodded in agreement. Together, they motioned the other men back.

"Claire, are you—" Traask began.

"I'm okay. Just . . . just give us a moment."

Traask didn't like this. Something was wrong. He silently struggled to get a better view up the stair, but it proved to be futile.

Adam also moved closer, straining to hear, but nothing was coming to him.

They had no choice but to trust her.

Meanwhile, Claire remained frozen next to Champ in the shadows. This was her opportunity. She knew him better than anyone.

But it was Champ that broke the spell. In a raspy voice, he ordered: "Go on. Get out of here." His voice was tender, almost friendly. To her astonishment, he released his hold on her.

He began to move away, but she reached out and seized his arm.

"No. I can't leave," she told him. "And neither can you."

In his escape, he had encountered a small patch of light that illuminated some blond hair and a forehead. "I know."

Most of his face was obscured by the shadows, but finally—finally, she could see his eyes. They were studying her with a calm sadness that told her he had already made plans. "Go on," he urged. "It's over for me."

He pushed her away lightly, and she released her hold. Bracing herself against a bookcase, she struggled to keep him near.

"No, it's not. It's not too late."

But he had stepped back farther into the room, surrounded by the puddles of thinner. In an instant, he produced a flame from a blue tip match—like a magic trick. He cradled it in his cupped hand.

All at once, Claire realized his plan and desperately tried to dissuade him.

"Michael, no! Don't do it. Just ... come with me."

A faint smile played on his lips—the only thing she could see in the darkness between them.

"I can't."

He tossed the match.

The liquid immediately ignited in bright flames of blue quick fire, racing along to attach itself to nearby tarps and tables. Ribbons of flame traveled across the surface of the pools, revealing the pattern in which Champ had carefully emptied the cans in preparation for this moment.

In the few seconds before the flames cut off the path between them, Claire was finally able to see the face of the man she had been searching for, in its entirety. It was clearly outlined in the bright illumination of the fire.

So clearly, in fact, that there was no mistaking it.

Adam had been only half right. It wasn't the young, fresh-faced Michael Corbett, the Arizona sheriff who walked off his job in the middle of a shift.

It was an older version of the same design.

24

All's Well That . . . Ends
July 1st—Courthouse Rotunda
13:19

"Claire!"

Traask made it to the top of the stairs.

But she couldn't take her eyes from the curtain of flames. They were beautiful . . . and consuming.

And Michael's older brother was in there . . . somewhere.

So close and yet so far. They had the right man all along, sort of. Something must have happened to Michael Corbett to force his brother to take such a stand. Immediately, Claire ran scenarios of conjecture through her mind. Was Michael still alive? Had he simply walked off or had he gone straight to his brother with this wild idea of starting this trail of vigilantism?

They might never know.

But Claire suspected that the pain this family had felt over the loss of their sister had run deeper than any one of them had imagined.

The fire had risen to the maple bookcases, and the resin popped and hissed from the sides. Even the banister had caught. Traask reached the top just in time. The heat was tremendous.

"Claire ... come on!" Traask urged, tugging on her arm. That's when he realized that she had been injured and was unable to walk.

Claire refused his help at first, continuing to stare at the flames.

And when she could take the heat no more, she reached out to Traask, allowing him to carry her down the twisting stairway. Once on the ground floor, she balanced herself between him and Adam, and together they crossed back to where Joey lay.

Bennie appeared, running to them. "Is everyone all right?"

Paramedics had entered, rushing to Joey's side. More emergency personnel dodged between the riflemen, positioned on the floor, aimed at the balcony, now fully engulfed.

"Get everyone out!" Traask yelled to Bennie.

Bennie crossed to the double-door entry that had been previously locked tight. He kicked it open with a mighty shove.

Just across the street from them, a fire station stood with its bay doors open. "Hey!" Bennie shouted. One of the men at the station working on a truck heard him. "Why don't you back it on over here and cash a few checks while you're at it?" Bennie taunted.

The fireman registered shock at the black smoke that billowed out around Bennie, soon concealing the doors of the rotunda.

"Jesus H. ...!" The fireman scrambled to sound the alarm, alerting others inside the station.

Claire noticed the flames were everywhere now. Small explosions of paint cans and thinner, igniting and reigniting.

The body of Eddie Jefferson was loaded onto a stretcher and carried out.

"Claire ..." Dan insisted. "He's gone. Come on. It's over."

Adam followed her gaze to the balcony. It was an inferno.

Reluctantly, she broke her stare at the wall of fire, and nodded in concession.

She took one last look in Joey's direction, satisfied that paramedics were getting her out fast.

Traask and Adam assisted Claire out of the building, just as a dozen firemen were entering.

Claire signaled one of them, pointing to the balcony. "There's someone still up there."

The fireman looked to the spiraling wall of flame.

"Up there?!"

He quickly grabbed two of his men, and together they tugged a hose toward the stairs, making their way up.

Dan then lifted up Claire, carrying her from the building and heading over to the same ambulance that Joey was bound for. Adam followed from behind, watching in amazement as the building spewed clouds of thick black smoke.

Dan helped Claire into the ambulance, where paramedics took over, examining the gash to her foot.

Underneath the oxygen mask, Joey acknowledged weakly, "I'm okay."

"I'll follow," Traask offered.

Claire considered this for a moment, but something inside of her stirred.

"No . . ." she replied. "Stick around."

"Why?"

Her face betrayed her concern. She wanted to say more, but for now, all it was, was another hunch.

Nobody could survive those flames.

"Just . . . keep an eye out," she said.

Traask stepped away from the ambulance. He nodded, giving her one last, long look, then began walking back toward the building.

As the doors to the ambulance were closing, Adam rushed up to stop them.

"Wait!" he ordered. Then, turning on Claire, he asked, "I gotta know. Were we right? Was it him? Was it Corbett?"

Claire hesitated before answering. She drew in a breath and let it out.

"Almost," she replied.

"What?!" Adam exploded. Claire motioned to the men to close the doors. They moved around Adam, forcing him out of the way.

"Claire . . . wait!"

She didn't.

The ambulance took off, and the siren began to blare.

The paramedics began to treat Claire's wound, but she paid them no attention. Instead, she focused on her partner, taking Joey's hand in hers.

With her good arm, Joey reached up and removed the plastic mask so she could be heard.

"You . . . okay?"

Claire nodded reassuringly. "You're the one in the stretcher, remember?"

It was difficult for Joey to speak. But a satisfied, if somewhat sarcastic smile began to build. "So . . . I finally got you in bed—with me."

"Hmmm . . . yeah, well—don't let it go to your head. Shut up and relax for once, will you?"

Claire put the oxygen mask back over Joey's nose and mouth.

"Whuh?" came the muffled inquiry.

"Relax," Claire repeated.

Eyes closed, Joey did as ordered. Several moments passed. Claire feared Joey might be losing consciousness. "Joey?"

Joey looked up at her partner, whose alarmed expression was instantly relieved.

"It wasn't him, Joey. It wasn't the cop from Arizona. It was the older brother . . . I can't remember his name."

"Chulss," Joey said from behind the molded plastic cup.

Claire leaned down and pulled back the mask so she could hear.

"Charles," Joey repeated. The rest came a little more breathlessly. "Worked construction. A boxer. Had a nickname . . ."

A rueful smile came over Claire as she recalled.

Yeah . . . *Champ.*

"Man down! Man down!"

The firefighters were having a tough time getting into the

thick of it. An additional unit had been sent in to fight alongside them.

Traask stood near the open rotunda doorway, watching the proceedings as the fire captain pushed past in a hurry. He raced to assist two others as they hauled out one of their own.

It was a firefighter clad in full heat-resistant gear, with an oxygen tank and assembly strapped loosely over one shoulder. His coat and helmet were seared, and his mask was so blackened, he couldn't see. He had barely made it out alive.

"Alexander, did we get him?" the captain asked the official on his right. "Did you recover the other guy?"

Alexander stepped forward to reply, but the soot-streaked firefighter coughed repeatedly, shaking his head.

"We tried to get to him, but the stairway just collapsed," Alexander told the captain. Then he nodded at the man in the scorched helmet and said, "He had to jump. Cap, the upper level's gonna go any time now."

The captain assessed the situation, agreeing. He called to the men on the hoses.

"Bring it back ... let her go, boys. Number two, shut her down. We're letting her go."

Adam followed Bennie and Dan as they were asked to step from the entry over to a couple of squad cars in the parking lot.

They watched as the firemen piled out of the doorway and coiled their hoses. A crowd had gathered on the sidewalk by the construction fence.

Traask doubted they knew half of what had really gone on here today. He watched as the scorched fireman was led over to the paramedic truck and treated for burns to his neck and shoulder area.

Brave guy, Traask thought as he studied the badly burned skin on the young fireman, *I could never do something like that.*

The man coughed hard, his lungs working to clear themselves, then arched his back from the painful burn.

"You gonna be okay, man?" one of the firemen asked. "I'll get the paramedics." Another handed him a cup of water. He took it gratefully.

Bennie jogged over to Traask after speaking with the fire captain. "That's it. He's toast. They don't even know if they'll recover a body, Dan."

Traask studied the flames and smoke with ill ease. Claire's final words were haunting him. Could she really think anyone would escape? Escape to where? The man must have wanted to die.

"Let's go," Traask commanded. He wanted to get to the hospital. He wanted to be sure everyone on his team was being taken care of. And when it came right down to it, he just didn't want to be here anymore.

Frank was dead. The Cannibal was dead. Jefferson was dead.

The nightmare was over.

Traask would have to report all the appropriate facts to the bureaucracy—but that was later. Adam could wait.

Bennie followed as Traask crossed the parking lot. Together they climbed into Traask's car and pulled away into traffic as still another news van arrived alongside the fire truck.

The wounded fireman was tossed a clean T-shirt, emblazoned with the fire station's ID. He indicated his thanks and moved off, trying not to be seen by the cops. Suddenly, there was Adam, busy speaking with one of the wounded officers.

The last thing he needed right now was to be recognized, so he skirted around the FBI man and continued on. To avoid the news crew and their cameras, he crossed behind the truck, pulling the shirt over his head as he went.

Stepping from behind the truck, he continued out of the parking lot, onto the sidewalk and past the bystanders and news cameras ...

His plan had worked.

The street was jammed solid with cars and spillover from

the crowded sidewalks. Several cops were out in the middle of it, attempting to curb traffic, but when they saw the fireman trying to cross back to his station, they waved him on through.

Once inside the station house, he walked to the back ... and kept right on walking.

Epilogue

The Elephant and the Eye of the Needle
Claire's Townhouse—Washington, D.C.
Eighteen months later

"I love you, Claire," Traask reassured her.

Claire's phone machine had his sexy intonation down pat.

"You know I love you," the recorded message continued. "Every time you leave—it's the same. And even though I've just put you in the cab for the airport, I can still feel you here. I want you with me, Claire. We have to talk about this. We need to be together."

Together ...

Claire sat alone in her darkened bedroom, flight bag not yet unpacked, listening to the message Dan had left on her answering machine only hours before. His scent was still on her clothes, his voice was following her here. A sad smile grew as she recalled the past five days she had spent with him, five perfect days that had ended all too soon.

So this is how their life had turned out? Stolen moments during weekends and vacations that ended without much discussion regarding their future? Something had to give.

Their romance had long since evolved into a solid relationship, somehow circumventing the usual negotiations with distance and time. There was no denying it, they were going to be together. Someday.

And yet here they were, going on two years from the start, and there were no plans between them to bring this waiting to an end.

It had occurred to Dan that Claire might want to request reassignment to be closer, but what would that do to her relationship with Joey? He didn't want to pressure Claire, so the subject never came up. He had hoped . . . with time . . .

But she had remained based in Dallas. It was her choice.

Now Claire was in Washington. This wasn't a bad compromise, it was half again closer than Dallas had been, which made a short duration trip easier on the traveler, but she didn't like Washington, and everyone knew it. It was full of memories, full of politics.

Full of shit . . . she thought to herself.

Things were not going easy with Claire. More and more, something remained unsettled within her. It wasn't just this town, it was everything. Something was nagging there, outside the fringes. It was as irritating and unruly as a lagging shoelace, and yet each time she stopped what she was doing and stooped to retie, everything appeared to be in perfect working order. It was frustrating as hell. Yet it was out there . . .

She was on the cusp again. Things were about to change.

Claire stripped out of her clothes and stepped into the shower, allowing the soap and water to carry away the last bit of Dan that she had managed to bring back with her. They had made love only ten minutes before the cab arrived to take her to the airport. It was a strange kind of lovemaking, a kind of flurry full of necessity that started by the front door and ended on the floor of his living room. It was ripe with all the things they could not say in the few minutes remaining. Each secretly vowing that this last act would bond them together until . . .

It was a last, desperate denial of impending separation. It was the only way they could say good-bye.

She knew that eliminating his scent would not erase him from her thoughts.

As she lay on the bed afterward, she cradled a pillow to her side, knowing full well it was time for some difficult decisions. Although she had only recently arrived in Washington, she didn't have to accept the promotion. She could seize the opportunity to negotiate, and somehow pave the way for an eventual exit from the whole dog and pony show.

Is that what she wanted? Is this what it was all about? Quitting? Surely they couldn't go on like this, but who was to say that quitting was the best means to an end?

What was she thinking tonight? Her thoughts were coming in aberrant waves, and she realized they lacked sufficient reasoning to consider them any further.

Sleep found her fitfully, and several times throughout the night she awoke with a start, sure that something was there—not in the room exactly, but certainly within her grasp.

At three-thirty, she arose and found her way to the kitchen. Filling a glass of water from the tap, she drank it down thoughtfully, remembering with some amusement the first night she had spent at Traask's apartment in Cincinnati. How thoroughly unprofessional she had been, entering his living room in the middle of the night wearing only her undies, a tank top, and a loaded .45. It was indeed, a strange way to seduce a man.

Claire had brought the glass to her lips one last time when a strident burst broke through the quiet. Muffled though it was, a phone was ringing in the next room. She quickly determined it wasn't her home line but the FBI cellular she packed for her fieldwork. Joey jokingly referred to it as "The Bat Line." It had come in awful handy over the past few months.

Claire found the device tucked inside her flight bag and silenced the little menace. "Randall here."

"Claire Randall?" a masculine voice inquired.

"Yes," Claire affirmed, "who's this?"

There was a brief pause at the other end. "We have a problem . . ."

The voice was calm and full of strength—as if it carried with it some bad news it was going to deliver tenderly, and yet ... Something was familiar about it. Claire was busy trying to place a face to it ...

"Are you still there?" the voice asked.

"Yes. I'm here," Claire replied, listening intently for identification purposes. "Who is this?"

Another pause. "Are you still on the case?" His tone was casual. Quiet. Waiting.

The hair began to rise on her forearms. The voice was not finding its way home. Something was wrong here. Claire was good with names, voices—people. With each sentence came another clue, but she was drawing a blank. Chances were it was just a fellow agent, but ...

"What case?" Claire asked, becoming a bit annoyed.

Silence greeted her on the other end of the line as the realization came to her all at once.

"You're not an agent, are you ... ?" Her speech was halting as she announced her conclusions.

"No," he replied. "I'm not. But I'd make a damn good one."

She had to think fast and gather as much as she could. "Still, your voice sounds familiar to me," she admitted while crossing the room quickly, heading for the white home phone line on the bedside table. She activated the speed dial and brought the receiver to her other ear, now using two phones simultaneously.

"You're more familiar with my work," he corrected her.

A cold hand moved across her heart with his admission. He was a killer. Claire was determined to keep the patter light.

"Well, I'm not very good at guessing games. Why don't you ..."

"Yes you are. It's what you get paid for." It was a bold statement, made all the more bold because it was true.

"It's one of the things I get paid for." She stalled. "I get paid mostly for sitting around waiting for the phone to ring." Which was by now, quite comical because the other line was ringing.

"And now ... it has," he said with relish.

"Yes ... it has," she agreed with some sarcasm.

In her other ear Claire was now listening to the automated switchboard at FBI headquarters.

My, but wasn't she good.

Still cradling the cellular with her left shoulder, she muffled the white receiver with one hand while punching its touch-tone keypad with the other. Within seconds she had access to one of the most powerful mainframe computers in the country.

"So tell me, what's this all about? Obviously you want something. What is it? Do you want to turn yourself in?"

She input a series of touch-tone commands into the main computer, punching in numbers like a master accountant. And when she was done, all she could do was wait.

"Turn myself in?" he repeated with some amusement. "Nah. I couldn't do that."

With her other ear, Claire could make out the confirmation tones of the central computer over the white receiver. She smiled. At this moment, the central computer was tapping into her cellular line and recording their conversation while simultaneously tracing the incoming call—all by digital commands over her home phone.

Biting her lip with repressed triumph, she tossed the white receiver away onto the bed and turned her energies to keeping this caller engaged.

"Why not? Maybe we could cut a deal." She tried not to sound too eager. "You'd save us a lot of trouble that way ... if you turned yourself in. People do it every day."

"Dead men can't turn themselves in."

Claire swallowed involuntarily, the sudden dryness in her throat nearly choking her. "Are we talking suicide here?" she asked with a lilting tone. She was eager to turn the tables, trying hard not to let him get to her. After all, it's what he wanted. "Is *that* why you're calling me in the middle of the night? I think you might have the wrong number then. This isn't ..."

"No ..." he chuckled softly. "I've got the right number."

Then he turned on the disappointment act a bit too thick.

"Don't you remember me, Claire? We did some of our best work together."

His mocking tone drew a shudder from deep within her.

"I'm ready to do some more."

His performance was chipping away at her veneer.

"Who are you?" Claire demanded, tiring of this game.

He laughed again, so softly against her ear that she closed her eyes against it. He was trying to seduce her with the sound of his sickness.

"Don't be mad ... don't be mad at me, Claire. I *need* you." Then he let the dam break. "Don't you remember our time together in Cincinnati?"

Claire's mind ran a marathon inside of three seconds.

Dead men can't turn themselves in.

Nobody could have survived that fire!

She glanced down at the scar on the inside of her foot where the ugly cut still made its mark on her skin.

"I've been away, but I'm back now."

She wanted to scream, to shout that he was insane—that the nightmare had ended there in Cincinnati and there was no room for new beginnings.

"Then I guess we do have a problem," she stated flatly.

"Yes," he agreed.

Dead men can't turn themselves in. And they never did find a body . . .

The thought of it rumbled past her senses, dulling her perception. Her silence was making him nervous, and she knew it.

"I have to go now," he told her suddenly and without humor.

"Go where?" Claire blurted out to keep him talking. She needed more time. "What are you going to do?"

His voice took on that tone again, that paternalistic quality that only madmen and lovers share with the ones closest to them.

"Don't you know already? That's why I'm calling."

Claire's voice hitched in her throat and before she could respond, the line had gone dead in her hand.

His last words still hung in the air.

"I'm going back to work. See you around, Claire . . ."